'Rendered with loving exactness . . . formidably talented writer relaxing into his voice' *Daily Telegraph*

'Compassionate, tragic and breathtakingly beautiful . . . I cannot remember reading a more exhilarating or emotionally affecting novel. A masterpiece' *Sunday Independent*

'The tender, disquieting autopsy of an unsophisticated and commonplace marriage. What a touching, honest and courageous book!' Jim Crace

'Intelligent and interesting. A powerful indictment of the bruising social upheavals of the Thatcher years' *The Times*

'Tim Lott seizes the irreconcilables of the Thatcherite legacy [and] out of it he spins a bigger picture – of social turmoil, family division, racial and sexual convulsion. Cleanly and compulsively told the story reaches its conclusion with a satisfying and painful thunderclap' *Evening Standard*

'A moving, beautifully observed tale' *Mail on Sunday*

'Nothing John Mortimer, David Lodge or Michael Frayn have written – or Nick Hornby, for that matter – comes close to the considerable breadth of what Lott has achieved here. He has given us a modern English novel with a life of its own . . . an English version of Updike's "Rabbit" books. A very funny, yet genuinely tragic story' Eileen Battersby, *Irish Times*

'Acute and disconcerting . . . once opened Lott's novel is hard to put down, and even harder to forget' *Sunday Herald*

ABOUT THE AUTHOR

Tim Lott was born in Southall, Middlesex in 1956. He attended Greenford Grammar School and Harlow Technical College, after which he joined the local newspaper. He subsequently worked as a pop music journalist, a publisher and an entrepreneur. In 1983 he attended the London School of Economics as a mature student and achieved a degree in history and politics, after which he worked as a magazine editor and a TV producer before turning to writing. He is author of *The Scent of Dried Roses*, which was awarded the 1996 J. R. Ackerley Prize for Autobiography, *White City Blue*, winner of the 1999 Whitbread First Novel Award, and a second novel, *Rumours of a Hurricane*, all of which are published by Penguin. He is divorced, has three daughters and lives in north-west London.

Rumours of a Hurricane

TIM LOTT

PENGUIN BOOKS

PENGUIN BOOKS

Published by the Penguin Group
Penguin Books Ltd, 80 Strand, London WC2R ORL, England
Penguin Putnam Inc., 375 Hudson Street, New York, New York 10014, USA
Penguin Books Australia Ltd, 250 Camberwell Road,
Camberwell, Victoria 3124, Australia
Penguin Books Canada Ltd, 10 Alcorn Avenue, Toronto, Ontario, Canada M4V 3B2
Penguin Books India (P) Ltd, 11 Community Centre,
Panchsheel Park, New Delhi – 110 017, India
Penguin Books (NZ) Ltd, Cnr Rosedale and Airborne Roads,
Albany, Auckland, New Zealand
Penguin Books (South Africa) (Pty) Ltd, 24 Sturdee Avenue,
Rosebank 2196, South Africa

Penguin Books Ltd, Registered Offices: 80 Strand, London WC2R ORL, England

www.penguin.com

First published by Viking 2002
Published in Penguin Books 2003

1

Copyright © Tim Lott, 2002
All rights reserved

The moral right of the author has been asserted

Set in Monotype Dante
Printed in Great Britain by Clays Ltd, St Ives plc

Dedicated to Jeff Lott, my absent friend

Thanks to
John Amlot and Garden Railway Specialists, Princes
Risborough, the Littlewoods Catalogue Company, Paul
Griffiths at English Partnerships, Mick Kitson, Nick Oatridge,
Penny Jones and all at DGA for keeping me bucked up,
Lesley Levene, Juliet Annan for her consistent enthusiasm
and support, David 'Mr Music' Godwin for going beyond the
call of duty on this one, and Rachael Newberry

Tempora mutantur, nos et mutamur in illis
Times change, and we change with them

Prologue

It is 1991. Winter. The woman sits, writing, at a desk in her office in the New Town. The office is one of two rooms in a prefabricated cube that sits at the easternmost perimeter of a small car park. A fleet of nearly new cars sits outside, polished and gleaming in the chilly sunlight. Atop each there is an identical plastic sign, 'M&P Driving Centre', picked out in red, white and blue.

The woman stops what she is doing and looks up. She scrutinizes the cars with a matronly, protective gaze. Her glance lingers on one of them, newer than the others, a brand-new Ford Fiesta in Cobalt. This particular car has a special significance. The school took delivery of it only today and it is their twentieth vehicle. The roundness and cleanness of this figure, 20, she finds seductive, rolls it around in her head like a cool green marble.

She notices one of her team of driving instructors leaving a simple breeze-block staff room which squats plainly on the opposite perimeter of the car park. The man makes his way briskly towards one of the neatly parked cars. With faint disappointment, although she knows it is a good and inevitable embroidering of the scene that she surveys, she watches as the car is occupied and begins to roll away to pick up the first of the day's customers. By midday, the car lot will, as usual, be empty, before the cars are all sucked back in during the late evening, like particles breathed in and out of a lung. The cars leave as carbon and return as oxygen, as profit.

In a town like this, where everybody needs to drive, and which is expanding at a rate greater than anywhere else in Europe, everyone needs to have this everyday skill. The growth in demand is demographically predictable. Yet the disruption of the grid of the twenty vehicles, laid out in a five-by-four rectangle, disturbs her enjoyment of the neatness of the scene.

The woman relishes geometrical arrangements. It is not obvious from her appearance, which shows none of the outward signs of asceticism that one might expect from an enthusiast of informal mathematics, from a devotee of the proper ordering of things. She is tanned from a recent foreign holiday, a real tan topped up now with a tone from an expensive bottle. Other than her heightened colour, her most prominent quality is that of density. She wears a thick gold chain, has a thickly powdered face, thickening thighs and thickly plastered lips. There is nothing angular or parched about her. She is clearly middle-aged, but seems sprightly and satisfied. Her suit is bright red, with a black collar and slightly padded shoulders. She wears court shoes with medium heels and fake Chanel earrings. Her hair is auburn, her eyes, which suggest a strange mixture of both softness and buried, implacable determination, miss nothing. In front of her, two bound ledgers, arranged exactly flush to the edge of the embossed green leather-topped desk at which she sits. Her right index finger makes circular patterns on the cover of the left-hand ledger, a kind of foreplay to her imminent teasing and massaging of the figures into the book-keeper's bliss of perfect symmetry.

The phone rings and she considers ignoring it, since it is only eight o'clock in the morning and she has not finished her coffee and fresh raisin Danish pastry, bought from the hot-bread shop in the large shopping mall to which her office is juxtaposed. After due consideration, she makes a mental pact: if it continues after ten rings, she will answer. On the eleventh, she picks up. A soft northern voice emerges from the earpiece.

Is that Mrs Buck?

Yes.

Good morning, Mrs Buck. My name is Julie from British Telecom. I'm sorry to bother you, but we were wondering if you would like to take this opportunity to avail yourself of some of the new services which we are –

No, I'm sorry. You've made a mistake.

I beg your pardon –

I mean, I've made a mistake. This isn't Mrs Buck.

I do beg your pardon. I thought you said –

I used to be.

Oh.

Not any more.

Maureen hangs up. She wonders how long it will take her to stop being Mrs Buck, and hopes it will not be too much longer. Her fresh life suits her. And it is fresh, feels fresh and warm, like the pastry she delicately devours in small bites rounded off by elaborate mouth-cleaning oper-ations with the napkin she has been offered to accompany the pastry. She drains the last of the contents of her cup with a smack of her lips, since no one is there to hear her transgress the good manners that she has tried hard to cul-tivate since she was a young woman. Then she turns to the ledgers and opens the one that her finger has been caress-ing. The news contained inside it, she knows already, will be good.

As she opens the ledger, fifty or so miles away to the south a man stands under a flyover in London, swaying slightly back and forth from the balls of his feet to the flat of his heels.

He keeps this rocking movement going for five, maybe six minutes. There is no sunshine here, only a steady dull downpour.

People hurrying by on the way to the nearby underground station entrance avoid looking at him. The pointlessness, the giant inappropriateness of his smile, the rock, rock of his ruined body put them on guard, register him as mad, render him invisible. His smile widens; something like a laugh emerges, but is obliterated by the rumbling of the tube train.

The smile dissolves. He takes a long, deep draught from a can that is clutched in his left hand. Then he crushes the can and lets it drop to join the five or six empties that he has previously let fall there. He stops rocking. His face is still, at rest. He closes his eyes.

His face, now expressionless, exposes clearly the topography of its damage. Thin, vermilion blood vessels snake across his cheekbones and nose. There is the remnant of a serious bruise there, and his hair, of which there is a thick mass, stands up with caked grime as if gelled and set. The effect is that of broken feathers on the back of an injured pigeon. His mouth is thin and inclines down heavily at either end. The impression is not so much of sadness but of anaesthesia. There is not the animation any more to drag the lips up at the extremities, to continue the pantomine of a private joke being shared with the battering rain.

His eyes are still closed. People hurry past. The rain strengthens and the wind that drives it pulls sheets of water whipping under the flyover. Yet still the man does not move. Another train arrives.

His clothes are soaking now, on every side. The damp seems to neutralize their colour, so that they appear not colourless but unidentifiable as any shade of any hue in particu-

4

lar. It is the colour of that which has fallen from the secret edge of the world.

A pale flicker of the smile reappears. Then the eyes open once more. They are shot. They were once cornflowers but now have come to resemble the damp non-colour of the man's clothes. Yet briefly they seem to blaze with some light, a light that is somewhere at the dark end of the blue-green spectrum and that sends out messages nobody is there to read. The lids widen slightly. Then the man closes them again. And takes a step forward. The flow of pedestrians redirects itself to avoid the obstruction, forced now to momentarily recognize the man's existence and thus recalibrate their own.

The traffic boulders down the main road at an urgent pace, each pair of windscreen wipers battling the downpour, the moment-by-moment flicking between clarity and opacity. When the trains pass and the traffic is growling, the sounds combine to make a thick, tumbling wall of noise that blocks a human voice pitched at the normal level. Car and train, train and car, the systematic indifference of machines. The man takes another step forward. The pedestrian flow redirects automatically.

The man reaches the kerb and he stands there, steadily, waiting until the trains and cars combine to create the necessary duet of obliteration. The quality of the noise is the cue he has given himself, pointless and nonsensical. He considers this apt. The 8.03 is late. A mechanical failure at Stratford is responsible.

Eventually, however, the man hears the train approach. He swallows. And again, then blinks, once. Although very drunk – he has been very drunk now for one and a half years – he feels, unexpectedly, a subterranean bolt of fear. This means he muffs his step slightly when he leaves the kerb, the ghost of a second thought hobbling him. So the lorry, when it hits, does not take him full on, but propels him from the shoulder, at an angle, twenty feet into the distance. It is not enough. Instead of the warm darkness which he hoped for, there is a cacophony of world-obliterating pain.

As if the rain were adrenalin, the crowd, a moment ago so united, so careful in its indifference, so discerning in its chosen horizons, flows undammed towards him. He hears himself screaming, and he hears voices babble around him, words that are rendered meaningless and incomprehensible by his agony.

The pain has not merely failed to kill him. It has brought him vibrantly alive, made him aware of the oldest edict coded into his genes: to survive. His cry sounds from somewhere he had not previously understood to have existed. The deadness of his spirit is in momentary retreat. For the first time that he can remember, at the chosen moment of his death, he wants to live. He is beyond registering the irony.

It is some time before an ambulance arrives. After the first excitement of the incident, which will be translated into a hundred anecdotes, each of them inaccurate in its own particular way, each inadequate to the size of the event, people are embarrassed. Many have moved on, refusing to let a wino's fate admit entropy into the grooved regularities represented within their loose-leaf appointment books. Others are fascinated by the blood which still pours in extraordinary quantities from several wounds on the man's head, chest and what is left of his right leg, and their initial shock has been replaced by an irrepressible voyeurism. A third group are paralysed by a need to do something and, countervailing that, a complete inability to do anything at all.

But to move on seems more callous than staying. So they shuffle from foot to foot, and they chatter concernedly, in lieu of more positive action. The dying of this man is too extraordinary a spectacle to leave; and yet now they want to be released from it, to glide back into their lives and consign this to memory, and then forgetfulness.

Some few of this third group try to talk to the man out of whom life is leaking, but their words emerge as diminished, shrunken by the dimensions of this event. *Where does it hurt? The ambulance won't be long. Can you move your leg? You'll be OK.*

This last, tender lie is the most profound of the deceits woven into the scene, so violently does it disagree with the remnant that is prostrated on this cracked and bloodied pavement. The words are uttered by the lorry driver, whose eyes are wide with surprise, who never expected to kill a man today. He is delivering plastic canisters to a feed manufacturer in Wakefield. Despite his upset, he worries that he will be late. He takes out a cigarette and lights it, and almost immediately puts it out again. The point is in the doing.

The consoling sound of an ambulance can be heard now. A wash of relief begins to crest above the spectators; they want their responsibility for this event to end now. But the siren turns out to be a police car, on another mission entirely. It passes by and the siren fades.

The right leg is almost severed below the knee. Corals of bone, shocking white, have appeared. One spectator finds it too much and the sound of retching joins the chorus of anxious muttering, motor engines, seagulls, descending planes. Another train arrives. Traffic is moving as before, drivers sequentially irritated by the hulk of the lorry stopped on zigzag lines.

Now the ambulance really is coming. Announcing itself by sound and light, sad cavalry approaching through the rain, it screeches towards the site of what will be logged in the driver's record book as an 'incident'. Neutral, painless-sounding.

The ambulance pulls up behind the lorry. Two men emerge, wearing yellow reflective vests over their uniforms. They take in the sight without registering shock or revulsion. They are both experienced; carnage is banal.

They go through the routine. A glance is enough to trigger the first part. One man, who is big, red-faced and naturally angry-looking, radios the hospital, ensuring that surgeons will be at the ready at the anticipated arrival time of around fifteen minutes. He speaks calmly, even delicately, despite the fury of his face. The fury is an illusion; he is a kind man who finds his work taxing and doleful.

The other man, smaller and younger, is attending to the shivering heap on the pavement. He mutters some words to him; takes various appliances from a bag, prepares an injection and administers it. The patient quietens down somewhat. He whimpers now, instead of screaming, but he remains frightened; the drug is not strong enough to erase this primal directive.

Within minutes he is loaded on to a stretcher, his half-severed leg, now tourniqueted, loaded on almost separately, nearly an afterthought. It is obvious to both the ambulance men that the leg is beyond repair. It is obvious to them also that the man they are now guiding into the small holding cell that is the rear of the ambulance will not be needing it anyway in a short while. A day, maybe two. Perhaps not even that long – a DOA.

The possibility of organ donation automatically crosses the mind of the older ambulance man, but he almost laughs at himself for making such a slip. The parts of a wino are detritus, particularly one of this age; early sixties, he guesses, subtracting ten years from what the face shows to allow for the wear and tear of street life.

No donations. The beating heart, the grey filter of kidneys, the soft sponge of lung are always too hardened, too softened, too punctured and fatty and gristled. And the liver of course . . . No. These are not prime cuts. No patient, even a dying, desperate, breathless, dialysis-tethered one, would embrace such maimed offerings.

The journey to the hospital is uneventful. In the wake of the ambulance, a few of the abandoned pedestrians are still staring at the brown penumbra of blood, are still guiltily enjoying the excitement. The paramedics are thinking about how long is left on their shift. The man on the stretcher is delirious. His thoughts are like scattered, broken glass, each containing a reflection connected, yet unconnectable, with a larger picture. He thinks of a wide boulevard dotted with yew trees. He thinks of a woman with auburn hair removing a plucked and trussed bird from a microwave oven. She is smiling, but unhappy. He thinks of an overheated room and a barometer shaped like a Spanish guitar. He hears the sound of cascading orchestral strings.

At the hospital doctors and nurses crowd around him as he is unloaded. Something in him is grateful for the attention, even flattered by it. He thought he had forgone such privileges long ago. Injury is elevating. People grant you respect.

Soon after the unloading, the man loses consciousness. He has been given a general anaesthetic. The surgeon, a cynical, hunched-over sexagenarian with a hatred of life that has somehow been generated by its endless sluicing through his hands, can hardly find the wherewithal to operate. He has taken his saviour's knife to too many street roughs and drunks and hopeless cases with their ruined insides, keeping him from spending valuable time on those he thinks of as more valuable people, those he believes misfortune, rather than personal weakness, has laid low. He hates what he tries to save; a futile drain on resources.

He immediately forms the conclusion that this man is probably going to die. The vital functions are too far gone. It is a waste of time. He removes what is left of the leg, out of a sense of propriety and tidiness. Then he closes the man up again, half hoping for a flat line there and then on the screen. But a weak pulse continues producing its sharp green hills. Another misuse of a hospital bed.

The man is moved to the intensive-care ward. Although he has a National Insurance card identifying him as Charles William Buck, no relatives can be traced. An old digital watch, newly smashed, is removed from his wrist. On the back it bears the inscription 'From Mo to "Rock"'.

There is no money in the pocket of his wallet. The only content is a torn and yellowed newspaper cutting, an old obituary. The headline reads 'Goodbye, Mr Music'. The orderly who is responsible for these matters, thinking it worthless, throws it in the rubbish bin alongside a batch of used dressings.

No one is there to watch this stricken coda to the life of Charles William Buck. Or almost no one. There are professional carers who visit the ward, death angels. They are predominantly women acting out of mixed motives. To comfort the dying, but to comfort themselves, who are also dying, at a more sedate pace. They look for a way of believing themselves good. They look for a way of being useful in their middle years, now that the children have left home and are off to university, or in their first year in respectable jobs. They flit from bed to bed, seeking out misery to alleviate, consciousness that can be fleetingly connected with.

One of them stands by the bed of Charlie Buck. There is a radio playing in the room. It is broadcasting a speech by the Prime Minister, John Major, who is making a national address in order to prepare the nation for war in the Gulf. The woman, who is fifty-three, the wife of a circuit court judge, has regretful, unfocused eyes. She sits on the bed. The man, who is on a ventilator, seems to exist merely as an extension of a network of clear tubes removing and supplying various kinds of fluid to what is left of him.

The woman talks to the mutilated contour under the blanket, his face distorted by the tubes and by the sad encrustations of his sixty-one years of lived life. She knows from the wreckage of the parts of his face that remain uninjured that he is a drunk.

She is puzzled by grief and madness. She has completed courses in counselling, she has sat in on dozens of sessions with weathered, slightly embarrassed men and woman declaring their names and their afflictions: I am an alcoholic, I am a drug addict, I am my illness.

Charles Buck, she says, in a voice so soft that she imagines even a fully conscious patient would not be able to hear her. *May I call you Charlie?*

She waits for a few seconds, imagines a reply.

*What **happened**, Charlie?*

She thinks: he was a child once, running to the corner shop for sweets, hugging his mother's knees. The thought makes her want to cry. She is sentimental. Emotion is part of her income for attending here. It is a kind of recreation.

To her surprise the man in the bed seems to show a response. It is as if he is attempting to frame a reply. But if there are words, she cannot catch them. She thinks, after a few seconds, that she imagined them. He is too far gone.

No more. Other unspoken words are interrupted by interior darkness.

She leaves the bed, sighting out of the corner of her eye a flickering of awareness in a stroke victim three beds along. The radio stutters, background noise to join harmonies with the soft mechanical and electronic devices that, defying nature, maintain life.

John Major is finishing his speech. The words Charles William Buck hears, but cannot make sense of, before a disturbance on his electrocardiogram triggers an alarm at the nurses' station, are:

Goodnight, all. And God bless.

PART ONE

London

I

3 May 1979. The truth that confronts us every day in the twenty-first century, that pushes in on our worlds through every crevice and loophole in our lives, is still, in this as yet unacknowledged fulcrum of a year, a kind of secret.

The secret truth is this: that things change. That things *are* change. And, hard as it is to reimagine, standing where we do on the precipice of an avowedly and perpetually crumbling world, this reality is, at the end of the 1970s, still under the carpet. People are beginning to trip up on it; but looking round, they are still puzzled by the cause of their bruises, their damage. It is a stranger place than you might expect, this remembered country. Recognizable, of course, yet oddly distorted, at odds, for a past so slightly receded.

Inflation, decimalization, the three-day week, industrial chaos, oil-price hikes, Irish terrorists taking their deadly suitcases and shopping bags to the streets and litter bins of England – the age is replete, like all ages are, with weird multiplicities of denial. But contradicting the fact that *things happen* is the popular embrace of a bigger, more established and comforting fact that *things stay the same*. The Queen reigns and is loved by all her subjects, with the exception of a few loudmouth punks. England stumbles on, making the best of a bad job. The unions fight with the bosses, and the government, Tory or Labour, steps in to sort things out when the two of them can't manage it themselves. Coffee is instant. Bread is sliced. Weather is rainy. Car, for Charlie Buck, is a plum-coloured 1973 Triumph Toledo with a starter motor that is always jamming.

Charlie, on this particular day, is on strike. Charlie, like his father before him, is a compositor at Times Newspapers. And, like his father before him, Charlie quite routinely finds himself on strike. It is a matter of no great alarm or surprise. Striking is much bemoaned by the politicians, and the public and the newspapers alike, but it is part of the texture of life in this particular version of this particular country. This fondness for industrial action will never change, just as prices will not stop rising, just as beer will remain warm and dark brown and tasting of the industrial processes that produce it. If the English have a common belief, it is a belief in certain kinds of inevitability.

Charlie Buck blows on his hands in an attempt to keep out the unseasonably cold weather. He has stood on the picket line in London's Gray's Inn Road for more than seven hours now. A coal brazier burns on the street, outside the entrance to the newspaper's offices.

His threshold for boredom, like that of most of his countrymen, is necessarily high, yet he finds himself all the same becoming restless, scoured by tedium. At the beginning, the strike – which is unusually protracted – had, in a strange way, been fun. It brings back to him his faint memory of the war. When that had started, no one had had any doubt that they would win in the end, and, even when danger had seemed imminent, it was often more monotonous than anything else, waiting out the time until the certain victory would arrive.

Victory was certain here, too. The management would cave in. They always did, they always had, they always would. Then Charlie and the rest would get back-pay, and things would be the same as they were before.

He checks his watch. Time to go home. He gathers up his possessions – a white plastic shopping bag containing the remains of a sandwich packed by his wife, a Thermos of coffee and a book by Sidney Sheldon. He straightens up, then raises a hand towards the six or seven other strikers. There are mutters of farewell. Two hands are raised in return. One belongs to a tall, slightly stooped black man in his fifties, with grey beginning to penetrate the dark thickness of his hair. The hand is mutilated, has the index and middle fingers missing. The other belongs to a young man dressed in jeans smoking a roll-up cigarette. His overcoat is too large on him, has a herringbone pattern and displays signs of tattiness. Yet he wears an expensive watch, a Rolex.

See you, Snowball.

Bye, Charlie. You keep well, bwoy.

Mike.

Don't forget to vote. You've got till ten.

They're all the same, says Charlie.

What about the card game? says Snowball.

Charlie catches the man called Snowball's eye, throws him a look.

There's a card game? says Mike.

I've got to get off, says Charlie.

Charlie turns his back and begins to make his way towards the bus stop. Without looking round, he raises a hand in farewell.

What card game? says Mike.

But Snowball has moved to another section of the picket.

Five miles to the south west, in a small municipal park, Charlie's wife, Maureen, runs. Her trajectory takes her away from the small council flat she lives in with Charlie and their son, Robert. She is dressed in a pale blue nylon track suit and white running shoes. Her lungs burn fiercely, her legs ache. Shortly, when she reaches the children's paddling pool that has been drained of water leaving only green scum, she will turn and begin the return journey. This is always the hardest moment for her, just before the homeward stretch, when there is more ahead of her than behind her and her whole body is complaining. But she is determined. She tightens her lips and narrows her eyes to focus on the paddling pool, which still seems impossibly distant. She listens to her breath harshly drawing, feels her breasts rise and fall with the rhythm of her footfalls.

She runs towards a young woman navigating a pushchair through a line of concrete bollards. In the pushchair a toddler, a little girl, is kissing a pink rabbit. She looks up at Maureen and holds the rabbit out towards her as she approaches. Despite the increasing pain in her chest, Maureen smiles, lessens her pace slightly. The girl smiles back, then drops her rabbit in a puddle and begins to cry. Maureen stops, picks it up, wipes it off and hands it back.

Now Maureen begins to run once more. The paddling pool is closer. Seagulls perch on the climbing frame that is constructed ten yards to the right of the pool. She feels sputum in her throat, checks that no one is watching her, then hawks and spits carefully into a litter bin. The gobbet misses the interior of the container and hits the side. Maureen immediately stops, finds a paper handkerchief from her pocket and carefully wipes the tiny stain away, then drops the tissue into the bin.

She picks up pace again. The paddling pool grows larger. She wants to stop now, wants to rest on a bench, drink oxygen. But the magazine article she has read insists on a minimum of twenty minutes' aerobic exercise, four times a week. This is if it is to have the desired effect of increasing her metabolic rate and thus easily burning off the pounds. She is worried that her looks and body are folding into the indiscriminate uniformity of middle age. She is thirty-eight years old, ten years younger than her husband.

She reaches the paddling pool, does a circuit of it, starts to head back. Her body hurts as much, but psychologically it is easier. She even ups her pace slightly. A woman she recognizes as a neighbour approaches, pushing a shopping trolley.

Hello, Mrs Jackson.

Maureen. Here. Did you hear that —

Can't stop. Charlie's home in a minute. I've got to put his tea on the stove.

You be careful. You mind yourself.

I will.

She pushes on, checks her watch. Charlie will be back in an hour. He likes to have things just so. She needs to find a recipe for tonight. Robert complains that she is not adventurous enough.

She leaves the park and goes out into the street. A dog barks, worries her heels. She stops momentarily, at the same time anxious that any interruption of the activity will negate its effect. Nevertheless, she pats the dog, ruffles his coat. She is outside the greengrocer's.

That mutt is always making a nuisance of himself.

He's a nice dog, Frank. You should look after him.

He's a mutt. What you up to?

What's it look like?

I dunno. Running.

That's it.

She pushes off. Frank is a decent man, but he is sloppy with his weights, overcharges when he can get away with it. You have to watch people.

Her breath is coming in great gasps now, but she is determined to sprint the last few hundred yards. Her breath rasps, her legs feel shaky. There's a bunch of kids hanging around the entrance to the estate as she approaches. They begin to laugh and jeer as Maureen comes into view. She stops to remonstrate but cannot find her breath. The kids run away, laughing. She knows where they live. Later, she'll have a gentle word with their parents.

Last few hundred yards now. She does not let up, checks her watch once more. Exactly twenty minutes. Mission accomplished. She slows to a walk. Robert is on the porch, smoking a cigarette. He is five ten, skinny, mussed-up red hair. Eighteen, but looks older. He smiles as she approaches.

Can't be good for you, he says to his mother.

At least I try, says Maureen.

I'll give you that, says Robert, drawing deeply on the cigarette. *You have a go.*

Charlie walks the few hundred yards to the bus stop and waits for the bus to take him home. After twenty-five minutes, a double-decker appears. By now there is a ten-yard queue, but the bus that arrives is completely full. It drives past without stopping. The queue shuffles and a few words are muttered. Then it settles back down, as if a single animal, into disconsolate resignation. It is just the way things are. After fifteen more minutes, another bus appears on the horizon. This time he just makes it on, last but one. He leaves behind him a queue of twenty people. The bell sounds, the bus trembles and moves forward.

It is a forty-minute ride to Fulham, where Charlie has lived for the last fifteen years of his life. London rolls past him as the bus progresses in fits and starts, engorging and disgorging its cargo at a dozen or so chilly bus stops, where long queues shuffle and mutter. He begins to enjoy the roll and sway of the old Routemaster, and although he gives up his seat to a woman holding a baby, he feels quite comfortable and has a good view through the window, which, incomprehensibly, is clean whereas the remainder on the bus are too grimy to see through.

Although he has lived in London all his life, he has no love for the clogged-up streets, sagging shops and dirty pavements. London is a place he has always dreamed of escaping from, to somewhere there is air and light and the sound of birdsong to wake you in the morning. He likes to watch birds, finding the cataloguing of their varieties, their shapes and colours and strange modes of existence comic and graceful. He has a pair of binoculars for this purpose. A gift from Maureen, Christmas 1975. Or was it '76? Or was it Christmas at all? His memory, he decides, is not what it was.

The bus travels through Knightsbridge. He watches Hyde Park go by on his right-hand side and the military barracks. He thinks of the wealth that flanks him without envy. It would be as pointless to envy the birds. The species are as different, as alien.

The bus conductor whistles a tune from *South Pacific* as he collects the fares with a cheerful efficiency. He has sandy hair and freckles and a likeably snubbed nose. When he disappears to the top deck, Charlie finds himself continuing the song in his own head.

Down the Cromwell Road, out towards the west. The great museums stand as testament to the history that somehow holds the country, holds it together, holds it back. Charlie notices them separately – the V & A, the Science, the Natural History – and, as he often does, makes a mental promise to pay them a visit soon. He likes to think that he is keen to expand his horizons and yet finds it boring when he tries. The promise, he half-knows as he makes it, will not be kept.

The bus turns off the Talgarth Road at the junction with North End Road, heading south. Charlie has finally found a seat, but now rises well in advance of his stop. He likes to be prepared, worries that things will fall out of control if he is not. He presses the Stop button and allows his finger to stay there for several seconds, concerned that the driver will not hear. But the bus slows as it approaches his stop and the familiar topography of his neighbourhood comes into view.

The shops seem tired, crammed together, indifferent to the disposal of their contents. There is a cluttered electrical supplies shop, Frank's greengrocer's, a fish and chip take-away which has now begun selling Jamaican patties as well as saveloy, cod and grey rock salmon, a newsagent's where Charlie buys his cigarettes and copy of the *Daily Mirror* every morning. There is a hairdresser's and an off-licence.

A pub stands on the corner, the Eagle, which has recently been repainted and now sells Sumptuous Cold Collations instead of ham and cheese sandwiches. Charlie visits here regularly and disapproves of the refit, which features mock-antique sporting goods and fake Victorian shop signs. It has driven many of the locals away, to be replaced by a younger crowd. But he accepts the development as he accepts most of the substance and detail of his life. Acceptance is what has been placed in the vacuum where for others there is choice. Such dreams as he has are small and, on most days, are comfortably hidden from his own view.

Alighting from the bus, he is assaulted by a smell which, over the last few weeks, he has become almost accustomed to. Like the bus drivers, and Charlie himself, the local binmen are in the midst of a dispute. This does not seem extraordinary to Charlie, merely an irritatingly private blip in an otherwise consistent pattern of public life. *Snafu*, thinks Charlie, his mind skipping back to army language. Situation normal, all fucked up.

As he walks, the smell seems to separate into three strands: decomposing food, baby shit from disposable nappies and the remnants of bottles and cans of booze. On each different day, a different smell is dominant. Today it is the contents of a thousand discarded Huggies.

He progresses past the six-foot-high pile of rubbish bags a few yards from the bus stop. It has been two weeks now since the last collection. Although Charlie feels dutiful about his own union, he makes a distinction between himself and the binmen who have gone on a work-to-rule after the local authority tried to keep their wages beneath government wage caps. They are unskilled labour; he, as a compositor, is a craftsman. Seven years' apprenticeship. In part of his imagination, the binmen are layabouts and drones whose 'struggle' – as Mike Sunderland, the young man in the herringbone coat on the picket line, would have put it – has little connection with the dignity of his own.

He makes his way past several other depositories of bursting bags, all attended by small squadrons of orbiting flies and bluebottles. The block of flats in which he lives, Ramsay MacDonald House, is constructed of yellow-brown bricks and is four storeys tall. Thin balconies connect the doors on the upper floors and these balconies are edged by rusting fences. A six-year-old girl fell from the second floor two months ago when some welding gave way at the joints. She broke both legs. Still the gap yawns, unrepaired.

Charlie lives on the ground floor. His neighbour on the right is Mrs Jackson, a septuagenarian who lives alone with four cats and who pops in for cups of tea two or three times a day. Popping in, it seems to Charlie, is the central occupation of her life. Her first name, Violet, is never used. She is pleasant and helpful, although Charlie finds her nosiness irritating and makes himself scarce when she appears.

On the other side, a young unmarried mother with a six-month-old baby. The mother has bleached hair and a pierced nose. Her name is Carol. Her last name is unknown to Charlie.

She wears clothes that Charlie thinks of as threatening and punky, but she is friendly and most of the time plays her music at a reasonable volume. She keeps a clean house. She is outside her flat when Charlie arrives, washing her windows with soapy water. The baby whimpers intermittently from the doorstep of the flat – the flat which, Charlie knows, is in all essentials the same as his and Maureen's, Mrs Jackson's and all the others in the block. She turns as she hears Charlie's footstep behind her. She is wearing a blue faded boiler suit with a badge on the lapel that has the insignia ANL. Charlie is not sure what this stands for but has seen Mike Sunderland wearing the same insignia.

– *Hello, Mr Buck.*

Hello, Carol.

There is a pause. Charlie wonders whether he has said enough to fulfil his commitment to politeness. He removes his hat and shifts it from hand to hand. Printer's ink stains his fingers, long-ingrained in the whorls at the tips.

They always smear.

You don't want to use soap.

You don't think?

Plain water and vinegar.

Vinegar?

Sarson's.

I don't want my windows smelling like a bag of old chips.

Carol laughs, showing good white teeth. There is a slight northern twang to her voice which Charlie takes as Geordie, although she is in fact from Leeds. He thinks, as he often does, about what it would be like to have sex with her. Young women now would do anything, he imagines. The world's gone sex mad. Charlie indicates behind him. The nearest pile of refuse stands only a few footsteps from the door. When the front windows are open, a rich, thick stink penetrates the kitchen.

I'd take a bag of chips over that any day, kiddo.

I'll give it a try. How's Robert?

Charlie shrugs.

Who knows how Robert is? He's indescrutable. Like a Chinaman.

He seems a bit down, says Carol.

It's his hobby, says Charlie. *If he smiled it would put a crack in his face.*

He's not so bad. He's got a lot on his mind.

Charlie gives a short laugh.

That's right, says Charlie. *I don't know where he keeps it all.*

The baby starts crying. Carol reaches down and picks it up, makes little clucking noises.

Shh, Nelson, says Charlie. He is uneasy with babies.

There, there, says Carol, rocking the baby up and down.

He was a great man, says Charlie, unable to think of anything else to say.

Who? says Carol.

Admiral Nelson, says Charlie, puzzled.

That's not who he's named after, says Carol.

Nelson's screams increase in volume. He writhes and bucks.

I'd better be going, says Charlie.

Say hello to Robert. From me, says Carol.

*We don't talk much. He doesn't **listen** much. Anyway. I'll try to remember.*

Bye then, Mr Buck.

Bye, Carol. Bye, Nelson.

It is gone six o'clock now. The light is fading. The front door of Charlie's flat is gunmetal grey – exactly the same as all the others. The council bought a job lot from a marine salvage company at a knock-down price; it has become the livery of Ramsay MacDonald House.

Charlie puts his key in the lock, turns it and enters. Inside, the barometer designed to resemble a Spanish guitar shows a prediction of moderate-to-mild. Within the flat, the same law of economics has determined the interior design. In the front room the walls are of diluted brown, which has the effect of compressing and darkening the space which they encompass. This has also been bought in bulk by the local authority. Maureen hates the colour, but, like the other council tenants, she and Charlie are forbidden from making any changes to it, as they are similarly forbidden from altering the door furniture or frames, or the cheap fireplace that surrounds the log-effect gas fire, or any of the plastic light switches that come with the flat.

Although they have lived here for fifteen years, their status is clear, and testament to that status stands plain and stark in the colour of every wall, in the shape and unalterability of each particular fitting. They are the guests and creatures of the council and are subject to the whim of unseen, unnamed men at the town hall whom neither Maureen nor Charlie ever has any luck in raising on the telephone from the booth on the corner of the street when a pipe bursts or the walls leak damp in the winter.

Maureen is in, as he expects, and also, as he expects, the table is laid for tea. The radio is on at a moderate volume. It plays the 'Pina Colada' song. He can see through the serving hatch into the kitchen that she is done up to the nines – a red dress that she has slightly outgrown, a fake-pearl necklace. He knows that she will be wearing high-heeled shoes, bright lipstick, hair brushed and set with the setting lotion that she gets from the local hairdresser's.

Charlie knows that the outfit is not for his benefit. Even in her prime, which Charlie ruefully dates as expiring several years ago, Maureen would not have dressed up for him while staying in. Maureen is dressed up because *Dallas* is on the TV tonight, sandwiched between *Terry and June* and *Petrocelli*.

Charlie can never really understand why she gets herself up in her best clothes just to watch a TV programme, but that was women for you. They weren't rational, like men were. But they were better in their hearts.

Charlie feels he has done well with his wife, better than he could have expected. He is realistic about his own charms, and although he is proud of his full head of hair, grey kept at bay by Grecian 2000, his once trim body overflows at the waistband and lines seem to multiply daily around his forehead and eyes. The choice of a younger wife was a good one. She is, he decides, neither plain nor a nag, and she takes care of the home and has been a good mother to Robert.

No sign of Robert. Charlie feels sure he is in his room. He is always in his room. There or next door with Carol, listening to her awful, furious records. He returns to base at mealtimes, but Robert's appearances in the communal areas of the flat have become rarer and rarer over the past couple of years. He gets up late, listens to the radio, reads magazines. He has had no job since he left school two years ago with two O-levels.

Charlie takes off his coat, puts it on the hanger and smooths out the creases. Without turning, he calls out to his wife.

Hiya, kiddo.

He now turns and sees Maureen divided into vertical bands by the gaps in the multicoloured 'Walk Thru' curtain-strip door. Hearing Charlie's voice, Maureen feels suddenly aware of the soft spread of her body; the jogging is not having the desired effect. She wrinkles her nose in disappointment, then composes her face and turns to Charlie.

Hello, Rock.

The 'Rock' is a private joke. Rock Hudson has been her favourite movie star since before the time she met Charlie. Rock Hudson, the embodiment, for her, of manhood. She used to think that Charlie looked like him, but any slight resemblance that existed has now been effaced by age. Nevertheless, keen to please, she dredges up the old nickname from time to time. Charlie is always flattered.

She smiles in acknowledgement of the joke. She possesses a battery of smiles; it is her default. They contain a series of inflections, defaults-within-the-default. Apologetic, encouraging, puzzled, concerned, defensive, even flirtatious. All merge into one for Charlie, combine into the underlying message, which is of compliance and a determination to please. In a way, Charlie has married her for that smile. He does not notice its mutation over the years they have been together, its sliding away, its slight curl of disappointment. For him the smile merely indicates what it is in fact carefully designed to display – that his wife is happy, and that all is well within their marriage of nineteen years.

She walks with a slightly exaggerated delicacy because of the smartness of her clothes. Her hair is thin and auburn, and the helmet-like style vaguely mimics Purdey in *The New Avengers*. Her face is unexceptional. Age has robbed it of distinguishing characteristics. Ten years younger than Charlie, she nevertheless seems well into middle age. Her sexual fantasy, apart from Rock Hudson, is Patrick Mower.

What's for tea, then?

Hold your horses.

Charlie sits down in the chocolate-coloured cord-effect wing three-seater. Next to it is the sole bookcase in the house, with four shelves. The bookshelves are full of bound books by nineteenth-century English authors – Dickens, Hardy, Austen, the Brontës. Their spines, embossed with gold, please Charlie. Some day he is resolved to read one of them. They are entirely decorative, bought by mail order – £15 for the lot from the Gratton's catalogue.

He removes his work boots – Tuf Big T – and places them

in the cupboard by the door. Then he [...]
on the black-and-white television, whic[...]
produces a picture full of ghosts. He has be[...]
colour for years now, but Maureen is happy en[...]
old set. Like her husband, she is suspicious of both cha[...]
hire-purchase agreements – the 'never-never'. They have [...]
little bit tucked away and they don't like to see it eaten into.
Maureen keeps a sizeable sum of money pared from Charlie's
wages hidden under a loose floorboard in the bedroom.
Although inflation eats away at it, she does not trust banks.

Charlie parades around the room holding the aerial aloft,
but the ghosts will not be exorcized. From next door, for the
first time, he notices the faint thud of music. He is unable
to identify the particular record as 'Spiral Scratch' by the
Buzzcocks and the low-level vibration is filed away in his mind
as merely part of a whole incomprehensible panorama of
music that emerged sometime during the 1960s which offends
him both aesthetically and, for reasons he himself cannot fully
grasp, morally.

He stares at the wall. He continues staring, as if beaming a
certain variety of dangerous radiation towards Carol. It is not
like her, so he feels it would be rude to knock on the wall, yet
he finds the noise increasingly intolerable. As if his presence
has been registered, the volume lowers fractionally – enough
for him to drop his gaze, then, gradually, move back and lower
himself on to the sofa and put his feet up on the square-quilted
spongeable black PVC pouffe – the 'poo-fay', as he pronounces
it.

He inspects the room around him. It seems reasonably clean
and tidy. Three places, as usual, are laid at the splay-legged
Ercol table.

A nest of three coffee tables stands next to the sofa. On the
largest of them, one copy of *Reader's Digest* and one of *National*

s the tip of his finger across part of the
...e result. Absolutely clean.

...ng with the table settings. Always concerned
...e is careful to set out the cutlery perpendicular
...ge of the table and exactly spaced. The knives are of
...ordinary sort. *Good*, thinks Charlie. *No fish*. Maureen folds
napkins into precise cylindrical shapes and puts wheat-
coloured table mats carefully down, in exact alignment with
the knives and forks. Charlie runs his tongue around the soft
corners of his mouth, which feels dry and tastes sour. He
notices that Maureen is putting out glasses.

Have we got any beer?

We've run out.

It occurs to Charlie that he is not feeling himself today.
Normally, and consistently, he is of the view that his life is
better than most, that his life is an oasis of stability and quiet
certainty. Respected in his home and at work. Job for life.
Family intact, wife and child. Good health. But he finds himself
unable to help but be mildly inflamed by the cumulative
oppressions of the stink of the rubbish and the noise of 'Spiral
Scratch' and the persistence of the television ghosts and the
absence of beer. He is also aware that the impending election
is playing on his mind for some reason but cannot understand
why. He is not 'political' like Mike at work. The prospect of
change, however, unsettles him. When he speaks, it is quietly,
but with an edge.

*Jesus God Almighty, Mo! I did ask you to get some in. I did
specifically say . . .*

Maureen smiles apologetically.

*I didn't have enough money, Charlie. Not after buying the
food.*

Charlie's face becomes a mask of genuine puzzlement.

But I gave you ten pounds an' odd not three days since.

*Everything keeps going up. And the money from the strike fund,
it's not very . . .*

Charlie winces.

Hold on. It's not right to –

*I'm just **saying** –*

I'm just fighting for a decent wage. I'm fighting for . . . for . . .

He throws his hand out around the room, around his world,
in a gesture to take in the cheap sticks of furniture, the dull
walls.

For all this.

The sentence comes out portentous, bathetic. The desire
to laugh invades Maureen; she pummels it down.

Charlie, I didn't mean to –

*I want a beer. I've been standing on the picket line for hours
listening to the . . . blather of idiots, and now I need a drink.*

What about the home-brew?

Charlie has bought a Hambleton home-brewing kit recently
and been making his own sour-tasting concoction in a plastic
bucket kept in the airing cupboard. His younger brother,
Tommy, makes gallons of the stuff, sells off the surplus,
watered down. Tommy's always one for the main chance. It's
cheap, it tastes OK.

It's nowhere near ready. It's got two weeks to go.

With this, Charlie stands up, puts on his coat and begins to
walk towards the door. Again, the smell of the rotting rubbish
assails him.

But dinner's nearly ready.

I'll only be a moment.

He feels angry, then guilty about being angry, then angry
about feeling guilty. He pauses as he approaches the exit to
the hall. The ghosts in the television settle into something
viewable. It is nearly the end of the six o'clock news now;
although the picture is unfocused, the audio is loud and clear.

The newsreader is Kenneth Kendall. Charlie likes and trusts him for his reassuring manner and beautiful pronunciation. The one on ITV always seems drunk. Kendall is saying that voting is continuing, that the turnout is higher than average. He is trailing the election special that is taking place on BBC 1 after the polls close. Charlie makes a mental note to watch it, if he can stay awake that long. He hesitates.

Have you voted?

Maureen's voice responds from the kitchen, raised over the tone of the whistle of a boiling kettle.

Is it today?

You know that it's today. Of course it's today.

I don't know, Charlie.

Charlie shrugs. Maureen isn't very political either. When she bothers to vote, she votes the same as Charlie. He can't quite decide whether to vote himself, since it's a five-minute detour away from the off-licence and it's a cold night.

I'm going to make my mark. Be back in about fifteen.

The tea – it's going to be ruined.

The news is finishing now. The expression on Kenneth Kendall's face changes from gravitas to restrained and dignified amusement as he describes the exploits of a Siamese cat who both enjoys and is adept at low-level parachuting. Charlie leaves, the echo of a soft, tinny miaou pursuing him.

Charlie, as he walks to the local school where the polling station is set up, tries to get his thoughts clear. Charlie Buck is not a philosophical man, although he tries to have points of view. A man without a point of view, he feels, is not much cop.

Charlie's points of view tend to mutate and contradict themselves according to circumstance, peer pressure and his intake of alcohol. Nevertheless, his central and most constant point of view is that a lot of people, wealthy or poor, black or white, short or tall, are up to no good. That you have to keep your eyes skinned or you'll get well and truly turned over.

He thinks bosses are on the make, he thinks politicians are on the take. Judges are perverts, juries are fools. He *knows* policeman are bent. His brother, wide-as-a-barn-door Tommy Buck, used to be one, a beat copper in Romford. The proceeds, legit and otherwise – mainly otherwise – bought him his three-bedroom terraced house in Theydon Bois. It would have been a detached with double-glazing by now if he hadn't left the force after losing his volcanic, hooligan's temper with the station sergeant. Put him in hospital, put Tommy on the dole queue. Tommy never was good with authority. Now he was a builder. Don't talk to Charlie about builders.

Yes. People are up to no good. Armies of them, marching in their millions, skiving, cheeseparing, thieving, pilfering, exploiting, loitering, cheating, lazing. Charlie thinks he is an exception to this rule, that he is an honest man in a den of thieves who has been turned over two or three times too often in his life. Decimalization, which he thinks the biggest con trick of the century, has been a set up by big business to raise prices at the expense of the working man. Call them working men, of course, but most are layabouts. Inflation, which he considers the greatest threat to modern life bar nothing, ensures price rises for house-owners, a group within society that Charlie feels he has little hope of joining. Trade unions, with the important exception of his own, hold the country to ransom.

Women's liberation is all very well and good, but it is, like communism, against nature. He has no particular objection to homosexuals, so long as they get up to their business in private. Larry Grayson makes him laugh, and John Inman, and so does Frank Spencer, although he is not so sure that Frank Spencer is really one of those. Homosexuals, nevertheless, are also indisputably against nature. He does not consider lesbianism probable, and thus it is beyond the reach of his prejudice.

Then there are foreigners. Southern Europeans he finds amusing or hysterical. Northern Europeans have a pleasantly enlightened attitude to nudity and sex. The Germans are the only cross-Channel community that he thoroughly dislikes, for all the conventional reasons. The Swiss and the Belgians are boring but make good chocolate.

He is frightened of young black men, but has no particular grudge against blacks as a group, so long as they don't take on too much front. Snowball at work is the perfect black man: neither young nor contrary, speaks English with a proper accent, rations his patois. Indian Asians, just defined in his mind as Asians, are peace-loving and hard-working, but they smell strange and are too interested in money.

Such are the points of view of Charlie Buck, family man, union man, craftsman. Without, in fact, finally bearing any of them in mind, he marches into the polling station. He does not have to think where to put his cross, even though he blames Callaghan's pay policy – which his employers are insisting on sticking to, suppressing the printers' wages – partly for the strike on which he finds himself.

He does not take into account policy or listen to speeches or weigh up differences in political nuance. He strides purposefully into the secret polling booth, feeling momentarily important, and inscribes a cross, clearly and heavily, so that a dent shows through the paper on the other side. He votes Labour, as he always does. He assumes that enough other people similar to him will do the same for Sunny Jim to be returned to power. He cannot imagine any woman occupying Number 10, despite the contrary indications of the pollsters.

He leaves the school and heads towards the off-licence, feeling strangely elated by the assertion of his democratic right. He fantasizes that the election in their ward will be won by one vote – his. However, he simultaneously recognizes that this is unlikely since the majority stands at some 16,000; it is one of the safest Labour seats in London.

At the off-licence he examines the shelves. He takes his time; he wishes to punish Maureen for crimes he is nevertheless not sure she has committed. A Bristol Cream Sherry box for £3.75 a gallon. He translates the 75p into fifteen shillings, a habit he cannot quite lose. Good value. A special offer. He is tempted, but there are not enough Christmases.

He moves past the Melcher's Advocaat, the Van Huyten Cherry Brandy, the blackcurrant rum, the Domecq Double Century, the Cossack Vodka, the Lord George 'His Own Special Reserve' Rich Old Port. Sam, the proprietor, a fat man with a fixed, all-purpose grimace and a perpetually wet mouth, sits uncomfortably behind the counter. Charlie has been coming here for ten years, but Sam still barely acknowledges that he is any different from a customer walking in for the first time off the street. They do not chat. However, on this occasion, Sam graces him with a small nod of recognition. Charlie nods back, encouraged.

I've been down the polling station.

Sam nods again, but otherwise does not respond.

Exercising my democratic right.

He says this with slight sarcasm, as if the words 'democratic right' were in inverted commas. Still Sam does not respond. He moves his bulk on the stool, trying to find some elusive centre of gravity. The discomfort of his weight is a constant oppression. Now Charlie feels vaguely embarrassed at the silence that has been thrown into relief by his venturing to speak in the first place. He cannot help himself filling up the gap.

Still, I suppose they're all the same as one another really, more or less.

He feels perplexed that he has been manoeuvred into stating a belief that he does not, in fact, hold, simply to gain acceptance from someone he does not, in fact, care about. A long pause ensues in which Sam shifts his weight once more, then smacks his wet lips twice, then, finally, speaks.

Not this time.

Now Charlie feels trapped and foolish. He did not expect Sam to have this opinion, did not credit him with the strength of mind. He *agrees* with Sam, is suddenly desperate to take this unusual opportunity for some kind of connection with this fat man he has seen practically every week for as long as he can remember. But there is no space for him to retreat into. To agree that Sam is right will be ridiculous now. Will expose his need.

Well, says Charlie. *Well.*

This country needs a bloody shake-up, says Sam, getting off his stool, something Charlie has hardly ever seen him do before. *No bones about it. I voted for Mrs T. She's the one for the small businessman. She'll knock this place into shape.*

He laughs to himself, something that Charlie has also rarely witnessed.

Well, says Charlie again, knocked off balance once more by both Sam's sudden fit of good humour and his proclamation of enthusiasm towards someone he vaguely perceives as an enemy on several fronts: Tory, female, anti-union. There is a brief silence. Charlie imagines that in this silence he is meant to make some expression of agreement with Sam. It is, he perceives, a test of loyalty. He fails it.

Charlie suddenly wants to get out of the shop. He cannot see his normal bottles of Worthington Pale Ale behind the counter to the left, where they usually are. Instead there is a stack of large cans of Double Diamond. Blindly, he points at them.

I'll have four of those, please.

Sam reaches behind him and takes the cans off the shelf. Charlie senses suddenly that the shopkeeper has fallen back into himself, that the gate of communication, briefly opened, has firmly shut once more. He passes the cans and curtly announces the price. Charlie fumbles for his wallet and takes out a £1 note. There is a disappointingly small amount of change. No bag is offered.

Almost scurrying now, Charlie turns to leave the shop.

Toodleoo, he says. Immediately, he feels like kicking himself. Not 'goodbye' or even 'bye' or even nothing at all. *Toodleoo*. A woman's farewell. He cannot be sure whether Sam responds or not; there is a slight change in his breathing which may or may not indicate some kind of acknowledgement.

He checks his watch. He has been gone half an hour. He feels now that the punishment he is meting out to Maureen is overly severe, and a shiver of guilt runs around the walls of his stomach. He quickens his step. As he turns the corner of the main road towards Ramsay MacDonald House, there is a man in a grey mac selling bunches of pink and red carnations from a trestle table.

They are a flower he finds prissy, but he stops and buys a bunch to make amends to Maureen. The man in the mac winks at him as he hands them over; Charlie has no idea what this indicates, but he gives a half-smile of acknowledgement nevertheless.

2

As Charlie approaches the doorway to the flat, he notices that the dominant smell from the black bags has changed from the heavy tang of soiled nappies to the earthy stink of decomposing food. He cannot decide whether or not this represents an improvement in the air quality. His key turns in the lock. The sight that greets him is of Maureen sitting at one end of the living-room table, a hostess trolley parked parallel. The smartness of her dress, the dark thickness of her melting make-up, juxtaposed with the strange sadness of the trolley, bring out another pang of regret in him. She looks up, with a version of a smile, one that is hollowed out and tinged with anger. But it begins to dissolve into something more real when she sees the flowers. She gets up from the table, wobbles on her heels, nearly falls, then steadies herself.

I'm sorry, kiddo. Being off work so long is getting to me. It's not your fault.

He holds out the flowers. Maureen takes them, reaches up to kiss Charlie on the cheek. He smells scent that he recognizes as perpetually Maureen's but is unable to name.

It's not easy for a man to have no job, says Maureen.

Charlie feels his pale repentance colour immediately into something darker.

*I **do** have a job, kiddo,* he says, finding it hard to keep the irritation out of his voice. *We're just in dispute.*

You know what I mean, Maureen says blithely. *Five months is a long time.*

As long as it takes is how long it takes.

Maureen nods. She still isn't sure what Charlie does at work. He has tried to explain, but she cannot visualize it. Once she visited the print rooms. The noise was deafening. All the shouting gave her a headache.

Maureen goes to put the flowers into water. Charlie removes his coat and makes to sit down at the table. The gas fire on the opposite wall has all three panels lit, yet there is still a chill on this side of the room. There are central-heating radiators, but they are supplied by a central boiler for the whole block. The boiler has not been working for the last two weeks.

The light from the overhead bulb is not muted or diffused by the tasselled lampshade, but merely contained and sent downwards instead of in all directions. The light is harsh, but Maureen likes it bright during mealtimes. Charlie would prefer the softer, yellower light of the standard lamp in the corner. This, he knows, will not be illuminated until after tea, when television viewing begins in earnest.

He hesitates before sitting down, then, instead of lowering himself into the chair, goes across the room to the Alba Stereogram and inspects the LPs that are arrayed in the mock-teak cabinet. Between Jack Jones, *The Essential*, and Jim Reeves, *The Intimate*, are three discs, all by Annunzio Mantovani – *Mr Music*, *Mantovani Today* and *Some Enchanted Evening*. Charlie loves Mantovani and has a collection of some fifty of his albums.

He changes his mind about the LPs and examines instead the smaller rack of 45rpm singles that abuts the album section. He takes out three records, wipes them all carefully with a yellow anti-static cloth, then stacks them on the spindle of the record deck. He switches it on. After a few seconds of mysterious whirrings and clankings, the first record drops, then the playing arm moves across, magically locating the first groove. Charlie feels a small sensation of lushness, of greenery, as the first notes seep from the speakers. He turns. Maureen has returned with a glass for his beer. He pours it, sits down at the table and takes a deep draught as the warm blanket of the music cossets him. He adds the words to the soundtrack of the Mantovani record, which he has loved since it was first released thirty years ago.

Charmaine . . . my Charmaine . . .

Maureen calls out to the back of the flat.

Rob!

Charlie smiles contentedly at Maureen as she takes a dish from the hostess trolley, walks over to where he sits and removes the lid from the dish. The smell is unfamiliar.

Surprise, she says. *A new recipe.*

Never a dull moment with you, is there?

Now it is Charlie who calls down the corridor, much louder and more threateningly than Maureen.

Robert, your dinner's ready! Come on, you bloody layabout!

I got the recipe from an advert in the TV Times, Maureen is saying. *It's called Lumberjack pie.*

What's in it?

See if you can guess.

The mush that is put on to the plate is an odd mix of orange, pink and pale yellow. The smell is stronger now. Charlie finds it faintly sickening, but has made up his mind to feign enjoyment if necessary. Maureen has placed a minuscule portion on her own plate and a vast pile on Robert's.

There's potato, says Charlie tentatively.

Maureen can wait no longer to give up her secret.

It's instant potato, Spam, baked beans and Cheddar cheese.

Is that so? says Charlie.

The whole thing only cost 72p.

There is a noise in the corridor. Robert appears, taking

small, reluctant steps towards the table. He smiles weakly at his mother, but does not look in Charlie's direction. He is dressed in a black T-shirt and straight black jeans. He has clearly not shaved that morning. His ginger hair is unkempt. There are several pimples at the point where his nostrils join his pale, etiolated face. He says nothing, merely sits down and regards the slowly spreading contents of the plate.

Charlie looks at him, irritated. He puts on a fake voice.

Hello, Dad. How lovely to see you. And Mother. What a wonderful meal you have prepared for us. So, Father. Please tell me all about your day fighting for a better standard of living for your wife and son.

Robert does not rise to this, but pushes the mess around with his fork.

Leave it, Charlie, says Maureen. *He's depressed.*

He's depressed? I'm bloody depressed. But I don't moon around in my room all day like a slug with a broken leg.

Robert fakes puzzlement.

They don't have legs, he murmurs.

Maureen silently dishes up some supplementary vegetables. Carrots, sliced and boiled. Cauliflower, frozen peas. She fills up her own plate with these. A thin cloud of steam drifts into Charlie's face. Charlie takes a deep swig of the Double Diamond. His belly sits over his belt by two or three inches. Underneath his nylon shirt, he can suddenly feel the pattern of his string vest, which makes him feel momentarily uncomfortable.

Robert is still staring at his plate.

What is it?

Lumberjack pie, says Maureen brightly. *It's instant mashed potato, Spam –*

Pet food, says Robert.

Don't you dare start, says Charlie, jabbing his knife in his son's direction.

Where's yours? Robert indicates Maureen's tiny portion.

I'm watching my weight.

Do you think Mum's fat, Dad? Robert turns to his father for the first time.

What?

Do you find her a little on the heavy side?

Of course not.

Why'd you buy her an exercise machine for Christmas?

Because she wanted one.

Why do you always get her dresses too small for her?

Charlie clenches his fist around his fork.

Listen, you –

Stop it please, you two, says Maureen, primly. *Let's have tea, shall we?*

I mean, it's not as if you're body beautiful, Charlie.

That's enough. And that's enough of this 'Charlie' business. I'm your father.

OK, Chuck.

Charlie unfolds his napkin and places it on his lap. There is a jug of Quosh orange on the table, a drink that Maureen uses as a substitute for wine, since she does not drink except on special occasions. She pours herself, Robert and Charlie small glasses, then sits down. 'Charmaine' is finishing on the record player, the strings cascading then fading into scratchy silence, before a new record falls and engages – 'The Song from Moulin Rouge', another classic. Mantovani, the soundtrack of Charlie's dream life: enfolding, warm, soupy, luxuriant.

Robert pushes the food around his plate. He takes two peas and a carrot, makes eyes and a nose in the mashed potato. He scoops an indent for a mouth, ups the ends into a smile, then down into a grimace. He mutters to himself.

Happy. Sad. Happy. Sad.

Just as the music begins to reach its first peak, a thudding begins again from next door. It sounds identical to the first noisy penetration from Carol the Single Mother's flat, but in fact it is X-Ray Spex rather than the Buzzcocks – 'Oh Bondage Up Yours'. The difference is lost on Charlie, who stares at his glutinous tea-time meal morosely. The Mantovani strings are being polluted. He stares at the wall. This time the radiation he tries to summon up has no effect.

Never mind it, Charlie, says Maureen. *Try your pie.*

Charlie digs a fork into the mulch on his plate and propels it into his mouth, past teeth yellowed by age and thirty Capstans every day. His tastebuds have been damaged by the smoking, but he has a vague sensation that what is in his mouth is not particularly nice. Although he likes Spam as it comes, or grilled on toast, in this incarnation it seems greasy and unpalatable. Nevertheless, he nods in approbation, but almost immediately takes a draught of the beer to erase the taste.

Robert picks only at the vegetables, but Charlie dutifully finishes every last mouthful of the rapidly cooling pie. The cooler it gets, the less palatable, as more artificial flavours seem to emerge. He tussles with the problem of being polite to Maureen while ensuring that this meal is never, ever presented to him again.

Robert has picked up a copy of *Tit-Bits* from a nearby coffee table and is reading the cartoons. Charlie looks at him sharply.

Found a job yet?

Yeah.

What?

Airline pilot.

*Did you **look** for a job?*

Why? So I can go on strike? It hardly seems worth the effort.

He has not taken his eyes off the cartoon. Charlie feels the muscles in his back tighten.

You can't keep poncing off us for ever.

I'm not poncing off you.

Yes, you are.

I make my own money. I'm on the Social. Plus Uncle Tommy gives me a bit for helping him out now and then.

*I forgot that you're fleecing the taxpayer. And what do we see of that? You spend all that on fags. And as for your Uncle Tommy . . . well, you don't want to end up like **him**.*

*I like Uncle Tommy. He's a laugh. And he does all right. Got a nice house. Owns **his** house.*

He's a laugh all right. He'll laugh you all the way to Wormwood Scrubs.

He's all right. Sees me all right.

Charlie feels himself going red in the face.

*That **chancer**. Listen. Tommy only does anything for himself. You should keep away from him. I told you that.*

Happy. Sad. Happy. Sad.

What?

Keep your hair on. Anyway, don't you like your little brother?

Don't you smart-talk me. We put a roof over your head, we –

Feed me, look after me, supply me with hot water and soft toilet paper. Change the record, Dad.

You need to face up to your responsibilities.

Change the record.

What record?

I fucking hate Mantovani.

*Don't you **dare** swear in front of your mother.*

You won't have to put up with it much longer.

There is a silence. He looks at Maureen, who is staring down at her plate. Charlie decides to try and lighten the atmosphere.

Mo, Carol next door. Who's her baby named after?

When Maureen answers, it sounds as if she is distant, thinking unrelated thoughts.

Nelson?

Yes, Nelson.

Don't know. The sailor, I suppose.

No. She said it wasn't.

Maybe the father is called Nelson.

The father's called Trevor.

Nelson Riddle? says Maureen.

She wouldn't know of Nelson Riddle.

Robert yawns.

He's named after Nelson Mandela, he says.

Who's he when he's at home? says Charlie.

What do you mean, we won't have to put up with it much longer? says Maureen finally.

Robert blinks. He had thought the remark had been forgotten.

Dunno, he says.

You don't know.

There might be a place.

Now Maureen begins to fidget with her necklace.

A place? she says.

It's not far, says Robert. *Might not happen anyway.*

Oh, happy day, says Charlie.

But Maureen is punctured by the thought of her only child leaving home. She slowly clears away the plates and returns with cling peaches in syrup. There is a tin of evaporated milk, perforated on either side.

Are you all right, Mo?

Sorry about the tin, Charlie. I broke the jug today. It slipped while I was washing up.

Butterfingers, he says, not unkindly. Then he turns back to Robert. *How you going to afford the rent on this place, then?*

Isn't any.

What do you mean, there isn't any?

It's a kind of . . . squat.

Maureen looks shocked.

You can't live in a place like that.

Why?

It's with a load of other layabouts, is it? says Charlie.

Not everyone who lives in a squat is a layabout.

Charlie bites back his anger in deference to Maureen's obvious upset. He dispenses the thin white liquid on to the peach slices and begins to shovel them into his mouth. He likes the flavour more than that of fresh peaches, just like he prefers instant coffee powder to percolated. He finishes a second can of Double Diamond. He is experiencing some mild effect from the alcohol now and feels himself growing slightly expansive.

Are you really going? says Maureen.

Of course he's not, says Charlie, who then decides to switch the subject, to take Maureen's mind off it.

Would you like a coffee, Robert? says Maureen.

Thanks, says Robert, desultorily finishing off his peach slices. *Got any percolated?*

Yeah, and get him a glass of champagne while you're about it, says Charlie. *Then you can feed him some grapes.*

There's only instant.

I'll pass then.

He rises from the table.

Where you going?

Thought I'd go and see Carol. Sounds like she's got some new records.

You and her pals, are you?

Not really. She's just got some good records.

You could clear up, says Charlie.

It doesn't matter, interjects Maureen brightly. *You go next door.*

Thanks, Mum.

Robert gives his father a triumphant look, grabs his jacket and sweeps out of the flat. After a few moments, Charlie and Maureen hear the bell ring next door.

That kid, says Charlie, hacking at his peach slices with the edge of his spoon.

You're too hard on him.

*He never makes an effort. Just drifts. He's eighteen years old. He's a **man**, for God's sake. I was in the army at his age.*

If you keep telling him he's a failure, then that's what he'll learn to be.

Charlie barely hears her.

He's just like my brother. Never sticks with anything. Floats around. Ducking. Diving. Chancing it. No wonder he's so fond of Tommy.

*You're his father, Charlie. **You're** who he looks to.*

He treats me like dirt. He treats us both like dirt.

*He does look for jobs. He **does** try. But he doesn't tell you about it, because every time he gets another rejection he thinks you'll throw it back in his face. He thinks that if you don't see him trying, then you won't see him failing.*

You're too soft, Mo. You give him an inch, he'll take a mile. Or a kilometre or whatever it is nowadays.

Charlie finishes off his peaches. As they disappear, so his mood dissipates. He regards his wife fondly as she carefully separates the sugary syrup from the peaches before eating them. He leans over, pecks her on the cheek.

How's your day been then, kiddo? says Charlie.

Nothing special, Charlie. I saw Mrs Jackson while I was out running.

How is the old busybody?

She's not so bad. I helped her do her hair. She's suffering most terribly at the moment with the arthritis. She can hardly move her hands. They're like claws. All bent like claws. Her sons aren't much use either. *The last time she saw either of them was about three months ago. She's all alone.*

Not much of a life, is it?

She wouldn't want any pity. She's got a lot of pride. She brought me a box of crystallized fruit.

That was nice. Still, she can't be nasty really, can she? Lonely people can't afford it.

We can have some later, if you like.

Maureen slowly finishes her peaches, chewing each mouthful at least twenty times, as she has read is best for digestion, then makes her way back into the kitchen, taking empty plates with her. Charlie settles back in his chair. Maureen returns and places a cup of instant coffee in front of him, and a jar of Coffee Mate. She can never quite get the proportions right, so she lets Charlie do it himself. Charlie places exactly one and a half teaspoons in, watches the powder dissolve. He prefers the taste to that of fresh milk.

Maureen leans over and wipes a few crumbs from the dinner off the corner of his mouth. Somehow he always leaves residues of food on his face; Maureen has made this tender gesture a thousand times.

Mucky pup.

Charlie smiles in acknowledgement. Maureen hurriedly tidies away the last of the cutlery and plates. Her eyes are darting towards the television screen. Although the sound is turned down, the TV remains switched on and she can see the opening titles to *Dallas* beginning to flash up, Larry Hagman grinning like a friendly devil.

I'll do the washing-up, kiddo. You settle down, says Charlie.

Thanks, Rock.

Charlie opens his throat to dispatch his third can of beer. He lights a cigarette, allows it to rest in his mouth. Shards of ash fall on to the plates as he clears them away into the kitchen. At the heart of the cigarette, a blaze like a star. Charlie has that day read in *Reader's Digest* that everything we are made of was forged in the stars. He looks around him at the Formica work surfaces, the Brillo pads, a jar of chutney. Impossible to believe.

On the windowsill by the sink there is a photograph of Robert when he was about fifteen. Charlie glances at it as he watches a cloud of bubbles develop in the sink. To Charlie's eyes, his son is not good-looking, with a weak mouth, pale unhealthy skin. Maureen tells him that girls find him attractive, want to look after him. He finds this incomprehensible.

The familiar *Dallas* theme tune pipes into the room from the lounge, now attaining its crescendo and ending. Charlie pictures his wife, as he scrapes Spam and Smash from the cornflower-pattern plates, seeing her fade into the television, into the world of oil wells and company duels and sex. This television version of Maureen has lips that are moistened, predatory. In his imagination, Charlie thinks her sexual once more, before familiarity wore down that perspective, before she became distilled into mother, provider, housewife. He doesn't care to watch *Dallas* himself, finding it not real enough. The Yanks always had to go over the top.

But as for Maureen, nothing could get her out of the room on the nights when Southfork manifested itself into the corner. Her evening classes, on Mondays and Wednesdays, are movable feasts, dispensable, born out of a need to fill space in her life rather than true enthusiasm, Charlie suspects. Still-life painting and yoga. *Dallas* was different. Maureen's brother died a few months previously; she had left the wake almost as soon as arriving rather than miss the programme. She had kept her funeral gear on until the closing credits.

He had asked her once what it was she loved so much about it.

I don't know, she had said.

Then there had been a long pause. Charlie was leaving the room, having abandoned hope of receiving an answer. Then, a murmur.

It's something about power, I think.

That was the last word he ever got out of her on the subject.

Charlie finishes the washing-up and then completes the drying also, with a tea-towel that is a souvenir from Ireland and is imprinted with shamrocks, shelalaghs and leprechauns. Finishing, he folds it carefully, and inspects the shamrocks, mistaking them for clover. He still looks for a four-leaf one when he sees a patch of them. But his superstitions tend to be less overt. He avoids certain thoughts in case the act of thinking them will bring them about. When a goal is scored against his football team, Fulham, he sometimes thinks it is his fault. Sometimes he is at the centre of his own magical universe and believes that what he thinks has a mysterious effect on the wider world.

Back in the sitting room, JR is arguing with Sue Ellen. Charlie stares at Sue Ellen's lips, and wonders momentarily what it would be like to experience her performing fellatio. Maureen won't do it. It is one of the few regrets of his marriage. JR is shouting. His eyebrows working up and down. JR storms out. Cut to Bobby. He is a good man in a difficult situation. Charlie identifies with him.

Charlie decides to go to the spare room. He loosens his belt a notch and sips at the fourth can of beer. He doesn't like Double Diamond much: too gassy. He wishes he had been more assertive with Sam.

In the spare room, he opens the door, which he has rehung to open outwards. He reaches his arm in and round the corner to switch on the light. Inside, a complete miniature world. There is a grey and white mountain that dominates one corner of the room. Behind it, a vista of blue sky and rolling hills painted directly on to the walls. Charlie has taken a chance that the council will have no cause to check inside and has broken the rules.

There are figurines clustered around a small wooden-roofed railway station building in the centre. They are dressed in Victorian attire. A young woman holding a yellow parasol with a bonnet. A man with a high collar and a top hat. A working-class family: tykes, a barrel-chested man with a cloth cap, a plain wife. A fat matron, a parson, a grandfather and grandmother. Two babies in prams.

The world spreads in all directions. There are several small illuminated buildings that fill with light the moment Charlie bends his arm into the room and hits the switch. There are trees, made of sponge and wire, a level crossing, perfectly miniaturized road signs. Milk churns, red fire buckets. The small world fills the room.

Thirty minutes after the end of *Dallas* and Maureen has changed into a nightdress and dressing gown. She hears the soft thud of music from next door, nurses a mug of cocoa that she sips to help her sleep. It is not long before her bedtime. She contemplates doing a few exercises but rejects the idea, though promises herself that she will do double the number in the morning.

She hears Robert's key in the lock. He sees her immediately, comes and sits in the chair beside her.

Want a biscuit with that?

Maureen says nothing. She suffers from mouth ulcers; runs her tongue now around a small crater on the inner surface of her bottom lip.

What's the matter?

Maureen looks up. There is lipstick on Robert's neck. She gives the smallest of smiles.

Have a nice time next door?

It was all right. What's the matter?

I don't know really.

Robert nods.

Is it about me leaving?

I suppose so.

Dad's right, you know. I can't stay here for ever.

She reaches for her son's hand. To her surprise, he lets her take it.

Why don't you like him, Rob?

Dad?

Yes, Dad.

He's all right.

He thinks you hate him.

Robert shifts uncomfortably in the chair.

I don't hate him. He just winds me up all the time. He's got me marked down. He thinks I'm a big fat loser.

I'm sure that's not true. I'm sure he doesn't think that.

He wants me to be a brain surgeon or something. You know, I'm not all that . . . clever. It's not easy getting a job. He should try it sometimes. I don't know. He just makes me feel . . . like . . . He makes me feel . . .

Like what?

I don't know. Like giving up. I suppose.

Robert removes his hand from Maureen's.

That's silly, Rob. You're only eighteen. Your dad loves you, you know. He just wants you to . . . fulfil your potential.

I think he over-estimates my potential.

Rob, will you do me a favour?

I'm listening.

Try and make it up with him a little bit, will you? Especially if you're leaving.

Maureen pauses, hoping for a retraction from Robert. There is only silence.

*You **are** leaving, aren't you?*

I think so. Yes.

Well, then. You don't want bad blood between you and your father.

Robert sighs.

I'll have a go, Mum. But he . . .

I know. I know.

The gas jets that supply the fire hiss. Charlie's footfall can be heard from his room.

Is the pep talk over? says Robert, smiling.

It's over.

I'm off to my room, then. I've got to get up early to help out Uncle Tommy.

What are you doing there?

A bit of this and that. Site dogsbody really. A bit of hod-carrying. Tea-making. General bodging.

Why don't you tell Charlie about it?

You know how he feels. He thinks Uncle Tommy's a bad influence.

But at least he'll know you're trying.

*He doesn't see me working with Tommy as **trying**. He sees it as betrayal.*

Maureen nods, sips the last of her cocoa.

I don't like keeping secrets from your father.

Perhaps I shouldn't confide in you any more. Is that what you want me to do?

No.

Robert takes his mother's empty mug to put in the kitchen.

Something will come along. Don't worry. G'night, Mum.

I know. Good night, Rob.

Charlie goes over to one of the cottages that stand at the edge of the room. He flicks back the roof to reveal a small array of switches. He engages one; immediately there is a soft sound from the far side of the room. A locomotive pulling a series of three brown-and-cream-liveried coaches begins to move along the OO-gauge railway that curls round the edges of the room. A whistle emerges from the engine; wisps of smoke appear, generated by the small heating element in the chimney.

Charlie sinks down into the middle of the array and watches the train navigate the route. He finds its progress reassuring. Up the mountain on rack railway of the sort that helps trains climb the Alps. This is what the mountain is supposed to represent, although the small world is otherwise British. There are red post boxes, a station clock, British signal boxes. Occasionally Charlie changes the points on the track to send the train on a slightly different circuit. But he enjoys the way the journey is always more or less the same.

He picks up a model box that has a small set of unpainted figurines. The box reads 'Seated American Tourists'. He takes out a man in a Homburg hat with a confident expression and a square jaw. Then, with the flat edge of a screwdriver, he opens a small tin of Humbrol enamel paint and begins to carefully apply a brown glaze to the man's hat. His tongue protrudes slightly as he concentrates. The train continues whistling and clicking on the track. It rises and falls on the mountain. The Victorian figurines watch mutely, never to board.

It is ten o'clock before Maureen puts her head in the doorway. The seated American tourist (male) is now wearing a blue-grey suit, a yellow tie and a cream shirt. Maureen's make-up has been wiped off. Night cream has been applied, making her ghostly in Charlie's eyes.

Do you want a cup of cocoa, Charlie?

He thinks of the skin forming on the top of the coloured milk and the idea suddenly revolts him. He declines the offer, wishes he had more beer, even Double Diamond. He feels woozy, hungover. Hair of the dog is what he needs. But the off-licence will be closed now. The corner shops are all closed by five o'clock, earlier on a Wednesday.

Some biscuits?

What is there?

Royal Scot. I think a few Rich Tea, but they're stale.

Charlie shakes his head, disappointed. He was hoping for a shortbread finger.

I'll be up in a while.

Maureen leaves. She always goes to bed first. She is usually asleep by the time Charlie joins her, in his flannel pyjamas decorated with vertical stripes the colour of lightly stewed rhubarb. She snores lightly, not enough to keep Charlie awake but it irritates him none the less. Charlie wants to stay up tonight and watch the election results, but he feels exhausted. He smokes another cigarette, moves the trains around the track again. Once more round, twice. It is enough.

He switches off the light in the room, checks the lounge and kitchen. Everything is switched off. Light from the orange streetlamps swamps the room. Deep pools of shadow are cast by the sofa. Charlie turns and closes the door behind him. The wood of the frame has swollen and it is a struggle to jam it shut, but Charlie works on it, believing it to reduce the risk of a fire spreading.

He goes to the bathroom. As usual, the sight of the pedestal set his wife has purchased from the catalogue offends him. It is her area, her territory, so he doesn't complain. There it is. Nothing to be done. Bright blue chunky-twist pile fabric, like a massed gathering of worms, covering the toilet seat, the waste bin, the toilet roll, the space in front of the lav. Maureen insists on calling it a toilet, not a lav. She corrects Charlie frequently.

The blue fabric looks alive, as if it could spread and take

over the house, eventually colonizing the lounge suite, the Marigold 'Curtina' net curtains, the quilted Terylene eiderdown with frilled sides that double as a valance, three-layer rouched trim, the Mandarin floral roller-blinds. It would all one day be blue worms. It would bring final unity to a flat that was a tender farrago of mismatched, copied, imitated styles, eras, fashions, materials, none of which bore any particular relationship to the others.

Charlie stands in front of the bathroom mirror. He cannot see his toothbrush. He opens the door of the cabinet. Hai Karate, Burley, Tabac Original. Presents bought for him years ago but still there, as he suspects they will be in ten more years. Maureen's sanitary towels. He wishes that she would store them separately. A marriage was like a life. You could only afford to contemplate a certain amount of it.

Maureen's Tryptophan, for her nerves. Calamine, Betnovate C for a rash on his bottom. Maureen's AYDS tablets, to help her lose weight. Like the exercise, like the calculation of calories, they didn't seem to be working. He wished it didn't matter to him. Medication for her verrucas and her mouth ulcers. Both plague her. Robert's various acne treatments litter the bottom shelf. No sign of his toothbrush.

He closes the cabinet, then studies his face in the mirror again. Not bad, he decides. Good, full head of hair. Wrinkles, of course, but less than some he knows who are older. Eyes muddied by drink, but still a sharp blue. He could pass for the same age as his brother, he decides.

From the corner of his eye he sees his toothbrush. It has fallen on the bathroom floor, by the toilet seat, and is half hidden by the tufts of twist-pile fabric. When he removes it, there are fine blue hairs intermingled with the bristles. He thinks there may have been urine in the twist pile which has now been transferred to the brush. Robert is careless when he makes water. He reluctantly tosses the brush into the pedal bin and makes up his mind to buy a new one in the morning.

Charlie squats on the toilet now, tries to move his bowels, but cannot. His mouth feels polluted. He thinks of the old advert for Gibbs SR, the tube bursting through the block of ice in a transforming explosion, and momentarily wishes his life were like that, that it would burst through its frozen crusts. But then he decides the thought is wrong. His life is not frozen, it is tepid. And it is his natural temperature, it's the point at which he survives best.

He rises, pulls up his trousers, but does not bother about doing up the button; after all, he will be changing into his pyjamas in a moment. He carries a book with him in one hand, the unfinished Sidney Sheldon, and a cup of water in the other. In the night his mouth gets dry.

As he makes his way across the corridor, he feels his trousers begin to work their way down towards his knees. By the time he has completed the navigation to the door of the room where Maureen waits, inert, Terylene-cosseted, the trousers have sunk to his calves. Rather than stop and put everything down, he moves in tiny pigeon steps. He feels ridiculous, but is too indolent to do otherwise. He is conscious of a slight but noticeable erection, caused by the rubbing of his pants against his groin.

At this point, to Charlie's consternation, Robert appears suddenly from his room, wearing only a pair of torn jeans. He looks his father up and down. Charlie tries to outface him. Robert says nothing, but coolly examines the spectacle of his father with his trousers round his ankles. Robert's tongue curls around words that he does not deliver, his mother's injunction to make peace with his father restraining him.

Up to watch the election? says Charlie casually, feeling his face reddening.

No, says Robert. *Did you vote?*

Of course. Did you?

Monster Raving Loonies.

Tailor-made for the likes of you.

Robert's eyes flick downwards. Charlie suddenly becomes aware of his own present absurdity. He decides it's best not too push this spat too far.

Must be turning in.

Good night, Dad.

Good night.

And Dad . . .

Charlie feels the stiletto being unsheathed, braces himself for impact. He feels the cloth of his trousers chafing his ankles slightly. It was surely too good an opportunity for Robert to miss.

Sweet dreams, eh.

Right.

And Robert is gone.

Relieved and reluctantly grateful, Charlie tries the door, which is on the latch; he fumbles at the handle with the heel of the palm which is still holding the glass of water. After a few attempts, he manages, and shuffles through into the half-lit room, which is illuminated only by a small white spotlight screwed to the headboard of the bed.

He puts the glass and book down on the Melamine dressing table, then swiftly removes his clothes, putting his underwear in the wicker laundry basket. He notices faint streaks of brown there and wonders if Maureen will notice them. He expects that she has learned not to look.

His pyjamas have been freshly washed and are warm in the airing cupboard. It makes him feel protected against the cold air in the room. Charlie curses the council and their inability to fix a simple boiler. With the bosses and the government, they make a triumvirate that confines and presses down on his life.

Climbing into bed, Charlie almost unconsciously runs his hand gently through his sleeping wife's hair. His eyes rest on her *Dallas* outfit, carefully folded by the bed. Prompted by this, Charlie thinks suddenly of the crimson passageway that is Sue Ellen's mouth. Unexpectedly, a full erection flowers on the vine of his imagination, making a lone drumlin halfway down the bed. This is a relatively rare event, a pleasurable conundrum that is usually solved by Charlie secretly masturbating, holding his breath to guard the silence as he ejaculates under the bedcovers into ready-waiting stippled, florally embossed kitchen roll, which he then disposes of in the toilet bowl. Or he will go and find the copies of *Men Only* and *Penthouse* that he keeps hidden from Maureen in the base of his tool box and lock himself in the lavatory. But on this occasion, although Maureen sleeps on, Charlie decides to instigate sex with her for the first time in several months. His frustration is a burden; he thinks sometimes of visiting prostitutes, but is afraid of herpes and of shame. Permissiveness everywhere. The world, he concludes once more, is going sex mad.

The moves feel well rehearsed, doomed. He starts by fondling Maureen's breasts, which are on the small side, like teacakes, and then kissing her neck, making a moue that brushes and vacuums her skin. He smells night cream and peppermint toothpaste. Having completed what he considers to be sufficient foreplay, he reaches down between her legs. What he feels there is dry. Her legs do not part to his touch. She begins a light snoring, like a distant earth-mover, and he wonders if this is actually theatre. Maureen acquiesces rarely now to his touch; there is a sense in which he is grateful. In the past, after the act was finished, he always felt that something needed to be said, something he has no words for, and so there was always a pang of loss.

But on this occasion he is not ready to give up. He thinks of Sue Ellen again; of Sue Ellen and Lucy Ewing together in bed with him, JR and Bobby unaware in their shining towers that Charlie Buck was stealing them away to his love palace in Ramsay MacDonald House, SW6.

He considers hauling himself on top of Maureen/Sue Ellen and attempting to have sex with her despite what he now considers to be her feigned sleep. His erection feels overwhelming to him; it is something to do with not working, he briefly considers. He needs to show himself a man.

Charlie continues to play with the pink space between Maureen's legs, a space which he now fantasizes as belonging to the blonde homunculus Lucy Ewing, her stumpy, full-breasted body pressing against his. Sue Ellen watches, mesmerized with desire. He feels unsure down there, confused still as to the exact nature of women's anatomy. He remembers once or twice during their marriage, when they were younger, and Maureen had seemed more generous with what was once a firm and smooth-skinned torso, that he had discovered places at the fork in her body that seemed to provoke daring, uncontained movements, and a loudening and lowering of pitch of breath. He had thought, briefly, of talking to her about the location and geography of this place, and how he might encounter it more often, but the words had died in his throat, strangled by the embarrassment that has been and remains the frequent, subterranean companion to their marriage.

He plays with her breasts once more, inflates them in his mind, this time rolling one of her nipples between his thumb and forefinger, then kisses her neck again. He is running out of strategies. Still no response. Lucy dissolves suddenly into the Terylene bedsheet and Sue Ellen's attention is wandering.

Some part of his spirit shrivels another degree. He feels his erection. Sue Ellen has abandoned him now. Trying to be as silent as he can, he rubs himself. But the blood has drained softly back into the ocean of his body and he is limp. Maureen snores again and turns to lie on her back. There is a tiny fly settled on the corner of her lips.

Before the retreating moment is lost entirely, Charlie redoubles his imaginative exertions, peremptorily summoning up Lucy once more. In this manifestation, she is being sodomized, doggy-style, by a panting, priapic JR. He has never suggested anal sex to Maureen, but the idea appeals to him while simultaneously revolting him. Sue Ellen, also reconjured, looks on, straddling the MFI dressing-table chair, her legs spread, masturbating with a long, scarlet-tipped finger. The summoned picture works; his erection returns as proud as before. JR is close to orgasm, his face bright and luminous. Those frightening eyebrows rise and fall. Lucy gasps. She wants more. Charlie rubs himself roughly, hoping to prevent the moment sliding by. Seconds later, he feels himself loosen, explode at the centre. JR, Lucy and Sue Ellen softly dissolve into the ceiling. He pauses, recovering himself, then goes to reach for the kitchen roll.

At this moment, Maureen stretches across and puts her arm over Charlie's stomach, resting herself in a puddle of freshly delivered semen. Immediately, as if she has been awake all the time, she sits up. She inspects her arm fiercely, not understanding. Droplets gather and fall from it. A faint bleachy smell rises.

Charlie feels no option but to confess.

I . . . I think I had one of those dreams. You know . . . one of those . . . dreams.

Maureen's face changes from confusion into a vague disgust that is diluted only by her understanding that Charlie is looking up at her as if a lost, dismal child. She composes herself, even manages a particular and rarely used smile that attempts to combine the opposites of anger and summary forgiveness. But it is unconvincing. Distaste, however modified by compassion, remains uppermost.

I'm sorry, says Charlie, unable to look at his wife.

Not knowing what to do, he feels the wetness at his centre, overflowing into their bed, a billion unrealized children expiring in a Terylene wilderness.

Maureen, without another word, gets out of the bed. A car passes, illuminating the room. He catches sight of her face, tightened, sad. He sees her go, to the bathroom, he presumes, to clean herself off. He knows this is also a strategy to give him a chance to re-establish the status quo. There is limited time. He rises from the bed, takes a pair of soiled underpants from the laundry basket and wipes himself clean. He rubs at the undersheet, but he knows the stain will show yellow in the morning, confirming his disgrace.

He hates Sue Ellen for what she has done. He finds a plastic bag that lines the rubbish bin – it is empty – puts the pants in them, ties the top and puts it in the pocket of his car coat in the wardrobe. He will dispose of it in the morning.

When Maureen comes back, he pretends he is asleep. This, he knows, is expected of him. Time and silence may begin to cauterize the moment. Yet moments, he knows, may have lifespans; some endure years. Within a few minutes, he hears her heavy breathing once more. He waits until he is sure she is genuinely asleep. But Charlie remains alert, a mile away from sleep now. Endorphins flood his body.

A small ball of anger has formed in the centre of his chest. He feels humiliated. It was normal, wasn't it, for a man to want to have sex? It was perhaps even his right. He wouldn't have done what he did if it wasn't for her. If she hadn't been dried up. Frozen. The word makes him think of the toothpaste tube bursting through the ice once more. Suddenly what the image means is obvious to him.

Careful not to awake Maureen, he extricates himself from the bedcovers. His pyjamas are damp. He makes his way to the door, gently opens it and walks towards the front room.

He feels his pyjamas adhering to his stomach. He thinks of rejection, and betrayal, and of a world falling out of the proper controls. Inflation. Decimalization. Loony lefties.

Then he decides that he has let his wife down. He seeks forgetfulness.

He lights a cigarette and switches on the television for *Decision '79*, with David Dimbleby and Robin Day. The picture is good. He searches through the cupboards in the kitchen for any kind of drink. There is only some advocaat left over from last Christmas. He hates the yellow stickiness of the stuff but pours himself a glass anyway. A large one, in a tumbler that features nineteenth-century scenes of a coach and horses racing from somewhere to somewhere else. The horses and footman are alive, vital with forward energy.

Charlie sits in front of the TV. The people in the studio seem very excited. Robert McKenzie attends his swingometer, an expression of enthusiasm and childlike glee on his face. Charlie is amazed at how some people get so worked up.

It is two in the morning and Charlie sips the advocaat. Politicians from each side queue up to state their viewpoints. There are shots from earlier in the day of Margaret Thatcher outside a school in Finchley.

Charlie likes the way her eyes hood when she is expressing concern, the way she cocks her head to one side. The odd dowdiness of her hairstyle makes her appear attractively ordinary. The way her face seems to break down into separate, discrete expressions each aimed at a purpose. She is respectable and decent, but not his cup of tea, not really.

Women push and jostle her. They carry placards that read 'Mrs Thatcher, milk snatcher' and 'We want women's rights – not a right-wing woman'. This latter slogan strikes Charlie as an awkward pun. *Lezbos*. The anger on the women's faces frightens him. He is glad that his own wife is so mild.

By three a.m. it is clear that his side has lost. In his own constituency, a massive majority has been overturned. The Conservative candidate has won by 1,500 votes. Yet despite defeat for his own team, Charlie enjoys the spectacle, the moment when all the double talk in the world can't hide the unvarnished truth. Union leaders, talking to the camera with all the authority of Cabinet ministers, seem only mildly dismayed; they imagine it will soon be business as usual. Callaghan smiles jovially as if nothing untoward has happened. The swingometer moves still further east.

Well, thinks Charlie, *a change for a while won't do any harm. Shake things up a bit.*

He is surprised to find himself vaguely invigorated. The advocaat is warming his stomach. He smokes three cigarettes one after the other. The flat smells perpetually of ash, boiled vegetables, tea, escaped gas. The piles of rubbish in the street still leave a trace in the air, despite the careful closure of the windows.

There is a shot of Mrs Thatcher appearing in her own constituency. Charlie thinks she is both stern and motherly, and is unable to muster dislike. Give the other bunch their turn. It's the way things keep their balance. She turns and smiles at the camera. She is spruce and excited. Charlie knows that the world will wear her down.

He switches off the television, drains the last of the advocaat and heads back to bed, hoping that Maureen remains asleep.

He does not wish her to smell the alcohol on his breath. She thinks that he drinks too much. Part of him agrees. He should cut down. A little change would do no harm.

3

31 March 1980. Charlie is back at work. The dispute between Times Newspapers and the array of unions ranged against them has ended after a year of battle. It has been a tussle between armed camps over what turns out to be a very small amount of territory. Some of his colleagues have lost their jobs, but it has not been a deluge. More a drizzle. Charlie has received back-pay, and increases in wages of a fifth. He is now making £200 a week – well above the national average – but this rise falls slightly short of inflation, which is surging as ever. The money comes in a small brown paper envelope, which Charlie hands over to Maureen, after deducting some drink money. Maureen continues to save for their retirement, in the gap under the floorboards. Neither of them believes spending to be as virtuous as saving. Saving conserves energy; spending disperses it. Maureen also has a sum put away with a building society. Thus she is covered both ways. She has shopped around, found 19 per cent. She imagines the interest piling up, free money, if it weren't for inflation.

A year of struggle. However, within a few weeks of the newspaper starting production again, wildcat strikes and stoppages begin once more. An agreement has been made that there will be a switch from the hot-metal composing rooms to an electronic composing room, but the agreement is showing few signs of sticking. The union chapels have, as ever, proved themselves both irascible and indomitable.

Charlie has a late shift today, so he is enjoying a bit of a lie-in. Maureen has gone for an early appointment at Divine

Creations, the hairdresser's on the main road. She is contemplating a complete restyle. Robert has left, is living in a squat somewhere in south London. Six months ago to the day, Maureen stood in the doorway as he moved his things out, fighting to hide the desolation that she found suddenly within her. She put on a brave face. She wrought a new smile for the occasion. Yet after Robert left, her exercise and diet regime collapsed. Self-hatred grew, a living culture on the surface of her loss. Her weight ballooned.

Maureen finds determination once more, flowering in the dryness within, the toughness of cacti. Eventually, her running resumes, increases from three to four times a week, despite the plague of her verrucas. Weekly, she hacks at the dead skin around the tender cores with their malignant black pinpoints. Sometimes it feels as if her feet are pitted, cratered, scooped out. She has substituted yoga for still-life painting on Wednesdays. In yoga, she tries to empty her mind, but Robert seeps into it, the memory of him taking his first steps, being tossed in the air and caught.

On this day, Charlie rises from bed. It is still hot. There is again something wrong with the radiators. Having so long been cold, now they will not turn off. The council, as ever, is proving elusive and tardy about remedying the situation. Charlie and Maureen are soon to have a telephone installed; this will make the never-ending tussle with the local authority weighted slightly more in their favour. The endless trips to the telephone box, the waits outside as teenage girls talk dim-wittedly and for ever to invisible friends, wear both of them down. Charlie decides it is an investment worth making.

Feeling the sweat on him, he takes a shower. The water comes out, as ever, in a sad trickle, impeded by gravity. He washes with unperfumed soap and dries off on a canary-yellow towel which he carefully folds and replaces on the heated towel rail. He is shaving with a disposable razor; there are six or seven of them already in the Tidybin. It is Robert who will eventually explain to him that you can use them more than once. A girl with big eyes holding a kitten stares down at him soulfully. The picture is called *Innocence* and it is by an artist called Mojer. It is Maureen's choice.

He returns to the bedroom, removes his maroon dressing gown with piped edges and puts on a wheat-coloured Arnold Palmer slimline shirt, a pair of dark blue Yorkers trousers with a slight flare and a 'Sweden'-front cardigan with Acrilan back and sleeves.

In the front room, he picks up his copy of the *Daily Mirror* from where it lies on the brown coir Welcome mat. The news is not good. A fourteen-year-old has murdered his disabled grandfather. The steelworkers' strike is continuing. Charlie Drake is successful in the West End. The Yorkshire Ripper is still at large, mocking the police. All men are considered by an ever increasing number of women to be rapists. T-shirts announcing this discovery are selling well. Charlie briefly wonders if he could rape anyone, then dismisses the thought as absurd. Inflation and unemployment are continuing to rise. The train drivers of the London Underground are on strike after 200 teenagers wreck a train in Neasden.

There has been a budget the previous week. Now Maureen has to pay £1 for her Tryptophan. The council are raising rents after Michael Heseltine cuts back their grants. There is talk of £50 a week. Charlie is outraged by the fact that Social Security is to be withheld from strikers – why should his family be penalized for something that is management's fault? There is a billion in cuts. Margaret Thatcher, as Mike Sunderland at work had predicted, is hated, and is magnetizing unrest. However, the girl on page five in the bikini looks as irrepressibly chirpy as ever, and Charlie is cheered as he examines the contours of her breasts while he stirs his tea.

The print world is a small world. He imagines he probably knows the compositor who laid out this page with Luscious Lucy from Luton, turned from beckoning flesh to solid metal then 10,000 tiny shaded dots on 5 million newspapers. This thought he finds comforting, feels a direct connection with the pulp that his blackened fingers grapple with as he chews on a slice of toast and margarine.

He begins to attack his boil-in-the-bag kippers. Charlie loves kippers, even the bitter silver-black skin underneath. He spreads the liquefied butter over the orange-stained surface of the split fish. The aroma he finds wonderful. He cuts a first slice, but then feels his mouth go suddenly slack. There is a small double-column story on page seven. It is headed 'Goodbye, Mr Music'. He swallows, stops chewing. Butter stains the edge of his mouth. There is a picture of a man with grey and white hair, a crooner's smile, dark, quizzical eyebrows. He reads:

The King of Easy Listening, Annunzio Mantovani, died last night at his home in Tunbridge Wells at the age of 74 after a long illness. In 1951 his first big hit, 'Charmaine', showcased the big 'cascading strings' sound that he developed with arranger Ronnie Binge.

Mantovani was the first act in the music business to sell over 1 million stereo recordings, and he far overshadowed his light-orchestral rival, Semprini.

Before his recording career took off, Mantovani served as musical director for a number of long-forgotten British musicals and plays, including several by Noël Coward.

Charlie feels a dryness in his mouth. He reads the paragraphs again, as if the story might alter on the second reading. Then he leaves the rest of his toast and kippers uneaten. The tea grows cold. A full five minutes he sits in his chair, barely moving.

Eventually, he gets up and he goes into the kitchen. In the Frigidaire, at the back, there is a bottle of Asti Spumante that he was saving for Maureen's birthday this weekend. He decides that he can always buy another and uncorks the bottle. It is 10.30 a.m. Foam cascades down the neck. Charlie finds a glass, wide as a saucer, in which he believes champagne should be properly served, as he has seen on an advertisement for Babycham. He takes both glass and bottle into the main room and sets them upon the table, where the molecules in his tea are slowing, losing energy. Then he goes to his stereogram, carefully takes out his copy of 'Charmaine' and sets it upon the turntable. He turns the volume control to High. The liquid strings fill the room. He raises his glass towards speakers that issue this preserved remnant of a dead man's imagination, silently makes a toast, then drinks the Asti down in one swig and refills the glass.

Charlie has switched the record to Replay, so 'Charmaine' comes on again and again. The second glass of Asti sets him to brooding in a way he cannot remember doing since the death of his parents, who, although both in their seventies at the time of their demise, he had considered to be functionally immortal. As he tears out the cutting from the *Daily Mirror* and places it in his wallet, those earlier losses seem to flash back. In his mind, he sees himself standing over each of their coffins and experiences the disturbing sense that life was much odder and less located in time and space than he had grown used to thinking. The death of Mantovani, whose warm, soupy music had acted as a soundtrack to his adult life, is troubling him in the same way.

He is just pouring himself a third glass, smacking his lips

and wiping them with the sleeve of his cardigan, when the doorbell rings. He assumes Maureen has forgotten her keys. But when he opens the door, a man in blue overalls and a second man in a cheap-looking suit with dandruff traces on the shoulders are standing on the doorstep. The second man carries a clipboard. The expressions on their faces are indifferent, but something in the way they carry themselves, a kind of cocked stance that seems to contain authority, makes him wary.

Mr Buck? says the man in the suit. His voice is thin and sharp.

Yes.

Council.

Yes?

Charlie is bewildered. He is grieving, slightly drunk.

We're here to see about the radiators, says the man with the overalls. His voice is gravelly, south London tough.

Charlie nods, suddenly comprehending.

About blinking time, says Charlie, emboldened by the drink.

Sober, he would be unlikely to risk provoking the council. They are too powerful. The man in the suit stiffens. A slight unpacking of muscle that seems to raise his height half an inch. Charlie stands back to let the men in. As the suited man crosses the threshold into the hall, he appears to register the smell of alcohol on Charlie's breath. He recoils slightly, then takes a handkerchief out of his pocket and blows. Then he neatly folds it and returns it to his pocket. All this time there is complete silence. Finally, the man turns to Charlie, without looking at him. His eyes scan the detail of the flat.

I understand there is a malfunction.

That's it, says Charlie.

How long has the unit been failed?

*It's not exactly **failed**,* says Charlie.

The man in blue adjusts his shoulders, which look massive even under the looseness of his overalls. He looks up at the suited man, who is three or four inches taller than him.

It states clearly here that there is a thermal loss.

Uninvited, the overalls man begins inspecting radiators. He produces a spanner from a kangaroo pouch at the front of the dungarees.

How does it seem to you? says Charlie, to the taller man.

I beg your pardon?

It's Hawaii in here.

What?

It's high season on the Costa del Sol.

A small rivulet of sweat is forming at the base of his back. 'Charmaine' still plays. Bubbles in the Asti bottle softly explode. His eyes drift to the Spanish guitar barometer on the wall. It predicts fair and warm.

The man in the suit seems irritated and confused.

Mr Buck, you have a reported a fault. I have it noted. Now you are saying there is no fault.

That was last time, says Charlie. *The radiators broke last time.*

He's right, Mr Huxtable, says the man in overalls. *They're functioning 110 per.*

OK, Stan, says the man with clipboard. He makes a note.

I exist, says Charlie, turning on overalls man. *Don't talk over my head. There's no need for that I'm-the-king-of-the-castle type of attitude. Listen, the problem isn't that they don't **work** . . .*

The man in the overalls, again uninvited, has disappeared into the corridor that connects the bedrooms.

It's just that you can't turn the bloody things off, says Charlie in frustration.

There's no need for language, says Huxtable. He purses his lips.

There is an uneasy silence. Charlie is not sure what is meant to happen next. He feels a free-floating nervousness under the hard skin of his pique.

Stan has reappeared from the corridor.

I'll have to make a report, he says.

Central maintenance or peripherals? says Huxtable.

We'll copy it, says Stan.

*Aren't you going to **do** anything?* says Charlie.

Huxtable looks wearily at Stan but says nothing.

I'm making a report, Stan says, in a slightly different tone, less deferential. Charlie has to guess that it is pitched at him, since Stan is looking away.

Why can't you fix it now? says Charlie.

Stan again addresses Huxtable rather than Charlie.

We can send a chit to the boiler people.

Is that procedure? I don't think that would be procedure.

*Why won't you talk to me? You bloody **people**.*

Charlie bites his tongue. His self-awareness, his protectiveness, close in through the cloud of drink.

I'm sorry. I didn't mean any unpoliteness.

But now Stan is looking directly at him for the first time, with disinterested malice. He slaps the spanner into the palm of his hand. Phlat.

One thing here, Mr Huxtable. I think you should take a look at it. There's something in the tertiary unit.

Stan turns and walks back down the corridor. Huxtable takes short, brisk strides in his wake.

*This is my **home**,* says Charlie desperately.

It's council property, says Huxtable, without turning his head.

Stan has reached the door of the spare bedroom. He walks in and Huxtable follows.

The three men stand in spaces in the island in the centre of the train track. Stan shifts his foot; a Victorian Woman with

Parasol disappears under the shadow of his rubberized sole. There is a barely audible *crick*.

What are you doing? says Charlie.

You will have to make restitution, says Huxtable, indicating the carefully painted wall of trees and valleys. *This is in contravention. Without question.*

Stan has picked up an Andrew Barclay locomotive for the Campbeltown and Mackintosh light railway.

Does this actually run? he says to Charlie.

Of course, says Charlie.

I mean, is it a real steam engine?

No, says Charlie, a faint note of regret edging his voice. *Though you can get those. I can't really afford it. That's what they call live steam. A real miniaturized engine fired by butane gas. They run to hundreds and hundreds of pounds though. That's **without** the casing. A bit out of my league. Now, if you look at these engines over here . . .*

Live steam or no live steam, it's a fire risk, says Stan, putting the engine to one side.

This whole contraption is a fire risk, says Huxtable. *It's too . . . It's too . . .* He frowns, looks questioningly towards Stan.

Big, says Stan, matter-of-factly.

Big, says Huxtable. *Absolutely. Toys, of course, are a permissible . . .*

*It's not a **toy***, says Charlie.

Toys, repeats Huxtable, *within certain limits, are . . .*

*This is my **home***, says Charlie. *I want you to leave.*

He grabs the lapel of Huxtable, who shakes him off.

You'll be hearing more from us, says Huxtable.

He does not move, and makes notes on his clipboard. Stan has moved in between him and Charlie. The spanner strikes his hand once more. Phlub.

This is wasting council time, says Stan. *The boiler is operative.*

Get out, says Charlie.

Huxtable and Stan, in what they make clear is their own time, leave the room, and Charlie goes to follow. He notices the Victorian woman and parasol in pieces on the ground. Huxtable has turned.

This door has been rehung. You must make . . .

Restitution, says Stan.

Charlie is examining the broken figurine.

This took me two days, he says, more to himself than to the men, who have now left his sight. He waits a few seconds, hears the sound of the front door closing.

He cradles the remnant of Victorian female passenger. He makes his way to the door. He trips on a miniature railway crossing; again there is the sound of breakage. He ignores it. He makes his way out into the corridor, raises his fist.

This is my home!

Mantovani has stuck in the groove, repeating the same brief cascade of strings endlessly. Charlie walks back into the living room. The broken woman is in his palm. He places her gently on the table, next to the bottle of Asti. He drinks directly from the bottle. The woman's back is smashed and is beyond all repair.

Maureen Buck sits in the middle chair of five at the hair-dresser's. She picks up magazines as she waits for the dye to take on her hair. There are copies of *She, Woman* and *Cosmopolitan*. Confined in this chair, she seems to feel age scraping at her, time's emery board. Her skin appears loose and grey to her gaze. A new ulcer has appeared on her tongue and she flicks it between her teeth.

Marie-Rose, her stylist for the last ten years, is chatting. Her real name is Elsie. The rebranding has been inspired by the sauce in which prawn cocktails are suspended. Maureen has asked Marie-Rose to cut and dye her hair in the style of Sue Ellen.

Maureen is on the F-Plan diet, but Marie-Rose recommends combining. She says it's all a matter of the correct relationship between carbohydrates and proteins. The issue of roughage is no longer prime. Calories are prehistoric. Marie-Rose has lost five pounds in a week. Maureen considers this a miracle. The F-Plan plays havoc with her bowels. She has lost three pounds, but suffers explosive flatulence and dislikes the pulses and baked beans which Audrey Eyton prescribes. Charlie is beginning to complain.

Marie-Rose finishes her glowing peroration of combining. She is only slightly Maureen's junior but wears clothes that are years younger – on this particular day, a rah-rah skirt and an all-in-one leotard, with white moccasins decorated with tiny coloured glass beads. A ragged sexuality hangs about her. She owns the salon and is confident and outspoken in a way that Maureen admires but finds hard to emulate. Marie-Rose moves on to another client while Maureen waits, her auburn hair, now tinted red, damply piled upon her crown.

Maureen inspects the magazines on the ledge in front of her. She has already read *Woman* and she considers *Cosmopolitan* slightly outside her sphere of interest. She picks up *She* and flicks through the pages.

The large-format magazine has changed from the innocent cookery and short romantic story format that she remembers. Now there is much about orgasm and possibility. The fashion seems extravagant. Oral sex features in one of the articles. Maureen reads her stars. A long-overdue change is imminent. A friend she holds in high esteem will disappoint her. She is advised to keep a clear head through present troubles, which will in due course be resolved. Marie-Rose returns.

What about that Meg?

She is talking about the owner of the Crossroads Motel.

I think she's being unfair to Sandy, says Maureen. Sandy is Meg's crippled son. *He was only saying what he thought.*

You can be too honest, says Marie-Rose, examining Maureen's roots.

Is he genuinely crippled? says Maureen.

Sandy? says Marie-Rose.

Is he normal in real life?

I don't know, says Marie-Rose. *I **think** so.*

Meg has to be strong, doesn't she? says Maureen.

Don't we all? says Marie-Rose, laughing. *It's a woman's lot. We can wash this off now.*

I admire her, says Maureen. *It must be wonderful to run your own business.*

It's not all champagne and lunches at the Rib Room, says Marie-Rose, gently manoeuvring Maureen's head back over the sink.

You've made a go of it, though, haven't you, Elsie?

She hesitates as she feels the hands that are in her hair roughen their pressure.

. . . Marie-Rose?

It's not easy, Marie-Rose says, pointing the nozzle of water at a space behind Maureen's ear.

It is almost scalding hot, but Maureen is reluctant to complain. The position she is in, bent backwards, renders her almost completely submissive.

No. But all the same . . .

Marie-Rose stands in front of her, hands on hips.

Why don't you get a job, now that Robert has gone?

She leans over Maureen and applies Elseve Balsam.

I don't expect Charlie would like it.

Well, he can lump it, then, says Marie-Rose.

You don't know Charlie. Anyway, what could I do?

There must be something. You're not stupid, are you?

Oh, I've not got all that much upstairs, I don't think.

Cock and bull, says Marie-Rose.

I suppose I do get bored sometimes, says Maureen.

Time on your hands.

Of course, I keep myself busy. You'd be surprised how much work —

You can sit up now. Hold still. Excellent. There we are. What do you reckon?

Maureen's colour is more vivid than she has expected, but it pleases her. She nods in approval. Marie-Rose falls silent and begins to tease at the hair with a dryer. Maureen picks up the copy of *She* once more. It falls open at one of the several articles on orgasm. Marie-Rose leans over her shoulder.

Picking up a few tips, are you? says Marie-Rose, winking.

I think me and Charlie are past all that, says Maureen. She imagines the menopause approaching, like distant cancer.

You're a young woman, Maureen. What are you talking about?

It's different for you, says Maureen.

You don't know what you're missing.

This, it strikes Maureen, is precisely true. She has never quite understood the magnetism of sex, although now it seems to gesture at her from the most mundane of advertisements: breakfast cereal, cutlery, even pension plans. Charlie has never exactly located her clitoris, she ponders. She does not blame him. It is unwilling to be discovered, like Shangri-La. Imagined others may strike this chord, but Charlie's investigations have proved fruitless. Now he is disheartened, has abandoned the quest.

Marie-Rose lowers her voice.

Have you ever had a multiple?

Maureen is momentarily puzzled.

A multiple what?

Orgasm, of course.

Maureen laughs out loud.

I'd be chuffed with the occasional single.

Marie-Rose joins in. But Maureen feels a constriction around her heart, as if an invisible hand is squeezing there.

I've nearly finished now, says Marie-Rose, standing back to admire her handiwork.

Maureen's hair looks only marginally different; tidier, the flecks of grey stripped out. She fears anything more substantial.

You could help out here if you like, says Marie-Rose.

I shouldn't let me near a pair of scissors, if I were you. I'd cut some poor devil's ear off in a week. Butterfingers, Charlie calls me.

I need someone to do the books. Are you any good with figures?

Maureen remembers at school, the way she could move numbers and symbols around in her head, manipulate them, make them come out right. She remembers how it used to satisfy her.

I'm quite handy. But doing the books . . .

It's easy, says Marie-Rose breezily. *Just putting things into columns. And there's a bit of you-know-what of course. I need someone I could trust.*

You-know-what?

Come on, Maureen. It's a cash business, isn't it? Everyone does it.

Oh.

The thought of cheating the taxman obscurely excites Maureen. The powers that be which determine her life bamboozled for once.

You think it over.

I'll have to talk to Charlie.

*Oh, **Charlie***, she says, raising her eyebrows. *You don't want to let men walk all over you, Maureen.*

Charlie is my husband, says Maureen.

Marie is unimpressed.

You think it over, she repeats.

Maybe I will, Els – Marie-Rose.

With a flourish, the pink sheet that covers Maureen's shoulders is removed. She feels a renewal that is greater than her hairstyle. She looks forward to seeing Charlie later that day. Yet she doubts that he will notice any change.

On the third floor of the *Sunday Times* building, Charlie hunches over the stone on which he makes his page layouts out of slugs of metal. He has to read it back to front . . . 'Prophets of Doom Predict Economic Gloom' in 72-point Roman.

A few yards away, the men on the Linotype machines are setting type out of hot metal, which drips from a suspended ingot into a pot containing a plunger. The noise as the molten metal is punched into the matrices creating the slugs is deafening, a constant thud and hammer. Alongside the Linotype machines is a group of Ludlow machines which are used to create the headlines in blocks of metal.

These Linotype operators are the aristocrats of the printing trade. They make small fortunes, tubby middle-aged men driving Jags and owning holiday villas. You have to know the right people to get that job. Charlie doesn't know enough of the right people, and anyway he feels happy with what he does, his easy mastery of his own skill.

Close by is an office bustling with proof-readers, copy-holders and revisers, who check the galleys of type and pages as they are set and made up, who hold the copy for the proof-readers to read. Everything is divided precisely into functions. Journalists come down here, and woe betide them if they try even to pick up the wrong piece of paper or touch the wrong piece of machinery. The unions – SOGAT, NATSOPA, the NGA – are powerful, and watchful, and protective of their demarcations. Any infraction of the arcane rules can easily result in tools being laid down. When a dispute does arise and time is lost on the newspaper, it is often settled by the management bribing the union involved by paying money into a 'pool' as an inducement to make the time up. Then the day will come when you get a nice little tickle, when the pool money is redistributed among the chapel members involved.

Another perk which Charlie has enjoyed is known as a 'tap day', when he gets a tap on the shoulder from the FOC and is told to take the day off. The FOC is the 'father of the chapel', the head of the particular section of the particular union. It's all a bit moody, but nothing to compare with what goes on in warehouses around Fleet Street, or the van drivers and their bucks, the men who bundle and unload the papers from the vans. Some of them are small-time villains, or hold second jobs as cabbies, which amounts to the same thing in Charlie's mind. Big, surly men from Orpington and Bexleyheath. Some of these men, mostly SOGATs or NATSOPAs, sign on for work under another name. These non-existent workers are known as Mickey Mouses, Dicky Birds or Charlie Chaplins. The shift men will entice these spectral workers out of the pubs on a Saturday night to put down their name on the rosters before returning to the pub. The £75 a night will be split with the men on shift.

Charlie doesn't think about all this any more, it's normal practice, it's just the way things are. He checks his watch. It is time for a break. Charlie has a hangover from the morning. He is anxious about the men from the council. The vision of the Victorian Lady Passenger with Parasol shattered oppresses him. He looks up and is pleased to see Snowball George approach, chewing a pencil. Snowball, a machine minder in the print room, has been on holiday for three weeks. He looks relaxed, healthy, extraordinarily young for a man of fifty-three. A Bajan, light-skinned, he is tall with a slight stoop. Tendrils of grey invade his neatly cut hair. He removes the pencil and grins.

Snowball, says Charlie, but the word is completely swallowed by the cacophony around him.

Snowball mimes drinking and eating. Charlie nods and gestures towards the stairwell. Snowball's real name is Lloyd, but nearly everyone at the print works calls him by his nickname. Charlie finishes up what he is doing and joins Lloyd at the top of the stairs that lead down to the ground floor. He slaps him on the back with inky fingers.

You're looking good, Snowy. Like Sidney . . . what's his name?

James?

Poitier.

Charlie, you look like you died and someone dug you up. He takes one of Charlie's cheeks and chucks it roughly. *What's vexing you?*

Nothing. Nothing. Just a bit of nonsense with the council. Let's get something to eat.

Outstanding. After all that fresh fruit and grilled fish, I can't wait for a soggy chip.

With gravy.

With Brussels sprouts and baked beans.

How was the holiday? Where did you go?

We went to Lido de Jesolo. Fantastic, I tell you. Those Italians know how to live. We went to Venice. A day trip. My God, the water. We took a gondola. How's Maureen?

She's all right. Keeps herself busy. You and Hyacinth should come over. Maureen's a cordon bleu cook now.

Ah, you know Hyacinth. Not much for the socializing. More for the churchgoing.

She's going to find out you've been gambling one day.

Not so long as I keep winning. And I'm too good with those cards to start losing, bwoy.

We need to find some mugs for a new game.

Ain't we already got some? Gaz and Baz just love giving their money away. They should get registered as a charity.

Gary and Barry Philimore are twins, warehousemen Charlie sees from time to time in the Printer's Devil pub. Both are terrible at cards and feckless with money, and are thus frequent visitors to Charlie's long-standing once-a-month game. Charlie shakes his head.

Gary's been transferred out of London and Barry won't come without Gary. We need some new mugs.

Anyone in mind?

Charlie shrugs.

No one ideal. My brother, Tommy, is always after a game, but I suspect he's a bit handy. Also . . .

Also, you don't like him.

He's all right, I suppose. He's a crook, that's the trouble.

What about that son of yours? Nice kid.

Mo's always after asking me to invite him along. It's a bit lambs to the slaughter.

*That's what lambs are **for**. And who better to teach you than your dad?*

They walk through the swing doors into the staff canteen. Immediately they see Mike Sunderland sitting by himself at a table, working his way through an enormous lasagne and reading a large book. Mike is a sub-editor on the newspaper; from time to time Charlie has worked with him on the stone, and the three of them have chatted on picket lines. Both Charlie and Lloyd are suspicious of him. His vowels are too rounded, his hair too long, his principles too ostentatiously worn. Mike looks up, catches Charlie's eye, raises a hand in acknowledgement. Charlie has no choice but to raise one in return. Mike beckons them over. Charlie reluctantly nods and gets behind Lloyd in the queue for the canteen food.

We've been got, says Charlie.

He's not so bad, says Lloyd.

He's a bit arty-crafty. One of those do-gooders.

Piety, saieth the Lord. All is piety. Something like that. In the good book.

Maybe he'll be gone by the time we've got the food.

Why not give him a few card lessons?

Him? Look at the state of him. Dirty old jeans. Shoes look like they've been picked out of a dustbin. You can always tell a man by his shoes.

Not always. His watch must be worth a few hundred pounds. And his voice, bwoy. I'm telling you, there's money there. He's a mug. A real live patsy. He's asking for it.

I dunno.

Look. He's one of them socialists, isn't he? Reads the **Guardian** *and that. He wants a pet darkie as mate. And what with you in the council house, it's two niggers for the price of one. Let's teach him a thing or two about the redistribution of wealth.*

He gives me the creeps. Hello, Connie. Shepherd's pie, peas, carrots and beans please. And don't be mean. I'm starving. I'm dying of hunger here.

You'll get the same as everyone else. What about you, Harry Belafonte? Connie, the woman behind the serving counter, says, turning to Lloyd. She looks pale and harassed as she stirs a heated tray of baked beans with a long metal spoon to bury the skin that has formed on top of them.

Give me the sausage and mash, Connie, says Lloyd, winking at Charlie. *A big pork sausage. You like a big pork sausage, Connie? A big old banger in your mashed potato.*

Connie doesn't even look up as she hands Charlie his plate and begins ladling mashed potatoes on to Lloyd's.

I do, luv, but it's all I can do to get a chipolata nowadays.

You're with the wrong man, girl. You come and see Snowball. I like the big girls. Something to get hold of.

One shepherd's pie. One soss and mash. Next please.

Lloyd and Charlie both laugh, pay for their food and scan the restaurant for a table. To Charlie's disappointment, Mike Sunderland is still where he was. He has recently grown a beard, and it ages him ten years. It does not summon up the revolutionary air that he clearly hopes for, but makes him resemble Dave Lee Travis.

Lloyd and Charlie make their way over to join him. He closes his book. Charlie reads the title: *Principles of Political Economy.*

A real page-turner, says Charlie.

He has the new Jeffrey Archer in his back pocket. Mike smiles, puts the book away in his briefcase. Charlie puts his plate of food on the white Formica table.

How are things upstairs, Mike? says Lloyd.

There are rumours, says Mike.

What kind of rumours? says Charlie.

Mike lowers his voice slightly.

The whole place is going up for sale.

I've heard it all before, says Charlie.

This time it's different. I've started looking around. The **Guardian** *are interested. **Very** interested.*

Sounds like a marriage made in heaven.

There are practical difficulties.

They won't pay you as much, says Charlie.

You're a cynic, says Mike.

There are worse things, says Charlie.

Piety, saith the Lord, says Lloyd, loud enough for Charlie to hear. Mike seems oblivious.

How are you, anyway, Charlie? You look a bit under the weather.

Charlie's vexed up. Something about the council, says Lloyd.

Really? says Mike, craning forward, screwing up his face as if this was the most fascinating information imaginable.

That's right, says Charlie, unwrapping his knife and fork. *Telling me I couldn't do this or that.*

Mike nods vigorously. He looks at Lloyd.

How was your holiday, Lloyd?

All right, says Lloyd, taking an enormous mouthful of mashed potato.

Mike nods vigorously again, then falls into silence. There is a damp slick of tea around the moustache of his beard.

I'll tell you. Give them a clipboard, it's like they're suddenly Napoleon, says Charlie.

Mike smiles, leans forward towards Charlie again.

*I hope you don't mind my asking, but what's it **like** living in a council flat?*

Charlie shrugs. *Not so bad.*

*I can't **believe** what Thatcher is doing. She's destroying the stock of social housing. Selling them off in that fashion. It's completely inappropriate.*

Charlie grunts, takes his copy of the *Daily Mirror* from his pocket and begins turning towards page five.

She's just trying to appeal to the worst in everyone. People are better than that. That's why people hate her.

Charlie nods. Caroline from Carshalton is disappointing. The open friendliness of her smile somehow erases sex.

Is yours a nice block?

About average, says Charlie. *Fair number of slags. Slags, tosspots and loafers. Like my bloody son.*

*I didn't know you **had** a son.*

Not so much a son. More a species of root vegetable. More of a potato than a man. Living on the Social. Holed up in a squat.

A squat! says Mike. He is clearly impressed. Noticing Charlie's disapproving look, he modifies his expression.

Pass the salt, Snowball.

Mike frowns, nibbles at his lip. The hair of his moustache is too long; gobbets of unidentifiable food are suspended in it.

How does that make you feel? says Mike, in a soft, polite voice.

Lloyd pretends not to hear, takes another forkful of mashed potato.

Do you think it's appropriate to refer to Lloyd in that way? says Mike, this time to Charlie.

What way's that, then, Mike? says Charlie, turning the page of the *Daily Mirror*.

You know, says Mike. '*Snowball*'.

Am I offending you, Snowball? says Charlie, still not looking up from the newspaper.

Not really, Charlie.

Well, says Mike, a little more conviction in his voice now, a little more push. *You should be. You ought to be offended.*

He takes a pack of cigarette papers out, extracts one, then a pack of tobacco. He focuses his attention on constructing the cigarette. Charlie sighs, looks up.

The trouble with you, Mike, is that you don't know real people. You live in a different world.

I don't think that's fair.

Charlie takes a deep breath.

Is what you're saying I'm a racialist, then?

Mike finishes the cigarette, puts it in his mouth, lights it and draws.

It's unavoidable.

Is it?

*It's not necessarily your **fault**.*

Does that include you?

In what sense?

Are you a racialist?

I try not to be. I make an effort.

Hear that, Snowball? We're all racialists. Except for Mike.

True, man. I'm a fucking racialist. I'll tell you who I hate.

Who's that, then?

You ever been to Guernsey? Can't stand 'em, the Guernseys. Sweater-knitting sons of bitches.

Lloyd and Charlie laugh. Mike looks puzzled. Then he smiles and nods.

I've got to go to the ghazi.

What? says Charlie.

Mike's eyelids quiver slightly.

The ghazi. You know. The loo.

Lloyd and Charlie burst out laughing again.

Back in a minute.

When he is gone, Lloyd and Charlie finish their meals as quickly as they can.

What a prize lemon, says Charlie.

Let's get out of here before he takes us on one of them protest marches.

It takes only a minute to clean their plates, but before they can make their exit Mike comes striding towards them from the toilets. They try to hurry past him, but he positions himself in the centre of the small space through which they must move in order to exit.

Do you like boxing? says Mike.

Boxing? says Lloyd. *I **was** a boxer. When I first come over here, the boat was full of boxers. I was going professional. Marquess of Queensberry Rules.*

Lloyd takes up a formal boxing stance, legs apart, fists raised, head high.

But in the end I didn't want to mess up my pretty face. You know what they used to call me?

Rice Pudding, says Charlie. *Like what you couldn't punch the skin off.*

The Yellow Devil. Because my skin is so light, see? High yeller. Man, those bad boys had to watch me. I was a viper.

Lloyd is dancing on the spot now, ducking, punching the air. Charlie yawns.

Now you've gone and done it. You've started Snowball talking about the good old days.

Lloyd bobs and feints. Although he is a little heavy, it is clear that he has trained.

Pow. Pow. I knew 'em all, bwoy. Johnny Edge. The gunslingers. The gangsters. No one messed with Lloyd George.

Mike looks nonplussed.

*Lloyd **George**.*

That's his surname. Why do you think he don't mind being called Snowball?

Lloyd goes into a clinch with Charlie, nearly knocking him off his feet.

Get off, you . . . old man, you, says Charlie, laughing.

Mike shuffles uncomfortably.

I was just wondering . . . You see, sometimes I get boxing tickets from a friend on the sports desk. I thought . . . well, I thought you might be interested.

Lloyd and Charlie come out of their clinch.

I'm listening, says Lloyd.

It's not exactly official. We have this story about unlicensed boxing. At the Finsbury Park Astoria. Quite an experience, apparently. Anyway, if I get tickets, I thought you two might like to come along.

Lloyd looks at Charlie. Charlie returns the glance.

Can't wait, says Charlie.

I'm there, says Lloyd.

Mike's face breaks into a wide grin.

Terrific. Terrific.

Yeah. Terrific. See you, Mike.

See you . . . lads.

Mike heads back towards the third floor, a spring in his step.

People like that . . . says Charlie.

Free tickets, says Lloyd, *is free tickets.*

And he takes up the boxing stance again, dancing, dancing, puncturing the air.

4

Christmas arrives, rounding off the first year of the new decade. Yet what was the 1970s still persists strongly, as a mental habit, a hidden coastal shelf of long-held assumption.

Times Newspapers, as Mike Sunderland predicted, is up for sale. The deadline for proposals is 31 December. No buyers as yet have been found. William Rees-Mogg, the editor of *The Times*, has turned down Robert Maxwell because, according to Rees-Mogg, he isn't *the right sort of person*.

Still Charlie feels confident about retaining his job and salary. His imagination falters at any alternative. Stasis is what he understands, what he expects, what, on a deeper level, he is in love with. His secret fear is choice.

The new government reinforces Charlie's belief that the world is not mutable – by its very attempts to prove otherwise. The revenge of stasis is mighty; Mrs Thatcher is hated, is plummeting in the polls. Unemployment has hit a post-war high, over 2 million. Inflation rages. All these occurrences result in the diminishment of Mike Sunderland's fashionable *Weltschmerz* by several degrees. In his world bad news is good, it proves all his points. Michael Foot has been elected as Labour leader. The droop of Mike Sunderland's moustache picks itself up a further millimetre or two. Charlie thinks Foot may be a bad choice; he seems like a dithering old fool in a donkey jacket. He prefers Denis Healey, is attracted by the strength in his eyebrows.

Maureen is trying to guess who shot JR. Mark Chapman, in a parallel universe, has shot John Lennon dead in New York.

This continues to be overshadowed for Charlie by the death, nine months earlier, of Annunzio Paolo Mantovani.

There are traces of mourning even now for this loss, while a younger world eulogizes Lennon. Charlie's grieving for Lennon is purely recreational. He simply enjoys the size of the event. He thinks of Lennon as a Scouse herbert who couldn't pen a tune to save his life.

Now, on Christmas night, he is asleep, his wife by his side in bed. The presents are wrapped. Tomorrow, they expect the arrival of his brother, Tommy, and his wife, Lorraine, for Christmas dinner. Robert has also promised to come, in a rare phone call from his squat in Battersea. Since moving, he has hardly been seen or heard from. Maureen lives with the ragged hole he has left, a hole that feeds into a vacuum.

Charlie's breathing is soft as Christmas dawn approaches. He is dancing with his wife, across a parquet floor, with a mirror globe sending out specks of coloured light into every corner of the immense room – so immense that the walls seem to blur with distance. Maureen is dressed as if for *Dallas*, except for her shoes, which are running shoes.

He looks down at her shoes, thinking them a poor match for the outfit, and sees that the floor is now made of ice. Hairline cracks are appearing, and puddles of water. He feels unnerved, but continues the dance. The music is 'Some Enchanted Evening', Mantovani's version, but oddly rearranged so that there are loud rhythmic beats interspersed with the drifting melodies. This distracts him, makes it hard for him to keep his step. The music changes again.

What is that . . . what is that damn music?

Then he recognizes it, sung by children, heartbreaking somehow. It is 'Oh come, oh come, Immanuel'. Charlie sang it at Christmas as a child at school. He has always loved it, its sadness and its promise.

Oh come, oh come, Immanuel
Redeem thy spirit Israel.

The floor is water now, but still Maureen and Charlie dance on the surface, desperately trying to keep their footing. They begin, very slowly, to sink. Then the water is closing over their heads. Charlie cannot breathe. He reaches out for Maureen but cannot find her hand. He tries to shout his panic, but water rushes in.

Charlie opens his eyes, tries fiercely to locate himself in space and time. He focuses on pinoleum blinds that let the morning light through as ever, and woodchip wallpaper that was once white but has faded into magnolia. He comes awake.

Pausing for only seconds to acclimatize to the day's fresh consciousness, he rises from the bed. The dream is not remembered. A carol is issuing from the radio alarm – 'Oh come, oh come, Immanuel'. It is uncomfortably warm. He puts on his dressing gown and opens the windows of the bedroom. The glass in the frames is sweating, and dozens of rivulets of liquid trickle on to the inside windowsill, leaving dozens of small pools of water. The light which illuminates the room is greyish-brown. Early, not far off dawn. He has always been an early riser.

He wipes his brow with the sleeve of his flannelette dressing gown. The perspiration he finds there leaves a slick on the material. It is stuffy. The radiators are on and they still cannot switch them off. Outside, it is an unseasonably warm day.

He turns to look at his wife, still asleep in their king-size divan bed. Her hair is drawn tight into curlers and she is snoring lightly. A small droplet of liquid has gathered at the base of one of her nostrils, some kind of bodily fluid. Behind her, a headboard in quilted gold-coloured vinyl. To the left of the bed, a Goblin Teasmade begins to dispense hot water into the waiting cups.

He walks over to her and plants a chaste kiss on her cheek. They made love the night before. Charlie wondered if it had been Maureen's Christmas present to him. Or perhaps it was the job at Divine Creations which Charlie had reluctantly agreed to her accepting. A few months after Maureen began, her sexuality had flickered momentarily. It had then receded, but had subsequently revived on several occasions, usually after she had completed some fat ledger or balanced two particularly intransigent columns of figures.

Last night, it had been over very quickly, and he had sensed that Maureen had been relieved afterwards. Now Charlie observes her as she shifts slightly under the covers. A thought strikes him, evaporating as soon as it is observed.

I love my wife.

The moment passes. Charlie feels a pressure inside his bowels and moves towards the bathroom. He walks with a slow, slightly awkward gait. He never feels quite at home in his body, never feels that it is designed for him but rather for someone else entirely. He feels that his head is too small to hold the thoughts he sometimes has. His legs are thin and pasty, and are beginning to display the odd baldness on the calves that heralds decay. His arms and chest he has been trying to build up using a Bullworker 2. It was both isometric and isotonic but still didn't seem to work. It was boring and made his back hurt. He was amazed that Maureen kept this exercise business going.

He opens his bowels and studies the results. Someone has told him that the Germans have shelves in the toilet bowls for this purpose. It adds to his impression that the Germans are dangerous, efficient, borderline insane.

The stools are small, like rabbit pellets. Wiping himself,

then rising and washing his hands, he studies his face in the mirror and feels oddly depressed. The more you were meant to enjoy a day, the more sad it was. Always the way. The face stares back, the same as every morning, nondescript, mottled, oddly apologetic. The fullness of his hair. A fleck or two of dandruff. Another year going by. Tommy always said Charlie played it too safe. Maybe he was right. Maybe it was true. Life bogged down. But that is how safety feels, he decides.

He returns to the bedroom, where he sees that Maureen is now awake and moving around the bedroom like some skittish animal whose livery is quilted vermilion.

Hiya, kiddo.

Maureen returns Charlie's smile.

Happy Christmas, Rock.

He pecks her cheek, then gestures towards a large box in the corner of the bedroom. Maureen is in her housecoat. Her slippers are pink, and upon each is attached a cotton-wool powder-puff ball. It was her present this time last year, along with the machine that had stood unused in the corner of the bedroom for the last six months: the Helitron 'Trim U Fit' Deluxe Electro Vibro Massager. It rankles with Charlie how quickly she has lost interest in it. He even senses that she had not wanted it, although she had given every appearance of being enraptured at the time. But now her gift was a sure-fire winner, he felt certain.

It's awfully early to be opening presents.

It's never too early for Christmas.

Maureen regards the amateurishly wrapped box quizzically.

It's very big.

Open it, why don't you?

Maureen goes to the box, attempts to lift it.

Heavy, too.

See if you can guess what it is.

I couldn't.

Go on, have a poke.

Oh, Charlie, I don't know.

*Come **on**.*

Charlie shifts his weight back and forth from the balls of his feet to his heels. He anticipates his wife's forthcoming joy and surprise.

A microwave oven?

Charlie feels a sheet of anger illuminate him darkly from within.

Just open it.

*It's **not**, is it, Charlie?*

Maureen seems to sense vaguely that she has said the wrong thing, and increases the pace at which she is removing the wrapping.

Oh, it is. Oh, Charlie. You shouldn't have. These are terribly expensive.

Don't worry about that. You deserve it. Having to put up with me.

He leaves a pause for her denial, but it does not arrive. He continues.

Look at that. It's top of the range. A Creda 40131. You wouldn't believe this thing. It can cook the dinner in ten minutes. It's got a browning tray.

How does it work, then? asks Maureen, carefully peeling off the last of the layers of wrapping paper, folding the pieces up, ready for another occasion.

It's all done by radiation. It actually cooks the food from the inside.

Charlie is gesturing at the large metal box excitedly.

It's the greatest labour-saving device since the washing machine. The radiation agitates the . . . er . . . the protons in the food.

Maureen gives this some thought.

What's a proton, Charlie?

A proton. **A proton**. He shakes his head in disbelief. He is amazed that Maureen is holding down this new job. *It's like an atom, only a bit smaller. The oven itself doesn't even get hot. And you can roast in it. It's got a browning tray. It defrosts. It can soften butter. See inside? That round thing rotates so that it cooks evenly.*

Maureen is reading her card. It has a photograph of a bunch of roses on the front, which stands out in relief from the rest of the card. Inside, gold script describes a short poem:

> For you, my love, on this special day
> Who makes my life happy in every way
> I hope that we may always be
> Together, you and I, eternally.

In a scrawl, underneath, Charlie's signature. It was illegible, but Maureen knew what it said: *C. Buck*. Charlie is reading the manual.

Simple as pie. We can take it easy this morning, kiddo.

That's right.

Maureen places the card on a shelf in an alcove in the corner of the room which otherwise supports an arrangement of silk flowers and peacock feathers. Then she pauses, turns and squints at Charlie.

What do you mean?

Charlie is still reading the manual and hovering over the oven. He looks up, picks up a cup of cooling tea that is still waiting by the Goblin Teasmade and frowns slightly.

The Christmas dinner won't take nearly so much time now. This thing can knock off a turkey in no time.

Maureen flushes and she begins to fidget with the buttons of her housecoat.

Oh, I don't know, Charlie. I think it might be best if I got used to it first.

Nothing to get used to.

Charlie bites his lip. He regards Maureen. She is a wonderful woman, he decides. A wonderful woman. A child she has borne him. Keeps a perfect house. Not one to complain. Never a nag. He just wished sometimes she'd show a bit more . . . get up and go. Initiative. That was what was lacking in this household.

Come on. I'll set it up. It's got to have a plug put on.

Charlie. It's wonderful. It's just . . . I think . . . best to start on small stuff. I'm not very good with these gadgets.

*It's not a gadget. It's **modern**.*

All the same.

For the second time, Charlie feels vaguely cheated. Bloody Christmas. He decides he will have to play his trump card.

That 'gadget' was £250.

You're joking!

That's right.

But we can't afford that.

Nothing's too good for you. You'll love it, you'll see. Come on. I'll put it through its paces.

Charlie seems more excited than Maureen. He lifts the oven up and cradles it in his arms.

But Charlie, don't you want your present?

Let me just take this for you. I'll be back in just half a mo.

Charlie staggers into the kitchen. He places the microwave oven on the Formica work-top and takes a screwdriver out of the drawer. By the time he has finished attaching the plug he is sweating.

So hot.

At this moment, Maureen walks through the door of the kitchen, carrying a parcel with a card attached to it. She holds both out towards Charlie.

I wasn't sure what to get, so . . .

Look at this, Maureen. Get a mug of water. Put a tea-bag in it. Go on.

Maureen deflates slightly, but Charlie does not notice. She puts down the card and the present and goes to the tap, fills a mug decorated with cornstalks with water. The water travels through a pink rubber attachment that is attached to the nozzle. She adds a tea-bag, then hands it to Charlie, who places it into the microwave compartment. He closes the door and rotates a plastic knob on the right-hand side of the oven's fascia. He turns a second knob anticlockwise to High. A light comes on inside the box and a humming sound begins. The mug can be seen rotating inside.

See that, Maureen! It's going round! The protons are all shaking about like billy-o. It's pure energy.

After a minute, the oven makes a loud pinging sound. Charlie opens the door and carefully removes the mug with a tea-towel. Steam pours from its surface.

Look at that. You can make a cup of tea in a minute.

He puts in a cold spoon to stir the tea-bag. The water reacts to the coldness by suddenly overflowing, boiling liquid pouring out on to the work-top.

Bugger it, says Charlie, feeling that the display has been ruined. He doesn't like to use bad language in front of his wife. He dabs at the boiling liquid with the tea-towel.

Maureen retreats from the kitchen, puts Charlie's present and card under the Christmas tree. The moment for giving has somehow passed.

There is a knock on the door at midday. Charlie, now dressed in a smart casual jacket, shirt, knitted tie and permanent-press brown trousers, opens it. But there is no one there. Suddenly, a big red-faced man jumps out from the left-hand side of the doorway. He wears an Adidas track top, Wranglers, blue

Dunlop 'Superflash' trainers, a leather blouson jacket with elasticated cuffs and a Mandarin collar. But on his face is a huge fake white beard. His hair is concealed by a red felt Santa's hat. Over his shoulder a bag weighed down with presents.

Ho fucking ho, you cunt.

Tommy Buck starts laughing, his great belly wobbling from side to side. His wife, Lorraine, slim, a little over five feet tall, emerges from the other side of the door, shooting Charlie a despairing look.

Come on, Charlie. Crack a smile, you miserable twat.

Tommy pulls off the beard. At forty, he is ten years younger than his brother, and Lorraine is younger still. They are childless. Charlie is not sure of her exact age, but she cannot be much over thirty. Her cheeks still bloom. Under her coat she wears tight Gloria Vanderbilt jeans, stretch denim indigo. A white blouse thin enough to see her bra through.

Come in, Tommy. Lorraine.

Now Tommy peels off his Santa hat, revealing close-cropped hair. He hands his bag of presents to his brother.

Stick those somewhere. I want to show you my Crimbo present.

From who?

From me to me.

He shouts past Charlie's head, towards the kitchen.

Oi, Mo! Happy Christmas, love!

There is no answer. Maureen has Radio Two on loud, and cannot hear. Lorraine pecks Charlie on the cheek and takes back the presents. Tommy makes a beckoning gesture towards Charlie.

Come and have a goosy-goosy-gander at this.

I haven't got any shoes on.

You got your slippers on, haven't you? Come on, don't be such an old fucking crock.

Reluctantly, Charlie follows Tommy outside. Twenty feet away, parked in the road, a sky-blue car gleams immaculately.

What is it? says Charlie.

Astra. When I was a copper we used to drive these. Fucking good motors. Course, they've improved even since those days. Those halcyon fucking days.

Charlie nods as they approach the car. Already Tommy is huffing and puffing with the exertion. Charlie calculates he must be fifteen or sixteen stones.

Must have set you back.

Three and half fucking K. With extras.

What's it got?

Strut front suspension. Phosphated body shell.

Charlie doesn't know what either of these is but nods sagely. Lorraine hovers on the pavement, looking nervously at two young black men who pass them without comment. She finds the way they walk irritating, too sassy. One of them turns and looks at the Astra, smiles. Lorraine hears something.

Pussy wagon.

Claat.

She tightens her lips as the men walk on. Tommy is continuing, as Charlie nods, uncomprehending.

Aerodynamically designed. Hydraulic tappets.

Looks like a gravy guzzler.

28.8 m.p.g. at fifty-six.

That'll do. On the never-never, is it?

It's on tick, sure. Got a good deal on it. A red-hot deal. Friend of mine's in the business.

Poke?

Nothing to sixty in 12.6.

Charlie admires the interior, the new-car smell, the ashtrays, the design of the gear stick. Eventually he generates sufficient admiration to satisfy Tommy and they withdraw inside.

Charlie insists to himself that such things are unimportant. But the gleam of the blue paintwork stains his eye. Tommy puts his huge hand round Lorraine's waist, gives it a squeeze. She wriggles to extricate herself.

You still driving that fucking Toledo?

Charlie nods.

*Rustbucket, a **fucking** rustbucket. Why don't you get one of these, Charlie? I've got a mate at Vauxhall. He can do you a deal. A good deal.*

How come?

Tommy leans close.

Actually, he's not really at Vauxhall. To tell you the truth, they're nicked. Well, not exactly nicked. I mean, it's safe. They're from fucking Cameroon or somewhere. No chance of tracing them. It's a right steal, I'm telling you, three and a half. Let me get you one.

It's not really me, Tommy. I've not got the money spare.

*Come off it, Charlie, you boring fucker. You fucking **square**. You and Maureen must have saved up a pretty penny over the years. Spend some of it for once.*

That's not really the point.

*Oh, it's the fine upstanding citizen routine, isn't it? Get with the fucking programme, **Charles**. This is 1980. Every man for himself.*

No thanks, Tommy. And the money I've got saved is for retirement. Or a rainy day.

It's always a fucking rainy day, says Tommy.

*The trouble with **you**, Tommy –*

*The trouble with **you**, Charlie boy, is that you're fucking frightened of fucking everything. You think life's dangerous.*

*It **is** dangerous.*

What's anything without a few chances?

Tommy drops his beard and removes his blouson jacket. He bellows.

Mo! Happy Christmas! Where the bloody hell are you?

Maureen finally emerges from the kitchen, wearing an apron with 'The Boss' printed in yellow across the torso. Tommy encloses her in a tremendous hug, so that she almost seems to disappear beneath his folds of flesh.

There she is. Laughing girl. There's my lovely Mo. You've lost weight, love. Nothing of you. Ain't cheerful Charlie feeding you?

Hello, Tommy. She extricates herself from her brother-in-law's grasp. *Happy Christmas.*

Happy Christmas, sweetheart. Tommy looks around the room. *Here, where's that no good son of yours? Where's that lanky fucking carrot-headed bastard?*

He'll be here later, says Maureen quietly. *He wouldn't miss seeing his favourite uncle.*

*His **only** uncle,* says Charlie quietly, half to himself.

He'll be here all right. Not going to miss out on his old mum's cooking, is he?

Not so much of the old, thank you, says Maureen, grinning none the less.

Everyone's old when you're a teenager, Mo. Even Lorraine's old to Rob, ain'tcha, Lol?

Suppose, says Lorraine, who has removed her coat and is sitting down, crossing and uncrossing her legs.

If I'm that lanky streak of piss's favourite uncle, Robert's Lorraine's favourite nephew, ain't he, Lol?

He's a nice boy. He's got a nice face. Sensitive.

He's a fucking ginger, that's what he is. Tommy pronounces both Gs hard. *Nah, he's a good boy all right. Clever. Don't know where the fuck he gets that from. Has to be all from Mo, eh?*

He laughs uproariously, as if this were the biggest joke in the world. Charlie ignores it. Tommy is doing well, or claims to be. Charlie suspects it's all HP, all show. He and Lorraine have driven here from the Barratt house in Theydon Bois.

Tommy and Charlie might not get along, but *family is*

family, irregardless, as Charlie has said to Maureen on countless occasions. Tommy the builder, the ex-copper, the jack of all trades. He is not, in Charlie's eyes, a good man or a craftsman. Both are titles he guards jealously for himself.

Tommy is all crocodile smiles and large, expansive gestures. He has meaty arms, breasts larger than Maureen's. He wears a West Ham supporter's shirt; on his right hand, one letter crudely inscribed just beneath each knuckle: WHUFC. Tommy frequently turns up with cuts and bruises. Today there is a purplish mottling the size of an orange on his neck. He is fond of recreational violence.

Charlie finds his brother vulgar, disreputable and loud, but he envies him his wife, whose body is tight under the close-cut outfit. Her lipstick is frosted, her hair bundled up on to her head. She has a thin, mean mouth. When she walks, she takes small, self-consciously dainty steps.

Did you get a nice Christmas present from Charlie? says Lorraine to Maureen.

Come and see, says Maureen, moving towards the kitchen.

Hold on, says Tommy. *This I got to see. Saucepans, was it? Gold-plated fucking Brillo pads?*

Tommy follows Maureen and Lorraine. He can barely squeeze through the door into the kitchen without moving sideways.

Lorraine is studying the microwave admiringly.

Oh, yeah, they're great. I wouldn't be without mine.

What is it, a Creda? says Tommy. *Who's Creda, then, when he's at home? We got a Japanese one, didn't we, Lol? Those fucking Japanese, boring little yellow bastards, bridge over the River fucking Kwai, but they know their white goods. Great fucking cars, great fucking electricals.*

I'm not sure where it comes from, says Maureen.

At least Maureen knows it's not off the back of a lorry, says

Lorraine. *It's probably got a receipt and everything. Six months' guarantee.*

A year, says Maureen.

A year's guarantee. How come none of the stuff you get me has ever got a guarantee, Tom?

What you need a fucking guarantee for? It's all kosher goods. It all works. Proper stuff. Advertised on TV.

Police Five, says Lorraine.

Lorraine returns to the living room, sits down on the sofa. Tommy follows her, huffing and puffing. He sits down by her side. The springs creak under his weight. He rubs her leg lecherously.

All right, girl?

She sniffs.

Hang this up for me, will you, Tom?

He takes the voluminous cardigan that Lorraine has draped over her shoulders. It has a picture of Tintin's dog, Snowy, knitted into the pattern on the back. Tommy hands it up to Charlie as if lord to vassal. Charlie bridles, but bites back his irritation on account of it being Christmas. He hangs up the cardigan.

Lorraine, who has been looking after the presents, gets up, removes them from the bag and carefully places them under the artificial silver Christmas tree. An angel straddles its peak at an obtuse angle, as if its wings are unable to support it. The expression on its face suggests that it is posing for a snapshot on a celestial package holiday.

Tommy is holding something in a plastic bag. He removes an album from it.

Present from Lorraine. Thought I might give it a fucking twirl, eh, wot wot wot?

The record is *War of the Worlds* by Jeff Wayne. Without waiting for permission, he removes *The Mathis Collection* from the turntable and turns up the volume a couple of notches. Charlie glances at the cover: aliens in machines. He finds the music irritating, but again shies away from confrontation.

Would you care for a drink? he says to Lorraine.

He stands by his cocktail cabinet. It is covered with quilted PVC Con-tact in silver, with splayed 1950s-style legs.

Campari and Britvic please, Charlie.

We don't have any Campari.

How about Baileys?

I could do you a Kahlúa.

That's more of an after-dinner drink, isn't it?

I don't suppose it matters.

Can you do me a gin and tonic, then?

Okey-doke.

Ice and lemon.

There's no lemon.

Lime?

Charlie is growing irritated.

We've got some Jif lemon.

That stuff that comes in the plastic fruit?

Lorraine wrinkles her nose and picks at a bowl of peanuts.

Got any dry-roasted?

What we've got is what we've got.

I'll have a Whisky Mac, thanks, Charlie.

Tommy, sensing the tension, seeks to defuse the situation. Then he goes back to reading the telly pages for the day.

Ice?

As it comes.

Charlie fixes the drink, pouring a large glass of Cossack Vodka for himself, mixed with tonic. The second of the day. Robert is late. Maureen emerges from the kitchen.

Should I give Robert a ring, Charlie? I can't imagine where he's got to.

His phone's probably been disconnected again.

Probably still in bed, says Maureen. *I'll give him a try anyway.*

Maureen picks up the phone and dials. She wears a smocked, elasticated bodice-style dress with narrow straps.

Four minutes later, Maureen is still hanging on the phone.

What are you doing, Maureen? says Charlie.

I'm waiting for him to get off the phone. It's engaged.

Charlie blinks in astonishment.

Maureen, in all the times you have ever phoned anyone who is engaged, have they ever come off the phone?

What?

Tommy and Lorraine are watching now.

Has it ever been your experience that anyone has come off the phone while you've been waiting for the engaged signal to stop?

Maureen seems flummoxed.

I don't . . .

They don't come on the phone when they hang up. The engaged signal just continues. Even if they stop the call.

Charlie suddenly realizes that he is humiliating his wife and tries to sugar things.

I don't suppose, using the payphone all the time, you had much . . .

But it is too late. Tommy has started laughing, great gusts of noise.

It's that fucking microwave, Mo. The radiation gets out, see. Fries your fucking brain like a rasher of streaky.

Lorraine giggles in tandem. Maureen replaces the receiver and disappears into the kitchen without a word. Charlie, feeling a blazing shame under his string vest, follows her.

Maureen, I . . .

Maureen is biting her lip. She never raises her voice to Charlie, but she knows how to brew an atmosphere, knows how to generate certain kinds of silence that accuse and reproach. Charlie tries to put his arm over her shoulder, but is shrugged off. He begins to speak, but suddenly there is the sound of the doorbell. Maureen shakes herself, begins to tease her hair.

Sorry, kiddo.

You'd best answer the door.

Charlie knows he is unforgiven, but decides to leave his offence to the unpreventable erasures of time. He opens the door to a man wearing a red motorcycle helmet and an all-in-one leather suit. He carries several badly wrapped parcels under his arms. For a moment Charlie cannot solve the conundrum of who this might be. Then Robert removes the helmet, gives a broad grin.

All right, Pops? he says.

His face is scrunched and clenched, as if by the wind and the cold. He attempts a smile, to show gappy teeth.

What you dressed like that for? says Charlie, bewildered.

*He's a fucking poof. A **kinky** poof. All the leather gear,* says Tommy, who's come up behind his brother.

What time d'you call this, anyway? says Charlie, jabbing at his watch.

Robert ignores his father, walks through the doorway. Immediately, Tommy picks him up and throws him over his shoulder head-first, until he is nearly inverted. Robert starts laughing.

You fucking ginger poof.

Robert struggles, but it is hopeless against the size and strength of his uncle.

All jacket and no bike.

Stop it, Uncle Tom! I'm going be sick.

Come on, Lol. Give him a tickle. He always loved a tickle when he was kid.

Lorraine begins to chuck him under the arms and Robert begins to scream delightedly.

No . . . Hold on . . . Cut it out . . . Aunty Lol!

Faintly embarrassed and regretful, Charlie watches these scenes. He has not yet touched his son.

Finally Tommy puts Robert down. Robert is still laughing.

You fat bastard, Tommy.

Enough of that, ginger nut. Or I'll get your Aunty Lol on to you again.

*All right then, Twiggy. Hold on though. You **have** lost weight.*

Despite himself, Tommy looks pleased.

You can't be more than a ton and a half now.

Jokingly, Tommy raises a fist and Robert whacks him in the stomach, but the blow bounces off.

It's like hitting a bloody space-hopper.

The pantomine over, Robert struggles out of the leather one-piece. Lorraine helps him. Underneath, a pair of camouflage trousers, DM boots, a T-shirt with a badge decorated with an eagle and the word 'Bundeswehr' inscribed beneath. The clothes look filthy, encrusted with grease and food stains.

Bike wouldn't start.

Those fucking rinky-dink mopeds are a nightmare, says Tommy, grinning.

It's a Kawasaki 800cc, says Robert.

That must kick, says Tommy, nodding gravely. *What was the damage?*

Worth about seven fifty.

Where did you get that sort of money? says Charlie, shocked.

Saved up of course, says Robert.

Oh, right, says Charlie, in a voice heavy with doubt, with suspicion.

He glimpses the gleaming motorcycle out in the yard, next to his brother's Astra. His Toledo looks sad, ridiculous.

Robert. Maureen advances on her only son.

What can it do? says Tommy.

Hundred and twenty in six seconds.

Maureen embraces Robert, will not let go.

Tommy whistles between his teeth.

Phew.

Maureen surrounds him with her eyes. His leaving is the greatest grief she has known. Each return is a miracle.

I love the leather suit, says Lorraine. *Kinky. Can I have a go on the bike?*

Robert shrugs.

Don't see why not.

Fuck me, she's gonna end up spread all over the road. Strawberry fucking jam, says Tommy.

Robert gives his mother a kiss.

Happy Christmas, Mum. You're looking gorgeous.

That's where you get it from, says Lorraine.

Robert steps back outside, and Lorraine grabs her coat and follows.

Charlie catches a glance between Robert and Lorraine. Tommy is now outside inspecting the Kawasaki. Robert climbs on; Lorraine spreads her legs behind him, wraps her slender arms round his waist. They begin to move forward, Lorraine squealing with laughter. To his father, Robert looks rat-like, emaciated. His teeth are badly stained; one that had been intact on his last appearance is missing. How did he get the money for the bike?

Then Robert and Lorraine are gone, in a flash of red. Tommy turns to his brother.

I know a man who does those half price. Safe. Unfucking traceable.

5

Maureen studies the manual of the Creda 40131. Charlie has insisted on this. For reasons she cannot really fathom, it seems important to him. It is as if it renders the Christmas dinner his achievement somehow, rather than hers. But Maureen identifies this as an ungenerous thought, and she is always concerned to do battle with ungenerous thoughts. *I must*, she thinks to herself, in an incantation she has taught herself, or been taught, *leave this world a better place than that which I came into*. This is the mark of a successful life.

And so she casts the bad thought out and replaces it with the more comfortable notion that Charlie is only thinking of her in the end. But the thought chafes with her somehow; if not a total lie, it does not feel completely true. Yet she puts this down to a failing in her own character, a lack of the goodness she feels she somehow expects herself naturally to possess.

Maureen regards the microwave anxiously. It all seems perfectly straightforward; too straightforward. Quite unbelievable in fact. You put the bird in, pressed a couple of buttons and the whole thing would be done in twenty minutes.

The turkey just about fits into the small box of an oven. She rehearses what Charlie has told her – it cooks from the inside, through jiggling the atoms or what-not, so it keeps all the juices sealed in. This makes it better than ever.

It was terribly expensive, this gadget, she knew, and this reassured her that the meal would be successful. It was very generous of Charlie to buy it for her, and she is grateful for the amount of time it would clearly save for her so that she could get on with other activities.

But what activities? The truth increasingly presses down on her that, without the labours of her life, she is at a loss. They do not satisfy her; in fact, she dislikes them much more than she would ever be prepared to admit to Charlie. But they stopped a hole, held back a flood. Now, all the accumulation of time-saving devices brings to the fore a long-suppressed conundrum. What to do with the time after it is deposited into her ever-swelling account? This, it seems to her, is the puzzle of her middle years.

She is no *women's libber* – this is the phrase she uses to herself, women's libber, borrowed from Charlie – but she feels that there must be a place to escape to, not just a place to escape from.

Working at Divine Creations has surprised her. Marie-Rose thinks she is good at her job, sings her praises loudly. Maureen enjoys the neatness of the columns, the quietly mounting figures tallying so elegantly with one another. Income, out-goings, a world under control. Marie-Rose thinks she should train as some sort of accountant. There are evening classes, postal courses. Publicly, Maureen pooh-poohs the idea, it seems way out of her reach. Secretly, she covets the prospect. The money Marie-Rose pays her feels different to her touch from that which Charlie gives her. Although she considers all income as belonging to the marriage, she keeps the banknotes in a different place from those he has earned.

Tentatively, she rotates the circular plastic knob on the fascia of the microwave and it begins emitting a soft hum. A pale light gleams reassuringly within. Perhaps it will be OK. She turns away to concentrate on the vegetables. Lorraine is helping peel some carrots, her eyes bunched up with blank concentration.

How you and Tommy getting along? says Maureen.

All men are the same, says Lorraine. *Bloody great kids.*

All women are the same too, says Robert following his voice into the room. *Give 'em a fast ride on a motorbike and they melt like half a pound of Anchor. All that power between the legs.*

Lorraine laughs.

You're filthy, you are.

Robert, peel a few of those sprouts, will you?

Robert picks up a knife, positions himself next to Lorraine and begins cutting at the pile of Brussels sprouts. Maureen checks through the serving hatch; Charlie is deep in conversation with Tommy.

You didn't tell your dad where you got the money for the bike, did you?

Nah. I think he thinks I nicked it.

He can think what he likes, so long as he doesn't think what he ought not to think.

What are you talking about, Mo? says Lorraine. The waist of her jeans is touching Robert's hip.

Charlie doesn't approve of me giving Robert money. Says he's got to learn to stand on his own two feet.

You paid for the bike?

Sort of. I promised I'd give him a pound for every pound he earned himself. He worked hard for that bike.

I bloody did, says Robert. *I was running two jobs. Security guard and removals man. Try telling Dad, though. He thinks I'm a layabout from top to bottom.*

I can't see you as a security guard, Rob, says Lorraine.

Actually, I quite like it. I like the uniform and that. And people listen to what you got to say. It's all right. Better than working in removals.

Why don't you tell your dad?

He wants me to be a bloody brain surgeon or something, doesn't he? Or a doctor. Some mate of his at work's got a son who's a doctor. I'm supposed to be impressed.

The potatoes and parsnips are already roasting. The arrival of the microwaved bird is imminent. Maureen is unnerved by the lack of aroma, of roast flesh; it must all be confined within the white box. The humming remains soft, but now it sounds threatening. She can smell the potatoes and parsnips in the oven. Peas, carrots and sprouts are in saucepans ready to be boiled. Robert adds the last of the sprouts. A hostess trolley is parked and ready. She checks the LCD clock on top of the fridge. She checks the time remaining on the microwave dial. Everything is perhaps going according to plan. Robert notices Maureen's worried expression.

Don't worry, Mum. It'll be fine.

Course it will, Mo, says Lorraine. *I'll finish putting the crackers out.*

Maureen helps herself to a second glass of Van Huyten Cherry Brandy. She is not meant to mix it with the Tryptophan that she takes for her nerves, but Christmas cancels all bets. Anyway, her nerves are playing up. She doesn't trust the turkey, which means, on a deeper level, that she doesn't trust her husband to make it all right. It is this deeper thought that leads her to the second glass. She lights a rare cigarette to accompany it, adding to the fug and heat that fill the room. She is suddenly exhausted.

It is twenty minutes before Maureen feels ready to make the announcement. She puts her head through the hanging plastic strips and speaks in a singsong voice.

Come and get it.

Brought out in advance, steaming bowls of vegetables: sprouts, peas, parsnips, potatoes, carrots. Charlie sits at the head of the table, Maureen's chair is empty at the other end. Tommy sits next to Lorraine and is rubbing her thigh with wide, circular strokes. His face, purpled by lust and drink, is the colour of an erection. Charlie, having dropped his Christmas cracker, is aware of the gradual progress of Tommy's hand towards Lorraine's groin after he stoops to retrieve it. He experiences a bolt of envy. In order to disguise or diffuse it, he rises to give Maureen a hand. Lorraine has undone three buttons of her blouse and her cleavage plunges towards a moist heaven. Robert sits opposite Tommy and Lorraine, drinking a glass of Carling Black Label. His eyes stray towards Lorraine's cleavage. They all await the centrepiece, the turkey.

Charlie goes into the kitchen. Maureen is standing over the bird, not moving. Steam rises from it. It is faun in colour rather than brown, but otherwise it looks to all intents normal, although the aroma is not as pungent and enticing as Charlie would expect.

I told you it would be all right, says Charlie, cupping his arm around his wife's waist. He still seeks forgiveness for his earlier transgression.

I hope so, she says shakily.

She inserts a skewer violently into a point between the breast and backbone. Charlie flinches. Clear liquid oozes. This encourages her. She nods to Charlie to take it through, while she brings in hot plates on the trolley. It is her best set, Avalon by Hostess, decorated with large orange and yellow flowers.

Charlie enters the dining room carrying the large but slightly anaemic-looking bird. He sets it in the middle of the table. Maureen emerges from the kitchen looking flustered but with a happy smile on her face. The mixture of tranquillizers and alcohol is successful even though it says on the bottle not to mix the two.

Amazing. It only took twenty minutes, says Charlie.

What model you say it was? says Tommy, slurring slightly. He and Charlie have both been drinking heavily.

Creda 40131.

You should try one of the Japanese ones. Yeah.

Lorraine's breasts tug at the fourth button. Robert's mouth is slightly open.

Charlie nods, tries to concentrate.

Mitsubishi. It's got an automatic wave-circulating system, says Tommy.

What's its golf handicap? says Robert.

Tommy ignores him.

No, but not trying to be funny. You need that. To cook evenly.

Looks delicious, says Robert, his eyes remaining firmly on Lorraine's cleavage.

Nice and juicy, says Lorraine, again glancing up at Robert.

It's a bit pale, says Maureen.

It's the method, says Charlie. *Microwaves don't change the colour so much.*

You can't judge a book by its cover, says Lorraine.

You sure it's fucking dead, Charlie? says Tommy, grinning wolfishly. *Looks like it's going to jump up and do a runner any fucking moment.*

Lorraine slowly licks her lips. Robert drops his knife. Charlie ignores all this, concentrating on slicing the turkey, while Maureen dishes out the plates and the guests help themselves to vegetables. For the slicing, he has an electric carving knife that does much to drown out further conversation. The flesh cleaves. Charlie feels confident about the bird, despite its sickly appearance. They have followed the instructions exactly.

The meat falls off the bone. Plates are passed in turn to Charlie and he layers the meat on to each one. No one starts to eat until he's finished. Maureen is seated now. They all have wine, glasses of pale Vinho Verde.

Before we start, says Charlie, *a toast to Maureen for the wonderful meal.*

Maureen.

Maureen.

Mum.

Maureen blushes.

Come on. It'll get cold.

Robert takes a bite of the turkey first. His expression freezes, is unreadable. Maureen takes a bite. She almost has to spit it out, so hot is the meat. But the strange thing is that alongside the heat there is cold. It is both uncooked and overcooked. The meat is tough, almost to the point of inedibility. Maureen tries to keep her face from falling.

It's . . . says Robert. But then stops. He looks to his Uncle Tom for help.

Tommy chews determinedly on the turgid meat. He nods at Maureen encouragingly, though not quite able to speak the required lie.

It's horrible, mutters Maureen.

Course it's not, says Charlie.

He wishes desperately now that he had spent the extra £30 on the automatic wave-circulating system. He helps himself to a large quantity of breast meat, then makes a performance of taking a large chunk. Recognizing its inedibility immediately, he nevertheless manages a broad smile.

Outstanding. You'd never get that much flavour in an ordinary roast.

Lorraine says nothing, but is manifestly not touching her meat. Maureen takes a sip of the wine that is in front of her. She readjusts her face into an expression of cheerful indifference.

No. It's horrible. Never mind.

She disappears into the kitchen and comes back with a large plastic bowl and begins picking up the plates one by one and scraping the meat into it.

Charlie looks outraged.

Jesus God Almighty, Maureen, I tell you it's OK. Don't take mine.

Come on, Charlie, give me your plate.

No. It was a top-of-the-range oven and it worked just fine. It cost £250.

Dad, it doesn't matter.

Robert hands his plate to Maureen. Taking their cue, Tommy and Lorraine do the same.

This is the best turkey I've ever tasted, insists Charlie, and forces another forkful into his mouth.

Maureen returns to the kitchen, where she stands, breathing heavily. Although disappointed by the failure of the turkey, the kick of the tranquillizers keeps her functioning. But she has no idea what to do now. Then Tommy appears at the door. He enfolds Maureen within his enormous bulk.

Don't you worry, Mo. It's only food. Not your fault, is it? You needed one with . . . a microwave with . . . never fucking mind. Anyway, I've got a solution. There's a fucking monster handy Gandhi I know around here. We'll have Christmas lunch Bombay style!

I don't know, Tommy . . .

Come on. What you fancy? Three alarm or four alarm. They can't make 'em hot enough for me. You cheer up. You put your feet up. Tommy'll sort it all out.

He turns his back, affixes the fake beard, then turns to Maureen again.

I'm fucking Santa after all, ain't I?

Half an hour later, the living-room table is covered with foil canisters, poppadoms, chutneys and naan breads. The smell of spices and chutneys fills the room. Robert, Lorraine, Maureen and Tommy pile their plates high, but Charlie, who has insisted throughout that the turkey is perfectly fine, sits there with an empty plate, having finished his Christmas dinner alone.

This is delicious, mutters Robert through a mouthful of lamb korma.

Fucking ought to be. I bunged the cook an extra tenner to do us something special. These guys know their stuff, I'm telling you. Christ, this vindaloo is almost too hot for me. Fan fucking tastic. How's your tikka masala, Mo?

It's good, actually. Very tasty. She feels herself brightening up, feels a swell of gratitude towards her brother-in-law.

Best curry house in west London, I swear. Pass us three of those poppadoms, Lolly.

Charlie sits staring at his plate.

I'm going to get some more turkey.

You really should try this bhuna ghosht, says Lorraine. *It's marvellous.*

The turkey's fine. I'm going to have some more.

Charlie disappears into the kitchen and returns with a plate defiantly piled with slices of sweating turkey, fresh from a reheating in the microwave. Tommy looks at Robert, raises an eyebrow. Robert nods in acknowledgement of his father's stubbornness.

So, I hear you got a job, Tommy says to Maureen. His eyelids droop.

*Not **exactly**,* says Charlie.

What do you mean? says Maureen.

The booze and pills are wearing off. She feels irritable, provoked, cheated of her proper laurels for preparing the Christmas dinner. Her cracker motto raises no laughs.

I only mean it's part-time.

Does that make it not a job? says Maureen sharply.

All right, says Charlie. *It's a job, then.*

It's nice to keep yourself busy. Now that 'trouble' here has flown the coop, says Lorraine. She winks at Robert.

It's not 'keeping busy'. It's a job, says Maureen. *Book-keeping.*

Cash business? says Tommy.

Hairdresser's, says Maureen. *Divine Creations.*

Perfect *cash business. I bet you get to use your imagination. I bet you tell more stories than fucking* **Jackanory**.

Maureen smiles conspiratorially.

Maureen wouldn't do anything like that, would you? says Charlie. *She doesn't go in for that kind of thing.*

Ah, bollocks, says Tommy. *No flies on our Mo, are there, Mo?*

Well . . . you know. I try to be flexible.

I had mine done at Sassoon last week, says Lorraine. *What do you think, Robert?*

It's all right, says Robert, not meeting Lorraine's eye.

Very nice, says Charlie.

What about mine? says Maureen.

What? says Charlie.

I had mine done last week and you didn't have a word to say about it.

You have to pay for quality, grunts Tommy, helping himself to the last peshwari naan. He keeps one hand on Lorraine's groin.

You still knocking yourself out cheap? says Robert, picking at his fingernails.

Cheap? says Tommy.

He takes his hand off Lorraine's groin, flexes the fingers.

Nothing cheap about me, says Tommy. *My rate's £30 a day. That's what you have to pay for a craftsman.*

Charlie snorts.

I was hoping you could help me sort out my house a little bit.

Nothing I wouldn't do for my favourite nephew, even if he is a ginger little poof. What sort of place is it?

It's a suite at the Hilton, says Charlie.

It's a squat, says Robert.

Sounds quite romantic, says Lorraine.

It's a dosshouse, says Charlie.

You've never even been there, says Robert.

You've never invited me, says Charlie.

There is an uneasy silence. Charlie holds out a cracker to his brother.

Come on, Tommy.

Tommy hesitates, then pulls. The paper separates without a bang. The crackers were cheap, from North End Road market.

Look what I saved, says Robert.

He holds out the turkey wishbone to Lorraine. Lorraine puts her little finger in it and pulls. She gets the smaller part.

Make a wish, says Lorraine.

Robert squeezes his eyes tight closed, pauses a few seconds, then opens them again.

What did you wish? says Lorraine.

*I'm not telling **you***, says Robert mysteriously.

It has to be a secret, doesn't it? says Maureen, chucking Robert under the chin. *Or it won't come true.*

Robert twists his face away.

I'm not a kid any more.

You're all grown up big and strong, says Lorraine.

How's the toy choo-choos, Charlie? says Tommy.

*They're not **toys***, says Charlie. *Shall we have some Christmas pudding?*

Dad had to get rid of them, says Robert.

What? says Tommy.

Council says they're a fire risk.

***Fucking** council*, says Tommy.

I don't know how you put up with it, says Lorraine. She is correcting her lipstick with the aid of a pocket mirror. *To have your own front door . . .*

We've got our own front door, says Maureen.

Yeah. Same colour as all the others. Can't change so much as the letter box. Look, I'm not trying to be snooty. All I'm saying is, it's nice to have your own.

We don't like the debt, says Maureen. *Do we, Charlie? We're just old fuddy-duddies.*

That's right, says Robert. *Mr and Mrs Keep Your Nose Clean and Steady As You Go.*

Slow and steady wins the race, says Maureen.

Charlie feels a hotness inside him. He notes that Tommy's hand is back on Lorraine's lap. His other hand strokes her Sassooned hair. The Kawasaki and the Astra are outside, shaming him with their newness, their naked expense. Tommy and Lorraine will drive home to their own house. He fumes at having had to dismantle his railway. The microwave lacks an automatic wave system for the protons. The turkey is foul. It is his fault. But Tommy sorted it all out, Tommy is the hero of the hour. When he speaks, it is with a thought at the back of his head that seems to have arrived from nowhere.

The trouble with you, Maureen, is that you're old-fashioned, he says. *I'm no fuddy-duddy.*

Maureen is shocked. She had been certain of agreement.

Am I, Charlie?

I've got a Christmas surprise, Mo. I've gone and got the forms.

What forms?

Charlie pauses, wonders momentarily if he can carry this off. But it is too late to back-pedal.

The right to buy. It's discounted 40 per cent. You can't go wrong. The repayments are less than the rent now that they've put it up. And then we got capital.

Good move, Charlie, says Tommy gravely.

He claps his hands together as if in applause. A plate of Christmas pudding steams in front of him and he applies custard and brandy butter.

Maureen's eyes dart back and forth from Tommy to Charlie. She is shocked that this private secret has been made so suddenly public, that this information has been withheld from her.

Are you having a laugh? says Robert, genuinely surprised.

No, says Charlie, pursing his lips.

Robert gives him a crooked half-smile.

You just made it up. You're just trying to impress everyone, he says.

That's rubbish.

Charlie is suddenly terrified of being found out. He resolves to get the forms first thing in the New Year.

Get on the property ladder, says Tommy. *That's the thing.*

The market's on the up, says Charlie.

I might buy something myself, says Robert quietly. He is privately impressed by his father's unaccustomed daring.

Hark, says Maureen. *The three wise men.*

The washing-up having been dispatched, it is time to open the presents. Charlie, as has become traditional, prepares to distribute them. The rest of the family sits around in a semi-circle. Drink and food blur each of them. Charlie starts to experience a slight but noticeable pain in the centre of his stomach. He hopes that the protons have not poisoned the turkey.

OK. This one is from Robert to his Aunty Lol.

Lorraine takes the gift and begins unwrapping it. It is a T-shirt. On the front, in large letters, is written 'Whoever Has The Most Money When They're Dead Wins'. Lorraine laughs, and goes across and gives Robert a loud kiss on the lips.

It's the truth, she says.

Lolly loves her lolly, says Robert, grinning.

She's a yumpy, says Charlie.

What's that? says Tommy.

I read it in the paper. Young Upwardly Mobile Professional.

Charlie picks out another present at random.

Us to Lol. Lucky Lol gets all hers first.

Pick out another, Charlie. I can wait.

Luck is luck. Go ahead.

Lorraine smiles and opens the gift. It is a thin gold bracelet like a knotted rope. Surreptitiously, she checks the hallmark. It is 18 carats.

Thanks, Charlie. Maureen.

She does a poor job of hiding her disappointment. The heavy atmosphere weighs down.

If you don't like it, I've still got the receipt, says Maureen.

No, of course I like it.

Of course, it's hard buying jewellery, says Charlie.

It's fine. It's lovely. Thanks.

Lorraine slips it into her pocket. She never wears anything less than 24 carats.

The distribution of gifts continues.

Maureen gets a Pifco 'Super Callboy' kettle, a Rima Toasted Sandwich Maker, a glazed ceramic fruit pyramid and twenty porcelain 'Miniature Whimsies' by Wade, including a spaniel, a kitten, a duck and a corgi. Lorraine gives her a bottle of Rive Gauche perfume, which, like the anklet, will never be worn.

Charlie gets 200 Benson and Hedges, a Black and Decker drill from Maureen and a bottle of Tabac Original to add to his collection. Tommy gets him *The AA Book of the Car*, with a washable silver cover, and the *Reader's Digest Book of the Road*. Charlie slips £20 into Tommy and Lorraine's card – Tommy always insists on a bit of cash, seeing Christmas as essentially practical and transactional.

Robert gets a pair of Nike Tailwind trainers from his uncle and aunty. He grunts his appreciation. He has bought Tommy a silver beer tankard with the West Ham club logo on it. One of the last gifts to be distributed is from Robert to Charlie. Charlie opens it and feels a small sweet spark at the centre of his chest.

Sorry I couldn't afford the whole thing, says Robert. He seems fiercely embarrassed.

It's . . . wonderful, says Charlie.

And he is truly touched. It is the casing of a Leek and Manifold (Peak District) locomotive in chocolate brown. The beautifully crafted bodywork that Robert has bought him is designed to be fitted around a live steam engine, the miniaturized locomotive that burns butane and pours out real plumes of smoke.

I know you haven't got the engine for it, Dad. I know it's for live steam and that. But one day, when I've got myself on my feet, I'll buy you the rest of it. The running chassis with wheels and valve gear. The boiler. All the ancillaries. Then you'll know I've arrived. Then you'll know I'm not a complete dead loss.

Thanks, says Charlie.

He is surprised and moved. He leans over to ruffle his son's hair, but cannot quite reach.

*I **know** you think I'm a flop. But you'll see. I'll get you that engine one of these days.*

Charlie is speechless. Unable to ruffle Robert's hair, he goes to shake his hand instead, but Robert misunderstands the signal and leaves his hand where it is, so Charlie just pats his shoulder.

Thanks, son. It's very special. And . . . I don't think you're a flop.

Yes, you do, says Robert quietly.

There is a silence. Then Charlie says, *I've got something special for you too.*

He hands a small parcel to Robert, about four inches square. The paper that covers it depicts joyful reindeer. Robert prepares himself; he expects his parents to get it wrong.

He is surprised to find that the calfskin wallet within appeals to him. It is plain black, elegant, with no unnecessary detail. He inspects the pouches and pockets, trying to work out what to put where.

Thanks, Mum. Dad.

Keep looking, says Charlie.

Robert checks behind the coin pouch, expecting maybe a £10 note. Since it is his only gift, he thinks a little cash will make up the difference. There is a piece of paper protruding slightly. He removes it, surprised to see that it is not money at all. Charlie smiles at his secret.

I had to go through hell and high water to get that.

Robert is perplexed. He studies it, then finally calculates what it is.

It's a meal ticket, kiddo. A job for life. I had to wheedle the FOC for months. Very hard to come by. But once you're in, you're in for the duration. You get overtime. Short days. Plus the old Spanish customs.

He touches his nose conspiratorially.

Robert turns the NGA union card over in his hand. He glances up at the look of expectation on his father's face, ready for approbation in front of the small, vital audience.

Hoy, cloth ears. Can you hear what I'm saying?

Your dad spent days and months on end sorting that out, says Maureen, noting the puzzled look on Robert's face.

Shhh, says Charlie furiously.

Robert nods, chews at his fingernails. Finally, he speaks.

Thanks, Dad. There is sadness in his voice. *Thanks for putting yourself out like that.*

You know what I'd do for you, son, says Charlie tenderly.

Robert places the card on the sideboard.

I've wangled a meeting with one of the boys from the machine room. He'll sort you out.

I . . .

Robert runs out of words.

Charlie looks at Robert, sees suddenly what the silence indicates.

It's a job for life!

There's no such thing any more.

Robert suddenly feels something within him coalesce, a tender defiance. When he speaks again, it is softly but firmly.

Anyway. Don't take this wrong, Dad. But your life isn't the life I want.

Charlie feels a shooting pain in his stomach, then a hotness invading his entire body. He sees his brother's face, thinks there is the ghost of a mocking grin. When he speaks again, he cannot keep the bitterness from his voice.

I suppose you've got the right to mess up your own life however you want. But the trouble with that dropout type of attitude is that it's all very well when you're young. But sooner or later you're going to get old. I know it's hard to believe. I never believed it myself.

I'm not a dropout, says Robert, turning his head away.

Obviously not. Obviously not. I mean, you've got a brand-new motorbike, for instance. The Social must be giving out Christmas bonuses this year.

Come on, says Maureen. *I'm sure Robert . . .*

You been taking a few lessons from your Uncle Tommy in villainy, have you, son? Is that the life you want? Taking the piss out of Joe Public the rest of your life. Thinking the world is just a collection of mugs waiting to be taken advantage of.

Leave off, Charlie, says Tommy. *Robert's not got the head on him for villainy. Worse luck for him. Takes after his dad. Old goody-two-shoes there.*

Thank you, Tommy. I know you understand my son far better than I do. I'm only his father, after all.

The silence that follows is long and awkward.

Anyone fancy a cup of tea? says Maureen finally. *Or coffee?*

Have you got Earl Grey? says Lorraine.

I'll have percolated, Robert says to Maureen.

Your mother's got a name, says Charlie darkly.

Yeah, says Robert, not so loud that his father can hear. *Mandingo.*

What's that? says Charlie.

Later the television is switched on. Charlie and Tommy want to watch the Queen's speech. Robert is in what was once his bedroom, listening to records. Lorraine has gone for forty winks in Maureen and Charlie's room. Maureen is handing out glacé fruits, dates and chocolate plums to Tommy and Charlie. Charlie pours himself a large Scotch, then sits in the empty armchair, although it only gives him a 45-degree view of the screen. The picture is colour and sharp; Charlie has invested in a new set to celebrate his return to work after the strike year.

The Queen says that the world can never be free of conflict, but that Christmas draws attention to all that is hopeful and good. It speaks, she says, in a voice that Charlie thinks of as serene and gravely wonderful, of values and qualities that are true and permanent, and it reminds us that the world we would like to see can come only from the goodness of the heart. The expression of this sentiment takes twelve minutes. The National Anthem sounds. Before it is finished, Tommy snorts.

What a lot of cock.

She's all right, says Charlie.

He likes the stuff about values being true and permanent.

He thinks of goodness of the heart and feels himself soften towards Robert.

I like Charles, says Maureen. *It's nice to see him having found love at last.*

Do you reckon he's a poof? says Tommy.

I shouldn't think so, says Charlie. *That Lady Di is a little cracker.*

That don't mean nothing. I reckon he is. I reckon he's gay.

What do you know about it? says Charlie.

When I was a copper, I met a bloke who used to do some bodyguarding for him. Said he tried to touch his arse and everything.

Charlie shakes his head doubtfully.

The thing about homosexuality, says Charlie thoughtfully, *is that it's against nature.*

You'll never believe this. Do you know what I heard the other day? says Tommy. *From this feller in the pub, used to be a driver for a film company. This bloke told me that Rock Hudson is gay.*

Maureen pushes him with the side of her hand. She is still in love with Rock Hudson. Her most prized possession is a signed photograph.

I've never heard anything so daft, says Maureen. She is laughing, but she is obscurely upset by this extraordinary suggestion.

It's true, apparently, says Tommy. *He knew all about it. A right arse bandit.*

It must be true, then, says Charlie, *if he was in the business.*

Cary Grant too, says Tommy.

Can we change the subject? says Maureen.

I hate poofs, says Tommy mildly.

They don't do any harm, I suppose, says Charlie, removing a remnant of chocolate plum from between his teeth.

That's not the point, says Tommy.

What is the point? says Charlie.

That's not, says Tommy, and lapses into a curt silence.

Charlie feels another dreadful shooting pain in the side of his stomach. He almost doubles up.

'Scuse me, he says, and scuttles towards the bathroom as fast as he can.

Entering the bathroom, Charlie kneels in front of the toilet seat. His abdomen contracts and he vomits. Vomits again and again, until only a thin trickle emerges, until he is dry-retching. In the pan, visible carrot, Brussels sprout. He tries to muffle the sound as best he can, does not want Maureen to know that either the turkey or a rogue proton has done this. A drum beats in his head. Bile is in his mouth.

He stands, wipes his mouth with pink tissue. He does not understand why a puppy advertises this. He flushes the toilet. Brushing his teeth to try and remove the taste, he feels the mint mix with the slick of bile. He runs a comb through his thick dark hair.

He thinks of his life in the composing room, the sweat he has shed. How today his son has made it seem to count for nothing. He thinks of holding Robert in his arms after he was born. The warmth and smell of talcum and faint blood. Now it is Tommy who puts him over his shoulder, it is Lorraine who tickles him and makes him shriek with laughter.

He reaches in his pocket for a cigarette. The pack is empty. There are 200 stored in what was once Robert's room. He feels drowsy, half drunk despite the sickness.

He turns the handle into the room. The light is poor. He is about to flick the light switch when he notices two moving shadows in the corner. He waits for his eyes to adjust. He cannot make sense of what he sees at first, of exactly what Aunty Lorraine is doing with her nephew. Why his eyes are closed, why he is breathing so heavily. Why his Aunty is on her knees, her head bobbing back and forth. He thinks she has dropped something, then, suddenly, the scene makes sense, makes awful sense.

Without a word, he closes the door, returns to the bathroom and begins retching once more.

6

Maureen winces as she dabs Bonjela on to a small but painful sore on the tip of her tongue. Her body, it seems to her today, is the bitterest of enemies. It never responds to treatment. It never recalibrates its shape. It bleeds and sweats and emits odours. It is out of control, and she hates it for its soft wilfulness, its wilful softness. A new line has appeared by the side of her mouth today, faint, the thickness of baby hair, but noticeable. Her body was once so powerful, could pull men towards her, bend them to her will. Now it is punishing her, squeezing her within, threatening her very existence.

But she will not give up. It can be tamed. If life strips her of her power, her body can still be her slave. It is simply a matter of willpower. *Willpower, Maureen, willpower!* This time she savours the bite of the ointment on a second ulcer, on the inside of her cheek. The pain refreshes her, reactivates her sense of purpose. No one beats Maureen Buck that easily. Certainly not Maureen Buck herself, certainly not that pink amorphous mass of muscle and bone and fat.

Maureen has just finished her aerobics class at her local community centre. There is a mirror there that covers an entire wall; she examined herself as she stretched and jumped and bent and straightened. She compares herself with the other women, fares badly. They are for the most part younger, do not have the knowledge that she possesses, the knowledge that it all fades and slackens. The knowledge that gravity pulls us all down in the end, down towards the magnetic earth. Her running kit lies in a heap on the bathroom floor. She will place it in the washing machine before she leaves, and dry and iron the clothes when she returns from work.

Work. She checks her wristwatch. Twenty minutes before she has to be at Divine Creations. How grateful she is to Marie-Rose for providing her this lifeline. She has an office to herself at the back of the shop, her domain. Now it is no longer a matter of just the monthly books. She helps do the annual income tax returns and sorts out the VAT, making calls to Customs and Excise to soft-talk the distant, powerful men on the other end of the phone. She files receipts and does the wage slips, filling brown envelopes with their salaries. Her empire outside the home increases. It is a small empire to be sure, but it is real, it feels real. Sometimes she thinks her life at home with Charlie is ghostly compared with this, the real substance of work, paid work.

She gets ready to leave, taking her coat from the hook in the hall, grabbing a slim briefcase from a space next to the umbrella stand. The veruccas make her limp slightly, but the discomfort today is not too bad. It seems to be less acute when she leaves the house, seems to disappear by the time she reaches the shop.

She checks herself in the mirror. Smart cream slacks, a candy-pink blouse, brown sandals with one-inch heels. Her coat is a raincoat from British Home Stores, Elderberry. The outfit, she decides, strikes a nice balance between the business-like and the informal.

She is just about to leave when there is a ring at the door. She checks her watch. If it's Mrs Jackson, there's no time to gossip. But when she opens the door, it is Carol who stands there, dressed in a violent-pink fluffy jacket and black leather trousers. Her hair is dyed orange, but her face is plain, without make-up. She looks anxious. She is hugging herself as if she is cold, but the day is warm enough.

Hello, Carol.

Mrs Buck, sorry to bother you.

Maureen is caught between the twin impulses of a desire to be polite and a determination not to be late.

Carol, I'm just heading off to work. I'm sorry, but I can't invite you in.

Oh, that's OK. I was just wondering if you have a number for Robert.

Robert?

Yes. It's just . . . I've tried to call him. And his phone seems to be cut off.

I didn't know you were still friendly with Robert.

Well, you know. We try to keep in touch from time to time. Only I've got to reach him.

What's the hurry?

There is a pause. Carol feels in a pocket of her jacket, brings out a badly crushed packet of cheap cigarettes.

He left something in my flat. I've got to give it back to him.

Really? He was at your flat?

Carol lights a cigarette. Maureen checks her watch again.

That's right.

Odd that he didn't come and say hello. Look Carol . . . perhaps if you drop round this afternoon.

I mean . . . you don't know if he's changed numbers or anything.

I don't think so. He hasn't said anything to me. Carol, I have to leave now.

Maureen steps out of the flat, closes the door behind her. Carol moves aside, still hugging herself.

Are you all right, Carol?

Oh, yes. Fine.

She attempts a weak smile.

Well, then . . .

Tentatively, Maureen steps past Carol towards the main road.

Do you have his address?

I've never been there, love. He's never invited me, to be honest. I know it's somewhere near Battersea Park. And it's . . . got a blue door. He sent me a photograph. But he's . . . Robert's not given me an address. He can be funny like that. Secretive. Look, if he calls me, I'll tell him he's forgotten his . . . What is it that he's forgotten?

His . . . his watch.

Watch? I didn't know Robert had a watch. Says that people are too 'hung up' about time.

Oh. Well, maybe it's someone else's, then.

Even if it is his, I dare say he can do without it for a week or two, eh?

And with this, Maureen strides purposefully towards the exit of the estate. She has only five minutes to get to work, and she hates to be late. Fortunately the verruca on her heel seems to be diminishing. She can make it, she thinks. A few minutes shy at worst.

Bye, Mrs Buck.

Carol turns, mutters something under her breath. She does not make her way back to her flat, just stands there. The thin complaint of Nelson, her infant son, sounds from her kitchen window.

When Maureen arrives at Divine Creations, she knows immediately that something is wrong. It isn't the fact that all the chairs are empty – trade doesn't usually begin to pick up until late morning or lunchtime – or the fact that Marie-Rose is gesturing angrily to whoever she is talking to on the phone. It is the fact that there is no music playing. Marie-Rose, from the moment she arrives at the shop to the moment she leaves, always has music on. She believes that without it the atmosphere in the shop is sepulchral, and there is something in this; the available light is reduced by the presence of a large decorated awning and the paintwork is maroon. The whole place needs lightening up and Marie-Rose believes that music is the only method that works. The dozen or so spotlights seem ineffective against the gloom. The compensation is that the light is very flattering. Each mirror presents each client in the best possible incarnation. Even before their hair is attended to they experience an improvement.

Marie-Rose slams down the phone and turns to Maureen.

Where the hell have you been?

Maureen checks her wristwatch. She is precisely three minutes late, the amount of time she spent on the doorstep with Carol.

I'm sorry, I didn't . . .

Oh, never mind. It doesn't matter.

Marie exhales and crumples down on to a bench. The shop junior hovers in the background, nervously arranging hair products on shelves.

I'm sorry to snap, Mo. The thing is, we've got a bit of a problem.

What sort of a problem?

Customs and Excise. A man was waiting for me on the doorstep when I arrived. Wanted to check all the books.

Maureen sits next to Marie-Rose, pats her gently on the back.

Don't worry, love. I've kept everything in order.

I know you have. You've done a good job. But you know and I know that the books are not . . . precisely everything they should be.

That's because you told me to . . .

*I know I told you. It's **all right**, Maureen. I'm not trying to blame anything on you. You've only done your job the way I've asked you to. And you've done it beautifully. Not a seam left unsewn.*

So what are you worrying about?

*Something I didn't think of. The **bastards**. They get you every time. How's anyone supposed to make a living?*

Why don't I make you a cup of coffee? Then you can tell me all about it.

Marie-Rose looks up. Although she is close to Maureen's age, she sees her as supportive, motherly.

OK. I'll put the Closed sign up. We need to work out what we're going to do here.

It sounds serious.

*It **is** serious.*

Maureen takes off her coat, puts the kettle on and spoons some instant coffee into two plain white mugs. She sits at her desk, puts her briefcase down, pulls at her cuffs. She does not feel panicked by Marie-Rose's obvious distress. The kettle boils. After a minute or two, Marie-Rose comes into her room, fingers fluttering in the air. Maureen hands her the steaming mug.

I've put an extra sugar in it. You look like you need a few comfort calories.

Thanks, Mo.

She sips at the coffee. Maureen sits calmly, and waits.

The thing is, Mo, he wants to see the appointment book for the last six months.

The appointment book?

*That's right. And I know, I **know**, I should have made up some cock-and-bull story about having lost it, I mean, what could they have done, but I didn't think. He caught me unawares.*

*You didn't **give** it to him?*

Oh, no, Mo. I'm not that much of a dummy. I said I'd left it at home. That sounds stupid enough, but he didn't have much choice but to accept it. He's coming back at one o'clock this afternoon to check it. That's in less than three hours! And if it doesn't marry up with the books, we're in trouble. I'm in trouble. The VAT men are *a **nightmare**, Mo. It's not just a matter of sorting it out with them, about coming to some arrangement, like with the Revenue. They prosecute. They take you for years of back-tax. I've got a friend who did three months in Holloway. Almost the same set-up. She was never the same. And her business, that went down . . . I don't know if I can ever –*

Elsie!

The use of her real name seems to make the woman in front of Maureen snap to attention.

Come on now. Pull yourself together. We can sort this out. Don't worry.

But how, Maureen? The book has got twice the number of appointments in it as are shown in the figures. It's a clear case of fraud.

We'll just have to get a new book, then, won't we?

*Oh, I've thought of that! It won't work, Maureen. It will **look** new. And what about the handwriting? It would all be different. You can't just sit down with a pen.*

We can do it. Get all the girls in. Get some pens and pencils sorted out. I know a stationer's that no one ever goes to – they've probably got books that look about a hundred years old, let alone six months.

It'll never work, Maureen. We've only got a few hours. Then it's all got to marry up with the patterns of income in the book-keeping. You'd have to be a bloody artistic genius.

Then you've got the right woman. Come on, get on that phone. We'll sort this out.

Marie-Rose wipes away a tear. She looks up at Maureen, who is already putting on her coat.

Do you really think we can pull this off?

Not if you just sit there blubbing, says Maureen, and bustles towards the exit.

*

When she returns from the stationer's just off the Fulham Palace Road, Marie-Rose and her four regular stylists are all waiting. Maureen is holding a large buff-coloured appointment book. It is dusty, slightly yellowed. The paper is curling at the edges. It is loose-leaf, with pages that detach from a retractable central spine. Maureen opens it.

It's not perfect, but it's something to work with. Everyone get a pencil or pen. Make sure the pens are different colours, different types. Here . . .

She reaches into her pocket and brings out a handful of different writing implements.

I'm going to go and get the books, then I want you to do what I tell you.

Maureen returns, carrying all the files she has available for the last six months. She opens the new appointment book at the first page. Then she opens her cash ledger, the one that the VAT man has inspected, and examines that also.

Right, Marie-Rose. Since you're the boss, you can go first. We need about fifteen appointments for the first day. You can have four, Sue can have three, and you two can have four each. Get on with it. Try and vary the handwriting a bit. Sometimes fast, sometimes slow. Sometimes less hard, sometimes lightly. We've got to make this look convincing, or we're all out of business.

Tentatively, Marie-Rose writes a name in pencil on the first page, one of her regular clients, 'Barbara – 10 a.m.'. She stands back and admires her handiwork. The other stylists all cheer weakly.

For two hours solid they work at the book, swapping pens, inventing client names and telephone numbers, trying to establish the proper degree of randomness. It is surprisingly difficult to make the book look authentic. Spontaneous, improbable patterns keep creeping in and need to be effaced.

By half-past twelve, the inscriptions are all finished and they marry up, more or less, with the patterns of cash flow that exist in Maureen's ledgers. Maureen studies the end result with a critical eye. The five other women in the room await her judgement.

It's not **good** *enough,* says Maureen. *It still looks too new. The writing is all right. We can get away with that. The pattern of entry is good. It matches up. It's the* **paper**. *There just isn't enough wear and tear. It still looks new.*

What are we going to do? says Marie-Rose. *He's here in thirty minutes. I might as well confess it all. It's hopeless. This is just going to get me into worse trouble.*

Quiet, Elsie. Lock the front door. Take the pages out. Move the chairs as far to the edge of the room as possible. Pull the blinds down.

What?

Come on. Snap to it. Help me, girls. Help me spread these pages all over the floor.

Maureen hands pages of the appointment book to each of the waiting stylists, who, puzzled, begin laying them out flat on the lino floor, while Marie-Rose pulls down the blinds and locks the door.

Now what? says Marie-Rose.

Now? says Maureen. *Now we* **walk** *on them. We walk on them for fifteen minutes, until they're dirty and torn-looking, and a bit rough at the edges. We walk on them until they look* **real**. *Come on. Get to it.*

There is a moment's pause. Then, as if one beast, the women in the room all start moving around on top of the pages, some jumping, some doing pigeon steps, some striding. Maureen walks briskly from one wall to the other. It is Marie-Rose who starts laughing first.

Oh, my God! What are we doing?

Then she bends over as the absurdity of the scene hits her

– five nearly middle-aged women parading around a deserted hairdresser's, stomping, hopping, kicking and scraping at the paper beneath their feet. Maureen joins in. Within seconds, the whole room is a cacophony of giggles and screeches of laughter.

Come on, says Maureen, through the gale. *March! March to victory!*

One of the stylists starts to dance on the sea of paper underneath and, seeing this, Marie Rose puts on the music. Then they are all dancing – jiving, bopping, twisting, funking together, throwing their arms in the air. The paper tears and crumples, soils and ages as they dance.

After ten minutes the women are left breathless. Maureen checks her watch, yells over the music.

That's it! He'll be here in a few minutes. Let's get these pages sorted out.

Together, they gather them up and systematically sort them back into the correct order in the appointment book. Maureen clips the mechanism on the spine, scratches at the metal a bit to make a few marks on it. Marie-Rose pulls the blinds back up and unlocks the door. Then the stylists adopt studiedly casual poses, reading magazines, arranging shampoos, wiping down sinks. Maureen inspects the book carefully.

Much better, she says, almost to herself.

She picks it up, ready to retreat to her room. Marie-Rose gives her the thumbs-up sign. Then, right on cue, a small portly man in a dark blue suit and carrying a combination-lock briefcase, walks in.

Sorry, I'm a bit early, he says, giving a vaguely malicious smile.

Oh, don't worry, says Maureen, approaching him, hand extended. *We're ready.*

★

Charlie sits in the corner of the pub. It is full to the extremities of hefty-looking men, some in dinner jackets, all looking vaguely threatening. There are no women. Apart from Lloyd, who is struggling to get served in the crush at the bar, everyone is white. He has been waiting for more than five minutes. Finally, he returns to their table, carrying two pints of bitter.

Tell me, Charlie. Can you see me?

What are you talking about?

I must have just rematerialized back here. I swear I was invisible up there. Five blokes standing behind me and they all got served before I did. Then they tried to overcharge me.

Well, busy, aren't they? I expect they get confused. Charlie raises his glass in Lloyd's direction. *Cheers, Snowball. I hope this is going to be worth spending an evening with the Tooting Liberation Front for.*

Ah, I can feel it all coming back. Lloyd, who is still standing, shuffles in his tiny space, throws a few punches in the air. *The Yellow Devil. Christ, those beers were expensive. When I first came to this country –*

Here we go, says Charlie.

When I first came to this country, you could get a pint of best for sixpence. Sixpence, man! Those were good days. People talk all the time about going back to the old country. It's nonsense, Charlie. As soon as I got here, I knew England was the place for me. Home of Shakespeare! Of Dickens! Of cricket! Of the page-three girl! Of Larry Grayson! Of course, it's going to the dogs all the same. Too many foreigners.

Ain't it the truth? says Charlie.

The Guernseys, Charlie. They're everywhere. Taking our jobs. Screwing our women.

Charlie laughs, pulls at his beer.

Guernseys. That's a good one, Snowy.

Knitting their bloody jumpers. Bastards. Not like in those days. No Guernseys then. And there was always work in those days. Not like today, millions unemployed. You know, when I came off the boat, I saw all these chimneys on the houses. And I had never seen a chimney on a house before, because they don't have them in Barbados. You know what I thought?

You thought all the houses were factories.

I thought all the houses were factories! You know, our family had to sell three cows to get me on that boat, Charlie.

That's right, Snowy. It was £28 10s, wasn't it?

Charlie yawns, looks up, sees Mike Sunderland come through the door to the pub, blinking through the smoke. He raises a hand, trying to get his attention.

*A lot of money. A **lot** of money. The youth today, they got no idea. That boat was full of boxers, the finest boxers. I wonder what happened to them all. They ate them up and spat them out, Charlie, that was what happened.*

Who did?

Jack Solomons, Ted Lewis. Those promoters, bwoy. Maybe this was the best luck I ever got.

Lloyd holds up his mutilated hand in front of Charlie's face.

*Because this way, I didn't hold on to no stupid dreams. **And** I stayed pretty. You know the first thing that struck me when I got here, Charlie?*

Mike! Over here! It was cold, Snowy. You thought it was cold.

It was warm enough, actually. I came in the middle of spring. No, what I thought was how ugly everybody was. Their faces. Men, women, children. Gargoyles all over the place, every shape and size. The Hunchback of Notre-Dame times 50 million.

Mike arrives at the table, breathing heavily through the cigarette smoke. He is wearing a donkey jacket, with a thick cable-knit sweater underneath. He hands one ticket to Lloyd and one to Charlie.

Sorry for the unpunctuality. My therapist's fault. He was running late.

Lot of crazies out there, says Charlie. *Fruit and Nut cases queuing for miles.*

Hey, Mike. Mike, is that a Guernsey? says Snowy, pointing at Mike's jumper.

Charlie smiles.

What?

Don't mind him, says Charlie. *What are you having?*

Well, yes. I'll have a dry white wine, if you don't mind.

Any particular year?

What?

White wine it is, then. Same again for you, Snowball?

When Charlie returns from the bar with the drinks, Lloyd and Mike Sunderland are deep in conversation.

You see, Lloyd, it's about guilt. I don't know, it's this thing . . . I mean, I don't know if it's the same in your culture. I don't think the same kind of sick mindset applies.

What culture is that, Mike?

Well, yes. That's a moot point, I suppose. What culture indeed? You see, even bringing it up, I begin to feel bad. I begin to feel wrong. Do you see what I mean about guilt? It's what white people grow up in, it's the . . . sea we swim in. Going to the therapist helps me to reimagine things in a different light. I mean, just because I feel guilty doesn't mean I'm always in the wrong. Of course, it's not the only issue. Self-esteem is another one. My father always . . . Oh, I expect I'm boring you with this.

You are a bit, yeah, says Lloyd, taking his drink from Charlie. *But I know something about crazy. Lot of people I know went crazy. They didn't take to this country too much. Even me. I went crazy a while. After this, I went a lickle bit crazy.*

He holds his hand up, inspects it as if this is the first time he's ever seen it.

*How did that **happen**?* says Mike, leaning forward over the table. *I mean, I hope you don't mind me . . .*

Got caught in a machine. I'm a machine minder, right? I was minding one. My hand got caught in it. Two fingers on the floor, in with the sawdust. Bwoy, it was something. You should have seen the foreman's face. Gargoyle having a heart attack. You ain't seen ugly till you've seen that.

Mike takes a small sip of his wine, puckers up his mouth, grimaces.

How's the vintage? says Charlie.

Mike grins.

The pub is beginning to empty. Mike checks his watch.

That's a nice timepiece, says Lloyd. *A real nice chronometer.*

Thanks, says Mike. *Of course, I didn't . . . I couldn't. I mean, I'd be perfectly happy with a Timex or something similar. It was a present from my dad after I came down.*

Came down on what? says Lloyd, genuinely puzzled.

Sorry. I mean when I graduated. From Cambridge. University.

*Cambridge University. You're an educated man. A civilized man. I **respect** that. Hey, Mike, ask me something. Ask me about any king or queen of England.*

Well, I don't think I really . . .

For God's sake, ask him, says Charlie. *Let him do his party piece. Then we can get out of here. The fights are going to start in a minute.*

OK. Who was king in 1103?

Henry I, says Lloyd immediately, grinning.

What about king in 1704?

Trick question. It was good Queen Anne.

You should be in a bloody circus, Snowball. Can we go now? urges Charlie.

School, you see. In Barbados. We had to learn every single English king and queen, or get licked. I learned. The Bajan man loves

England. They call it Bimshire. The finest and warmest of the English counties. How much is that watch worth?

Oh, I don't know. A thousand or so, I expect.

Mike looks fiercely embarrassed. Lloyd exchanges glances with Charlie.

You ever play cards, Mike? says Charlie.

Lloyd, Mike and Charlie make their way out into the north London night. It has been raining, but now the clouds are clearing away. They walk slowly. The Astoria is only a few minutes away. Lloyd kicks at a can, then punches the air a few times, blows air out of his cheeks theatrically.

What's the deal with this, then, Mike? says Charlie. *Not strictly legit, is it?*

It's perfectly **legal**, *says Mike. It's just not licensed by the board of control. There's a few that are over the hill, a bit punchy. And they jazz it up a bit. Razzmatazz, costumes, a bit like wrestling really.*

Look at that, says Lloyd, stopping, staring at the kerb. *I love that.*

He is staring at a puddle of oil that, spread thin by the rain, has converted into a gutter rainbow. When he speaks again, he speaks quietly, so that Charlie has to strain to hear him.

You know, when I first came here, after it rained . . . You know, they put glass into the pavements here, into the concrete or whatever it is. So when it rained, you could see the glitter of the glass in the pavement. When the rain washed off, I said to Hyacinth one day, I said, it looks like diamonds. Like a diamond pavement. Yeah.

Lloyd looks up, seems to snap out of his reverie, begins to dance again, then stops, holds the boxer's pose, then throws a few punches to within an inch or two of Charlie's face.

Let's go. Marquess of Queensberry Rules or no.

Inside, the Astoria seems immense, far larger than you could guess from the modest exterior. There is a smell of aftershave, and of sawdust, and of old beer spilled on to cheap carpets. Charlie, Lloyd and Mike make their way through a press of red-faced, mostly middle-aged men, many of whom barely fit into their dinner jackets. Mike leads, studying their ticket numbers. Eventually, he makes it to a row of seats about five away from the ring. He checks them again; it seems that someone is sitting in their seats. Charlie, checking his own ticket, gets an impression of the man in his seat – like a side of beef in a evening suit. He puts a hand out to restrain Mike from making a fuss, but it is too late. Mike is already tapping the man on the shoulder.

I do beg your pardon. There seems to be some confusion over the seats. I think if you check your ticket stubs . . .

The man has turned round now. His face is the closest thing to evil Charlie has ever seen. The skin is pockmarked and scarred, the eyes small, red, close together. Each line on the huge face announces that this is a man to whom the details that appear on a ticket stub are of staggering insignificance. He fixes Mike with a blank look that Mike is too stupid, too *cushioned*, to make sense of.

I think if you check your ticket stubs you'll find that those seats are actually . . .

Charlie pulls Mike back and occupies his space.

Sorry, mate. Our mistake. Terribly sorry.

But Mike blunders on.

Now just hold on a second.

Shut up, Mike! Charlie turns to the man. *Really sorry to have disturbed you.*

The man carries on staring for a few more moments, then finally turns back towards the ring. Charlie exhales. He turns on Mike, hisses.

You're not at a tea party in Hampstead, Mike. Now let it go.

That bloke would have torn you a new arsehole in ten seconds flat.
These people are villains. I know one when I see one. Christ, my
brother's a card-carrying member of the fraternity. They don't give
a fuck for you or your tickets. There's plenty of empty seats a few
rows back.

Eventually, the three of them find empty seats with a
reasonably good view six rows further back. They settle down.
In the ring, the fighting has begun. A short, heavy-set man,
who arrived in the ring in a battered raincoat and goes simply
under the name of Columbo, is fighting a younger, blond,
relatively tall fighter known as Iron Man. In terms of age,
reach and physique, the younger man should be winning
easily. But Columbo is letting him punch himself out, going
into clinches, easily absorbing short blows to the body. After
a couple of rounds, the young man is clearly exhausted and is
still trying to finish off the shorter, older one. Then suddenly,
out of nowhere, a great looping swing, starting way back behind
Columbo's head, connects with the Iron Man's jaw. His eyes
glaze, his legs crumple. He stays standing, but only just. The
crowd are on their feet, screaming. Columbo throws another
punch in the same surreal, scything fashion, this time connecting with his opponent's nose. Blood spurts everywhere.
The noise from the crowd now rises another ten decibels.

To his surprise, Charlie finds himself up on his feet and
yelling. He hasn't been at a boxing match for twenty years
and he is amazed at the transformative power of violence. The
blood excites him. The Iron Man begins to topple. Mike is still
sitting making notes in a ring notebook. Lloyd is shaking his
head, looking faintly sad. Columbo connects with Iron Man's
jaw again, knocking him down. The crowd, including Charlie,
roar. On the count of eight, Iron Man is back on his feet.
Charlie can hear Lloyd muttering.

Stay down, man, stay down.

Now Columbo comes forward step by step. The younger man's face is a purple mess. He is rocking from side to side. Even Charlie expects the fight to be stopped, but Columbo comes on. He seems to hesitate, as if out of pity. The Iron Man stands there, his guard not even up. The referee makes no move to stop the fight. Now Columbo gives a little 'what can you do?' shrug, and Charlie sees his right arm go way, way back behind his head, shudders as he anticipates what is certain to come. He sees the blow approach the Iron Man almost in slow motion, the glove taking him full in his once symmetrical face. The blow seems to almost lift him off the ground, cartoon-style, then he collapses in a bloody heap. The crowd are going insane. Charlie feels excited and then vaguely shocked at his own excitement. Mike just writes in the notebook spread open on his lap. The fight over, the crowd quieten down as seconds rush to attend the spread-eagled figure in the ring. Charlie sits back down, his heart beating nineteen to the dozen. He finally looks towards Lloyd, who has his eyes squeezed closed.

What's the matter with you, Snowball?

It's a massacre.

What were you expecting? Pat-a-cake?

Lloyd opens his eyes, blinks at the ring.

Bwoy, this is . . . I didn't expect this, Charlie.

They don't have to do it, do they? They choose.

*But it's not even . . . I mean, the kid didn't know **anything**. Against an old pro like that. He's going to be mincemeat. And the referee didn't even stop it. Let him mash the bwoy. It's not Marquess of Queensberry, it's a freak show.*

Quite right, says Mike, without even looking up from his notebook. *It's going to make a **terrific** story.*

The evening wears on. There are fighters dressed as cave-men, as super heroes, as cartoon characters. Against this theatre there is extreme violence. Many of the fighters are way past their prime, others seem massively inexperienced. Weights are mismatched, skills are randomly thrown together. The referee never seems to stop a fight before one or other of the contestants has been rendered unconscious. Most of the bout, Lloyd spends with his head in his hands. Mike is writing, filling up his notebook at a prodigious rate, but Charlie is just mesmerized. Despite being aware of a faint shadow of shame, he finds the spectacle of the fight hypnotic, extraordinary. He feels himself lost in the crowd, swaying with it, shouting and jeering with it. He roars, he sways, he exults. As they move further up the bill, the fighters get more skilful, and still more ruthless. The intervals between the fights are short. By ten p.m., they have witnessed six bouts. There are only three left. The last fight was disappointing, Charlie feels. As they wait for the next, he flops in his seat, pulls at a cigarette.

What's up next, Mike? he says.

Mike consults the small, amateurishly produced programme.

Jungle John versus the Viking Destroyer. Jungle John used to be a first division footballer, apparently, who's gone to seed somewhat. I don't know anything about the Viking Destroyer. He looks rather unpleasant from his photograph.

A rustle in the crowd announces the arrival of the new contestants. The PA begins to play 'The Lion Sleeps Tonight' at deafening volume. There is a chorus of boos. Suddenly, Charlie sees projectiles flying through the air, as the boxer who calls himself Jungle John climbs into the ring, then ugly laughter rattling round the auditorium.

The projectiles are bananas, dozens of them. One hits Jungle John on the top of his head. The laughter redoubles.

The boxer sits down, his face seems to burn with some closely held emotion. He is dressed entirely in leopard skin.

There is even some kind of bone pushed through his thick hair. His face is old, beaten. There is a terrible air of desperation about him. But he is big, over six foot, well built, not all his muscle has yet turned to fat. He gets up from his stool, begins gently to pick up the bananas that are still flying on to the canvas, gathers them up and hands them to his second. Charlie can see that he moves with grace, with a kind of residual litheness. Still the bananas come. One by one, the boxer sadly picks them up. Charlie looks at the faces in the crowd, faces compressed with hatred.

Then there is a roar. Out of the corner of the auditorium, walking down the aisle, comes a huge man wearing a Viking helmet and animal skins. He is six foot six at least, with a chiselled face, pure blue eyes. He looks arrogant and deadly cool. The music that is playing from the PA switches to 'The Ride of the Valkyries'. The man climbs into the ring to deafening cheers. He removes his helmet to reveal pure white-blond hair. He flexes his muscles, struts in the ring, eyeballs the other boxer, who does not join in the pantomine, just sits in his corner staring at the canvas, as if composing himself.

The fighters are brought together in the middle of the ring. The Viking spits at Jungle John's feet. The black boxer meets his gaze, but instead of staring him out just gives a smile, then turns and goes back to his corner once more, to a chorus of boos.

The fight is ferocious from the beginning. Each man goes at the other with extraordinary ferocity. The Viking is faster and stronger, but Jungle John clearly has a better technique and can soak up the punches. He is also graceful and fast, despite his age and weight. Every time he dodges one of the Viking's jab and thrusts, the crowd moans. Charlie feels the hate swilling all around him, the sheer energy of the anger. He finds himself lost in it, caught up in the sheer adrenalin rush of it. He is out of his own body, on his feet, swaying with each punch, roaring as each connection is made.

By the fourth round, the ferocity of the fight has not abated. The face of each fighter is covered in blood. The bananas which fell into the ring after the first three rounds have now ceased and the crowd is moving as if one animal. Charlie is lost, on his face a film of sweat, his fists punching the air as if he is in the ring himself.

The exchange of blows comes at an incredible pace now and it is impossible to decide who has the advantage. The Viking's face is a mess, his legs are tired, but he keeps clipping Jungle John around a cut eye. They use every inch of the ring. At one point, the Viking goes down, to shocked silence, but he is up again at the count of five. He counter-attacks. Suddenly Charlie can sense the black boxer's fear that the Viking has taken his best shot and come back up. The crowd senses it too and begin to bay. Charlie is there as well, up on his chair now, screaming. The Viking comes forward, one to the body, a heavy one to the solar plexus, an uppercut to the jaw. Jungle John is beginning to sway. Charlie is vaguely aware of the triumphant shouts and screams around him

Get that fucker!

Murder the cunt! Knock him back to the jungle.

And Charlie is vaguely aware of himself shouting,

*Finish him off! **Kill** him.*

Jungle John goes down to a swingeing right hook to his left cheek. It is immediately apparent that he will not be getting up again. He is flat out, legs spread, eyes closed, the referee counting him out above him. Jungle John's second is rushing to his side.

It has been a fight of extraordinary aggression and intensity. The noise from the crowd is astonishing. There is blood on the canvas, blood on the bodies. The Viking raises his hands in triumph. Worried-looking men begin appearing in the ring. Charlie becomes aware of stretcher-bearers approaching the ring from the opposite corner. Jungle John's second is shouting something from the centre, beckoning, his eyes alight with panic. The Viking is dancing in triumph. More bananas rain down on Jungle John's inert body. Someone thumps furiously at his chest.

Charlie comes back into his own body, looks round. Mike is still writing furiously. Lloyd is nowhere to be seen.

7

4 May 1982. Charlie is not working today. To the fury of Mike Sunderland, Rupert Murdoch is the new owner of *The Times*. Unlike Robert Maxwell, it turns out, he is the right sort of person. But Mike's pique has gradually ebbed, diluted by a generous pay rise, and News International seem to have done little to upset the union applecart. The money, the Spanish customs, all survive. *The players change*, thinks Charlie. *The game stays the same.*

It is on this day, twenty-two years earlier, that he and Maureen were married. Tonight they go out to celebrate. He has started the day with freshly boiled kippers, toast and tomatoes, all presented lovingly by Maureen, in bed. He is re-reading yesterday's copy of the *Sun*, which he has held on to out of admiration for the headline. The *Daily Mirror*, he has decided, is too stuffy nowadays. The *Sun* has a satisfying photograph of an Argentinian ship, the *Belgrano*, on fire. It makes Charlie smile with pride.

He is now out at the front of the flat with a paintbrush. Charlie wears a plastic Union Jack bowler hat that Mike Sunderland has bought him as a sardonic comment on his colleague's patriotic enthusiasm for the Falklands War, but Charlie, lacking irony, wears it with pride. He looks up and down the line of ten flats that make up the ground-floor layer of this block. For as far as he can see to either side and also above him, doors of gunmetal grey. Dripping from his paintbrush is a colour that is as close as he could come to the chocolate brown of the Leek and Manifold casing, the gift from Robert, which currently has pride of place in the railway set that runs once more in the spare room.

The day the deeds of ownership came through, the first thing Charlie did was to take all his models, trains and track out of storage and create a new layout. This repainting of the front door was the next thing he promised himself.

He dips the paintbrush in the tin, and stares at it as the sticky brown liquid drips off the bristles. Something moves inside him. The actual signing of the deeds, the moment when ownership transferred to him, Charles William Buck, had been an anticlimax somehow. Like Christmas, the anticipation outweighed the reality. He had felt no different, merely a strange sensation that combined both weightlessness and the crushing gravity of a debt that stood at some £20,000. But now, staring at the paint fall, an unfamiliar excitement comes upon him. He is a man of property! He can choose the colour of paint, put it where he likes. It is intoxicating. The council is no longer his master.

He feels a guilty gratitude towards Mrs Thatcher, but knows for certain, and with relief, that she will be removed next time round. There have been huge spending cuts, riots in Brixton and Toxteth, the biggest fall in industrial output since 1921. Unemployment tops 3 million. The country is buckling, as Mike has predicted.

He has prepared his door, rubbed it down, applied primer. This feeling of improvement, of change, is satisfying in a way he has rarely known. Carol, the single mother, emerges from her flat. She has a new baby in her arms, screaming. Nelson is at a nursery nearby. The baby clutches a Holly Hobby doll; noseless, it seems mutilated to Charlie. The plaits and bonnet are sucked and blanched of colour.

She seems harassed and pale. She looks up.

Like the hat, says Carol.

Got to support our boys, says Charlie.

What you doing? says Carol, noticing the paint. Her tone is suddenly clipped, slightly afraid.

I'm doing a spot of redecorating.

You'll have the council down.

Not any more, says Charlie. *We've bought it.*

Carol stares at him.

You've done what?

We've bought it. It's ours, says Charlie proudly. He believes that congratulations are inevitable.

Is that right? says Carol. *You'll make a nice little bundle then.*

Nothing wrong with honest profit.

There's no such thing, says Carol, *as an honest profit.*

She pauses, then without another word she turns and walks away. Charlie feels shocked. Carol has always been friendly to him.

Jealousy, thinks Charlie. It's only to be expected. A part of him relishes what he thinks of as her envy, but the larger part is disappointed. He does not want this moment to be sullied, so he now decides that she is also suffering from nerves because of the new baby. He applies the brush to the prepared door. He smiles, as if a great secret has been revealed. The door begins its transformation.

Inside the flat, Maureen is reading a book, *Teach Yourself Accountancy.* Her brow is furrowed in concentration, despite the soft chatter of the television in the corner. She has two bars of chocolate on the table beside her and is slowly making her way through them. On the television, a woman with a mad, ever present smile, is jumping up and down on to a step. She makes exercise look terrific fun, but Maureen, who is going through one of her periodic losses of interest in keep-fit, knows it is a cruel illusion.

Maureen puts down the book. She hears Charlie whistling

156

from the outside. It is 'Land of Hope and Glory'. She makes a few notes on a pad and examines her work. Marie-Rose, pleased with her efforts, has introduced her to other traders. There is a florist in North End Road she helps out four days a month. The fish and chip shop is interested. Maureen is gratified, and faintly amazed at the way she is taken seriously by these people. Her columns are neat, carefully constructed, with just the right balance of honesty and guile. Charlie thinks it is little more than a hobby for her, but something swells inside her when she contemplates each completed set of accounts. It is her creation.

I think you'd best shift, Mo. It's going to be like world war fucking three in here.

Tommy Buck is holding a lump hammer. His face is blackened and bruised from a weekend ruck on the terraces, making it appear distorted and discoloured as if viewed through mottled brown glass. The furniture has been moved out of the room or covered with plastic sheeting. Tommy is knocking down the wall that divides the kitchen from the dining room to create a kitchen-diner. He's doing it as a favour for his brother, who is willing but unpractised at home improvement.

Charlie comes in from outside.

You do know what you're doing, don't you, Tommy? says Charlie nervously.

Are you taking the piss? says Tommy. *Stop worrying. You're always worrying, you fucking old woman.*

Anyway, where's that ginger streak of piss? I thought you were going to get him to give me a hand.

Haven't heard from Robert for six months. He's got the hump about something.

I'm worried, Charlie, says Maureen. *He could be anywhere. Anywhere there's layabouts.*

Maureen retreats into the bedroom. The hammering begins immediately, and it is deafening. She gives up trying to study the book. In between thuds, she can hear Charlie following up his rendition of 'Land of Hope and Glory' with 'Charmaine'. The whistling is sweet, resonant. It touches Maureen. A sentimental cloud descends on her. On impulse, she reaches to the top drawer of a small chest and takes out a photo album.

It has been a long time since she has looked within. A layer of dust coats the leather binding. The images revealed as she turns the pages change her mood into a gathering sadness inside the nut of her chest. Charlie's grin looks wide, uncomplicated, certain. She seems vaguely frightened. This is the story, she thinks, of her marriage.

She wonders, for the first time in years, on this day of their anniversary, why she chose Charlie. She could have had others. At nineteen, she had felt plain, but she could see now that she was not. To her surprise, she sees an obvious sexuality there, a muted physical hunger.

Maureen remembers how before she got married, she went into the factory and how much fun she had in the big place, grinding out things she didn't even know the name of. The work didn't matter, but chatting to the other women was fun. And you got a pay packet.

But then after the marriage it was privileges withdrawn. Back in the kitchen. She didn't mind. Always wanted kids, anyway. A husband.

She didn't mind.

Suddenly the thought strikes her, as she turns the page and looks at a photograph of her holding Robert in her arms, that this is a lie, a lie that has fossilized, sunk, become incorporated into her.

Only there is nothing she can do about it now.

She turns the pages again. Sometimes, looking at Charlie, she wonders why they are together. Fate, she supposes. Luck, accident. What is the difference?

She had been running for a bus. She was an inch away from the bus, nearly, nearly. It was raining. She wore low heels. Seventeen years old, carrying a plain black umbrella. 1958. She missed that bus and tripped. Flat into a puddle. The umbrella blowing off down the street to the Lord knew where.

And there was Charlie, helping her up. He had even retrieved her umbrella. She had no idea who he was. She didn't think he was handsome. Good thick hair, large blue eyes, but a weak chin and sticky-out ears. Nevertheless, he was smartly turned out, in a serge suit. Smelt then as now of Brylcreem and something else which she couldn't name (it turned out to be ink). He had a handkerchief, pathetically small for the task, but he tried to dry her off. He lingered a little too long over her breasts, and, to her surprise, she found this exciting. She had never slept with a man, but she thought of sex quite often. Then you weren't meant to, but Maureen did. She played with herself sometimes, down there. She shocked herself.

Charlie offered to buy her a cup of coffee in the Kardomah coffee house which was next to the bus stop. She knew right away she was being picked up, but that was OK. They had coffee and cream slices while her coat dried off on a radiator. Underneath, her trim bust outlined by a cotton blouse. Charlie kept glancing while he picked the filling out of the slice.

They had a nice chat. He was very normal, very conservative with a small C. Didn't like the Tory government. Didn't like layabouts and oiks either. Him and Maureen nearly got into an argument – her whole family voted Conservative, always had. But politics wasn't nearly important enough to have a row about. It was just gossip. Everyone was entitled to their opinion. Not all Tories were swine, even though Charlie said that they were.

Charlie took her dancing at the Kilburn State, to the cinema, for walks in the park. They had only been seeing each other three weeks. Maureen didn't love him, but she thought he was OK, not the worse one so far. He was incredibly persistent. Also, he had his own flat, which was unusual. One of his three uncles rented it to him. Maureen didn't know anyone who had use of their own flat. The point being that she could tell her parents that they were going to the cinema and they could go to the flat instead.

That was how Maureen lost her virginity. She was bored with being a virgin, that was all. Sex was bound to be more interesting than everything else in life. And it was. It was more than interesting, it was wonderful, except that Charlie always reached his climax a bit too quickly and then fell asleep. Still, now that she had discovered it, there would be other lovers, better than Charlie, more accomplished. It was a whole new world.

Even then she wondered what other secrets were being kept from her. Like real work. To feel you were doing something that meant something in the wider world. Men kept that a secret.

She'd been out with quite a few men before Charlie. They were a strange breed, but she liked them on the whole. Their strength and containment, the way they controlled their feelings so effectively. She supposed that they did have feelings, but you couldn't be absolutely sure with men. You had to guess. Sometimes she would try to hurt Charlie just to see if he was alive inside.

Charlie was pretty much what Maureen thought of as the standard model – polite, respectful, a bit of a laugh after a drink or two, not very good with words, wanted a family, wanted a job for life, security, kept his nose clean. Nothing eccentric or odd at all about him except that in those days he smoked Du Maurier cigarettes, which was an unusual brand, expensive. It was the little part of him that he allowed to be different from the mob, but on the whole Charlie was happy with the mob, content to be just the way he perceived everyone else to be. He thought people had it too easy in the main. Charlie drank a little too much, was apprenticed as a compositor. He worked hard and he thought other people should work hard. There were too many immigrants, he said, but he didn't hate foreigners, didn't hate anybody really. Hate was a waste of energy, he said.

So they went to bed in his flat. Maureen had liked him well enough, and supposed he was all right in bed, although she didn't actually have anyone to compare him with. But she hadn't felt he was *all that*, and also they were in many ways different. So when she found out she was pregnant, she was at first distraught, half because she was unmarried, half because she might have to get married to Charlie.

Charlie, she was simultaneously relieved and disappointed to discover, was determined to stand by her. Offered to announce their marriage right away. Maureen felt she had no choice, and after a while didn't mind that much. She could do worse than Charlie, she supposed. He seemed nice enough. The world was full of accidents and one had just happened to her. She wondered if it would turn out all right.

In the end she lost the baby anyway, but she decided to go through with the marriage all the same. Too much momentum to retreat. She remains amazed at how a whole life can turn on one moment. On a gasp, a clutch, a narrowly missed bus. If a traffic light had changed a second sooner, or later, her life would have been utterly different.

Being with Charlie had become a sort of habit she found hard to break. She got pregnant again, six months later, with Robert. It was that that landed them their first council flat. She was huge. Charlie wasn't particularly proud, but he accepted it. He was good at accepting things, at letting life slide over him without him really noticing.

A terrible crash from the front room interrupts her thoughts. She throws down the album and rushes the few yards to where Tommy has been working. He stands in the kitchen, looking puzzled, his face a mask of fine white dust. There is a huge hole in the ceiling, and a mess of crumbled wood and plaster detritus covers the floor.

Your joists must be rotten, says Tommy amiably, giving Maureen a placatory smile. *Been fattening up the old woodworm. Place like this is fucking McDonald's for them.*

They've been all right this last twenty-odd years, says Charlie, who has emerged at the same time as Maureen from the other side of the room.

I'll call my mate Tony, says Tommy cheerfully. *He's handy on plaster. A dab fucking hand.*

Well, I hope he's cheap.

Charlie is breathing heavily, biting the nail of his thumb and shifting from foot to foot as if needing to spend a penny. Maureen recognizes these gestures; they imply a fury barely contained by will.

I'll talk to him. It won't set you back much.

Set me back much? What's it got to do with me?

Charlie is still unconsciously holding the paintbrush in his right hand. The shock of the noise and the collapse of the ceiling have made him forget himself. Droplets fall on to the new carpet that Maureen dipped into their savings to buy only a month previously.

Well, says Tommy, with guarded simplicity. *It's your ceiling.*

It might be my ceiling, but –

Charlie!

Maureen has noticed the paintbrush. She points wordlessly.
Charlie looks down.

Christ!

There is a trail from the door to where he stands. Maureen
is rushing across with a cloth.

It'll come out with a little drop of white spirit, says Tommy.

Charlie glowers. As a child, he had been protective of
Tommy, and Tommy had taken advantage, always taken
advantage.

It better had. Or you can stump up for a new carpet as well.

Hold on a cotton-pickin' moment, Charlie boy.

*Hold on! Don't tell me to hold me. You're not in my house but
ten minutes and you've brought the ceiling down. You're not a
builder, you're a cross between Roy fucking Rogers and Arthur
Daley. I should have got you a lasso for Christmas instead of giving
you those stupid Kevin Kline jeans.*

They were too small for me anyway.

I'm not surprised, you fat . . . you fat cowboy bastard.

At the word cowboy, Tommy bridles.

I spent years learning my trade. I'm doing this as a favour.

*Half-rate doesn't entitle you to smash my new house to bits.
Anyway, I've only got your word it's half-rate. Who's going to pay
forty sovs a day to someone who don't know how to prop a ceiling?*

Tommy nods violently.

I'm a liar too, then, is it?

Maureen has been rubbing at the carpet with white spirit.
The stain has become a penumbra spreading outwards from
the specks of paint. She stops rubbing for a moment.

Tommy . . . Charlie . . .

It's all right, Maureen.

Tommy is now removing his overalls.

I've got plenty of other work on that needs to be done where I'm not going to get this sort of grief.

Yeah, that's right. He's in demand is Tommy, says Charlie. *That's why they came and took his Astra back. Trading up, is it, kiddo? Roller on order from the factory, is it?*

Now Charlie and Tommy are squared up to each other like fighters. Tommy's voice can usually be heard halfway down the next street, but now it is very quiet.

I had a bad patch. They hiked the interest rates. It can happen to anyone.

It can happen to anyone who hocks himself up to the neck so he can show off to his neighbours in la-de-da land. What you got now? A '72 Allegro, isn't it? Lorraine must be chuffed up to the eyeballs.

Tommy thinks momentarily about punching his older brother, but he feels the taboo of being adult tugging at his bunched fist, and the calculation of what it might cost. Family is family. Instead, he looks at Maureen, gathers up his tools.

I'm off, Maureen. Sorry about the mess. We'll forget my dough for this morning.

No need for that, says Charlie, taking his wallet out and removing the entire contents, £65. *Here you are. There's an extra mark-up there for woodworm detection. That's how you work, isn't it, Tom? Go on, take it.*

Tommy sighs, holds up a hand in farewell to Maureen and walks out of the door.

This paint isn't coming off, says Maureen, still rubbing furiously at the carpet. She only succeeds in spreading the stain still further, unstoppable, the colour of drying mud.

To celebrate their anniversary, Charlie has chosen Los Caracoles, a tapas bar and restaurant just off Shaftesbury Avenue.

Mike Sunderland, who is familiar with eating out in restaurants in a way that Charlie feels he will never be, has recommended it as both intimate and authentic. Charlie and Maureen rarely go to restaurants, and when they do it is to steak houses or hotel restaurants or dinner dances in distant suburban brewery-owned fake barns. Charlie feels unhappy with the rituals demanded, feels threatened by a codified servitude that seems to him obscurely contemptuous.

Spanish food is, Charlie has been told, all the rage. On their yearly holidays in Alicante, Charlie and Maureen always eat English. But change is in the air and the wind blows everyone before it.

The restaurant is much smarter than Charlie has expected. He feels suddenly uncomfortable in his shirt and tie, Pringle sweater and brown Marks & Spencer double-pleated flannel trousers. He had wanted something informal, reassuring, but the room is plain and unwelcoming, and the other diners are clearly much younger and more fashionable than Charlie and Maureen. They are made to wait for several minutes before a waiter acknowledges them. He is theatrically Spanish: tight black trousers, red shirt, olive skin, slicked-back black hair. Handsome. He looks them up and down with a puzzled face. He seems genuinely confused that they are here.

We have it reserved, says Charlie, in a voice louder than it needs to be. *We're right on the button.*

They have been to see *South Pacific* in one of the theatres round the corner. Seeing the cinema version was their first big night out as a courting couple, twenty-two years earlier.

The waiter holds up his finger, as if in admonition.

Ranch?

Buck. Charles William Buck. We have a cubicle.

The restaurant has half a dozen small alcoves. Mike has sold it as very intimate. The waiter furrows his brow, shrugs.

One moment.

He disappears, while Charlie and Maureen fidget uncomfortably. In the distance, he sees the waiter talking to a man in a dark suit, who is shaking his head. They laugh together. After another wait of several minutes, the waiter returns. He gives a faint smile.

No cubicle.

Charlie feels annoyed, but intimidated.

But listen. We specifically –

Is impossible.

It's our anniversary.

The waiter nods as if processing this important information. Charlie feels a grain of hope.

There is no alcove. It does not say.

He holds the book out to show the reservation for Buck.

Well, I don't think it's my fault if one of your . . .

But the waiter is not listening. Instead he has started moving away from them, beckoning.

This way, please.

Don't make a fuss, Charlie, urges Maureen.

The restaurant is arranged in an L-shape and the waiter leads them through packed tables to a cramped two-seater in the middle of a row of similar tables. There is barely room to move elbows. Everyone seems to be making a terrific row. Charlie realizes that most of the people in the restaurant are Spanish and that they are speaking in their language. This is what Mike meant by authentic. It unsettles Charlie.

He hesitates, but the waiter ushers him firmly to his seat and his will collapses. Charlie and Maureen face each other. Both feel uncomfortable but trapped. Having accepted the seat, it seems impossible now to get up and leave. The waiter hands them each a menu and scurries off.

It'll be fine, Charlie, says Maureen encouragingly, as Charlie looks around him, tugs at his shirt sleeves awkwardly. *I think it's nice here.*

It's a bit arty-crafty, says Charlie. *Mike says the food is top of the range.*

Maureen makes an attempt to put some romance in the evening, which is feeling under threat. She leans forward over the table.

Happy anniversary, Rock.

Charlie responds, as best he can, although his heart isn't in it, what with the hassle from the waiter.

You're my rock.

He picks up the menu, is immediately shocked at the prices. He looks up at Maureen and catches her face in studied neutrality as she battles to understand the Spanish dishes, none of which are translated into English. Her lips move slightly. This gesture, the unconscious innocence of the action, brings forth a judder of affection in Charlie. It reassures him. He has sometimes been uncertain whether he loves his wife. He has never doubted that Maureen loves him, however, although she has not told him so for twenty years at least. It was natural for a woman to love; that was what they do, while he worked, and provided, and supplied the final word in difficult decisions. He is strong, and he believes that she admires this strength.

In the few seconds that he stares at Maureen, he thinks, *mine has been a successful marriage.* Of course, none of their friends have been divorced, because people like them, of their generation, of their *standing*, didn't get divorced. You saw things through, for good or ill. And mostly, it had been good. She hadn't complained, anyhow. And he has been satisfied. Also, tonight she looks good. A simple black dress, gold earrings, hair piled up. Although now forty-one years old, she stands up better than many, thinks Charlie. Under the thick powder, her skin has not lost all its elasticity and there is brightness still in her eyes, a direct connection to life itself that Charlie feels is the talent of women. Men put a defensive wall between themselves and living; they have no choice.

Charlie feels the tightness around his neck of the stiff collar. He isn't accustomed to wearing a tie and he notices that the people at the tables around him are dressed more casually. The noise from the nearby customers seems to be getting worse. There is Spanish music being piped that seems to have got louder since they arrived. He needs to almost shout to try and make his next words heard.

You look good enough to eat, says Charlie.

What?

You look good enough to eat.

I can't hear you, Charlie.

Charlie gives up.

It doesn't matter.

Maureen smiles back, then returns to the menu. Charlie ponders for a moment, then finds a pen and writes the compliment on a napkin and passes it over to his wife. She reads it, smiles, blows him a kiss, then returns to the menu once more. Charlie feels obscurely disappointed. He had expected more in return for his chivalry.

The waiter returns, looking harassed. He keeps glancing at other tables while he asks if they'd like an aperitif.

Do you have Pina Coladas? Like in the song?

Maureen is smiling grimly. Charlie feels a pellet of bile form in his mouth.

The waiter seems to retreat slightly.

Pina?

I don't know what's in it exactly. Coconut of some kind.

She looks at Charlie for confirmation.

Isn't it, Charlie?

Charlie takes a deep breath. The noise has abated slightly.

Maureen, they don't have that kind of drink here. You want something to, you know, clear your palate. What about a Campari and Orange? You like them.

Maureen's lips seem to thin slightly.

The orange juice hurts my ulcers. What about Midori? It's made out of melons.

The waiter intervenes. A smile plays about his mouth.

Of course, madam. I think we have some . . . somewhere. And for sir?

Whisky, says Charlie.

Which brand, sir? We have Glenlivet, Laphroaig . . .

Charlie is determined not to be wrong-footed.

Teacher's, says Charlie abruptly. *With Pepsi.*

We don't have that brand.

Charlie feels flustered now, and blames Maureen. If she hadn't asked for the Pina Colada, he would just have said yes to one of the ones that the waiter recommended. Now he can't remember what the brands were.

What you got again?

Laphroaig, Glenlivet, Glenmorangie . . .

Glenmorangie. That's a nice one. I'll have that. And make it a double.

With Pepsi, sir?

Charlie flushes. He isn't going to be intimidated, he decides.

Yeah, with Pepsi.

The waiter nods and retreats. Charlie feels a sense of relief. Maureen speaks again.

It's all in Spanish.

It's part of the atmosphere.

I don't know what anything is.

It's mostly common sense. Calamares fritos. That's like calimari, isn't it? Fried squid.

Too fattening.

You're always on this new diet. The trouble with you, kiddo, is that you can't accept yourself as you are.

But secretly he is pleased that she is still making an effort for him, that she will not let herself slide into lard. She is the most visible symbol of what he has or has not achieved, of his success or failure in life.

What's albond . . . albond . . . albon-digas.

I dunno. Have the paella. You know what that is.

I'm not all that keen on rice.

You like Chinese, don't you?

It's done differently.

Alitas de pollo. Pollo is chicken. It's chicken something. You like chicken, don't you?

What's macedonia? It's a place isn't it?

Eventually they settle on calamares for Maureen to start with and the gazpacho for Charlie. Then paella for Maureen and Charlie takes a risk on pulpo a la gallega. Even though he does not know what it is, he is determined to order it anyway as a bit of an adventure, to show Maureen that he is not the *fuddy-duddy* everyone takes him for. When the waiter comes for their order he does not understand Charlie's pronunciation, and makes a great theatre of shrugs and eyebrow-elevation. Eventually they are forced to point to the dishes in question, and the waiter repeats everything exactly and elaborately, as if to throw into relief Charlie's inarticulacy in Spanish.

Vino?

I'd like some Vinho Verde, says Maureen.

You got Vinho Verde? says Charlie.

Is Portuguese. I'll bring you the vino de la casa. Blanco o tinto?

Yeah, I'll have some of that.

What?

The . . . the blanco o tinto.

The waiter explains. Charlie's face, reddened by the stiffness of his collar, deepens a shade. He understands that he has to make up ground now, that he cannot accept the house wine.

Hold on. Haven't you got a wine list?

The waiter shrugs and disappears.

I don't mind what we have, says Maureen.

It's a special occasion, says Charlie.

The waiter returns with the wine list, which seems to Charlie to contain several dozen wines all outrageously priced. He'd thought Spanish wine was cheap. He gazes uncomprehendingly at the catalogue of Riojas.

Would you recommend anything?

The waiter is checking the other tables again. He answers Charlie while still looking the other way.

It depends.

What on?

On how much you wish to spend.

Goaded, Charlie snaps back.

The price doesn't matter. What's good?

Would you prefer something very dry . . . or light? Full-bodied? What are you having to eat?

Charlie finally feels his patience exhausted.

Look, you just write it down. You just bring us a bottle of decent red wine.

With the octopus?

What octopus?

Pulpo a la gallega.

Charlie swallows the distaste he feels.

I'm paying, so I can have whatever I ruddy well want.

Of course.

With this, he turns elegantly and heads back towards the kitchen.

Dagos. Onion-munchers. Fucking –

Shhh, Charlie.

Sorry, love.

Charlie tries to avoid swearing in front of Maureen, although he knows that such delicacy is nowadays antique. The collapse of the ceiling and the row with his brother still weigh down on him. He reigns himself in. He tries to concentrate on making what is left of the evening a success.

He tries to improve his mood by thinking of *South Pacific*. The tunes still leave a residue in him and a strange yearning. Can it really be like that in the South Pacific? Apart from Spain, he has never been abroad, and he finds it unimaginable that such a place can really exist, such colours of blues and yellows and strange women who did not mind showing their breasts. They make it all up, don't they? Probably the South Pacific was an s-hole.

As they wait for the food to arrive, Charlie struggles to make conversation with his wife. It is rare that they find themselves in this position, in such sealed-off intimacy where conversation becomes a necessity.

Are you still worried about Robert? says Charlie.

He never calls me. His phone is disconnected. Of course I'm worried about him, Charlie.

He'll be all right. He's a Buck. It'll all come out in the wash.

He thinks you don't like him.

I don't have to like him. He's my son.

I know you love him, Charlie. But he's sensitive. Why won't you make an effort?

What kind of effort? What can I do?

Well, you could invite him to one of your card games, for one thing. You've never invited him. Father and son spending the evening together. He'd like that.

But Charlie doesn't appear to be listening.

He should have taken that job I sorted him out. He'd have been sitting pretty.

The rejection of the union card that Christmas stings him still, and part of him seeks vengeance, wishes his son's destitution. But despite holding this view absolutely, he does not admit it to himself. The part of Charlie that is visible to himself wishes Robert well.

Charlie looks up as the waiter reappears with a bottle of wine which he offers to Charlie for tasting. There is a grain of cork in the liquid.

It's corked.

No, no. Is OK. Please to taste.

The waiter says this in such a steely tone that Charlie is cowed. He takes a tentative swig. The wine tastes OK, but he is uncertain what it is meant to taste of. He nods reluctantly. The waiter pours and disappears. Charlie wishes that he had stuck to his guns. He feels he has lost face in front of Maureen.

They lapse into silence. After twenty-two years of marriage, all opinions seem to be known, all prejudices and tender points and raw nerves have been noted and catalogued. Life seems simply a matter of floating predictably around well-mapped rocks in a flat, transparent pool. Charlie feels, without thinking it, that Maureen is a known quantity to him, as certain in her boundaries and workings as the stone in the compositors' room, reading the hot-metal letters back to front, something he had absolute confidence in his ability to do. Maureen, compositing; both solid, fixed, known and reliable. Also dull, but then Charlie has not been brought up to expect excitement from life, or even happiness. Things are what they are; the trick is to maintain them, to protect what you have.

Maureen sees breadcrumbs attached to the edge of Charlie's mouth. She wipes away the mess with a napkin. It is she who finally breaks the silence.

What's your happiest moment of our marriage?

Charlie feels caught off guard, taken aback.

That's a funny question.

Is it?

Charlie is aware that he is suddenly on delicate ground.

That's tough, Mo. So many of them.

He tests the truth of this statement, finds it wanting. He does not understand happiness, only its absence. Sadness is so much more dogged a force in the world. He knows an answer is required, scours distant maps of the past.

Give me a moment. What's yours?

Maureen answers immediately.

The day Robert was born.

That was something sure enough.

Charlie wasn't at the hospital when Robert was born. When he heard the news, he went out and bought himself a cigar. He didn't like cigars, but he went ahead and bought himself one anyway, because he had learned from the films that this was what you did when children were born. The smoke made him feel sick.

He had felt scared. He didn't know how he had found himself in this marriage. Going and getting her pregnant like that. He should have known better. Him and his Hampton Wick. It had got enough men into trouble before. Charlie had thought that he was smarter, but they all thought they were smarter, didn't they, until women got their fingers around the neck of your life.

Now it was just him and her for the rest of his days. Maybe thirty, forty more years. A long time. A bloody long time. But the world was full of things you couldn't deny, couldn't do anything about. War was one. Your place in the world was another. Marriage was another. Kids were another. You just had to fall in, didn't you? Fall in! He hears the sergeant-major's shout in his head, echoing down from when he did his National Service. He smiles to himself. Fall in. That was what life was about.

Have you thought of anything? Maureen says intently.

The true answer, he realizes, is the time Maureen went away for a month with Robert fifteen years ago to see her parents, who had moved to Australia. He had had his sole affair of their marriage, a brief fling with a secretary in classified advertising. Maureen had never suspected, and it had been pure excitement, with no price tag. He remembered waking up at the secretary's flat, where a magpie perched on the windowsill, then flew away. He had watched it disappear into a dot. The smell of coffee. Her perfume, like scented earth. The way she touched his face when they made love. Every day he thinks of her.

The secretary had left for a job abroad two weeks after Maureen returned and he had never seen her again. That had been the last time he had slept with a woman who wasn't his wife.

Yeah. When Robert was born.

They lapse back into silence.

What's the latest from work, then? says Maureen.

They're still playing silly buggers. Threatening this and that.

It occurs to her that in all their years together she has only ever been to Charlie's place of work once and therefore has very little idea what he does all day. He has tried to explain it to her but she finds it hard to follow. Not because it is too complicated, but because it bores her too much to concentrate. Of course, she would never reveal this to Charlie. There are many things she would never reveal to Charlie. She understands far better than he does what can and what can't be spoken.

*They've got all these fancy new . . . technologies that they're trying to bring over. From the States . . . Computers. They let you keystroke directly on to page layout. We've said all along that we have to keep control of the keyboard. Compositing . . . it's a craft, a craft that goes back **centuries**. You can't just dump that in the bin* *because big business lifts its little finger. It's a matter of politics. All they care about is maximizing profit. The working man counts for nothing. Well, they're not getting away with it. We're standing firm.*

He sees a familiar faraway look in his wife's eyes. He had planned to tell Maureen about demarcation and differentials, but noticing the look the words stop in his throat.

I have to use the little girls' room, says Maureen. She gets up from her chair, barely managing to squeeze through the gap that separates their table from the adjacent one. Her hips expanded after childbirth, and have continued to do so, despite the wide range of diets she has systematically placed herself on, despite the Trim U Fit massager, despite the jogging and the morning aerobics. Her figure remains the figure of the woman she is: a middle-aged mother.

Mother. Charlie watches her go, past two women in their twenties with hard bodies pressed into black dresses. He thinks again of the day this title was bestowed on her. Was it a proud day? What's to be proud of? Sticking it in was all it took.

Maureen returns. They have been waiting for their food now for half an hour. Both of them are starving. For want of anything better to fill the silence, he decides to continue his lecture on the printing industry.

He talks about demarcation agreements, piecework, Linotype, maintaining differentials. She has heard it all before. All she knows is that he doesn't seem to work that hard, or that often, and compared with most of the people she knows he produces a decent wage packet – around £330 a week. She has come to dislike the expression he has on his face at this moment, which is one of petulant morality. Charlie is upset that the 'bosses', as he likes to call anyone who occupies a senior position to him at the newspaper, should try and tell the union what to do.

*. . . of course, the **bosses** always try to push it. It's natural. If you're a union man like me, you learn that. They're not all bad. Marmaduke Hussey is a natural gentleman. But some of the others – the self-made men . . . people like Murdoch – got this idea that they're above us. They've got another think coming, I'll tell you that for nothing.*

Maureen shakes herself out of her encroaching trance, which she attempts to conceal, as ever, with a light, noncommittal smile.

But surely, Charlie, you can't stop progress. If they've invented these computers, they've got to come sooner or later. How can you stand in the way of that?

It is unusual for Maureen to offer an opinion so contrary to the one Charlie has expressed and a look of mild surprise crosses his face.

Kiddo, it's hard to explain. Of course the computers have got to come. But when? Now? Next year? In fifty years? Who's to say? Is it the management who has the only say?

Well, they've got a business to run, haven't they? If they can't run a business, you wouldn't have any jobs. It's uneconomical to keep things like they are.

At first amused by Maureen's contrariness, Charlie now feels irritated.

*You've got it the wrong way round. You can't run a business without workers to work in it. We **are** the business. They just cream off the profits, like their sort always have done. Sitting on their fat behinds, smoking cigars. They do all right. You have to make a stand whenever you can. Give them an inch, they'll take a mile.*

The wine is full-bodied, heavy. Maureen is not used to it on an empty stomach. She feels unable to put down the stick which she has picked up, despite sensing Charlie's dislike of her daring agnosticism.

But what if some other newspaper takes on the computers? Then they'll be able to do everything much faster and cheaper. And then what'll happen to you?

Charlie chews this over. Bearing in mind once again that this is a wedding anniversary, he decides to keep his pique disguised. He musters a grin for Maureen.

You know what Mike Sunderland at the paper would call you?

Maureen doesn't.

He'd call you a . . . what was it? A . . . petty barge wire zee. He'd call you a class traitor.

Really. Is that what he calls people who tell him stuff he don't want to hear, then?

Now Maureen finds it hard to conceal the spite she suddenly feels. Her smile has become brittle. Charlie lets out a long sigh. She is going too far. She doesn't understand anything about it. He is opening his mouth to speak, to put her right, when the waiter reappears with their first course.

Gazpacho.

Here, says Charlie.

He places the calamares in front of Maureen and the soup in front of Charlie. The portions look very small. Charlie stares at the waiter. Something about him – the way he carries himself, the slight moue on his lips – suggests hatred to Charlie. He studies his soup.

Please enjoy.

The waiter gives a small, thin smile that Charlie feels he is somehow intended to notice. He feels suddenly suspicious. He does not trust restaurants at the best of times, and has heard from Tommy, who does work for West End restaurants from time to time, that many are shockingly unhygienic, with rats, maggots and cockroaches vying for space among the fancy cheeses and caviare and all that. Charlie knew what went on.

He studies the soup again. Maureen is already tucking into her calamares.

Look at that, Maureen. See that?

Charlie indicates a small north-eastern region of the soup's surface, on which a slick of olive oil gleams.

This is very good. I wonder if they'd give me the recipe.

Recipe – what recipe? They stick it in a deep-fryer for five minutes. That's the recipe. Not much of it either, is there? Have a look at this now. What do you make of this?

What, Charlie? That bit of oil?

It's not oil.

What do you mean?

Charlie lowers his voice, looks around him as if the other Spanish customers are intent on listening in.

He's spat in it.

Maureen fights back a smile. But clearly this is something Charlie needs her to take seriously.

Do you think so? Well, you better send it back then.

I can't, can I?

Whyever not? Maureen has drunk three glasses of wine now and feels unusually free to speak as she pleases. They have ordered a second bottle of wine. *If the man has spat in your soup then I think it's only fair that he should bring you another bowl.*

She finishes her last piece of squid, then takes a piece of bread.

*Don't be stupid. He's not going to **admit** it, is he?*

The waiter returns, this time bearing the second bottle of wine. Maureen looks up at him delightedly.

My husband wants to have a word, she slurs.

The waiter raises an eyebrow and turns to Charlie.

Is there problem?

Charlie shifts in his seat uncomfortably.

No, not at all. It's lovely.

The waiter balefully regards the untouched soup.

You are not hungry?

During this phrase, he uncorks the bottle with a single, elegant gesture. Charlie, cowed once more, takes a spoonful of soup. He is convinced now that it contains sputum.

He looks up. He thinks he sees the waiter smirk. His eye is then caught by something past his shoulder: a Spanish flag with a large, clearly visible slogan. It reads *Viva Las Malvinas*. This both shocks him and clinches everything for him; his suspicions coagulate into certainty. He points an accusing finger at the waiter.

You hawked in it. You gobbed in my soup.

The waiter takes a step back.

I don't understand.

You heard me.

You are crazy!

You're the one that's crazy. We're leaving.

The waiter gives an indifferent shrug.

If you wish. I will fetch the bill.

The bill? Que? Que? Listen. You've been in our face all night, probably because we're the only English in here. You've been taking the piss because we've been kicking your jacksies in the Falklands.

Now the waiter really does spit, not in the soup, but on the floor at Charlie's feet.

Las Malvinas.

The Falklands. The Falkland bloody Islands!

The waiter reels back. Faces, nearly all of them olive-skinned, dark-haired, turn towards the table.

We kick your bloody arse, Winston Churchill, we kick your bloody arse, Maggie Thatcher!

*Hey, Pedro. What about **this**?*

He gathers the words that he has seen in the newspaper this morning, tosses them like a grenade.

Gotcha! How'd you like that, hey? Gotcha!

The waiter turns his back in disgust.

You don't like it up you, do you? They don't like it up 'em, Maureen.

All the customers are watching now. Charlie is pushing the table to one side. The manager is rushing over. Maureen stares down at her plate. An argument ensues. A man at the next table spits at Charlie's feet. Charlie throws him the V-sign. Then he roughly calculates the correct amount for the bill – even in this situation, a sense of obscure rectitude controls him – peels off a couple of banknotes and throws them on the floor. Maureen begins to cry. Charlie takes her arm and steers her out of the restaurant into the night.

On the way home, Maureen and Charlie sit silently in the front of the ailing Triumph Toledo. They are stuck in traffic. Charlie, although he has promised Maureen to stay sober, is faintly drunk.

Maureen begins to cry again. Charlie pulls the car over to the side of the road and tries to put an arm around her. She shakes it off.

I always thought you were different from your brother, but you're the same. Always picking fights. Tommy, this morning. Now this waiter – on our wedding anniversary, Charlie! You're not yourself when you're drunk. And you're drunk too often. You're drunk now. I hate it.

Charlie feels the acid of remorse in his stomach.

*I'm **not** like Tommy. But you've got to stand up for yourself. It's self-respect.*

Maureen shakes her head, does not answer. Charlie reaches in his pocket for something.

I'm sorry, kiddo. I'm getting to be a grouch. Got a lot on my mind. And I know I need to cut down on the drinking.

It's been a horrible day. Horrible, horrible, horrible.

Charlie brings out what he has been reaching for in his pocket. It is an envelope.

She is not prepared to forgive him in exchange for this. She knows what to expect, something bought in the last five minutes of a lunch hour on that same day.

But the card inside is not a shop-bought one at all. Fine cream handmade paper, Charlie has laboured at it, using the print machines at work and paint he uses for his models. It has taken him days to get it right, and he has had to throw nine or ten prototypes in the bin. It is meticulous in every respect, professional.

It depicts scenes from their life together. Their meeting at the bus stop, their wedding day, the birth of Robert – all are there in minute detail. He has finished the pictures with his railway modeller's brush, then glazed it with varnish. He holds it tentatively out towards Maureen, frightened that she will not take it.

I made it you. I was going to give it you after the meal.

Maureen takes it. She examines the card, understanding slowly dawning. She is first transfixed, then amazed. The vignettes are competent, even well drawn; both she and Charlie have faces that are recognizable. Forgiveness spreads slowly, mysteriously, through her chest, swelling outwards to every part of her body. She feels her eyes well up for the second time that night and then throws her arms around Charlie's neck.

Happy anniversary, kiddo, says Charlie, grinning and flushing at the same time.

Happy anniversary, Rock.

The reconciliation complete, the embrace dismantled, Charlie starts to drive again. The atmosphere has cleared, but the roads are terrible. It takes them nearly an hour to get to Earls Court. Charlie looks around him at the teeming traffic, the packed houses, the swaying crowds of youths on the street. He sees two scowling young men lounging by a traffic light, decides they are up to no good, locks his door. Police sirens wail. Charlie tightens his grip on the wheel, hoping they will not stop and breathalyse him.

Bloody London, he murmurs. *You take a short cut, and end up five times further away.*

True, says Maureen.

It's the way the cookie crumbles, he says bitterly. *The way it **always** bloody crumbles.*

He thinks of Tommy's place in Theydon Bois, the wide streets of the estate, the private gates, the trees outnumbering the houses. He remembers his childhood holidays with his parents on farms in Cornwall. He thinks of bobbies and red post boxes and smiling white shopkeepers in white coats dispensing gammon and Cheddar.

When they get home, Maureen goes straight to bed, but Charlie cannot sleep. He pours himself a large Scotch, adds a splash of Coke. He settles down in front of the TV. There are adverts on. Charlie likes the adverts more than the programmes sometimes. The beginning of this one shows a clown in red candy-stripe trousers on stilts. He has seen the ad before many times, but now he decides to concentrate. He loves this miniature film. Although he cannot say why, it produces a yearning in him.

The clown is in a shopping centre. He is giving out red balloons to children, his hands sheathed in white gloves. He wears a tall hat with a red and white band; the red picks up the colour of the balloons. A close-up on one face, an ordinary-looking white boy with tousled brown hair and an expression of innocent longing. Accompanying the pictures, a piano puts out tendrils to find heartstrings. Charlie feels chords being struck within him.

The boy, now with balloon, is seen walking past a group of other white children practising martial arts in neat outfits on the floor of the shopping centre. A bearded, avuncular policeman takes the scene in with a benevolent gaze.

The camera follows the progress of the boy and his balloon through a street market. Charlie sinks another mouthful of Scotch. The boy pulls on a pair of roller-skates and begins to glide on wheels through peaceful, empty cycle paths. A bridge across a main road looks down on surging, nearly new cars, unimpeded by other traffic.

Charlie watches as the boy glides past a group of children about the same age as himself. They attend to smart BMX bikes, which they mount. In the background music, strings are rising, restraining themselves, then rising to higher peaks. The boy glides past a fish and chip shop. The BMX bikes follow, through woodland and cycle paths, flanked by new houses that have been styled to look old.

A wall is covered by graffiti, but not real graffiti – it is a careful mural that represents 'street art'. The boy arrives home; he lives in a cottage. Charlie lights a cigarette. The BMX boys pull up outside his cottage. Charlie cannot understand why they have followed the boy, but it does not matter. They are friendly; and their pursuit is some form of tribute, not a threat.

The boy writes something on a piece of card in a nicely furnished front room. The red balloon still hovers in the foreground. Then they are both out on the road again, going along lush country lanes. Flutes arrive on the soundtrack now, adding a touch of urgency, as the boy crosses a rustic bridge. Birds can be heard singing as the boy greets a friend who is dressed for fishing, like a character from Mark Twain, complete with angler's hat. The boy leaves his friend, ties his balloon to a tree and skims stones across a glassy lake. The first time the ad was shown, at this point Charlie still did not know what it was that was being advertised. He had guessed bicycles.

The film cuts to a smiling bus driver. The boy is on board the bus. It travels down empty lanes; the red balloon flutters from the window. Then the bus arrives at its destination.

This is the bit that Charlie enjoys most, that never fails to produce in him a kind of bliss. The lone boy and balloon run up a flight of apparently freestanding stairs in what turns out to be a sports stadium of some kind. There is a heart-stopping moment when he reaches the top, and the camera sees his point of view: thousands of people, perhaps tens of thousands, and each of them holding a red balloon.

At last we see an indicator of the product that is being sold. A sign reads 'The Great Milton Keynes Balloon Race'. Close-ups reveal that the clown is here. He is orchestrating a countdown – five, four, three . . . At zero, there is a huge cheer and everyone in the stadium lets go of their balloon.

Charlie is on the edge of his chair, face like one of the child actors that he watches. The sky is blocked out almost completely by red balloons ascending. The faces of the children who have just released them are full of wonder. The bearded policeman gazes on, smiling. Children wearing T-shirts with corporate logos gaze skywards as the balloons fly free. Freeze-frame on the balloons and the sky. Voice-over: *Wouldn't it be nice if all cities were like Milton Keynes?*

Charlie is almost in tears. He sees that this city has it all – mobility and security, history and modernity, cars and bicycles, space and air. Above all, there is freedom. The balloons travel to heaven.

Bloody London, he repeats, and switches off the television. Watches as it fades to a faintly glowing blackness.

8

Maureen strides nervously along the Battersea street, checking her body language for anything that might announce her as a victim. She has had a terrible outbreak of verrucas on her right foot, six or seven clustered on the ball, and the tenderness makes it hard for her to walk with confidence, assertiveness, without displaying the slight tinge of fear that she actually feels.

But this is a journey she is determined to make, despite her discomfort. She is dressed down, in jeans and an old baggy overcoat, so she will not suggest any kind of prosperity, but she realizes that compared with the people who pass her on the street she must look well fed and comfortably off. No wonder Robert has not wanted her to visit. He knows that she will worry, and now she does, now she is worried.

She studies the photograph that she holds in her hand again. Robert sent it to her a few weeks after he moved in. It shows a large, slightly dilapidated Victorian terraced house with a blue door. She squints to try and make out either of the two numbers on the door, thinks she sees a seven.

She has been walking the streets around Battersea Park for more than an hour and is beginning to despair of ever finding Robert's house. She thinks that by now the door may have been painted a different colour entirely, or that it is not in Battersea at all, that Robert is duping her.

Then, suddenly, she sees it. Without even checking back with the photograph, she knows it is the right door. It is number 37, in the middle of a six-house terrace. The door is exactly the right blue. The arch above the door has a single plaster rose. Maureen stops, tries to take stock of it. The place is not the house of her imaginings. None of the windows are boarded up and there are no graffiti on the walls. It is certainly in a worse condition than most of the houses in the same terrace – the sills to the windows are crumbling, and there is a rusty bath in the small front garden – but on the whole it doesn't look too bad. Reassured, Maureen takes a step towards the front path.

She becomes aware of music coming from the interior, something vaguely familiar although she cannot put a name to it. It is loud, repetitive, urgent. The singer shouts, accuses, bellows. Music now is all made out of anger. Maureen cannot understand it.

She makes it on to the front porch and examines the front door for a knocker or bell, but there is neither. She pushes at the door. It is locked. The music continues, louder even than before. Taking a deep breath, she starts to pound on the front door with the smallness of her fist, but the noise she manages to generate seems pathetic. No one comes to answer.

She thinks of tapping on the window, but there is a basement to the house and it is impossible to reach the ground-floor window as there is a drop beneath the sills of about fifteen feet. The stairs down to the basement look filthy and dangerous. Maureen calculates, then removes her right shoe, holds it firmly by the toe end and begins hammering on the door.

This time the result is much more satisfactory. The music suddenly reduces in intensity. She hears a footstep approach. She prepares herself for Robert's reaction, whatever it is. But it is not Robert who opens the door, it is Carol. Both women stare at each other blankly.

Now Maureen understands why the music seems so familiar. She realizes that it is a record Carol has been playing incessantly back at Ramsay MacDonald House for much of the previous week. At one point she was driven to complain, and Carol very sweetly apologized and turned the music right down. She likes Carol, so she finds herself smiling and is the first one to break the silence.

Well, look who's here, is all she can think to say.

It's me all right, says Carol, apparently equally dumbstruck.

There is a footfall on the stairs behind Carol. Maureen looks up, sees Robert wearing a dark blue security uniform with a badge marked 'Tesco' above the right-hand pocket. He is holding a baby's bottle in his left hand. Now the music has quietened down, Maureen becomes aware of the sound of a baby crying from somewhere in the house.

Oh, fuck, says Robert.

The bottle loosens in his hand, begins to drip milk gently on the uncarpeted floorboards.

The four of them sit in the kitchen. It is a nice kitchen, thinks Maureen, airy and spacious. She holds a freshly made cup of tea. She is surprised at how calm she feels. Carol is holding the baby over her shoulder, purring to him.

Shh, Charlie.

Maureen smiles. Within her, a battlefield of competing, cataclysmic sentiment, and each separate emotion battles for dominance. The anger, at the moment, is crushed beneath the weight of Maureen's tenderness. She holds out her arms to the baby.

Can I hold him?

Of course. Of course you can.

Maureen holds the child, the child she has seen dozens of times before, in its pram, on the stairwells, at the shops. In front of her, Carol has always called him Chucky. How can she have been so stupid not to have made the connection.

I have to go to work in a minute, Mum.

What's your father going to say, Robert?

He's going to go mad. Please don't tell him.

How can I not tell him? I see Carol nearly every day. I see his grandchild nearly every day.

Robert's face sets in a determined grimace. Maureen recognizes that expression. It is inherited from her and so she knows how pointless arguing is. Robert sits on the chair opposite his mother.

*You **mustn't** tell him. Carol's moving in here next week, so it won't be such a big deal.*

Won't be a big deal! He's got a grandson and it's not a big deal!

You don't understand, Mum! Dad already thinks I'm the flop of the century. This'll be the last straw for him. I just want . . . I just want . . .

It's wrong, Robert, it's plain wrong. How can I keep a secret like that?

I just want him to know that I'm not worthless. That I'm not just working as a stinking security guard in Tesco, living in a squat with a six-month-old kid. I want to do the right thing, Mum. I just haven't had time to do it yet. I haven't had time to find out what it is yet. Give me some time to sort things out, to get myself on my feet. When he finds out about this, I want him to be happy, not furious.

*But what are you going to **do**, Robert?*

Robert looks suddenly crestfallen.

I don't know. Something. There's no jobs anywhere. The jobs there are – they're rubbish for people with my qualifications. Or lack of them.

You're a clever boy. If you'd tried harder . . .

If this, if that, if the other. This is how it is, and I've got to solve it the way it is.

You need to get in touch with your father. We haven't heard hide nor hair from you for months.

Robert bites his lip till the flesh turns white.

Come on, Rob. You keep telling me you want to face up to things. If you want me to keep quiet about this, you've got to make an effort.

Hmm.

Look. What about going to one of your dad's card games? As a first step. I mentioned it to him not so long ago.

And what did he say?

Nothing.

Right.

But I know he'd like to see you.

What am I going to gamble with, Mum? You don't get much spare cash out of security guard work.

Maureen reaches past the baby for her purse. Robert starts shaking his head.

No, Mum. I'm trying to stand on my own two feet.

Don't be silly. This isn't about you buying a motorbike. This is about you making friends with your dad. Take it. Lose it. Lose it to your dad, if you can. Take the first steps. Then . . .

Robert looks up, pleading.

Then I'll do what you want, says Maureen quietly.

Carol comes over, puts a hand on Robert's shoulder, toys with the nylon epaulette of his uniform.

Take the money, Rob, says Carol.

Robert takes three £20 notes from his mother's hand, brushing against her fingers. Carol reaches over and tickles the gurgling infant.

Robert's a good man, Mrs Buck.

You'd best call me Maureen now.

Maureen. A lot of blokes would have just pissed off. I mean, it's not that we love each other. We're just mates, really, and it . . . it **happened**. *But he knows that Charlie is his, as well as mine. And I know it too, which is why we called him after his grandfather.*

Robert's all right. He's not . . . Yosser Hughes. He'll get a job, a good job. He just doesn't know which one yet.

Maureen shifts position with the baby, cradles him now in her arms, looks down into the moon of his face.

I could speak to your Uncle Tommy. He knows people.

The wrong sort of people. I've spoken to him too.

You didn't tell him about the baby, did you?

No, of course not. Strictly about a job. Tried to get me to go and work on the building site. But I don't want to be a bloody hod-carrier. All the same . . .

What?

All the same . . . he did have one good idea. Nothing to do with the building trade. Totally legit. I might take him up on it. I really might. Good wages and getting better all the time. Respectable. Opportunities for promotion.

Sounds terrific, says Maureen.

*Not **that** terrific,* says Carol archly.

A hot evening, late August, Tommy's house in Theydon Bois. Tommy, Charlie and Mike are sat around a table.

Tommy is shuffling cards. *Hooked on Classics* by the Royal Philharmonic is on the turntable. Mike Sunderland is excited by the pronounced ordinariness of the surroundings. There are beers on the table and cigarettes. Cheese and onion crisps, Twiglets, silverskin onions on cocktail sticks. Already the ashtrays overflow and the room is softened into a deep fug. Lorraine is on a girls' night out at a wine bar Up West.

This mate of yours, handy, is he? says Tommy. He divides the pack into two, expertly flicks one stack into the other. *Bit of a fucking sharpie?*

Snowy? He's not a mug, but he's not all that good, says Charlie. *He's lucky, though. He gets the luck every time. I don't know how he does it. It **kills** me, the luck that man has. You know, he doesn't* play the odds, he kind of spots runs of luck, rides on their coat tails. It's black magic.

Tommy turns to Mike, who is quietly making a roll-up.

You play much cards, Mick?

Oh, I don't know. I used to play a little duplicate bridge from time to time.

Tommy laughs.

That's not fucking cards. That's old ladies waiting to die.

You'd be surprised. It's quite intellectually challenging.

Oh, la-de-da, pass the fucking champers, Maud. All your mates at work like this, are they, Charlie? Christ, if I had my head that far up my arse I'd be able to whistle Dixie with my farts.

Mike stops rolling his cigarette, looks suddenly taken aback.

Don't mind Tommy, Mike. He's never quite got the hang of manners.

Nah, don't you worry about me, Mickey boy. I couldn't care less where you come from, Hoxford or bloody old Cambridge, wot wot, so long as you bring your money. That's what we're here for. A bit of moving and shaking, a bit of the old fucking redistribution of wealth.

Tommy takes a big pile of fivers bound by an elastic band and slaps them on the table.

So, take that fucking plum out of your north and south and show us the size of your wad.

Mike nods, removes a small wallet from his inside pocket, and takes out four £50 notes, places them on the table opposite Tommy's.

I hope that's sufficient, he says quietly.

That's sufficient, yeah, that's sufficient, snorts Tommy. *That'll pay for a bottle of Bolly or two, wot wot, that'll pay for a new cigar lighter on the old Bugatti.*

The doorbell rings. Tommy gets up to answer it, wobbles violently all the way there. Mike is pulling furiously at his cigarette and is already making a new one as the old one expires.

You all right, Mike?

Well, to be honest, Charlie, I feel a bit nervous for some reason.

Don't mind my brother. His bark's much worse than his bite.

Tommy wobbles back into the room. Staring for the umpteenth time at the clear red mark that resembles the imprint of a set of teeth on Tommy's cheek, Mike finds this hard to credit. Tommy has his huge arm around Robert's shoulder and is squeezing him.

That lanky streak of ginger piss is here. Hope he's brought money and not fucking buttons. And tell him we don't cash cheques from the Social here.

Tommy laughs uproariously at his own joke, chucks Robert's cheek. Robert grins weakly. To Charlie's surprise, he is wearing a suit, has a scrubbed face and short, carefully cut hair. He looks vulnerable, extraordinarily young. Charlie suddenly finds himself unsure what to do it's such a long while since he's seen him. He has an impulse to jump out of the chair and embrace his son. But habit and pride get the better of him. He raises a hand in acknowledgement, stays where he is.

Hello, Dad.

Hello, Robert.

There is an awkward silence. Mike gives a small cough.

Robert this is Mike Sunderland. He's a sub-editor on the newspaper.

Mike rises, holds out his hand.

Very pleased to meet you.

Behind Mike's back, Tommy puts his hand on his hip, goes camp and mimes *very pleased to meet you.*

Robert ignores him, smiles at Mike, shakes his hand.

You too.

He sits down. Then he gets up again, removes his coat, looks round for somewhere to put it and, seeing nowhere, puts it on the back of his chair. He sits down again, then spots a coat-stand on the far side of the room and gets up once more.

Fuck me, it's Zebedee, says Tommy. *Do you want a drink, you ginger nut?*

A beer would be good, Uncle Tom.

What about you, Mikey boy? Gin fizz? Babycham? A spot of the old shampoo?

I'll have a beer too, thanks.

Tommy walks over towards the kitchen.

You all right, Dad?

Robert is sitting in the chair opposite his father. The table is oval and he sits at the point of the oval, the largest distance possible.

I'm fine, Robert. It's . . . He hesitates. *It's nice to see you.*

Nice to see you too, Dad.

Where the fuck is this other stooge of yours? says Tommy, returning with the drinks. *I'm not here for a getting-to-know-you event. Let's do this. Five more minutes, we'll start without what's his-name, Snowflake. How did he get a silly fucking name like that anyway?*

He'll be here, says Charlie.

Right on cue, there is a buzz on the doorbell. This time Charlie goes to open it. It is Lloyd, smartly dressed in a dark blue raincoat, and a yellow shirt with a sky-blue tie. He is breathing heavily.

Sorry, Charlie. Bloody buses.

You should get a taxi.

Not on my wage.

Come in, Snowy. Let me take your coat.

Lloyd removes the coat, to reveal a very low-waisted jacket

with padded shoulders and peg-top trousers with slit pockets. He looks flashy, smart.

Snazzy.

You won't believe this, bwoy. This is the suit I wore when I first came over here. Look! Still fits me perfectly. Ain't I pretty?

You're pretty all right. You're a doll. Snowy, meet my brother, Tommy.

Tommy, who is fumbling with ice from the ice bucket to put in his double Scotch, looks up. Charlie notices a kind of freezing of his stance. Lloyd strides over, holds out his hand.

Nice to meet you.

Tommy doesn't move. Finally speaks.

Nah, better not. Hands wet.

Then he heads back to the kitchen. Unfazed, Lloyd turns to the table where the other men sit.

Hello, Robert. My, you've grown. You was just a nipper last time I saw you. Now look at you. And you don't end up ugly like your father neither.

Thanks, Lloyd.

Do you want a drink, Snowy? says Charlie.

Do I? says Lloyd. *Rum and blackcurrant.*

Charlie shouts through to Tommy in the kitchen.

Tommy, get Snowy a drink.

There is a silence. Then Tommy comes back into the room, carrying more snacks – Hula Hoops and peanuts.

Where's Snowy's drink? says Charlie.

Did he want a drink? I didn't hear nothing.

Tommy sits down on the opposite side of the table to Lloyd. Charlie sighs, goes into the kitchen and returns with a drink for Lloyd. *Hooked on Classics* fills the brief silence in the room.

What's this mush? says Robert.

Music with a bit of melody. What's wrong with that? says Charlie.

I pity the fool, says Robert.

He likes to watch Mr T in the *A Team*, whose catchphrase this is.

Robert goes over to the record player, takes off *Hooked on Classics* and puts on a record from his bag. He turns up the volume. Spraying guitars invade the room.

A chorus sounds.

Jesus God Almighty . . . What is this? says Charlie.

Anti Nowhere League, says Robert, nodding his head to the sound.

Rubbish, says Charlie.

It's got fantastic . . . energy, says Mike Sunderland eagerly.

Punk filth, says Charlie.

I like it, says Tommy. *It's like . . . it makes you want to fucking chin someone.*

Oh, God, says Charlie.

Anyway, it's not punk. It's Oi.

Oi? says Tommy.

Oi, says Robert. *As in OI!*

Tommy laughs. Charlie gets up, pushes past Robert and takes the single off. He replaces it with Mel Tormé.

Bloody commotion.

Tommy shuffles.

Nice place you got here, says Lloyd to Tommy.

What's it to be then? says Tommy curtly.

What about Chase the Ace? says Robert.

Charlie shakes his head.

It's a kid's game, Robert. We're not at a Christmas party now.

Cool Hand Luke, says Lloyd, sucking at his teeth.

What's Chase the Ace? says Mike brightly.

Like I say, it's a kid's game, says Charlie firmly. *What about pontoon first?*

What do you usually play? says Mike. He is the solicitous head teacher at the sixth-form party.

Pontoon. Shoot. Stud poker. Sometimes a little gin.

Let's go for poker. Let's go for broke-a, says Tommy, grinning like a lizard.

He feels himself taking on a role, the chancer, the all-or-bust man. This is how he is in cards. Charlie is always more cautious, rations his bets, plays the odds, never wins or loses much.

Pontoon first, says Charlie.

Twenty-one it is, says Lloyd. *Let's have a lickle tickle.*

OK, says Robert.

He has taken his wallet out and is counting four £5 notes on to the table. There is a big bowl of change in the middle.

Is that the same as blackjack? You know, vingt-un, says Mike.

Charlie inspects Mike's pile of £50 notes. He wonders why Mike always dresses so badly when he is clearly so prosperous. He pronounces *vingt-un* in an aggressively authentic French accent. Charlie bridles slightly.

Pontoon is pontoon. No sticking on fifteen. Split and burn. Split any card. Burn on 14. You can buy the bank, otherwise we cut for it. Pontoon takes the bank. Minimum bet 50p.

I think I get the idea, says Mike, converting one £50 note into change.

One other thing you need to know, says Charlie.

What's that? says Mike.

Snowball uses voodoo.

Lloyd grins, showing teeth discoloured by the thickness of the blackcurrant cordial.

Just good play, bwoy.

Robert lights a cigar, feels good. Everything is fresh, no luck has played itself out yet. Lloyd gives a private smile.

Pontoon takes up the first hour of the evening. Robert takes the bank; the other players have to beat his hand. As predicted, Lloyd is lucky, pulling in around £30 over the period. Tommy is reckless and unpredictable, throwing large sums at mediocre cards. But he enjoys the drama, doesn't mind losing £20 at a pop. Mike Sunderland plays textbook: moderate bets on most cards, high bets on good, a bit of instinct, a bit of luck. Comes out on top. But Charlie plays as he always plays: cautious, marshalling resources, careful, fearful of loss, watching odds, not believing in runs. He always places the minimum bet unless the odds are heavily in his favour, then he always bets the same: a £5 note, which pays him back, in the long run, more often than not. At the end of the game, he has slightly more than he had when he started.

Doesn't look like it's going to be your day, says Charlie to Tommy, eyeing his shrinking pile, which Tommy now tops up by converting another note into change.

You are the most boring fucking card player I have ever seen, says Tommy gruffly. *At least I have a bit of fun. You got to take a few risks in life.*

This isn't life, says Charlie. *It's cards.*

Same thing, says Tommy.

Ain't it true? says Lloyd. He has taken out a toothpick and is gouging at a crushed Twiglet near the base of a molar.

What? says Robert.

It's true, ain't it? says Lloyd. *Your pops plays at cards like everything. No unnecessary risk.*

I can take chances, says Charlie, obscurely hurt. *I'm just not silly about it.*

If you aks me, says Lloyd, *you're a pussy.*

Unusually, Tommy makes some kind of response to something that Lloyd has said. He gives a small, dry laugh.

A little bit short in the bottle department, you might say, says Tommy.

I got all the bottle I need, says Charlie, throwing a glance at Tommy.

There is an awkward silence. Charlie starts swiftly dealing out cards.

So, your father tells me you're trying hard to find a job, says Mike.

Yeah, says Robert, staring at the pack of cards.

Mike shakes his head in apparent despair.

*It's **appalling** out there. The unemployment. It's a deliberate policy, you know. To drive down wage costs. The government **wants** high unemployment. It weakens the unions, it drives down wages.*

Right, says Robert, picking up his cards.

Have you had any luck finding anything at all? says Mike earnestly.

I've got a few things on the boil, says Robert.

He catches a sceptical expression on his father's face, feels suddenly enraged.

I'm in training right now, as a matter of fact.

Really, says Mike. *In what?*

The security profession, says Robert.

That's the place to be, says Tommy. *It's like the filth, only private. It's the future, private prisons, private screws, private fucking army. That's a proper job. You can crack a few heads. When I used to be a copper, it got so that you couldn't even give some hooligan a slap without some fucking social worker calling you to book. What a load of bollocks.*

Charlie shakes his head. He has heard from Maureen that Robert is working at Tesco. His son could have been a craftsman.

Is this a card game or is this not a card game? says Tommy. *Let's rock and roll. Let's shoot that shit.*

He sees himself as American when he is gambling, a pistol in his pocket, heroic and unafraid of danger.

Let's go for stud, says Charlie.

All righty, says Robert. He counts his pile. He is down £6.50.

Stud it is, then, says Tommy briskly.

He empties another can of beer, lights another cigar. Mike Sunderland looks at him in awe, the tattoos on his knuckles, the red flayed face. The real thing, pure and unsullied.

Tommy is as reckless at stud as he has been at pontoon, but he has a little more luck this time. Also he is good at bluffing and raises the stakes so high everyone is afraid to match them, apart from Mike, who calculates effortlessly, who is in fact a practised poker player. Tommy makes £20. Mike's luck is not good, but his tactics are flawless. He and Tommy both emerge as winners; Robert loses out again, and Charlie is slightly down after pushing three of a kind too far against Mike's full house. Lloyd does not like stud, and coasts through it, keeping the betting low. He comes out slightly down, but with enough resources to attack the final game, shoot, which begins at the end of the second hour.

Now this is where the drama begins, says Tommy. *This is when we talk the turkey.*

I don't think I know this, says Mike.

Very, very simple, even for a mug like you, says Tommy.

Mike glows, pleased that he has been accepted enough to attract friendly abuse, to be included in the banter.

Everyone puts a five spot in the kitty, says Charlie. *Then all you do is deal out two cards face up to everyone. Then you have to gamble on whether the next card dealt is going to be in between the two cards.*

So what if I get a five and a seven? says Mike.

Minimum bet is £1.

I've got to bet £1 even if there's only one card I can win on?

That's it. Even if you can't win, you got to bet, even if you got two cards the same, you got to bet. That's how the kitty builds up. And you can only bet as much as is in the kitty.

So the best hand is, what, an ace and a two, or a king and a two?

That's it. But if you shoot for the pot and the card that comes up matches one of your cards, you pay in double.

Mike nods.

So if I had a king and a two, and there was £50 in the pot and I shot for it all, I would have to put £100 in if a king or a two came up.

Bingo, says Lloyd.

Communism in action, says Charlie.

For the first half-hour, the game is uninteresting. The pot never builds up beyond £20 or so and every attempt to shoot it is successful. But then Robert shoots at a £25 pot with a jack and a three.

Go for it, Rob, urges Charlie. *You can buy me that steam engine at last.*

But he gets dealt a jack. Right away, £75 in the pot. Robert looks sick. A few hands later, Mike Sunderland gets dealt king–two. He hums and haws, wants to show himself a man in front of the boys. He shoots the pot. There is a gasp from all of them; it is a king. Mike blinks.

Bloody hell.

He hadn't anticipated losing more than £50. Now he has to put in £170. Suddenly there is about £255 in the pot. It is the biggest any of them can remember it making.

The atmosphere in the game has changed now. From being a lark, a bit of fun, it has become deadly serious. The pot gets chipped away at, Lloyd betting £50 on a queen–two, Robert putting thirty on a queen–three. But then Tommy draws a king against his king–four and his bet of £75 gets doubled into the pot. Now there is more than £300 in there.

Then Charlie gets dealt an ace–deuce. Next to him, on his left, Tommy gets a king–deuce. The atmosphere sharpens, closes in. The deal comes round to Charlie again.

Shoot it, Charlie! says Lloyd.

He won't do it, says Robert flatly.

Charlie studies the cards as if they will give up some secret. He glances at Robert, registers something obscurely, that this is important beyond the card game itself. Tommy is grinning, confident. Charlie looks around, thinks about which cards in the pack can beat him. Two of the deuces have gone. Lloyd has been dealt another ace, matched with a queen; no good to him, but eliminates another potential enemy. There are only four cards in the pack that can take him down. Four cards out of . . . what . . . he finds it hard to think . . . forty-three, forty-two. Four cards out of forty-two. Good odds. Very good odds. But he is afraid. To lose means he has to put more than £600 in the pot. It is an enormous amount of money. It is a decent second-hand car, it is a fortnight's holiday in Malta in a decent hotel with Maureen. Maureen would hit the flaming roof. He is frightened.

I haven't got the stomach, says Charlie.

He looks at Tommy's cards. He knows that Tommy will shoot for it. He senses that Tommy will win too. He glances again at Robert, expecting disdain to be registering in his face. But Robert looks worried.

Don't do it, Dad. It doesn't matter, he says quietly.

Come on, Charlie, says Tommy, himself sweating slightly. *You never take any **chances**. Life's a **gamble**.*

I think maybe we should just pack it up, split the pot and go home, says Lloyd.

Yeah, says Robert. *Maybe Lloyd is right.*

Don't be a sissy! bellows Tommy. *Go for it, Charlie. Shoot the fucking pot. Shoot it down in flames. There's only three cards in there that can take you out. Show us what you're made of.*

Charlie fidgets again. His whole nature militates against the play, but four cards . . . only four cards. To walk away with £300. To show Robert that he is fearless. To show Tommy and Snowball that he has enough bottle to open an off-licence.

Maybe I'll take £50, he says tentatively.

Tommy groans.

I'm going to take that pot, big brother. I'm going to fucking take it. I fancy it, I double fancy it. And I'm going to take it. Because I got the big fat hairy balls to. You poof.

OK, shoot! says Charlie suddenly.

Mike Sunderland makes a movement to deal the card.

No! says Charlie. *Let me think a moment more.*

He stops, his hand on the card. But there is nothing to think about any more. The odds have been calculated. The potential profits and losses are clear. There is only courage left. He feels the eyes of Robert on him, both wanting him and not wanting him to do it. Most of all, he feels Tommy mocking him, as ever disdaining his caution. He wants to do it. He wants to break the spell of his life, marshalling chances, job for life, always watching the rear-view mirror. Trains on tracks.

There is silence. He takes one last look at the deck of cards, as if it can reveal to him the card underneath with sufficient scrutiny. Then, softly this time, but his voice charged with a mixture of determination and resignation, he speaks.

OK. Shoot it.

You sure?

Shoot it.

The card turns slowly up. Charlie swallows. His throat is dry. No one is moving. The kitty is piled in the middle, a mound of notes and coins that practically spreads to the edges of the table.

Eight of diamonds.

There is a sudden cacophony of voices, a charge of released tension.

Old Charlie Buck, says Lloyd in a singsong voice. *He gets all the luck.*

I bet he drinks Carling Black Label! yells Robert, punching the air.

Balls like watermelons, shouts Tommy, slapping his big brother on the back.

Well done, Charlie, says Mike Sunderland, smiling, delighted at the authenticity of it all, despite his loss. Balls like watermelons.

Charlie sits there amazed, guilty at taking this money from his friends, from his family, but astonished that he was capable of taking the chance, and, having taken it, being rewarded. Not just the game but life itself suddenly seems cast in a different light. Tommy was right, is right, has always been right. He is too cautious. He pulls the money towards him in a daze. Although all of the faces around him must hide disappointment – it is *their* money he is taking – he sees nothing but admiration and a kind of delight. Winners are loved; this truth begins to dawn on him. He wants to win again.

Charlie Buck suddenly feels that he wants to win for ever.

PART TWO

New Town

9

1984. Orwell's year of communist nightmare. Charlie once read a Reader's Digest condensed version of the book, thought it was over the top. And so it proves.

Charlie and Maureen are approaching junction 14 of the M1. The Triumph Toledo has been replaced by an Austin Mini Metro, this time only five years old. The boot and the back of the car are packed with suitcases. Charlie can hardly see behind him in the rear-view mirror. The stream of traffic carries them, steel flotsam, until they take the turn-off marked Milton Keynes.

Charlie considers only a few days in his life to have been extraordinary. His first day in the army, his first job, his wedding, the arrival in the new council flat with Maureen after Robert was born. Each seemed too large to imagine as he was experiencing it, its true scale becoming apparent only looking behind him – a rear-view mirror unobscured by baggage.

But on this day a genuine sense of new beginning seems to shine, for behind each landscaped hedgerow, each flower bed on each of the seemingly endless roundabouts as they approach their destination, some two miles away from central Milton Keynes, in an estate near the array of concrete cows that is the town's only famous landmark. Charlie reflects that, as Tommy has always protested, he has been too cautious with his life. Today, choice seems to spread out magically in all directions, in three dimensions, and with it, beckoning, benign consequences. For once Charlie does not find this disturbing but invigorating.

The drive is dreamlike, as it had been the first time they came to search for property here. Charlie liked the architecture of the place; everything new, but designed to imply the past. Countryside, but not the frightening solitude of real country-side. Cars that could move, air that could be breathed without choking. A decent space between everyone. Privacy.

It was not, he knew, the paradise shown in the ads – Charlie and Maureen were too long in the tooth to believe in places like paradise, too many rings under their bark to believe in advertisements. But nevertheless, it was closer to paradise by a country mile than Ramsay MacDonald House, SW6.

Here there are shops increasingly full of wider and wider varieties of . . . stuff, all sorts of stuff, stuff nobody had thought possible when they were growing up. Here they would live, not in a council flat, not even in a private flat in a council block, but amid fresh air and open spaces, in a detached house, and with other pioneers like them; others who owned their own property, who had means, gumption, get up and go. Get up and go was what Tommy always said he'd never had. Now he was proving him wrong. He had got up and, Jesus God Almighty, he had gone.

They'd made a packet on the flat. Fulham, to his amaze-ment, had become what some people now thought of as fashionable. Shit had turned to gold. They'd cleared about £15,000 on the place. The figures had sat like miracles in his bank account for a few magical hours as the bridging period was crossed. He had never imagined that someone like him could have so much money. He noted down these five digits, stared at them; if he could understand their secret, he felt that a world of endless possibility would somehow be revealed.

Their detached three-bedroom house has cost them £41,000. It's a lot of money – a *lot* of money. But the beauty is, the money is still *there*, as Charlie sees it, dissolved into the mortar, soaked into the red of the bricks. It is like fissionable material. Energy can be extracted from it.

After a lot of thought, they go for an endowment mortgage rather than repayment. Tommy has a policy, swears by it. Their financial adviser – Charlie and Maureen can hardly believe they even have such a thing – is a nice man, sincere. He came to Ramsay MacDonald House, he drank their tea and ate two Digestive biscuits. Cleared up the crumbs afterwards and put them in the bin. He was even-handed about it all, but came down on the side of the endowment, because it was sure to leave them with a pretty penny on top at the end of the day when the mortgage was paid off. More money for nothing, a prize for simply joining in this wonderful new game.

The grid roads are named alphabetically and numerically. They travel along V11, then H5, get lost somewhere between H4 and V9. The roundabouts seem to be ubiquitous. They drive past the peace pagoda; there is a settlement of Buddhist monks here.

Well, says Charlie, *it's a spiritual place. You can feel it.*

The wide spaces open up the sky. Today a wind is blowing. No pedestrians can be seen. The city is invisible.

Robert was supposed to be following them in Tommy's builder's van, bringing most of the remainder of their possessions. They lost him somewhere around Hanger Lane but expect he'll find his own way.

Maureen is the doubter in this project. Charlie, having made the leap away from a lifelong caution in his own mind, having felt the touch of gloss paint on the door of what was once council property, has discovered the passion of the newly converted. He is not to be left behind, not here at the crest of the 1980s. He may be a *fuddy-duddy,* he decides, but he's no fool.

Charlie has a secret. He voted for Margaret Thatcher in the last election, following her triumph over the Argie menace. It made the Prime Minister swell in Charlie's imagination, it made him respect her. And there was more money appearing in his pay packet as income tax shrank, and he was sick anyway of the loony lefties, and although Foot was now gone Kinnock was a windbag and, worse still, he was Welsh, a bloody troll. It wasn't the Labour Party he used to vote for. Anyway, Charlie figures, he can always come back to the fold.

In the meantime, not a soul knows of his conversion. He is part of a large secret community: the Labour-supporting Tory voters. Tommy, who is open in his admiration of Thatcher, suspects as much, but nothing he can say will extract the admission from his older brother.

But it's clear to Charlie that Maureen does not understand or appreciate this new Britain. It takes all his powers of persuasion to get her to shift up to MK. At first she had said no. However, in '81 she had wanted to stop Charlie buying the council flat for fear of debt. But Charlie talked her into it, and her astonishment at the quick profit they subsequently turned has shaken her confidence in her own judgement, edged her closer to Charlie's point of view. They had doubled their savings without any work being done. It was extraordinary, money for nothing. It went against some inherited, deep-rooted idea of how the universe worked, but there it was all the same. Charlie promised her more where that came from. Tommy had never had so much work, had bought himself a five-series BMW, could you believe it? He said that there were good times ahead for property. They could move up and up.

Still, Maureen proved hard to convince. She hadn't wanted to leave her friends at Divine Creations, at her evening classes, at the local shops. She didn't want to leave Carol and Mrs

Jackson. She had her little jobs that brought in a tidy sum. The fear of debt that Charlie is beginning to shake off, to triumph over, continues to haunt her. She cannot drive.

She didn't want to be so far from Robert. But Robert has promised to come and visit regularly, just as soon as he finishes training in his mysterious new job. Maureen has warned Charlie to expect an announcement about Robert, good news by all accounts. Charlie finds it hard to believe. Maybe his son has been kicked upstairs to Sainsbury's, he muses bitterly.

Charlie has talked it all up. She could learn to drive; they would borrow the money to buy a second car. She would love the vast new shopping centre in MK. She could shop, not for bread and potatoes and kitchen flannels, but for the good things in life. She could shop for *pleasure*. Charlie has made a bargain with her that if she goes along with the plan, she would have not only a beautiful home but one full of beautiful things. He harangued, he cajoled and, above all, he bribed. Maureen wanted to carry on working, maybe even studying her accountancy. Charlie said that the Open University was right there in Milton Keynes, that she could study all that stuff to her heart's content. Secretly he thought it was all a waste of time, a hobby, but still. She could shop, and study, and all in a place that was as near as damn it countryside.

Finally Maureen gave in. She, too, was hearing stories, of friends from school, a friend who once worked in Woolworths, living in places not far off palaces. Places that were always rising in value, that had £10,000 kitchens. She has heard of acquaintances married to plumbers who were driving Mercedes. Rumour states that anything is starting to be possible. And Charlie has prised her caution off her, with the jemmy of his will, just as he has blown the caution off himself with the packed breath of envy for his brother. Envy: there is such energy there; if you could package it, you could light the country. And in a thousand homes, in a hundred towns, the same thing was happening. Money was there for the taking. You just had to have the courage, the nous, to reach out and take it. And you had to get ahead, or the lives of those around you would mock you.

They turn off one of the endless roundabouts. First, second, third on the right. Suddenly Charlie stops the car. He is studying something out of Maureen's sight.

What are you doing, Charlie? says Maureen.

I want to see the cows.

Then he is out and standing by the fence, looking at the famous sculpture. He is disappointed. There are only six cows, smaller than he expected and crude in execution. They are black-and-white friesians. Three are calves, one of which is half spread-eagled, as if invisible weights bear down upon it. Its concrete mother looks back at it dumbly. Cows four to six either gaze at nothing or nose at scrubby grass.

They're a bit rubbish, aren't they? says Charlie.

Oh, I don't know, says Maureen.

They stand and stare for longer than they need, to justify the decision to stop. They are bored and a cold wind blows. After a minute or two they retreat back to the Mini Metro. The house is very close now.

Past a row of trees, and another mini-roundabout. Right at the roundabout, then into a wide boulevard of yew trees. Charlie stares entranced, as he was the first time he saw them.

Astonishingly to them both, there are only twelve houses in the street. Theirs is the last. They stop outside; although there is a car port, they park in the street. It doesn't seem enough theirs yet to make a manoeuvre so intimate. The house is only ten years old. Children play quietly halfway down the street. One of them has a balloon. Charlie notes with disappointment that it is blue rather than the red of the

TV ad. Three houses along, a man about the same age as Charlie is working at a rockery with a trowel. He looks up as they go by, but does not otherwise acknowledge their presence.

Look, says Charlie. *Keen gardeners up here. Just think, our own garden. We can grow roses.*

Wordlessly, Maureen and Charlie leave the car. They stand and stare. Charlie takes a cigarette out of his pocket and lights it. Breathes in then out, displacing the smoke from his lungs. Replaces it with air made from distant light industrial chemical emissions, a million green trees, decaying matter, gases from space, exhaled breath. All combining into this browning and dampness.

Then they begin to walk at a slow pace down the newly laid path towards the front door, with its leaded light and plain, dark varnished wood. When they had viewed the property there was a carriage lamp outside, but this has been removed, leaving an unsightly gap in the masonry.

It seems that they will never arrive. There is no reason for this crawl along through the well-kept front garden. It is as if the gravitational pull of the front door, although finally irresistible, seems too weak to snap them to attention and pull them into what seems clearly mark ꞋꞋꞋd by this relocation as the second half of their lives, the final half. So they become sluggish and uncertain, a part of themselves resisting what they had thought they wanted. Charlie suddenly feels frightened, though he cannot say why. How could this new, brightly lit, geometrical world be dangerous?

The sounds. Familiar yet fresh, because out of context. A distant lawn mower. Unnamed birds, complaining mutts. Faint trains, receding airliner. Modern, ancient, urban, rural, mixed as if randomly. But almost nothing is random here. Nature has been tamed and corralled, imprinted upon precisely. This is what has drawn them to the place. Maureen particularly likes its order, its evenness of construction. She likes the alphabetically named grid roads, their emptiness. It is somewhere she feels she could soon learn to drive.

The sun is weak, but sharp and bright all the same.

This is it, then, says Charlie.

Yes. This is it.

They reach the front door. They notice that the brass letter box, like the carriage lamp, has been removed. The gap looks ugly. Charlie feels in his pocket for the keys, which seem light, insubstantial. They do not recognize their own significance. He removes them, tries the Yale in the lock. It opens easily. Maureen makes as if to walk through.

Hold on.

Charlie grabs Maureen round the waist, picks her up in a single motion. He still has the strength, and she gasps.

Come on, kiddo. Just like Rock Hudson.

He carries her across the threshold. Maureen is laughing. Charlie is worried about his back. He drops her almost the moment they go inside. She stumbles, and he almost falls, but saves himself at the last moment.

Maureen looks around her. It is darker than you would expect, given the late sun. The windows are small, to conserve heat. Her pupils expand, take in the scene. Her laughter dies in her throat.

Jesus God Almighty, says Charlie.

The house is not merely empty, as they had expected. Plastic light switches have gone, as have the handles to the windows. The skirting boards have been removed, the electrical socket covers have been ripped off. There are no doors, or even door frames. The effect is shocking, one of violation.

They can see from where they stand that there is no sink in

the kitchen. A brief exploration reveals that there is no bath in the bathroom. Some floorboards have been removed.

The Bucks have arrived into their new world to be confronted with an act of insane greed.

Well, at least they didn't hack off the plaster and chip out the mortar, says Charlie feebly, watching Maureen, who will not meet his eye.

I mean, effing hell. I mean, Jesus God Almighty.

He notices the connecting pipes where the central heating radiators used to be. He laughs bleakly, lights another cigarette, barely able to keep it still. Runs a hand through the fullness of his hair. Maureen's eyes are desperate. She presses at a fresh ulcer inside her cheek with her tongue. Charlie begins to gabble.

Aren't some people funny? Well, I suppose they're within their rights. It'll take a while to put this right. Never mind. If we . . .

When Maureen speaks it is in a flat tone with all emotion drained out.

They've taken the . . . the telephone socket is gone.

Charlie follows her eyes to the gap above where the skirting board once was.

They're lunatics, says Charlie.

Maureen is still staring at where the telephone socket should be. Something about the terrific smallness of the removal snaps her and she gives up the struggle for self-control. Water overflows the corners of her eyes. Charlie makes to say something. Walks across and puts his arm around her, to stop her dissolving. To breach the waterfall.

Don't fret, Maureen. It really is nothing. A week'll sort it. I'll do it myself.

Maureen holds him. There is the joyful hooting of a horn outside. Robert has arrived. When he walks through the door he is holding ten chrysanthemums.

For me? says Charlie, still trying to lighten the awful heaviness that this moment has acquired.

Five each, says Robert. *What in God's name has happened here?*

It takes them a week to get the house back to a state where it is habitable. Tommy, who is normally chocker with work, or so he says, comes up for a few days from London to help them. There is a pink sticking plaster over Tommy's ear where a burly Irishman tried to detach it with his teeth during a pub discussion about Ulster politics. On this day, Tommy and Charlie have been working all morning. Maureen appears with a shopping bag and, head down, makes towards the door. Charlie is finishing a ham and tomato roll. There are crumbs around his mouth. Maureen halts her stride and automatically wipes them away. It is raining outside. On the mantelpiece is a giant card illustrated with Charles Schulz's Snoopy reclining on his kennel in a First World War flying helmet. It reads, 'There's No Burden Heavier Than a Great Potential'. It is signed by all the women at Divine Creations.

There is a trilling noise from somewhere that Charlie cannot locate. Tommy reaches into his toolbox and pulls out a large heavy rectangle of plastic. To Charlie's amazement, he takes a handkerchief out of his pocket, puts it over his nose, then begins to speak into the box in a feeble but exaggeratedly polite voice.

Hello, Chigwell and District Loft Company. Hello there, Mr Jenkins! Yes, I'm terribly sorry I couldn't make it. I've had a touch of the flu. Didn't one of my secretaries call you? Well, I'll have a serious word with Samantha about that. It's not good enough. Yes . . . I am feeling a bit better actually. I've got the loft conversion pencilled in now for . . . hold on . . . for next Monday. No, Monday week. Yes. Yes. I know I've said that before. But . . . no, I'm afraid the money you gave me has all gone on materials . . . OK . . . There's no need for that kind of attitude, Mr Jenkins. There's no need to swear. Of course. I'll be there. Yes. I guarantee it. OK. Goodbye, then. Goodbye.

Tommy hangs up, catches Charlie's expression.

Save me the fucking sermon. I got bills to pay and there's mugs out there to pay them. What you think of the dog?

Charlie has not seen a cellular telephone before outside of American TV series. He decides to make no comment on either Tommy's business practices or the expensive gadgets that they enable him to acquire. But Tommy, of course, will not let the moment pass. He brandishes the object at Charlie.

You should get one of these. It's a godsend.

It's a gimmick.

They said that about television. This is the future. I'm telling you, Charlie.

They said that about eight-track. Of which you also had a fancy version. They said it about quadraphonic. How much did you blow on that? You even bought a bloody Betamax.

This is different.

And I'm a Chinaman.

I'll have a number 37 and a side order of egg fried rice.

Tommy, satisfied that his point has been made, that his prosperity has been displayed, replaces the device in his tool-box. Maureen, who has taken no notice, goes to leave.

I'm off, then.

Charlie holds his hand up. He has a way of evening the score with Tommy.

Hold on, kiddo. I've a surprise.

Charlie reaches in his pocket. Maureen squints to make out what he's doing. He takes out an envelope, thrusts it into Maureen's hand.

What's that?

Have a gander.

Maureen peers inside the envelope. There is a rectangle of plastic.

Came this morning, says Charlie. *Take it with you. Treat yourself to something.*

Maureen looks puzzled.

I've never used one of these before.

It's not rocket science, says Tommy.

You just give them the card. You have to sign it first.

Maureen puts the card on a sideboard, takes out a ballpoint pen.

I can't get my signature in that tiny space.

Course you can.

The pen isn't working properly and Maureen's first attempt comes out barely legible. Tommy hands her his pen. This time, the lines are thick and firm, and fit the tiny strip perfectly. Maureen holds it up to the light to admire it.

Now you've done it, says Tommy with a smile. *There'll be no holding her back. You've lit the blue touch paper.*

Maureen isn't like that.

It's like handing out heroin to teenyboppers. You should see Lorraine.

I'm not sure, Charlie, says Maureen. *It's not really necessary.*

I told you, Maureen. Just give it a try. You've been a bit down. Get yourself a nice dress or something.

I don't know.

Hope you've got enough credit on that bloody thing, says Tommy, nudging Charlie in the ribs.

Maureen puts the card into her purse, gives a faint wave, disappears out of the door and heads for the bus stop.

Tommy watches her go.

Up for a pint? says Tommy. *I'm fucking parched.*

I'm on the wagon, says Charlie.

*You're winding me **up**,* says Tommy. *It's mother's milk to you.*

Not any more. I've been overdoing it.

That's the whole fucking **point** *of drinking. Maureen get to you?*

I don't always do what she says.

Women have their methods.

I suppose.

Fucking thumbscrews.

The rack.

They laugh. Charlie giving up the sauce had been Maureen's condition of them moving home. If she was going to have to give something up, so was he. Charlie finds it hard, but the new start makes anything seem possible.

Tommy, Charlie thinks, has been in good spirits lately. He and Lorraine have moved to Chigwell from Theydon Bois, a house with a conservatory and a double garage. Always one step ahead of Charlie. Lorraine is pregnant. She claims to need the extra space.

Lorraine's giving me hell, says Tommy, as he applies a second coat of magnolia vinyl matt to the wall of the front room.

Don't talk to me about it, says Charlie. He is fixing shelves into an alcove. By his feet, ornaments ready to place there. Ceramic figurines. *There's no pleasing her at the moment.*

Tell me something I don't know, says Tommy, raising his eyebrows. *I've just spent ten K on a new kitchen. Fucking Poggen-something. Of course, it's all wrong. Six months ago, it was new carpets. Now she's decided she don't want them. The pattern don't match the curtains. She wants to tear them all up.*

Cheaper to get rid of the curtains, isn't it?

Not by much. It's those ruched ones.

Yeah. They're nice.

She'll get her way. The ayatollah.

Hormones, says Charlie. *It's hormones.*

Although Charlie isn't exactly sure what a hormone is, he

is convinced they have a significant and detrimental effect on his wife's behaviour.

What's it with Maureen?

I think it might be the Change. That time of life.

Well, there's a bright side. No more PMT. No more crimson fucking tide.

Tommy dips his brush in the paint again. The walls are good, the plaster firm. He wants to make reparations. Charlie hasn't quite forgotten about the ceiling. This time it's for free. Charlie puts down his screwdriver, turns to his brother. For all the space between them, for all the subterranean hurt, Tommy is the only person to whom he can confess his life. Sometimes he joins Maureen watching the American chat shows, is amazed by Americans and the readiness with which they unbutton their lives. Nothing to separate thought and word.

She looks on the negative. Here we are. A brand-new home. A fresh beginning. I get on the train into London, into the smoke and shit and dirt. Do my bit in the sweatshop, then I'm home, and it's all there. The trees and that. And Maureen is sitting in a chair in front of the TV, watching some soap. There's no . . .

Get up and go, says Tommy.

*Exactly, Tommy. **Exactly**. Last week I get back, there's not even my dinner. I've got to phone for a pizza. Says she's got nothing to do. There's a thousand things to do here. A million. Evening classes. You name it. This is a can-do place. That's the way you got to be.*

Of course, she can't drive, Charlie. That must make for limits.

*I keep **telling** her. It's as if she's scared.*

What's the buses like?

All right, when they turn up.

How often is that?

Not very often.

What's the neighbours like?

Who knows? You never see anyone.

One of them does driving lessons.

Charlie blinks.

You what?

I seen the car. It's got a driving school . . . thing on top.

Where?

A few houses along. It's there now.

Show me.

Tommy and Charlie walk out into the street, and Tommy gestures in the direction of the house where Charlie and Maureen saw the tall man with the trowel watching them on the day they arrived. There is no car visible.

It was down the side, says Tommy.

The car is parked in an alleyway by the side of the house. This is why Charlie has never noticed it. Sure enough, there is a sign running across the roof of the car: *Journeyz Driving School*.

Charlie notices a face at the window. It is the man who was holding the trowel. His face is impassive. He is sallow, with thinning hair and a small, full mouth. He gazes at Charlie and Tommy impassively. Charlie returns his gaze, gives a smile and holds up his hand, but the man does not respond. Instead he lets the curtain fall, as if someone has caught him acting improperly.

Private around here, aren't they? says Tommy.

It's no bad thing, says Charlie. *It's one of the reasons for being here.*

They hesitate, then walk up the path together. There is no bell, so they rattle the letter box. For several minutes there is no reply. Charlie and Tommy are about to give up when there is a fumbling behind the door. It opens a crack, held back by two security chains. A vertical segment of face appears behind it. No sound emerges from it.

All right? says Charlie.

He can see eyes now. They are wary, unconvinced.

The man behind the door speaks at last.

I'm not buying.

His voice is low, quiet, distinctly London. It has a slightly effeminate, faraway quality.

I'm not selling, says Charlie.

I don't believe in God, says the voice.

Tommy and Charlie are momentarily thrown by this metaphysical revelation. Then Charlie speaks.

Do we look like Jehovah's Witnesses?

What's it about then?

Driving lessons, says Charlie.

Oh. The man pauses. *Office is in the shopping centre.*

Tommy speaks at last.

*This is Charlie. He's your **neighbour**. Three houses along.*

What?

I live here, says Charlie. *Just down the street.*

After several seconds the door chains are unhooked. The door opens. The man's face is plain to see now. He is younger than Charlie thought, but dresses older. He has a pair of trousers with the creases sewn in and a Pringle sweater over a soft-collared shirt. He is tall but not fat, with a well-proportioned body for a man of his age.

I seen you, he says. *Sorry. I've had a few break-ins.*

You can't be too careful, says Tommy. *Lot of rogues about.*

The man hesitates another second, as if wrestling with a dilemma. Finally he holds out his hand.

Peter Horn.

Charlie Buck. This is my brother, Tommy.

Peter Horn's handshake is limp, crushable. When Tommy takes it, Horn almost seems to recoil. Tommy likes to test a man's mettle by the force of his handshake.

Would you like a cup of something?

They follow Peter Horn through a small corridor into the front room. The layout is precisely the same as Maureen and Charlie's. The house is extremely tidy, not a stick out of place.

Horn goes to the kitchen and starts clattering about, while Charlie and Tommy sit at a rectangular pine table with an arrangement of paper flowers on it. It is almost the only decoration. Everything else is functional, giving the space a hollow, faintly sad air.

There is something about the room, its neatness, that means they hush their voices slightly, as if too much volume will disturb the symmetry, throw up dust. There are framed photographs on a sideboard – three young children. There is no sign of a photograph of a wife.

On the wall there is a cabinet with four shotguns in it.

Horn returns with two mugs of tea and a plate of biscuits. Charlie nods at the guns.

You're taking no chances.

They're replicas.

I assumed.

I got real ones. Licensed. I'm in the gun club. Passes the time.

Charlie and Tommy nod. Horn looks around him as if to check that no one is listening.

Want to see?

Horn gets up, feels in his pocket for keys. Charlie looks at Tommy. They rise and follow Horn towards the back of the house. He talks, looking behind him.

You have to have a proper gun cabinet. Two separately keyed locks. Internal ammunition section with a third key. Fixed by four bolts to an exterior wall. Here they are. This is where I keep them. My equalizers.

He leans over, opens the gun cabinet. He seems half in a dream.

It's a wonderful thing, shooting. Got nothing to do with violence, really. It's the silence. The silence before you fire the gun. Just you, the gun, the sights, the target, and total peace.

He takes a pistol out of the cabinet, examines it.

Then BLAM!

He laughs. Tommy looks more impressed than Charlie has ever seen him.

It's a meditative experience, see. From silence to eighty dB of boom. From the stillness of the body to the recoil force. From serenity to destruction. It's all about contrast.

Are they safe? says Charlie.

Guns are not unsafe, says Horn, replacing the pistol. *People are. That's a Bernadelli .22 pistol. Got a lot of stopping power. And that's a Zabala shotgun. One of my favourites. People's choice. Not as deadly as it looks, but excellent intimidation value. The Kalashnikov 7.62mm is a semi-automatic. Nice gun. And then there's the classic Beretta 9mm pistol. That's a nice gun too. That's a beautiful gun.*

Can I . . .

Tommy reaches out towards the gun case, but Horn slams it suddenly shut.

Sorry. That wouldn't be right. Very strict rules. Want another biscuit?

Tommy nods morosely. The three men return to the living room.

Day off, is it? says Charlie amiably, taking a ginger nut.

I've got a shift this afternoon, says Horn, checking his watch.

We're not keeping you? says Charlie.

I've about twenty minutes. How are you and your wife settling in?

Now that he is sat down at the table, Horn begins visibly to relax. His smile is wide, suggesting relief as much as welcome. Another day unmugged.

Mind if I smoke? says Charlie.

I get asthma.

Oh, right. Sorry. Yeah, it's lovely here. My only regret is that we didn't do it years ago.

Up from the Smoke?

Fulham way.

You're joking. Anywhere near Munster Road?

Half a mile or so.

I grew up there, says Horn.

Get away with you, says Charlie.

Now, it seems, they are suddenly firm friends, although Peter Horn left the area thirty years ago, when he was fifteen years old. But he remembers shops, geography, that chime with Charlie. His father had a stall in the North End Road market, selling ornaments. Horn remembers him talking in backslang to the other traders.

He was a real cockney, the genuine article, says Horn proudly, his own voice free-floating, classless estuary English.

They both attack London, the joy of leaving. It is too big, too dirty, too crowded, too expensive . . . Tommy hardly gets a word in edgeways.

Peter is divorced. His wife left him five years ago. He hasn't seen his children since 1982 and now lives alone. She is in Melton Mowbray. He has, he says, a few lady friends, but nothing serious.

Do you want one more? says Charlie, bluntly now, trusting this man because of his accent, because of the way he insists on making a second pot of tea.

That all depends, says Horn, vaguely suggestive.

Nothing like that, says Charlie, unoffended. *I'm talking about my wife, Maureen. She needs some driving lessons.*

I'm not really meant to, says Horn. *You're meant to go through the office.*

Cash in hand, isn't it? A favour for a neighbour, says Charlie. *They can't begrudge that.*

They might.

That nit-picking type of attitude, it gets up my nose, says Charlie.

I suppose they wouldn't find out, says Horn.

What's the ecrip? says Charlie teasingly. He doesn't expect Peter Horn to get the joke.

Through the office, it would cost you a nevis. But I could do it for a rouf.

They both laugh in recognition and delight.

Shake on it. Four quid a lesson, says Charlie.

Done, says Horn.

I'll tell Maureen. She'll be made up.

Maureen is in the shopping centre. Thirty minutes' wait for the bus. If there hadn't been rain in the air, she would have walked. Milton Keynes town centre is only twenty minutes.

Now it is pouring outside. At the North End Road, she would be hunched against the weather. Here it is warm and bright. For the first time, she has a credit card in her purse. She is not even sure how to use it.

People hurry by. The spaces between them are wider than in Fulham. They do not bunch together to push past market traders who have taken too much pavement space, or to avoid the belching cars that squeeze down the road to and away from Fulham Broadway. There she would recognize faces, would smile and nod, exchange a few words. It didn't amount to very much, but she misses the sense she once had that her presence was registered by others. Mrs Patel in the newsagent's would always give her a smile, and they might even gossip. Then there was Marie-Rose, Frank in the greengrocer's. Dolly at the chemist's. She hardly spoke to most of them, but she knew their names and they knew hers. That was important.

Here, she is utterly anonymous. She sees clearly what this gleaming crystal construction is about, where it locates fulfilment. She thinks it crude, yet something in her heart responds. Perhaps she has not been selfish enough in her life. All the young women's magazines speak about self this and self that. She isn't used to thinking about her own life in these terms, but she half understands the language, like the way she can make sense of simple Spanish in Alicante.

Everything is loss, she thinks. Robert gone away. Her home left behind fifty miles away. She did it for Charlie. Her book-keeping jobs abandoned. She sees her face reflected in the plate glass of Boots the Chemist. The lining and stippling of her skin that comes too slowly to be seen yet, having arrived, will never depart.

She looks up and sees high, glazed galleries. There is Marks & Spencer, John Lewis, WH Smith. There are outlets just for ties, just for underwear, just for socks, just for your body. Shopping was focused, specific, separated into discrete desires.

She does her shopping for food in Waitrose. Fruit and vegetables are beginning to appear that she has never heard of, that she is too bewildered by to purchase. Starfruit, kiwi, unnameable orange gourds, strange canary-yellow spheres. Even the lettuces are confusing. The most shocking moment for her is when she finds ready-grated cheese. Such indolence leaves her breathless.

She sticks to potatoes, carrots, peas, oranges and apples. On impulse, she buys four passion fruit, hoping that Charlie will give them a try. Another part of her knows he will not. She bought sun-dried tomatoes a few weeks ago and Charlie refused to believe they were dried in the sun. He said no one would be able to tell the difference if they were dried in an airing cupboard.

The meat is sealed and unimaginable as part of an animal; in the butcher's in North End Road, entire rabbit carcasses would hang there, eyes accusing. She finds this plastic and polystyrene universe pleasantly reassuring, buys pork chops and chicken breasts.

She gets a few luxuries, a bottle of Le Piat d'Or and some of Mrs Bridges's jams and chutneys – Charlie always loved *Upstairs, Downstairs* from where the invented character of Mrs Bridges has been appropriated – and the food shopping is complete. She pays in cash, then sits down on one of the benches to take a breather. She looks around her. Shops aren't shops any more, it seems, but 'emporiums' or 'centres'. Centres are everywhere. She went past a museum earlier, only to find that even this had become a 'heritage' centre. And yet she now feels at the perimeter of her own life.

She checks to see how much money she has left. A few pounds. She slides out the credit card.

She suddenly wants to see how it feels. There is a women's clothes shop just opened in the centre opposite where she sits. It is having a sale and the colourful posters beckon her. She rises to her feet, holding the plastic bags. They feel lighter.

Inside the shop, an assistant immediately rises to her feet and smiles at her.

Would you like me to take that?

Sorry? says Maureen, not at all sure what the woman is talking about.

Can I take your shopping for you? It'll be easier to have a look around.

Oh. Of course. Thank you.

She hands the shopping bags over and the woman puts them down by the counter, then looks again at Maureen, who is simply standing there, fingering her purse. She has held on to her leather shoulder bag.

Is there anything you're looking for in particular? says the assistant.

Her smile is glowing and kind. She seems genuinely concerned that Maureen should make the right shopping choice. In North End Road they ignore you, keep you waiting to take your money.

Not really, says Maureen, smiling.

To cut the conversation short, she starts to self-consciously look at the racks of dresses that line the wall next to her. The clothes are expensive, but Charlie has told her to treat herself. She picks out three, all in a size 16, spots the changing room and disappears into it.

There is a full-length mirror inside. As she removes her clothes she glances at her reflection, but cannot bear to look for long. She sees only loose skin, discoloration, the slackened muscles. All her efforts at keep fit have failed. All her efforts at dieting have failed. She cannot see what others can see, what Marie-Rose repeatedly insisted – that she is still in good shape for her age, that she is still an attractive woman.

She quickly puts on the first dress but it does not suit her, makes her seem larger even than she imagines she is. The second dress is better, but an unflattering colour. She is about to try on the third when she notices a fourth item of clothing that has fallen under the seating bench. Someone has left it there.

She picks it up. The colour is azure, her favourite, and the size is 16. It is mid-length, with a scoop neck and slightly ballooned sleeves. She tries it on. She likes it.

The last dress is the third of the ones she originally brought in. It is purple, longer, more classic in style, in a heavier, slightly elasticated material. She likes this also. She holds the blue one up against the purple one, but cannot choose between them. Both are expensive. She has decided to take Charlie up on his offer, but there are limits.

As she changes back into her old clothes, she glances down at her handbag. She wishes that she could have both dresses.

Suddenly she realizes, with the clarity of truth, that she can. She realizes how simple it is. Without even a shiver of nerve she does something that thrills her. She takes the blue dress that she has found under the seat, folds it, puts it in her handbag and clicks the bag closed. In her other hand, she takes the purple dress. Then, suddenly confident and unafraid, she walks out of the cubicle. The smiling assistant is still there, still smiling.

Anything you like?

Maureen holds out the purple dress.

This one's lovely. I'll have it.

That is a gorgeous dress. Sexy. Special occasion? She takes it from Maureen.

Sort of, says Maureen. *We just moved here.*

Won't this be too big for you?

Maureen accepts the compliment, follows her to the checkout. She feels the weight of her bag. The woman is passing electronic readers across scanning equipment. The price appears in ghostly green letters. The assistant folds the dress carefully and puts it in the bag.

That's going to be £40.

It is now that Maureen realizes she has left her purse in her handbag. The blue dress is exposed on top of it. The assistant gazes at her.

Do you take credit cards? The regularity of her breathing increasing slightly. She is now hoping that the answer will be no.

Of course.

Maureen nods. Then, an icy calm comes over her. The handbag is deep. The assistant cannot possibly see from her position. Maureen blatantly opens the clasp top; the bag gapes. The dress is there, mute testament to her temptation and fall. She moves it aside, uncovers her purse and takes it out of the bag. She does not even close the bag again when the assistant takes the credit card and puts it into the swiping machine. Maureen signs the slip. The card is returned to her. To her amazement, the assistant does not even check the signature. She could be anyone. Quite casually, she replaces the card in her purse, drops it in the open bag, snaps the bag shut and picks up her new purple dress. She gives the assistant a smile even wider than her own.

Thank you very much.

*Thank **you**, madam.*

Maureen retrieves her shopping and then, at a consciously slow pace, leaves the shop. When she is round the corner, out of sight, she feels a joy rise up in her such as she cannot remember.

When she returns home, Tommy has gone. Charlie is in the back garden, which is big, at least seventy-five feet. He is laying track. The Alpine peak has made a reappearance adjacent to a scraggy patch of shrubs. Large-scale station buildings and signal boxes push up against a rockery and a rose bush. He has bought a garden railway, G Scale, the latest thing from Germany. The electric-powered steam-outline locomotives are American style, from the 1880s. He has just put up a miniature road sign next to a hypothetical carriage way; it says, 'Road Narrows'. Big Joe is the driver. Nearby is a farm with artificial dung heap, stable and cheese dairy. There is a smithy and a hay wagon. Charlie is enjoying his break from the more pressing redecorations; it calms him and centres him.

Maureen sees him bending in the garden, but he does not see her. She goes upstairs, almost at a bolt. Above the landing, there is a loft. Maureen hooks down the loft ladder and then ascends. In one hand, she holds her handbag.

There is a working loft light. Maureen, on all fours, makes her way into a far corner. There is an old piece of hardboard which runs astride two joists. Beyond it, only an old plastic shopping bag with the word Asda just discernible on it. Underneath, a wide, shallow gap. She removes the blue dress from her handbag, puts it in a plastic bag and places it in the gap, then replaces the hardboard. Maureen scrambles back down the ladder.

She is filthy. She looks out of the window and sees that Charlie is heading in. Panicking, she goes into the bedroom and begins to remove her besmirched clothes. A few seconds later, his foot is on the stair. She can think of no way to explain this behaviour to him. She sees the second dress, the purple one she has legitimately bought with the credit card, and quickly pulls it on. She sees herself in the mirror; it is flattering, even glamorous. Smoothing her hair, the anxiety gives way to an unaccustomed feeling of power.

Charlie walks in, stops when he sees her.

Dallas on tonight?

It isn't. Maureen flounders for an explanation.

This . . . this is for you, Rock.

For me? Charlie doesn't understand.

It's the dress you bought me. Maureen turns slowly round. There is something feral in her eyes that he barely recognizes. *What do you think?*

What do I think? Charlie swallows air; this moment is completely surprising to him. *I think I'm going to have to take a flipping cold shower, kiddo.*

He puts his arms round her waist. She puts her hands

over his. He moves under them slightly. A smear of dirt appears on the back of Charlie's hand. The combination of the dirt and the pristine, glamorous dress also excites him strangely.

What have you been up to? he says softly.

Maureen starts slightly inside herself, recovers when she realizes that Charlie cannot know what she has done.

Maureen sees Charlie staring at her hands.

I was clearing out some cupboards.

Charlie nods, then starts to kiss her neck. His hands travel towards the top of her thighs. The doorbell rings.

Jesus God Almighty! Leave it! mutters Charlie.

He smells dust on his wife, and sweat. Somehow it arouses him further, but she shakes him off. Her face is flushed, her hair mussed.

We can't. It might be something important.

Before Charlie can reply, she has left the room. Charlie hears her heavy footfall. He cannot work out who it might be, but he curses them. He smooths his clothes down, pats his hair. He hears a man's voice downstairs. Then he remembers who is expected.

He can see Peter Horn standing in the doorway, holding a bottle of wine. Maureen is blocking his path, looking uncertain. She hears Charlie behind her and looks up imploringly towards him. Charlie cannot think: he is amazed by this sudden budding of sexuality. Finally he speaks.

It's all right, Maureen. He's our neighbour.

Peter pushes the bottle at Charlie.

I tried to say. Tried to tell her. I think your wife thinks I'm some sort of weirdo.

Oh, it's not that, says Maureen. *It's just that I wasn't expecting . . .*

No, I told Peter to drop round. He's got a proposition for you.

Charlie winks at Peter. Maureen looks bewildered, continues to block the door.

Let the man in, for heaven's sake, Maureen.

Maureen moves to one side and Peter walks past her, smiling. He brushes against her dress, hands the wine to Charlie, then turns back towards Maureen.

I'm Peter Horn. I live up the road.

He's the man with the trowel, says Charlie.

The gardener. I remember, says Maureen. *What kind of proposition?*

You'll see, says Charlie.

They walk through to the living room, and Peter and Charlie sit at the table while Maureen goes off to the kitchen with the wine. Peter glances out of the window into the garden. He notices the train track.

That's unusual.

My 'toys', you mean?

They're not toys, are they? I've got a friend who does those. There's a real art to it.

Charlie sits forward. He is excited and surprised by this sudden acceptance. Most people make a joke out of it.

What's that one there?

He points to a Leek and Manifold casing to an engine which sits alone on the mantelpiece. It is the gift that Robert bought him, Christmas 1980.

That? That's nothing. Charlie finds this painful to talk about. Where is Robert? *Of course, there are people who are obsessed by the things. Gricers we call them. Never stop going on about their bloody train sets. For me it's just a nice hobby.*

Doesn't it all rust, in the rain?

No, it's made especially for outside.

It's impressive. I can see the appeal.

Most people can't. It's your own private world, you see. You can make it exactly how you want.

Unlike real life, says Peter.

Exactly. **Exactly.**

Maureen arrives with the open bottle, two glasses, and a mug of tea.

Not having any, Mrs Buck? says Peter.

I am, says Maureen. *It's him that's off the juice.*

It's true, says Charlie ruefully. *I'm happy with a cup of tea nowadays.*

Would you like a piece of cake? I baked it myself.

That would be a treat. It was all my ex could do to defrost a treacle tart from Tesco.

Maureen makes an outstanding jam sponge.

You're a divorcé, are you? says Maureen, retreating to the kitchen and returning with a covered cake tray.

Peter tells him about the woman in Melton Mowbray and their three children. Maureen sips at her wine, registers polite concern. The dress accentuates her breasts. She notices when Peter's eyes come back to them a second time. She sips her wine, cuts cake for Peter and Charlie. Again, she feels powerful. She thinks of her stolen dress, secretly above them.

Peter is a driving instructor, Charlie is saying. *He's offering lessons at cost.*

I've got quite a bit of experience, says Peter. *Been qualified for three years now. I've got a better success rate than most.*

Who's the worst driver you ever had? says Charlie. *I bet it was a woman.*

It was a man, funnily enough, says Peter.

Of course it was a man, says Maureen, finishing her wine, laughing.

He ended up killing a woman and her four-year-old child, says Peter ruminatively.

Maureen stops laughing. Charlie scratches his nose.

Did he pass? says Charlie.

There's a silence, and then Maureen begins to laugh again, then Peter, and then Charlie joins in until they are all chorusing, Charlie's dry, coughing laugh counterpointing with the tumbling liquidity of Maureen's and the odd hack-hacking of Peter's.

That's terrible, says Maureen eventually, when the moment is worn out.

Charlie pushes the remaining crumbs from his sponge around his plate.

What do you think, then, Maureen? says Charlie. *Fancy giving it a go?*

I don't see why not, says Maureen brightly. *I'll try anything once.*

IO

Spring, 1986. Maureen has a small biscuit tin which she has kept since the 1950s decorated with two cheery but fading Scotty dogs wearing vast tartan bows around their necks, like Valentine gifts. She takes it from the secret hiding place under the floorboard beneath the bed, alongside a large envelope bulging with cash. She still does not trust banks completely. There is a sizeable sum there, five figures.

The biscuit tin is full of mementoes, scraps of her life. Charlie knows of this box, but has rarely seen it, let alone looked inside it. It is private to her, one of the small fragments of her life that she has managed to keep undisclosed from her husband. She is beginning to understand that located invisibly within secrets there is compacted power.

Maureen opens it. There are a few love letters here, from pre-Charlie romances. Harry Smith, a big gimp of a boy whose letter was virtually illiterate. She had let him kiss her only once. His nickname was Donkey because of his ears. Jack Thomas, the greengrocer's son, hands everywhere, quite good-looking and sweet. He had run off with Henrietta Green and they had got married.

There are fading photographs of her dead mother and father, bus tickets from journeys to the Essoldo and the Gaumont when she was courting Charlie, a typing certificate from secretarial college. Most recently it has been joined by her first accountancy qualification, from the Open University, Milton Keynes. It has put her in good stead. She has part-time work, assisting with the book-keeping at Peter's driving school as well as at a small factory making ceramic models of old English villages that has recently opened in a nearby business park. One of these is also in the tin box. In her tea breaks, she sits and watches the production line taking what seems like an endless stream of these models on their journey towards the clay ovens and then, cooling, towards the painters and finishers. Her model is of a man sitting on a village bench with a pipe and an old beaten hat. She stole it. It was easy and satisfying.

Maureen has to dig down deep into the box for what she seeks. Past their wedding certificate, past Robert's birth certificate, past both sets of the ticket stubs for *South Pacific* when Charlie had taken her to see the film on an early date and when they had gone again, to the theatre this time, on their twenty-second wedding anniversary. She sometimes wonders what will happen to this box after she has gone, and if it will mean anything to anyone else, and what else will appear in it over the next thirty or so years of her existence to testify to her brief and puzzling stay on this earth.

Right at the bottom is what she has been looking for. It is an autographed black and white photograph of Rock Hudson. Her father, in one of his many professional incarnations, had been for a short while a doorman at the Dorchester Hotel, where her hero had briefly stayed in the 1950s. When he had presented her with the photo, she had felt close to fainting. It was like being almost touched by an almost god. His very hand had described these lines and curls in ink.

She does not believe what today's newspapers have said about him. What they have *implied*, for there is no proof. Heterosexuals could catch AIDS too, decides Maureen. If Rock Hudson could get it then no one was safe.

It wasn't long after his death the previous year that the stories started repeating the slander that Tommy had once uttered, which Maureen had shrugged off. Now, as then,

Maureen refused to believe them, turned over the TV if they appeared on the news. He had been married, after all. He was friends with Ronald Reagan. She had watched him in *McMillan and Wife*, in *Dynasty*, loving him even as the creases began to fold into his still-beautiful face. She thought of him kissing Doris Day in a dozen bedroom farces, she remembered when she saw him in *Giant*, how he made her tingle inside.

The way they went on about him being a homosexual was silly. If he was 'gay' – that was the new word, wasn't it? – then why had the papers not mentioned it earlier, all those years he was famous. Now he was dead, of course, they could just slander him all they liked. Jealous, vicious, petty.

She looks at the autograph to see if she can find any signs of effeminacy in his handwriting. It seems to her a strong hand, vital . . . *male*, for heaven's sake. Replacing the photograph and closing the box, she resolves that she doesn't want to hear any more of this nonsense. Everybody is always talking about sex. Like Charlie says, *the world's gone sex mad*. It was all around you, on the telly, selling you face flannels and verucca ointment. Sex has arrived like an IRA fragmentation bomb in the West End, penetrating everywhere. *Are you getting enough? Have you had any lately?*

She wonders if it is safe for her and Peter Horn to carry on making love without a sheath. She has had a coil in her uterus for years and sometimes she imagines that her change of life is under way. Lately, her periods have become irregular. She fears losing what it is that makes her a woman and Peter helps to reassure her that this loss is not irreversible, reminds her that there are other ways of being a woman. They are both lonely.

How did it happen? She had only had three lessons, when his hand covered hers where it rested on the gearstick and she let it remain there. When, instead of returning the car to the driving school, they went to his house and silently, fearfully, it seemed to her, he took her to bed.

The whole thing was extraordinary, improbable, but only for the first few minutes. Then somehow, very quickly, it became the way things *were*, and had been ever since. Peter was a weak man, and he was not particularly intelligent. But his need, his simple desire for Maureen, is like elixir. She feels him filling her up, pushing out the dryness of her years. Inside the walls of his house, inside the echo chamber of his bedroom, forgotten chords are struck.

She returns to the kitchen table, where she has a set of ledgers ready for tallying.

There is a mess overflowing from the rear extension that Charlie has been building. It irritates her. However much work she puts into it, the dust and dirt will not cease their invasion into the main part of the house. She notices a thin film of wood dust on the leather binding of the ledger.

Charlie has borrowed more money to make it possible, and the last of their savings, excepting the sacrosanct cash under the bed, has also gone into the house. A new kitchen, double-glazing. Maureen cannot understand what the point of all this is; the place is already too big for them, and it will take a lifetime to recoup the cost of the new windows on heating bills. But Charlie says it is an investment, freeing up your capital. And it is true the house is swelling absurdly in value, already worth double what they paid for it.

Rivers of wealth flow towards them. Charlie has bought shares in British Telecom with the money he saves through the tax cuts in his pay packet. They were worth triple what he paid for them. It is strange and wonderful, and yet Maureen often sits and thinks of their little council flat, Carol and Mrs Jackson next door, Marie-Rose teasing Maureen's hair into new styles that Charlie never noticed.

Now Charlie spends nearly all his spare hours in the back garden, rain or shine, working at the extension or moving his trains around the fixed track, adding model after model, sometimes whole villages, an entire infrastructure of artificial life. Building other worlds, while the real one remains in his peripheral vision, separately unfolding. He takes photographs of his efforts every week, dates and places the results in an album so that he will have a full record. On the first picture he writes, in black marker pen, 'Here we go! The "great bodge" begins!'

She picks up a perfect, round Florida orange, cuts it into four and sucks at the segments. Even now, it surprises her that she can do this without pain, but for some months now her mouth ulcers have been in unprecedented remission. A tube of Bonjela remains unopened in the bathroom cabinet. Her teeth tear at the flesh of the orange, separate it from the pith, and she swallows.

The taste of the orange is disappointing. Like most of the fruit and vegetables she buys from the hypermarket, the appearance is enticing, symmetrical, proportionate, unblemished, but the flavour is dilute, mediocre.

She is taking her driving test today. It is her third attempt. She will fail, not because she cannot pass but because she wishes to fail. It provides the ideal excuse for her and Peter to be together. They drive out to the countryside, sometimes stop in a tamed wood, and make love in the back of the Ford Fiesta. Peter tugs at her hair as he moves, and she wriggles to push him in further. He wants her to leave Charlie. She does not know what to do. Marriage is a promise that no one else seems to keep, and yet to her the words spoken at the altar carry a sanction that hangs heavy on her life, down all her wedded years and to this day.

Maureen checks her watch. Soon she must leave for work.

*

The workshop for Happy Heritage is much at odds with the products it produces. Instead of a thatched cottage, the works are enclosed within a prefabricated building rather like an enormous garden shed, only windowless, illuminated by huge sheets of chilly neon light. It gives the interior a stark, clinical appearance. There are around fifty people here, working on moulding, glazing, painting, firing, packaging. The figures produced by Happy Heritage are cheap 'collectables', a down-market version of the far more successful 'Lilliput Lane'. The goods are shoddy and break easily, but are individually numbered and hand-painted by a team of poorly paid house-wives who sit at the end of the production line, finishing off the figurines – dray horses, rustic idiots, village pubs and, of course, thatched cottages – at a terrific speed, since they are paid by the piece. The results, which sell through mail order for between £20 and £30, are surprisingly popular, particularly in new towns like Milton Keynes itself.

Maureen works from a small glazed area to the side of the main production floor, as an accounts clerk. On this day, she finds herself daydreaming, staring out at the endless lines of historical gewgaws which pass within her sight. Her boss has gone out for lunch, and she has finished the tallying and checking that are her function here and awaits new tasks. In the meantime she sits and toys with the model of three smiling children by a village pond that she has in her pocket, out of sight. It is worth very little, but, as usual, the theft of it gives her a strange glow inside. She will give it to Peter that afternoon, she decides.

She wonders what Charlie is doing on the picket line, wishes he was back at work. There is something awful, she decides, about a man without work. Not because they need it more, or deserve it more, but because for Charlie, for *men*, it is the best part of what they are. Maureen senses that she is more than what she does, but Charlie is not. What would Charlie be without his craft? She sees the fear in him, even now, that he might lose the battle, that he will be thrown upon the ever growing human scrapheap that hides behind the unemployment statistics.

She stares through the window at the multitude of figures. Most of them are women, with bad skin and cheap make-up. Women, she supposes, like herself. Some are fixed over their work with bleak, lined faces, but others are laughing and joshing with each other. She *likes* her own sex, she decides. Men have been ruined by the tight packing they are pushed into. They have the power, they have the money, but they are shadows somehow. Even Peter is a shadow, but Maureen believes he can be redeemed in a way Charlie could not; the grooves of who he is are not so deeply etched.

She yawns, checks her watch, sees her supervisor approach through a distant portal at the edges of the workspace. It's not like being with Marie-Rose and the girls. There's no fun in it. But the alternative, dabbling around the house all day while Charlie saws and plasters and screws and hammers at his pointless extension, seems to her the worst option, by far. She adjusts her clothing, checks her face in the mirror. How can Peter find it beautiful? But he does.

She returns at three in the afternoon. Peter has arranged for them to meet at his house. She sees his car in the driveway and knows that he will be inside. There will be fresh flowers in the bedroom. The articles in the cupboards, once chaotic, have been rearranged, all Maureen's work. Female touches have begun to appear in a stark and functional male environment. Pots of herbs, new curtains. She is seeping, like fresh blood, like water, into his life. Maureen has a drawer here with underwear, clean clothes.

She walks in, using her own key. Peter is lounging on the sofa, reading *Popular Mechanics*. He does not get up when she arrives, merely looking up and smiling.

You're early.

The bus was actually on time. She reaches into her bag. *I bought you a present.*

She hands the figure over to Peter, removes her coat.

That's lovely, Mo. Thanks ever so.

He places the figure in a space on the mantelpiece, then returns to the sofa and picks up his magazine again.

Make us a cup of tea, will you, while you're up?

Maureen blinks. She runs her tongue across the inside of her lip, searching for ulcers, but there are none. Peter's request hits her, for some reason, like a barely withheld slap. A quizzical look slides across her face. For the first three months of their affair, on her arrival, Peter always had a bottle of chilled wine ready and little presents for her. He fussed and complimented, he grabbed her the moment he saw her. Lately, as his confidence has grown, these attentions have been fading. Yet she is convinced that he loves her. She cannot believe she would have done something so enormous with someone who did not love her. The perfunctoriness of his acceptance of her gift also rears up within her. Then she feels a smile of supplication generating itself inside her, of service. It begins to find its way on to her features. Peter settles more deeply into the sofa. Maureen snaps the expression back, crushes it with her new will.

Make it yourself.

What?

You heard me. Make it yourself. Who am I, Mandingo?

Who's Mandingo when he's at home?

He's a slave.

Peter puts down the magazine, looks suddenly regretful.

To Maureen's surprise, instead of snapping back at her, he jumps up and grabs her by the waist.

I'm sorry, Maureen. What was I thinking of?

She is vaguely astonished. She had not known what powers lay beyond regretful smiles and the soft applications of guilt.

After a glass of wine, which Peter fetches from the fridge, they play a game of checkers. It is not always just sex now, though the wine is loosening Maureen up, softening her. She thinks about going upstairs. A vase of flowers catches her eye on the windowsill; the flowers are dying.

You should change the water, Pete.

They're too far gone now.

I'll get rid of them.

She goes to the window bay, and, as she gathers the flowers, she glances up. She sees Charlie's Allegro parked in the bay. She immediately takes a step back, flushes.

Charlie's back.

Peter laughs.

You look like you've been caught with your hands in the till. Don't worry. There's nothing peculiar about going to visit a neighbour for a cup of tea.

But why's he back? There must be something wrong.

I doubt it. He's probably gone on strike again for something or other. Maybe one of the journalists picked up one of the printers' pencil sharpeners.

He's already on strike. He's on a full day's picket. I'd better go.

Peter says nothing, stands up, walks to where she stands by the window and puts his hands on her breasts, in full view of anyone who happens to glance in.

You can spare five minutes first, can't you?

She shakes him off angrily.

Don't be stupid! People have got nothing better to do in this street than gossip with each other.

Peter takes a step back.

So what if he does find out! He needs to find out. He needs to be told. This is driving me up the wall. What's he got to offer you any more? You want someone who treats you right, someone who can look after you. All he thinks about are his silly trains. Trains and that extension . . . Half his life he's down the MFI warehouse, the other he's Casey Jones. You said yourself you're just going through the motions, you said yourself you hate it when he touches you, you said yourself . . .

Maureen pulls on her coat, her back to Peter, who is now jabbing a finger in her direction.

Shut up.

What?

*Shut **up**, Pete. Charlie is my husband. We've got a kid together.*

*A **grandchild**,* she adds to herself silently.

She thinks of little Charlie, with a stab of guilt beneath her heart. Robert has promised her he will tell his father soon, that he will be ready soon. The training for the new job is finished, he is respectable.

You don't just kick twenty-five years under the carpet.

*Twenty-five years, twenty-five minutes, what's that got to do with it? The past is all . . . it's all in your **head**, isn't it? It's happened, it's gone. It's what was. **Now** is what matters. Now this minute. You and me here in this room.*

*Yes, and now my husband – my **husband** – has come home, and I've got to go and see what's the matter.*

*I bet you'll make **him** a cup of tea,* says Pete with a sulky dip in his voice.

Maureen turns.

I will make him a cup of tea. And I'll give him a biscuit as well.

Good. You want to throw him a bone as well? He's like a bloody pet more than a husband. Anything he's ever done is because of you.

Goodbye, Pete.

Goodbye. There is a violent silence. *You **cunt**.*

She slams the door after her, tries to calm her breath. Pete swings the door open after her, his eyes wide with desperate regret.

Maureen, I'm sorry I said that. You just hurt me. I didn't mean it.

But Maureen begins walking. Pete runs out after her, grabs the sleeve of her coat.

Maureen, I . . .

The Sikh who lives opposite at number 7 and runs what Charlie says is a sweatshop out on a business park in Bletchley emerges from his front door. He raises a hand in greeting.

For Christ's sake, Pete. Behave, will you?

Sorry. Sorry.

He raises his hand in belated acknowledgement to the Sikh, and Maureen waves cheerily. Then she turns to Pete, hisses under her breath although the street is otherwise empty.

I'll give you a call later, Pete. Now let go of my coat and stop making a scene.

Peter, after holding on for a beat more, lets go and retreats, while Maureen, her face flushed, moves off towards number 12.

As she covers the hundred or so yards back to her own house, thoughts flash into her head unbidden. Despite her fury at Pete, she is amazed to find her own life so much like a soap opera, and is secretly excited. The shouting, the held arm. *Cunt.* It is as if, viewed through a new window, her existence has refracted into fresh colours. Emotions have become swollen. Risk scatters possibility in all directions. She is the thief of Peter's heart, of a widening range of designer clothes from carefully lit chain stores, of heritage figurines, of time itself. Now she expects a new drama. In her head there is an invisible spotlight illuminating her as she takes each step towards home.

Walking through the door, she knows something is wrong, because Charlie is sitting at the table. Simply sitting there, staring at nothing. This is something he never does. He keeps himself busy from the moment he gets inside, tidying up, setting to work on the house, painting his models for the American trains in the garden. If Charlie sits, it is with a newspaper or the television on, or one of his Mantovani records playing at a sensible volume. But now he just sits, doing nothing. It sends a tremble of apprehension through Maureen.

Something else she notices. He has a highball glass of clear liquid in front of him and she knows it cannot be water, because Charlie always drinks water out of a tumbler. In highball glasses he drinks spirits. She feels certain it is a glass full of vodka or gin. He has not had an alcoholic drink since they moved to the house. Charlie, still not registering her presence, takes a swig that drains half the glass. Maureen searches her vocabulary of phrases for the right thing to say. She has given up watching soap operas, finds them empty and pointless now, but nevertheless she wonders what Alexis Carrington would say, or Angie if it were Dirty Den. She believes with absolute certainty now that Charlie has dis-covered her affair with Peter. Hovering above her fear is a kind of excitement about the largeness her life is now attaining. Charlie looks up. His eyes are only slightly hazy. There is no accusation in them, only astonished grief. Then he looks down at the table again.

Charlie. What's wrong?

It is not the phrase she had hoped for. It seems inadequate and hangs thinly in the air. She waits for the laying to waste of their life. Maybe twenty-five years is nothing after all, just connections glowing darkly in the brain.

They sacked me.

What?

They sacked me, Maureen. They sacked everyone. Five thousand of us. Just like that.

Maureen can take enough of this in to feel relief, then registers guilt chasing it. The shame in her delight that Charlie has been sacked rather than discovering her affair.

Who sacked you? Why? she says dumbly.

Charlie still does not look up.

Mike Sunderland was right all along, wasn't he? They're only out for profit. They don't care about nothing else. The years I've worked for that firm. I got this letter. It's like one of those what-do-you-call-its. A form letter. I've got six months' notice. No offer of redundancy even.

Nothing at all? I thought they had an £80 million fund.

That was before we went on strike. It's been withdrawn.

It's a bluff. Isn't it? They're always bluffing.

Look at this.

He holds out a newspaper with a paragraph circled. A quote from an anonymous member of News International.

'Once these people go out, it will be the last time they do it, they won't come back, never, never.'

Maureen searches desperately for something to say now that will match up to the enormity of the event. But all she can manage is her lifelong default, her English embrace.

Oh, Charlie. Do you want a cup of tea?

Charlie sighs gratefully.

Yes. Yes, please. That would be very nice.

The uttering and execution of this familiar ritual is in fact comforting for them both. When Maureen sets the cup in front of him, she touches his shoulder with the flat of her hand. It is as close as she can come to an embrace, with Peter's memory so near. She feels the fierce sourness of betrayal in her stomach for the first time.

What are you going to do?

Charlie looks up, determination in his eyes.

I'm not going to end up down the dole, I'll tell you that. All that 'gissa job' type of attitude. No. I'm not my son. I won't be my son.

Charlie is shaking his head furiously. Maureen speaks gently, for fear of pushing him into some territory where no return is possible.

They call them job clubs now.

Now Charlie is practically shouting.

You can call a duck a sausage roll, but it's still a duck. Anyway. I'm going to fight it. We're all going to fight it, to the hilt.

How can they bring the paper out without you all?

It's the bloody electricians' union. Bloody scabs. They're doing our jobs. Nonces, untrained Herberts. If that Australian **convict** *thinks he can do things here like he does down under, he's got another think coming. We're going to smash his new plant to pieces. We're going to bring him to his knees. Our leader says he'll be on his knees in two weeks. We've got a right. A right to work, the right to do a job, the right to work at Wapping. We're going to rise, like, like . . .*

He takes another swig of the vodka, his eyes blur another degree.

. . . like rats from the rubble! That's it, Maureen, like rats from the rubble!

Maureen gently takes the glass of vodka out of his hand.

This ain't the answer, Pete . . . I mean, Charlie.

What?

Charlie looks up, confused, ploddingly processing the words he has just heard. Maureen feels panic rise up in her, but packs it back down.

Charlie, Charlie. Sorry, darling. I've been spending so much time on these driving lessons, I don't know if I'm coming or going. Pete's giving me extra lessons before my next test.

Charlie grunts. He feels no suspicion, merely resentment at the expense of the lessons and the inadequacy of his wife in being unable to pass the driving test.

Give the glass back, Maureen. It's just the one. I've had a rotten day.

You've not drunk since we've been in this house. Don't you think it's a bad idea to start again now? Please, Charlie, for me.

He looks at his wife, contemplates momentarily what his life would be without her. Something gives way within him. He nods.

Put it down the sink if you want. I don't even like the taste any more.

She leans over to her husband and gives him a peck on the cheek.

OK, Rock.

You're my rock. We'll pull through this, kiddo. You wait and see. Things are going to get back on course, Mo.

He looks at the extension.

I don't know how I'm going to finish that blooming thing without any money coming in.

We'll manage somehow. I've got my little bit of pin money. I know that you'll get your job back.

It's a good investment, Maureen. You'll see.

I know, Charlie. I know it is.

And she reaches across and kisses his cheek, smiling determinedly, relentlessly, as she does so.

II

Charlie, in a cloth cap and thin brown scarf, sits on a concrete bollard in the fading dusk, now being supplanted by blazing spotlights from within Fortress Wapping. He is surrounded by a jostling mass of bodies. There are thousands of people outside the News International enclosure. Charlie has never seen it so jammed up. He stares at the extraordinary mixture of ages and faces and expressions. But there are only six pickets allowed outside the gates. The rest of the 6,000 or so demonstrators and pickets are kept back across the Highway by the thousand or more police, some mounted, most on foot. Many carry shields and batons; kept in police buses for hours on end, they are bored and keen for a fight. Charlie thinks to himself he must invite Tommy along one of these days. He'd have a field day.

Like the last big action in '79, it has the texture of a kind of war: long periods of boredom, interspersed with moments of excitement, rage, even fear. The police here terrify him. He has seen women and children beaten to the ground. In the pub he was drinking in earlier, they came in mob-handed and pulled about two dozen people out, laid into them, no provocation. These police are not like the avuncular coppers he has seen on TV – they wave their wage packets at the strikers from their buses, laugh as they attack. He hadn't imagined there were so many Tommy Bucks in the Met.

Above and in front of him, the high fences, protected by rolls of razor wire sometimes three layers deep. The cutting steel butterflies wound through the thick cable. Around here, all the old warehouses are being turned into apartments. Tower Bridge is lofty, above the fray, in the middle distance.

He looks behind him and notes the banners that range above the crowd. Most are union banners, but there are also the SWP, Class War, Save the Whale. Some of Class War wear balaclavas and carry black flags. To his disgust, Charlie notes that one of them has impaled a pig's head on a spike on the railings.

He wonders what whales have got to do with anything. Charlie doesn't care about whales, about class, about beagles that smoke two packs of Silk Cut a day. He wants his job back. He wants the past, intact. He wants a brown wage packet with real money inside that he can give to Maureen every week, that she can squirrel away under the floorboards.

Lloyd stands next to him, shifting slowly from foot to foot. A Volkswagen Beetle passes, moving very gradually, plastered entirely with strike flyers and stickers, speakers blaring from the roof. In the air, the smell of cinnamon, from the old spice warehouses. There are dozens of familiar faces from the old print works at the Gray's Inn Road, and many more he does not recognize. Daytrippers. A scattering of football supporters that have somehow found their way into the mêlée. There are a number of women with kids. One revealed her breasts to him as he made his way along the lines. She has a sticker over each nipple: 'Don't Buy the *Sun*'.

He feels out of place, ridiculous. He wants to get on the train back to Milton Keynes, but this is a twenty-four-hour picket and he is committed to sitting out another five hours yet. He tries to concentrate on the book he has brought with him to pass the time, a Ken Follett thriller. He likes it, the way the plot moves along so fast, all so neatly tied up in the end. Life with shape, and justice, and retribution.

He decides he is hungry. A hundred or so yards away is one of several refreshment vans that regularly attend the picket.

Want a snack, Snowball?

From one of those vans?

No, I thought I'd pop round to the Savoy. Get some pheasant and game chips.

I'm not eating from those vans. Cat food. Food for dogs. Dogs in the food. Hyacinth made me up something. I don't like it tonight, Charlie.

You don't like what?

The vibe-ration. There's something ugly here.

I'm looking at him.

Lloyd grins, rubs absently at his nappy hair with his mutilated hand. The first time he saw it, it revolted Charlie, but now it is part of Lloyd, the absence comprises part of his friend. He would be disappointed if it were somehow made new.

This crowd is ugly. All you people are ugly. I'm the only, the prettiest man in Wapping, London. Cause I never did fight. Cause I looked after my beautifulness.

Charlie regards him. A spotlight is shining down on him from somewhere, making his skin shine. A thought comes that embarrasses him: Snowball *is* pretty, or at least handsome, a fine-looking man in his middle years. Tall, still powerfully built, with a nose that was angular rather than flattened out, big liquid eyes, high cheekbones. Perhaps his stories about himself and the ladies were true, that he *was* a blade, a one-time Notting Hill dandy. But Charlie dismisses the idea as too far-fetched. Snowball, of Snowball and Hyacinth, of Willesden Green Dominoes Club, hanging round with Johnny Edgecombe and the Keeler mob. Even the stories about him being a boxer he can't quite believe, although the footwork looks authentic every time Snowball does his party piece.

*See, even **you** fancy me, Charlie. I can see the way you look at me. But you too ugly, bwoy. Maybe I'll give Maureen an opportunity one day. A fine woman for a back-a-bus like you.*

Charlie shakes his head, measures the density of the crowd between him and the refreshment van. He decides it's worth a try.

Are you sure now, Snowball? Nothing at all?

Lloyd's smile has faded.

It feels bad here tonight, Charlie. I can feel it in my water, in my piss, Charlie.

Charlie's hunger gnaws at him.

We're too old for this kind of thing, Snowy. This is Mike Sunderland's department.

Not any more, says Lloyd bitterly.

No, says Charlie.

You know what he said to me, Charlie?

You saw him?

I bumped into him, yeah. On the street. Coincidence. I didn't want to talk to him much, but he insisted.

You talked to him? That scab? Wave a salary rise and health package and promotion, and he's so far up Murdoch's arse he could clean his teeth for him. Some bloody socialist.

*I **talked** to him. He was justifying it all, you know. Said his therapist had helped him to think it all through. That he was just suffering from guilt, see.*

*And the therapist **cured** him.*

*That's right. That's what he said. The therapist cured him. So now he could take the money, see. Because if he didn't someone else would, and that they would probably be a fascist and a racist and that he would be better inside working inside the system, he used that word, the **system**, than being out on strike and everything. That he would be more use.*

You let him buy you a cup of coffee?

No, Charlie. I wouldn't let him give me a glass of water if I was starving.

Or dying of thirst.

Or even that, yeah.

Talking of food, Snowball . . .

He turns away from Lloyd.

I'll be back in a minute.

He fights his way through the crowd to a tea van called the Costa Del Wapping. They offer the usual roadside standards, plus some local specials: 'Chilli Con Wapping' and 'Wapping Hot Pot'.

Do you want a coffee, mate? says the vendor, a short pale man with a thin head of greased black hair that curls over his collar and then flicks upward.

I brought my own.

Charlie holds up the Thermos that Maureen has prepared for him. As he does so, he feels a pressure in his bladder, the faint urge to piss. The Portaloos are a hundred yards away through the thickest part of the crowd. He decides to hold it till the crowd thins out a little.

What else, then?

I'll try the hotpot.

He nibbles at the hotpot as he makes his way back to his place. Not bad.

The police are zipped into boiler suits with no numbers or ranks to identify them. They are shifting around nervously. Charlie decides Lloyd is right about the atmosphere. Something sour in the air. He pushes through the dense crowd, reading the banners as he goes. 'Murdoch is Bad News', 'East Enders Reclaim the Streets'. The locals have had it tough, hassled, stopped and searched, just for living here. There are people selling badges and left-wing paraphernalia. In the distance he can hear the sound of a marching brass band, some far-off procession approaching.

The jostling increases. As he makes it back to Lloyd he hears a chant from some of the balaclava-wearers, but cannot make out what it is. There is a bus coming towards the gates. Charlie looks towards the line of policemen straddling the Highway. Behind them, mounted police, batons hanging from their saddles. It is strange to see them here, hundreds of them, when no crime has been committed other than to strike.

Behind the police lines there are raised terraces of benches on which the press and television crews arrange themselves, like spectators at an arena. At this moment, Charlie hates them as vultures, but thinks they are also maybe protection, although cameras and notebooks are sometimes snatched from them.

Now he can make out the words of the chant, which is coming, he thinks, from the Class War lot. Or is it the Trots? They are goading the police line.

Who's got the brain tonight?
The sergeant's got the brain.

The policemen's faces are tight, angry. Suddenly, without warning, the crowd begins to surge past the invisible barrier that stands at the edge of the Highway. The police tighten their ranks. An officer reaches for a megaphone. The reason for the sudden press of bodies, a coach full of strike-breaking workers, comes into Charlie's view. There are cries of 'scab' and 'blackleg' as it approaches the compound gates. It is becoming impossible for Charlie to read his book. He gives up and puts it into the pocket of his car coat. The noise increases. Lloyd leans over to him.

Who is it in there?

Can't see. Hacks, I think.

Pen-pushing pricks . . .

A few stayed out.

Twelve.

They think we got it soft.

We got it soft? Us? With their expenses? Sitting on their arses all day.

There is the sound of a breaking bottle, then another chant begins, something about Margaret Thatcher. Charlie is aware of the police advancing slightly.

What's she got to do with it, then? says Charlie.

What's the whales got to do with it and all? says Lloyd.

They're like printers, isn't it? Getting extinct.

Charlie and Lloyd are being pushed along by the force of the crowd now. They are coming closer and closer to the police line. The officer with the megaphone begins to speak. It is hard to hear what he is saying. Charlie strains his ears.

If . . . do not . . . vacate . . . ten minutes . . . consequences . . .

A man with an Anti-Nazi League badge pushes hard up against Charlie. He knocks the Thermos out of Charlie's hand. Charlie thinks he looks scruffy and needs to wash his hair. The man turns angrily.

Watch it, mate.

Charlie turns in astonishment, bends down to pick up his Thermos, grips it tightly. He feels suddenly angry.

Who are you to . . .

But when he straightens up, the man is gone, disappearing into the crowd towards the police.

A man with a megaphone is standing on an upturned box, appealing for calm. Charlie recognizes him as a SOGAT official. He looks harassed and confused. Charlie cannot understand what he is saying.

A flashgun goes off. There are reporters from other newspapers, lights for television cameras.

The crowd is acting as one now. A large bullet-headed man whom Charlie recognizes as one of the printers from the works at Bouverie Street is pushing past. He comes very close to Lloyd, is pushed right up against him. Amid the tumult he hears half a muttered sentence.

. . . coons doing here?

He looks up at the printer, who has now pushed past Lloyd, who does not appear to have heard. Charlie thinks of remonstrating, but the man is big and he frightens Charlie. The man with the cropped head turns to Charlie now.

This is a fucking circus. With pigs. He looks back at Lloyd. *Pigs and monkeys.*

Charlie nods, mutters that it is, gives an automatic, polite smile. The pressure in his bladder is worsening. The crop-headed man pushes past him.

Someone is standing on his foot. He feels garlic breath in his face.

Now a police megaphone is sounding, this time distinctly. The voice, even through the distorting filter of the amplification, is hectoring, edged with menace. This time, Charlie hears the message clearly.

Anyone in this area after I count to ten will be arrested.

Charlie wants to comply but is trapped by the crowd. Off to his right a sudden mêlée. He tries to see over the heads of the men in front of him but can make out only a disturbed ripple in the crowd about thirty feet off. There are shouts of anger, cries, indecipherable curses. Then the tussle dies down as suddenly as it flared up.

Behind him, there is some singing – West Ham Football chants. The confusion grows. The coach, windows covered by wire mesh, comes closer to the compound gates, still impeded by a wedge of bodies that have toppled police crowd barriers. Ahead, by the gates, the police stand firm, but Charlie gets a sense of tensing, of imminent release.

A bottle flies over his head and crashes in front of the police lines. Another shout:

Over the wall we go! All coppers are bastards!

And:

Pig! Pig! Pig!

The coach inches forward. Demonstrators are spitting and hammering on the sides. Charlie is aware that the police have begun to beat their shields. He sees a video camera being held over the heads of the swaying crowd. A policeman knocks it down. TV lights illuminate the side of the coach. He squints, and sees nervous faces at the window. He thinks that he glimpses a bearded face with a roll-up sticking out.

He checks again, is sure. Mike Sunderland, looking pale, face turned slightly away from the window. He has been promoted to chief sub-editor, features. Charlie sees him turn towards another journalist. Then he does something that shocks Charlie to the core. He laughs. He throws back his head and laughs.

You have five seconds to comply.

Charlie is freezing. He looks at the warm fug in the coach, feels a surge of intense, bewildering anger. The glint of a silver Rolex on Mike Sunderland's wrist. He feels the Thermos of coffee in his hand and, before he can think what he is doing, hurls it in the direction of the coach. His throw is weak and it falls short and to the left, hitting a policeman on the shoulder. The top, which is only loosely attached, falls off, and hot liquid spills on the policeman's uniform. The policeman winces and opens his mouth, bellowing. Charlie sees this clearly, feels shocked and regretful, then suddenly frightened, as the policeman points in his direction. Other policemen follow the direction of the finger.

There are ten policemen on horseback. They too follow the policeman's finger to where the flask of coffee came from. The moment holds, seems to be frozen, and then the coach progresses slightly more quickly now, nearly at the gates, which slide open behind the police lines.

Suddenly, the front line of police, the snatch squads in there to pick out troublemakers, start to move forwards and the horses break into a trot. The line of pickets bends and breaks, and in an instant Charlie is aware of truncheons being used some twenty feet in front of him, and screams of pain. The horses are headed in his direction and he feels a surge of panic.

Again, a bullhorn from the union representative, telling everyone repeatedly, uselessly, to keep calm. Missiles begin to fly towards the mounted police. Charlie looks round desperately. From behind him too, now, he sees police pressing the crowd in between riot shields. He has not seen fully kitted-out riot police before and their appearance is terrifying, inhuman. They are pressing the crowd together, squeezing it out. He looks forward once more. A brick has hit the coach as it moves through the open gates.

Scab! Scab! Scab!

Lloyd turns to him. His face, normally the warm colour of coffee cake, has drained into a sickly grey.

Let's go! Let's go! says Charlie.

But they cannot move. The crowd has pressed even closer, and they are being carried by the current of anger, retribution, the spirit of the ruck, moral indignation. Charlie cannot believe this is happening, feels it has nothing to do with him.

Lloyd is trying to say something else to him, but Charlie becomes aware of a police helicopter hovering above which swoops lower and lower, blocking out his voice. A searchlight comes from above now, dancing close to where he stands. The light is ghastly. On either side, police advance, half with riot shields and truncheons, half on horseback. Through the infernal row of the helicopter, he makes out cries of pain and anger. The police on horseback advance, raining down blows. He sees the crop-headed man fall to the ground under a blow from above.

Charlie feels his heart beating so hard it seems to be knocking against the thin cage of his chest. He does not know which way to turn. There is a blow on his head; someone has thrown a beer can at the police line and it has struck him. Warm liquid dribbles down his face. He assumes it is blood, gives a cry, raises his hand to the wound. He examines the liquid. To his amazement it is clear, yellow. He raises it to his nose and recoils. The can is full of urine.

An elbow is in his ribs. He feels he is going to faint. The noise is incredible. The coach is through the compound gates now. Suddenly things start to quieten and the crowd around him begins to loosen; the panic within him abates slightly. He looks around once more.

To his horror, the mounted police are continuing in his direction, pointing at where he and Lloyd stand. He can see the faces of the policemen on the horses now and they seem to him robotic, inhumanly determined. The horses are massive, steaming in the cold air. He turns the other way, but the line of riot police is still there. Another protester goes down under the horses' hooves. A placard with 'Reclaim the Streets' scrawled on it goes flying.

Charlie now feels an overwhelming, irresistible desire to piss. He looks around desperately for an alternative, then grimaces, relaxes himself. He feels a warm stain spread out from his groin. Then another sudden movement of the crowd, a clearing of the stream, and the horses are nearly upon them.

Charlie turns to try and move away; he hears voices from above. The policeman who got hit by the Thermos is right up in the front line of horses, shouting.

It was the . . . there . . . Can you see him . . . there! There! With the . . .

The policeman, Charlie realizes, is pointing at Lloyd. With amazing swiftness, the police at the front of the line move in his direction. An elbow hits Charlie in the guts. He buckles up in pain, then recovers himself, searches the horizon for Lloyd once more. He locates him immediately. Fixed plain in the field of his vision, a sight that liquefies his guts, stings his eyes.

Lloyd has taken up the boxer's stance, the stance he took in the pub before the fight at the Finsbury Park Astoria, legs apart, fists raised, chin high. In that moment he appears as a tableau, or a statue, lit by fierce blue spotlights, long shadows thrown on to the bodies behind him, elegant, poised, nothing but proud disdain on his face.

He looks like a photo Charlie once saw in an encyclopedia showing a Victorian boxer squaring up to an equally courteous and posed opponent. In front of him, three policemen, truncheons raised high in the air. Charlie almost seems to feel the blow as the first strikes Lloyd square in the face.

He wants to go back and *do* something, explain to them that it was all a mistake, that it wasn't Lloyd, it was him, Charlie Buck, and that the Thermos was aimed at Mike Sunderland, not the police, but instead he merely speaks at a pitch barely higher than his normal voice, a sound that is immediately swallowed up by the crowd noise.

Leave him alone.

A policeman nevertheless turns towards where he is, as if he has heard, and starts moving in his direction. He panics, turns, and so senses rather than sees Lloyd go down under three, four blows to the head. He is too scared once again to do anything. Suddenly a gap in the crowd opens, like a gasp of relief, and he is able to break through it.

He turns once more, sees Lloyd holding his head while he gets dragged away as if into the maw of a great blue, hydra-headed beast. In the direction Charlie is travelling, the riot police advance step by step. The line comes to an end about twenty yards to his left. Charlie makes for the gap, hoping that he can break past it and out into Wapping Lane, where the crowd has scattered into free-moving pockets.

He pushes and shoves. There are women in the crowd. One to his amazement has a baby on her back. Both the child and the mother are screaming. He stops and shouts at the woman, asks if she wants any help. Tears run down the woman's face. All he can hear is, *Fascists!*

Why has she brought a baby to a place like this? He wants to help her, wants to go back and help Lloyd, but he sees the end of the line, sees an escape from the terrible crush and threat.

He suddenly breaks through. A thirty-foot dash and he will be free. The last policeman on the line of riot police is moving into the crowd and away from him. A gap opens in the crowd and he runs to make his way through it. Out of the corner of his eye, he sees a single policeman peel off and shadow his course. He increases his pace and the policeman increases his also. He is shouting something.

He feels a huge panic squeeze the air out of his lungs and he tries to run, but trips over the kerb that is the only barrier now between him and the apparent freedom of Wapping Lane. He tries to get up, but he realizes without looking that the policeman is above him. He hears his breath, seems to feel his shadow.

He bunches his hands over his head, waiting for the blows

to come, arches his body downwards to protect his genitals. He winces and bends, catches the sour aroma of his own urine drifting up from his groin.

The impact does not come. Instead, he feels a hand on his shoulder. The helicopter has retreated and the sound begins to drop. Moments pass. He is vaguely aware that the crowd is drifting away from him. The hand is moving, trying to turn him upwards.

He gradually uncurls himself, waiting for the retribution that must now come. Risks a glance upwards in what is left of the light. The policeman is invisible behind a visor, but he sees that he is slowly, almost tentatively, lifting the visor up. As it rises, he feels the knot of fear in his stomach change its configuration. The sick sensation now is one of recognition, of gathering, horrified amazement.

Robert.

He reaches up to his head, brings his hand down, and sees it is covered in sticky darkish brown liquid, vaguely understands that he is bleeding. Robert's face is stricken. Other policemen behind him are beating their shields.

Dad, I've . . . There's a first-aid post . . .

Get away from me.

I wanted to tell you. I was waiting until . . . I thought . . .

He tries to get hold of Charlie's arm, but Charlie, eyes wide, shrugs him fiercely off.

This is Tommy's doing! Tommy put you up to this!

Charlie feels himself backing off, Robert becoming very slightly smaller in his vision, his perspective shrunk. Robert seems unable to move.

Uncle Tommy . . . it was his idea but . . . I'm not like . . . It's two years of training . . . a professional career . . .

How much you making? How much you getting? What's the going rate now for a tickle?

Nothing. Nothing, Dad. I'm not the same as Uncle Tommy, I'm just trying to . . .

You're just like him! You're just like him! You're just like him!

Then Charlie senses a space clearing behind him, sees Robert take a step forward, reach out an arm, and Charlie recoils, turns, runs, doesn't stop running until his breath chokes in his throat and he can feel the very trees and fronds of his lungs running with salt and acid and the bitterest of bile.

12

It was the only decent job he could get.

Charlie is lying in bed with Maureen. Maureen has told him the whole story – about how Robert has been training these past years, keeping it all concealed. About his unimagined grandson, about how Robert needs to support his family now. Charlie feels exhausted by all the new knowledge, scoured by it. He hates Maureen for her deception, but also understands it somehow, a mother's love for her son the strongest thing.

His pyjamas feel uncomfortable, twisted on his body, and he cannot get them straightened somehow. He has his hand down the back, scratching his buttocks. Stress expresses itself for him here, ignobly, in rashes and itches. Maureen notices but tries to ignore it. He and Maureen lie like this, six inches of clear space between them. The pillows, freshly laundered by Maureen, have a faint floral aroma that Charlie enjoys, better than real flowers.

What was he doing before?

Oh, this and that. Rubbish jobs, says Maureen sadly. *Like working in burger bars. Didn't have much in the way of qualifications. The manager had a degree from bloody Cambridge. What chance did he have?*

No wonder he didn't want to see us.

*He didn't want to see **you**, Charlie. Because he thought you'd be ashamed of him. So he heard about police recruitment – from Tommy, yes from Tommy, of which he didn't approve but went for an interview anyway. They **wanted** him. Can you imagine what it* *feels like to be wanted, when McDonald's don't even want you? Big call for police. He was on the miners' strike too. Made a fortune, he says. He says he likes it. He likes being a copper.*

What does he like about it? The kickbacks?

No kickbacks, Charlie. Robert's not like that. He likes the uniform. It gives him a bit of respect. You don't get much respect doling out Bender Brunchburgers, do you?

I can't believe he would go up against his . . . his own father, says Charlie.

Maureen watches his face, cannot believe that he is not slightly enjoying the melodrama, in the way that she has found herself doing lately.

Maureen tries to imagine the scene at Wapping, without success. While Charlie was being chased down Wapping Lane, she was in bed with Peter, having the miracle of cunnilingus performed upon her.

What's Robert going to do now, Charlie?

Huh?

Will he be able to come and see us?

Charlie looks at his wife, almost catching her eyes directly. They have not looked straight into one another's eyes for many years, both afraid of what they will see there. What he sees now is an ache that seems to slightly arch her entire body.

I don't know if I can forgive him.

For what? For finding himself a proper job. He had no choice.

*He had a choice all right. He could have been a **printer**. He would have worked by my side.*

It doesn't look like that would have done him a great deal of good in the long run, does it?

Instead he's Tommy. Son of Tommy, Tommy Mark 2, the sequel. What do you mean, it wouldn't have done him any good?

Maureen pinches the bridge of her nose, as if to more carefully contain her thoughts within her head.

You're not going to win, are you, Charlie? The printers aren't going to win. He's never going to have you back after all this.

It's not down to him. We've got to fight for the . . .

Charlie! You're not looking at it straight.

You don't understand, Maureen. The union will wear Murdoch down. We're not Australian criminals. Not like him. I'll have my job back. Everything's going to be like it was.

Nothing's ever like it was, says Maureen, and she turns and closes her eyes.

Charlie lies awake for another hour, staring up into the darkness. The six inches that yawn between him and his wife never narrow.

Excuse me . . .

I'll be with you in a moment.

Charlie stands awkwardly in the corridor of the hospital. A woman is parked on a gurney six feet from where he stands. He can't help staring at her. Streams of ordinary humanity drift past her, carrying gifts or wearing white coats, bearing syringes or anonymous packages. A child is crying, is placated by a lollipop. In the midst of this sputtering life, the woman on the gurney.

He does not want to catch her eye, or to make contact, so when he glances it is surreptitious, furtive. There is almost nothing of her to see. The bulge she makes under the white worn hospital sheets is tiny, like that of a child. But it is her face that draws his gaze. It is so extraordinarily ancient.

Her mouth hangs open slightly, a gap that once kissed, told of a good or bad day at work, spoke of small disasters happening to distant relatives. It trembles now, and a thin line of spittle like shredded spider's web hangs from it. Her skin is scored deep like a dry river bed. She is shrunken as if she has lain in a bath for a week and the skin has sagged to overwhelm the flesh. Charlie does not know why he cannot stop watching her. He decides it is the contrast between the shape under the white sheets and the bustling rivers of indifferent life flowing past. The way they refuse to see each other. He hopes suddenly that his life will never come to this.

Take me quickly, Lord, when my time comes, he mutters to himself.

He glances one last time. To his shock, she is staring right at him, right into his eyes. Her eyes are small and black, tiny scooped-out olives, dully reflecting the strip-lighting overhead. They terrify Charlie. They are not blank and lost, as he expected, not sad or dopey or distracted. They are horrified. They contain a universe of fear. They are utterly self-aware.

Just before Charlie tugs his gaze away, the arrangement of the woman's face shifts slightly. He cannot make out what the expression is, had thought that she was somehow incapable of expression. Then he sees it is a smile, just the tiniest of smiles, and he senses that it is directed at him. He shivers. He feels obscurely that she knows something awful about him.

Can I help you?

What?

Can I help you?

Oh. Yes. I'm looking for Lloyd George.

The receptionist, a woman, black and huge, the size of a manatee, isn't even looking up. Her tone is completely flat.

We're very busy. We don't have him, or Jim Callaghan, or Lord Kitchener for that matter. If you could please tell me who you're looking for, I'll direct you.

*His name really is Lloyd George. Not **the** Lloyd George. He's a coloured chap. Was admitted a couple of days ago.*

The nurse looks up sceptically.

He's black, is he?

Coloured, yeah.

He's black. Afro-Caribbean.

*Whatever. Whatever. Why's everyone so **sensitive** about every-thing nowadays? Why's everyone always **offended**.*

We're not all from Bongo-Bongo land.

*What you **talking** about? I never said . . . Look, luv, could you just tell me where he is, please.*

My name isn't luv.

Oh, Jesus God Almighty. Can't you just tell me where he is?

She pauses, then slowly and deliberately checks a ledger that is in front of her on the desk.

Florence Nightingale ward, second on your left.

Charlie turns towards where she has pointed. He sees, with relief, that the woman on the gurney has disappeared. He walks down the corridor. There are paintings by children decorating the walls. Charlie likes the effect, it cheers him up.

He sees doors opening on to wards spectrally full of half-hidden patients. This other world is making him more and more uncomfortable. He enters the Florence Nightingale ward and sees Lloyd immediately. His face is a mess. The nose is broken, a cheekbone fractured, the left eye swollen. His chest is tightly bound and there is a drip running into his arm. He sees Charlie, but instead of smiling raises an eyebrow, gives a small mysterious nod to himself. He mutters something inaudible.

Charlie stands next to the chair by the bed.

How are you feeling, then?

Lloyd does not answer.

Not too much pain?

The silence is awkward and long. Charlie's legs are hurt-ing.

Mind if I sit down?

There is a grunt from the bed that could be a negative or

a positive. Charlie sits down, crosses and uncrosses his arms.

So it's not too bad, then?

Lloyd grimaces. When he finally speaks, his voice sounds dry, hoarse, pressed down into himself.

*What do you **want** Charlie?*

A nurse comes by, smiles and makes a few adjustments to Lloyd's drip.

*How are **we** today, Mr George?*

Depressed.

Oh, come now, she says briskly, apparently registering nothing of this. *You'll be up on your feet again in no time.*

And with this she is gone.

Fair bit of crackling, says Charlie, struggling to stay bright. *Nurses, eh?*

Again, Lloyd doesn't respond. Charlie takes a deep breath.

What's got into you, then? Why you got the hump?

Lloyd shifts under the bedclothes, then winces in pain.

*I haven't got the hump. That's the one thing I haven't got. I've got a broken rib, a split lip, a busted nose, a bruised face and two fractured fingers, which leaves me only six in total. Nothing wrong with my **hump**.*

*But, Snowball, what's it got to do with **me**? Why have you got the hump with **me**? It's just the way the cookie . . .*

Just the way the cookie crumbles, kiddo.

Lloyd is mimicking Charlie's voice like a schoolboy tease.

*Well, what **has** it got to do with me?*

Apart from the fact I took your beating for you.

Yeah, well, I didn't mean . . . I mean, that wasn't my fault. It was Mike Sunderland. He was laughing, Snowball.

Lloyd nods again, as if to himself. When he speaks, his voice has changed. It is now far away, disconnected from the scene somehow.

You know, I've been doing a lot of thinking in my head. A good licking like that, it kind of sets you to thoughts, if you know what I mean. Clears the old brainbox.

Charlie, encouraged by the less hostile tone, smiles.

Like kicking the telly.

*If you want to think of my **head** as a telly.*

I didn't mean . . . The police just made a mistake . . .

No mistake. The reason they came after me is because I'm a black man.

Oh, I don't think . . .

Now Lloyd sits himself up a little, turns to look at Charlie for the first time.

*You don't know **nothing**. It was because I was a **black** man. You should have heard the verbal I was getting. Nigger this and nigger that. They was having the time of their lives. And then they fitted me up for it. 'How do you like it now, golly?' While they were making the statements. I said, I never threw the thing at the policeman. And you know what they said?*

What?

They said, 'Yeah, we know.' And they just had a laugh.

That's terrible, Snowball, that's . . .

That skinhead that walked past you. Just before the charge. I heard what he said to you.

What you talking about?

He called me a coon. A fucking coon. Then he said something to you. Said I was a monkey. And you smiled.

Charlie suddenly feels sick, never knew shame could make your stomach so tight.

Well, what was I supposed to do? I mean, it didn't mean I agreed with that type of attitude . . .

I don't know what you were supposed to do, Charlie. But that wasn't it.

I wanted to say something, didn't I, but . . .

Now Lloyd tries to sit up. He winces in pain. Charlie

reflexively reaches over to try and help him, but Lloyd bats his hand away with surprising strength. He has shifted position enough to look Charlie right in the face.

It wasn't the first time either, was it? 'Three times you did deny me.' That's what Jesus said too. Who was it, Charlie?

Jesus? What are you talking about?

*Paul, was it? Or Mark. Some white . . . motherfucker anyway. Three times. And I turned the other cheek. Hyacinth, she told me to turn the other cheek, because she believes in all that Jesus rubbish, that crosses and angels **thing**. The boxing. She told me, she said, 'Turn the other cheek, Lloyd. Charlie is your friend.' That poor man, that poor sad man in the animal skin, so humiliated, Charlie. And you were on the edge of the chair. I looked at your face, and you wanted him **dead**. You wanted to kill him **yourself**, kill him and scrape him off that canvas. I had to walk away, Charlie, there and then, because if I'd seen any more, well, I wouldn't have been able to fool myself any longer that you were different.*

Charlie becomes aware of the soft beep of the monitoring machine next to Lloyd's bed. He finds the steady rhythm comforting, tries to concentrate on it.

*Then you invited me to your brother's house, for cards, with Tommy, and your son, and Mike Sunderland, and your brother, he won't even shake hands with me, won't even fix me a drink. I am that much of **nothing** to him. And what do you have to say about it, Charlie? I listen, I listen for a word from my old friend Charlie, that you will not put up with this, that you will not **stand** for this, but all you do is play cards. All you do is play cards. All you do is win money so you can show yourself big in front of your son and your brother, your brother who you need to impress so much.*

*But, Snowball, I didn't **do** anything . . .*

*You didn't do anything. You didn't **have** to do anything. You didn't do anything at Wapping. You people **never** do anything.*

Lloyd begins to cough, so loud and harshly that Charlie thinks of calling the nurse, but it soon drops in volume, then disappears altogether. In the silence that follows, Charlie begins to try and pick some words to drop into the emptiness that he now sees gaping in front of him.

You're being . . .

*I know you think Mike Sunderland is full of shit, and he is, he is full of shit, right to his pasty little evil-shit right-on eyeballs. But on this one, he was on the **but-ton**. I thought it weren't like that with you but it is. I thought it was Marquess of Queensberry rules between you and me, but it ain't.*

Charlie feels another surge of shame, but also defiance, irritation, that Lloyd is being hysterical, unreasonable.

Steady on now, Snowball. It's all a bit much. Coloured people . . .

*What colour **am** I, Charlie? You're not no colour, is that right?*

Charlie is now completely bewildered. Lloyd has never talked like this before.

*Black people. **Afro-Caribbeans**.*

Now Lloyd's voice has taken on the faraway tone again.

Look at my face, Charlie. I'm a man who was beautiful, a man who could have been a boxer. If he didn't want to save his pretty face. Pretty funny, eh, Charlie? Especially with the face now. What a waste, eh? Now I'm as ugly as all of you. As ugly as you.

Charlie can think of absolutely nothing to say. Lloyd's voice has now quietened to the smallest of whispers. His eyelids are flickering. It is as if he's falling asleep, can hold on to his slender drift of consciousness no longer.

No. Not as ugly as you.

Charlie dredges at the cold ocean inside him for words, but the silver fish dart away, far from his net.

Snowball, we've been friends for nigh on fifteen years. Can't we . . .

And another thing, Charlie.

What. What is it? says Charlie numbly, leaning over to hear Lloyd's whispered words.

Don't call me Snowball.

I . . .

My name's Lloyd.

He holds his mutilated hand up, flaps it faintly.

You can go now. Tired. I'm tired.

What?

Tired.

At this moment, the nurse appears as if out of nowhere.

I think Mr George has had enough. I think you should go now.

Lloyd has turned over and has his face on the pillow, his eyes closed. Charlie adjusts his clothing, stares at the nurse, rubs his nose, tries desperately once more to think of something to say that will make this come right, but sees no possibility, not now or ever. He gets up from the chair, and when he speaks, he is surprised to find his voice relatively normal, if a little loud, a little brisk.

Right then, I'll be off. See you, then, Snow . . . Lloyd.

Lloyd makes no sign that he has heard him. Charlie looks up at the nurse, who smiles firmly and points towards the exit. Charlie just stands there. Then he holds up a hand, as if in farewell, lets his arm drop and walks slowly away.

13

January 1987. Maureen is on top of Peter, pushing her pelvis down upon him. She is amazed at the sensations she experiences now, powerful concentric ripples moving upwards and outwards within her that she thought existed only in the bodice-rippers and Black Lace novels that she used to read, in the soap operas that she used to live for but now almost never watches.

Peter makes the slightly high-pitched combination of a whistle and a groan that marks his moment of climax. He holds Maureen tightly by the hips, pushes her down upon him. She centres her gravity, feels him expand and contract within her. His face excites her, the way the lips are shot with blood, the deepening colour of the cheeks, the odd absence in the eyes. He is gone; she feels satisfied beyond measure, in control.

His body relaxes but she stays there, until she feels him begin to slacken within her, until the extraordinary fullness is gone. Only then does she climb off. Peter is looking at her, a face shocked with adoration. It is amazing to her, this look which Peter seems to summon almost routinely, a look Charlie has never given her. Maureen falls down on the pillow, smells the pot-pourri that is set by the bed. A thin shaft of sunlight streams into the room. She is, she is surprised to register, happy. A feeling forgotten for so long.

There is silence for several minutes, as if out of respect for what has occurred. To speak sooner would be a violation. They both stare at the ceiling, eyes open, holding hands.

I love your body, says Peter.

She has given up being bewildered at the adoration this man has for the grooves and swollen slackness of her flesh. The complete acceptance of her has left her free to stop exercising – no more running, jumping, stretching, stepping, power-walking, high-impact aerobics. It is an extraordinary relief, and a relief she feels Peter Horn has given her as a gift. She loves him for it. What else does Peter have that marks him out? Wounds. The deep understanding that things go wrong. Charlie has always had a certain blindness.

Why won't you leave him, Maureen?

Maureen finds this question increasingly difficult to answer with honesty. The fact that she and Charlie are married feels, in truth, less and less insurmountable to her, as she starts to gather and select and focus purely on information that she finds comfortable. Marriages, she has begun to tell herself, break up all the time. It has become, without anyone ever announcing it, almost normal. No two people could be expected to spend a life together now that people live so long. Outdated convention. People change. Her conviction that it is sacrosanct, untouchable, is tarnished. As Peter says, once you are being unfaithful, how sacrosanct can it be? And this is hard to answer. Nevertheless, she routinely makes the same reply.

You know why. I made a promise.

Now the real reasons for her intransigence unexpectedly surface within her. She feels pity for Charlie; she does not have the strength to be so cruel. She wants him to pick an argument, so she can blurt it out, but Charlie's even temper, his particular sense of fairness, stands in the way. Barely a cross word, a raised voice, in their years together. She tries to provoke him often now, but Charlie will not rise to it.

Also, she is scared. The slab that is their history, that is always on their horizon when she turns her gaze behind her, projects a shadow which almost blots out imagination. The complete uncertainty of a future without Charlie makes her heart race. But she tries to create runnels in her mind for the possibility to leak into.

I don't know how long I can go on this way, says Peter.

Why don't you leave that driving school? says Maureen.

This thought also comes from nowhere. Maureen finds herself more and more surprised by the subterranean parts of herself. It is not something she has previously considered. She is as surprised as Peter by the idea.

What?

You're always moaning about how hopeless it is. How they don't promote themselves, how the cars are breaking down half the time, how the drivers miss appointments.

They're going to offer me a partnership.

They've been going to offer you a partnership since year zero. It's not going to happen, Peter.

Oh, I don't think . . .

Maureen is surprised by the steel in her voice. New, unsuspected aspects of herself are surfacing all the time now, the surprise of spring crocuses.

It's not going to happen, Peter. Why would it happen? You've shown yourself as being prepared for second best. You've threatened to leave three or four times. They laugh behind your back. They know you won't do it. They'll never make you a partner.

Peter lies, his naked body soft and shapeless as an ink blot, his cock shrunk to almost nothingness. He seems stunned.

What are you saying?

I don't know what I'm saying.

But Maureen is tossing a thought about, fighting the temptation to deliver it. It is too large, too revolutionary. Yet it emerges all the same, the rough weight of the words threatening to chafe her throat raw as she speaks them.

Start your own business.

Come off it, Maureen. How am I going to get the money for that? The mortgage on this place is too big. I'm still paying maintenance for three kids. I couldn't handle the stress on my own.

What if you weren't on your own?

Maureen's eyes light up with the daring of her own idea. She thinks of Marie-Rose, with her business, she thinks of the excitement of moving those columns of figures around, all that energy turned to black hooks and spindles on the page. She remembers *Dallas*, the shining grail that is commerce. Oil wells. Fancy foreign sports cars. A fleet of six Ford Fiestas; the M&P Driving Centre. This is the name she suddenly favours.

Peter sits up at this point. His belly is loose and covered by a fine down. Maureen, too, is naked, flesh spreading in all directions. To each other they are holy.

What are you saying?

I could do the accounts. Help with marketing, administration. I'm good at all that. Charlie always says I'm an organizational genius.

Pete looks momentarily excited, then sinks back on the pillow.

Yeah, but . . . where's the money going to come from? It's a pipe dream, Maureen. It's Scotch mist.

Not necessarily. My and Charlie's house is worth well over £80,000 now, especially when the conservatory is finished. The mortgage is only £30,000. I've got some cash hidden away. If we skimped it, there'd be enough to get off the ground. I mean, if we . . . if we were . . .

She has never spoken the word before and finds it sticks on her tongue. She works to expel it. It is ugly, overwhelming in scale.

If we were divorced, I'd get half of everything, wouldn't I?

If you were divorced?

I'm not saying I would get divorced. I'm just daydreaming really. But it's not completely mad, is it?

I don't know.

How much is a car?

Slow down, Maureen. Hold on.

What?

I don't know if I'm cut out for business.

Maureen suddenly becomes aware of something she experiences as fierce heat along the pylon of her spine. It is excitement.

I am, though, Peter.

What do you mean?

*I could **do** it. I'm good with figures. I've got a qualification in accountancy. I understand about money. I could run the business side.*

You? But you're . . . but you're . . .

What? A woman?

Well. It's not that exactly.

*It **is** that. It's that exactly. Listen, Pete. I'm not going to spend the rest of my life making cups of tea and chit-chatting down the supermarket. I've had enough of that. If she can do it, then I can. She was a housewife, wasn't she?*

Who?

Her. Mrs Thatcher.

What's she got to do with anything?

Everything. Maybe nothing. I'm just saying. They snap to attention when she comes into a room. All those shiny men. When I come into a room, people ask me if I've got any digestive biscuits.

Peter looks blank.

Have we?

Would you leave your job, Peter?

It's a big risk.

Would you?

I don't know, Maureen. If I did it . . .

What?

If I did it . . . Well, it would be a hell of a thing, wouldn't it?

Wouldn't it, though? says Maureen, biting at the edge of his ear now and moving her hand down, down through the white-grey forest of his chest.

Charlie stands back, adjusts the F-stop, focuses, takes a photograph. The conservatory is complete. He already has ninety-six colour prints in an album that charts the progress of the extension from holes in the mud to this epiphany, this perfect moment.

The extension is Georgian hardwood, French doors included as standard, with three-point Espagnolette locking system. Full-coat microporous spray factory finish in deep mahogany. Double-glazed, of course. Pitched roof, powder-coated aluminium, with decorated crest finials. A 600mm dwarf wall. He inspects each feature with a deep sense of satisfaction, ticks the list off in his mind. The red brick matches the brick of the house almost perfectly. Sunlight pours in through the six glass panels of the windows. Although the whole thing is bought as a kit, it takes considerable skill and resourcefulness to put it all together. He wants to celebrate. Three feet from where the dwarf wall stands, the miniature railway track runs. Thus his invented world expands.

He wants to celebrate. The strike at Wapping grinds on and he feels that this is the only good and complete and successful thing he has done for the past twelve months. With his sleeve, he wipes at a smudge of fingerprint that he has left while fitting the French doors. Otherwise it looks just as perfect as it did the day he saw it in the London Modern and Traditional Conservatory Company catalogue. He considers how superior the world of materials is to the world of humans; how, finally, screws and cement and wood and steel bend to your will, take the shape of the promise delivered in blueprints.

Maureen!

Maureen is indoors studying *The Highway Code* for her next test. Sometimes Charlie thinks that she will never pass, but he admires her determination. Nothing seems to put her off her lessons. Peter Horn has even offered a 20 per cent reduction in the hourly rate, which strikes Charlie as decent, neighbourly and also a feat of superhuman patience.

Maureen!

Maureen emerges from the door that leads from the lounge into the conservatory. She is framed there in sunlight. She wears slacks from Principles and a plain white blouse. Charlie's glance extends to a gaze. He is surprised that he finds her beautiful and something chokes tenderly within him. The move to Milton Keynes, he decides, has suited her well, despite all her reservations. The open air, the promise and possibility of the place. The get up and ruddy well go. She pushes the French doors with bronze-effect handles and comes out into the chilly air. The worn copy of *The Highway Code* is gripped in her left hand. He walks across to his wife, kisses her on the cheek, puts his arm around her.

Guess what, kiddo?

What?

It's finished, Maureen. It's actually finished.

Maureen smiles. Her smile, Charlie has noticed, is different lately. Less perpetual, and yet this seems to indicate a greater happiness. When it comes, it has more force than before, more radiance.

That's marvellous, Charlie.

Irregardless of all the other stuff that's been going on, I feel . . . well, I feel satisfied.

She smiles, pecks him on the cheek, folds her arms, then stands back to examine her husband's handiwork. What she sees satisfies her. She feels genuinely proud. Charlie nods in approbation. She has not seen him this happy for a long time.

It'll put ten, fifteen K on the price of the house, easy.

I'm sure you're right.

You'll never guess what they sold that place up by the junction for.

Which one?

You know. Number 7, I think it is. A dog's dinner. No double-glazing. No car port. One less bedroom than us, I think. There was a board outside. Where the Pakistanis were.

They weren't Pakistanis, Charlie. They were Sikhs.

*The **Indians** then. With the skip outside. And guess what it went for.*

I don't know.

Go on, guess.

I couldn't.

Charlie feels a shimmer of irritation spoiling his moment of joy.

Guess, Maureen. Take a wild guess.

About £80,000?

Disappointment edges his mouth.

That's right.

There is a pause, while the exultation over the extent of their new wealth overbalances the disappointment at Maureen's prescience.

So what does that make us, Maureen? Hey? We've got an extra bedroom. And now this extension. This place has got to be worth over 100 K. Think, Maureen. The mortgage is only £30,000. We're worth £70,000. And it's going up every week. Every day!

Maureen smiles. She has already made her own set of calculations, involving division rather than multiplication.

Who'd have thought?

*Who **would** have thought?*

I think this deserves a celebration, don't you? A glass of bubbly.

Coca-Cola or Tizer? says Charlie resignedly.

Charlie is still discouraged by Maureen from drinking.

I think we could indulge in a little bit of the real thing, don't you? I'll nip down to the off-licence and get something.

Really?

You've earned it.

No need to go down the offy.

How's that?

When we first moved in, I had a few bottles. I wanted them out of temptation. So I squirrelled them away.

Fetch them out, then, Tufty.

We'll chill it down in no time.

Charlie moves past Maureen into the main part of the house. He feels complete, for once. He feels like a man.

*Where have you hidden them, you sneaky **thing**, you little **squirrel?*** says Maureen, giving a pout that she usually reserves for Peter.

Charlie is leaving the room now, grinning broadly.

In the attic.

Charlie is not there to witness the blood drain from Maureen's face. She whirls round.

Charlie . . .

But Charlie is already moving up the stairs. A few seconds later she hears the hooks at the end of pole that unlocks the loft ladder seeking the steel eyes. She scurries along behind him, gabbling.

I thought we'd get something special. Maybe some proper Moët.

This is the real McCoy. Vintage. I got it as a present from Tommy. A while ago. Top-of-the-range fizz.

Maureen scrabbles about inside her head for ways of

escaping this danger. She thinks momentarily of pretending to faint, but abandons the idea as ridiculous. Charlie already has the hatch open and is climbing through. She tries to calm herself. There is no reason to think he will find what she fears. She searches for an ulcer to probe with her tongue, but there are none. Along with her verrucas, they have disappeared, disorders neutralized by the newness of her life here.

The loft light has blown. It's dark as hell up here. Jesus God Almighty.

The light from the landing beneath just illuminates the attic enough for Charlie to move forward as his pupils dilate to allow in what available light there is. He cannot quite remember where he put the bottles, only that they are on the far side of the attic. He strikes a match and the attic space is illuminated by flickering yellow light. On the far side, under the strut of a roof beam, he can just make out the plastic Asda shopping bag that contains the bottles.

The pitched roof is low. He takes tiny steps, balancing on the struts that support the ceiling beneath, not wishing to risk the plasterboard. The match is extinguished by a sudden draught. He fumbles for another, and as he does so he stumbles and falls.

Damn and blast!

Still prostrate, he reaches in his pocket, finds the matchbox. He lights a match once again, decides this time to proceed on all fours. In the corner, just to the right of where the plastic shopping bag is, a sheet of hardboard rests across the struts. He crawls across it and reaches out a hand, gains purchase, then pulls the hardboard back. The match goes out again. He fumbles with the matchbox once more but drops it. His mouth is dry. He feels suddenly desperate for a drink, had forgotten how much he has missed the faint burn of alcohol on his tongue, its sweetness in the blood.

Jesus God Almighty.

Now using only touch, he feels about for the matchbox. There is a gap against the wall where the hardboard stops and he imagines that the box may have fallen in here. He moves his hand about, seeking, a tiny animal scuttling through the dark. Charlie is surprised at the texture he feels in the gap. Instead of dry dirt and wood, there is something silky. He registers, to his surprise, that a faint whiff of perfume is detectable. He rubs what he finds between his finger and thumb; some kind of cloth. Letting go, he continues his search for the matches, then realizes that there is more of the material down there. After another thirty seconds or so, he finds the matchbox. He strikes; the scene is illumined.

At first in the dimming yellow match-light he cannot make out what it is he sees. There are a few plastic bags. There are piles of material. He can just about make out the names – Next, Principles, Marks & Spencer. These are flotsam floating on a sea of coloured cloth. There are what look like scores of items here. Even in this struggling light, he can now see that they are clothes, brand new, apparently unworn. The match shears down to his fingers, burning him. He fumbles, lights another. Now his hand is shaking slightly. He sees that the colours in front of him all blend into a shadowy blur, but as he picks at the pile he can make out shapes. There are dresses, slacks, coats, underwear, tights, skirts, blouses. There are three pairs of leather gloves, two pairs of knee-length boots. Scarves, sweaters, cardigans. It is a whole collection. Charlie's mouth sags open, takes in dust. He swallows, feels a clogging there. His thirst redoubles, turns from simple desire into need. His mind works to make sense of what he is seeing. No explanation fits. His mouth closes, purses, opens again. When he speaks, his voice is croaky, hollowed out.

Maureen!

There is no reply.

Maureen! What the merry hell . . .

But when Charlie descends the ladder once more, back-wards, smeared and layered in dust, grime on his face, tragic champagne still in one hand, Maureen is gone.

Charlie sits and stares out of the front window. Maureen has been gone for five hours now. The light is fading, turning brown. He shifts uncomfortably, feels a hardness beneath him. There is a hammer which he has been using to finish up the extension that has worked its way under his pillow. He removes it, puts it by the base of the chair and settles back down. He pours the last of the second bottle of champagne into a glass and smokes the tenth cigarette of the previous hour. An overflowing ashtray is in front of him. There is a sour fug of smoke filling the room.

A newspaper is laid out in front of him, and three or four cans of Humbrol paint. His hand shakes slightly as he applies a final layer of red paint to the casing of an LGB American-style Mogul 2-6-0 Tender, a turn-of-the-century steam engine. Through sight slightly blurred by alcohol, Charlie scrutinizes his work. Paint runs in blobs and colour overflows into colour. The shell is a terrible mess. But he continues to paint, ran-domness incrementally gathering. A smear of red falls on the bare metal of one of the wheels. He does not bother to wipe it off.

When he finally hears a car pull up outside, he does not bother to do more than glance up. He sees the Journeyz sign on top of the Ford Fiesta and registers, without understanding the implications, that Maureen is driving the car unaccom-panied.

He continues to paint as he hears the key in the lock. Maureen walks in, and he sees her at the edge of his field of vision, staring at the clothes that cover the floor, that cover the chairs. Dozens of them. The colours are clear now. They are strong, unapologetic. Bright yellows and blues, echoing candy pinks, greens the colour of new sprouting leaves. The front room has become a soft, static kaleidoscope. Maureen picks her way through the items until she reaches a chair opposite Charlie. She sits down calmly. She looks at Charlie directly. He had expected an averted gaze.

Aren't you going to take off your coat?

It is all that Charlie can think of to say.

There's no need.

Charlie nods, as though he understands. In fact, he has no idea why Maureen does not remove her coat. He is expecting her to lighten herself, to prepare herself for contrition.

His head clears slightly and he feels that he needs to take a no-nonsense approach, that he needs to clear the air.

You stole these, didn't you?

He is surprised by the strength with which Maureen answers in the affirmative. There is no shame, no apology. He has an odd sense of his inner stance moving towards the defensive, but cannot understand why.

Yes.

There's dozens of them.

I expect so.

I've never seen you wearing any of them.

No.

Mystery mounts upon mystery. He reaches for his glass, but finds it empty. He is expecting words from Maureen, even imprecations, but nothing is coming, and this throws him off balance. He decides he must plough on through the heavy air.

Why? Why on earth would you do something like that?

I don't know.

You don't know?

Maureen's face is tight. Charlie is unsettled by the fact that it seems to contain not contrition but a kind of packed determination.

I don't know.

Right.

Charlie taps cigarette ash into an overflowing crystal ashtray. Instinctively, Maureen stands up and reaches for it, goes to empty it into the rubbish bin. Charlie grabs her arm.

Jesus God Almighty, Maureen. Leave that!

Maureen tamely puts the ashtray back down again, returns to her chair. Charlie sees lines on her forehead working as if she is processing something heavy and sour inside.

The trouble with you, Maureen, is . . .

*The trouble with **you**, Charlie,* says Maureen, suddenly cutting him off in a way that is unprecedented. Then her words hit some closed door, rebound. *Oh, what **is** the trouble with you?*

Maureen searches for language that has been locked down for so long that she has forgotten its location. Finally, in cool blue light, she discovers it.

*You know about . . . things. You can do your job. You can fix the house up. You can make – your special worlds, your railway worlds. You're a decent enough man. I'm no better than you. I'm **worse**. But there are whole parts of my life that . . . that you just don't **know**.*

Charlie nods politely, feels that he needs to go through the charade that this makes sense.

You should have just let everything stay the same, Charlie. You would have been better off. All these changes. Changing things is dangerous.

Charlie tries to ignore this.

*Never mind **me**. This isn't about me. Why did you steal all those things?*

When Maureen answers, it is without pause or reflection.

It felt good.

It did? says Charlie.

Yes.

*What did? What **exactly**?*

A lot of things.

What kind of things?

This is excruciating. He wants to take Maureen, to shake the knowledge out of her, but he has never laid a hand on his wife in all the years they have been together.

I don't know really. The taking of them. Getting away with it. They just put it all out in front of you. They make you want it, don't they? They build it into their budgets.

What?

Thieving. They allow for it. So it's not really all that bad. But actually it wasn't the taking of it. It wasn't really the stealing. That was just the exciting bit. But that wasn't what made me keep doing it.

A pause. The conversation is like a gun with empty chambers save for one live, deadly bullet. Each sentence is a trigger pulled. Charlie feels himself bracing.

What was it then?

Click.

It was the fact that nothing happened.

What?

I did a bad thing. And nothing happened. I did it again. Still nothing happened. I did it again and again and again. Nothing happened, Charlie. There were no . . . consequences. Do you understand?

Charlie looks, and feels, utterly blank.

What on earth are you talking about? he says desperately.

Click.

You can do things, Charlie. You can do things, and what the world says is going to happen doesn't. It makes all sorts of things possible.

Click.

All sorts of things?

Click.

Yes. And then . . . something else. It gave me something else.

I'm listening.

He tries to regain the initiative by sounding stern, in control, even as he knows he is a small boy waiting hopelessly in the headmistress's chamber, fateful cane looming on the wall.

When I came here, Charlie, I was so lonely. Everything was gone. My whole world was gone.

It was a new start. It was our new . . .

*It was just . . . it was like a big nothing. All the people I'd known. Everything I was familiar with. All gone. But I did it for you. I had nothing, though. You had your job, your trains, your new house to boast to Tommy about. Your cards, your damn extension. You had me. I even gave up my job. I know you thought it was pin money. That it counted for nothing. But it was my **job**. And I needed something else.*

Click.

You need to be a robber, do you? A villain, like Tommy?

Secrets. That was the best thing, secrets . . . When I stole, it gave me something of my own. Something that had nothing to do with you. And I had these secrets, and they felt good, and nothing happened.

Yes.

And then, I wanted more secrets. Or, if I didn't exactly want them . . . I wasn't afraid of them any more.

More secrets?

Yes.

Suddenly a piece of information collects and coalesces inside Charlie.

Click, bang.

When you drove here just now?

Yes.

Maureen knows what is coming. At last, she welcomes it.

You were alone?

That's right.

You can't drive alone. You haven't got a licence.

There is a long pause, in which Maureen alone knows that the entire span of her married life hangs in the balance. She can still step back. For the last time ever, she can step back. She draws breath one more time, cannot find the strength to stand between the hammer and the powder.

I have, Charlie. I've had a licence for a year.

*No, that's not true. **You haven't**.*

Then Charlie nods as if he fully understands and approves this information.

But . . . you didn't tell me.

No.

Why not?

Now the truth blows at him, bitter wind, but he turns his back to it, huddles.

Because . . .

Because you just wanted another secret, right? You wanted to keep it a secret that you could drive.

That wasn't the secret, Charlie.

The slug finds its way to Charlie's temple, begins to bury itself. Imaginary blood falls invisibly, mixes with the red paint around the blurred, treacled coating on the miniature steam engine.

It wasn't?

No. It was an excuse.

*For **what**?* says Charlie, although he already knows.

Peter. Me and Peter . . . Peter and I . . . we . . .

Charlie nods. The bullet has reached his brain, exploded with a blinding flash, with its terrible cargo of knowledge.

Charlie stands up quietly, prosaically, then pulls Maureen to her feet, feels his fist come back. It is as if he is outside himself, watching as the punch lands on his wife's sad, collapsing face. She falls to the ground. She does not make a sound. He wants her to scream, to beg for mercy, to accept retribution, to undo everything that has been done, but she does not make a sound. He kicks her once; she gasps. Her chest harder than he would have expected. She lies amid unworn clothes, seeming to turn the colour of parchment, but it is only the late afternoon light.

Charlie stops as suddenly as he has started, begins to cry. He has never cried in front of Maureen before, never cried at all, since he was a child. He falls to his knees. Maureen gives an almost-smile, tasting the blood in her mouth as she does so. She reaches up. She strokes his arm, even as she feels consciousness slipping away. She sees a crumb of food at the side of his mouth, feels herself reach up weakly to wipe the mess away. Outside, the wood in the conservatory creaks as it contracts. A snail crawls upon the roof, trailing silver.

Charlie puts his hand over Maureen's, then feels it slide away. He pulls back. He sees the hammer resting by the base of the chair. Slowly, as if in a dream, he picks it up. It seems graceful, weightless, yet reassuringly solid. He tests his grip on it, feels its firmness between his suddenly old fingers. He stares down at his wife, batting her hands feebly in the air. The moment holds.

Then Charlie turns and rushes out of the door, hammer still in hand. He runs, he runs, he runs, blindly, not sure where he is going, and does not stop. A cold wind batters him. He runs across one mini-roundabout, then another. A man in an anorak passes him but keeps his head down.

In two minutes, he is where he now realizes he wants to be. He hurdles over the fence at the edge of the field. He goes for the smallest first, the calf, mottled black and white like all the rest, takes a single swing at its stupid, blank, indifferent head. Three strikes are enough. The cows are more fragile than he had thought, chicken wire and spray concrete, the lumpen solidity only an illusion. The head falls into the grass.

He attacks all the other five before he is exhausted. Then he collapses in the middle of the decapitated herd, his breathing agonized, tears pouring out. Six concrete heads surround him like a ritual circle. What's left of the cows – neck, body and legs – still stands around him, mutilated, finally indestructible, entirely indifferent.

14

The divorce lawyer – greased, slicked-back hair, florid jowls, lips that always seem wet – gazes at Charlie with what aspires to be absolute neutrality. But Charlie feels sure that there is pity there and it frightens him. He feels shrunken inside his clothes, which are smart – grey suit, tie, a shirt too big for him, polished shoes. He is intimidated by lawyers, their unnatural brisk efficiency in the face of expanding human chaos. When Charlie speaks he barely recognizes his own voice. It is parched, small, like Maureen's once used to be.

What happens now?

I presume she'll file a petition as regards your unreasonable behaviour.

My unreasonable behaviour? She's been going at it with my next-door neighbour for the past . . . God knows how long.

It hardly matters whose unreasonable behaviour it is. The courts don't exactly take into account whose fault it is.

But she's been betraying me all this time.

Mr Buck, you beat her up.

At his words, Charlie seems to shrink further inside his suit, his neck seems to protrude like a turtle's from its shell. He puts his head in his hands.

She should get it all, after what I've done. All of it. I don't deserve a penny. I can't believe that I . . .

The lawyer cuts him off. He has heard it all. Human beings, he has discovered, are almost entirely predictable in these particular circumstances.

You won't always feel the same way. The future, as they say, lasts a very long time. Is she going to press charges?

I don't think so.

*Well, that's some good news anyway. It's not going to look **good** in the family court, though. But the bruises will have faded by then, thank heavens. Anyway, most cases don't make it that far. There's no question of custody here, of course. No dependent children. It's just a matter of a financial settlement.*

What's going to happen? What does it all boil down to?

There are two sides to this. Capital and income. Let's take income first. What is your employment situation? You are a . . .

The lawyer consults a sheaf of papers in front of him, makes a small moue.

You are in the printing trade. And you are currently involved in an industrial dispute. What is your legal status in terms of employment?

What you mean?

Do you have a job?

I'm not sure. Strictly speaking, we've all been sacked. It doesn't look good.

Is there any question of redundancy?

It's hard to say. There's some kind of fund being suggested. From what I hear it's peanuts.

Well, whatever it is – if it comes to that – you will be doubtless expected to make allowance for your wife – or ex-wife, as she may well be by then – in the final settlement. Of course, if you have no income, you will not have to pay her maintenance. But if you do start to get yourself back on your feet, then she will be able to apply to the court at any time for an adjustment.

What? You mean even if she's left me for another man, and he's looking after her, and she's doing nothing all day, I've got to pay her money?

I'm afraid that's the case, yes. Typically 20 to 30 per cent of your income.

Charlie nods. The collar is scratching at his neck. He is not used to dressing formally and it makes him feel awkward, forces his words out in a way that seems artificial to him.

And what about the matter of capital? says Charlie, giving a small cough.

What are your present assets?

Assets?

Let's start with the house. What's that worth?

Charlie feels himself puff up slightly, feels his status move a degree closer to that of the lawyer, whose professional objectivity he can't help but see as contempt.

Well over 100 grand. Maybe 120. And it's in my name of course.

I'm afraid, says the solicitor sadly, *that is irrelevant.*

How can it be irrelevant? says Charlie. *I worked my guts out to make the money to put up that deposit.*

Nevertheless. The law will see it as a joint asset. And the mortgage?

Thirty K. Just under.

And what else is there?

Not much. A few stocks and shares. Tell Sid, you know.

Charlie fills his suit out a little more. He is a shareholder, a possessor of financial products, something he never dreamed of.

Any proceeds from these, you will expect a proportion to go to your wife.

Shock is beginning to work now, all the grief of the last few months beginning to coalesce into this moment. Some events are not stuck in time; they unfold endlessly within. He stares out of the window, sees three birds he cannot identify standing next to each other in a tree he cannot name. They twitch and shuffle, open beaks for dumb, inaudible song. His mind drifts towards them. In the distance, he hears the solicitor's voice again.

Does your wife have any sole assets?

Maureen? What do you mean by sole assets?

Money or possessions that she might consider to be hers alone.

Charlie shakes his head confidently.

No, no. Well, only what she kept for both of us.

The solicitor raises an inquisitive eyebrow.

I'm not quite sure what you . . .

Maureen didn't really believe in banks. I used to hand her my wage packet every week. She'd take something out and put it in a box somewhere. It was a fair sum.

How much, precisely?

*I'm not sure **precisely**. Last I heard, it was about twenty-five K. That's a lifetime's saving. It was going to go towards our pension.*

The solicitor makes a note on the pad in front of him. Something about the way he bows his head makes Charlie anxious.

And where is this money kept?

Maureen puts it somewhere. Under the floorboards. In a box, a strongbox.

And it's in cash you say. Do you have any proof of its existence?

Charlie now feels bewildered.

Proof of its existence? Why would I need proof of its existence?

The solicitor brings out from a yellow buff file a thick wad of papers and begins to leaf through them.

As you know, I have now received Mrs Buck's financial disclosure forms and there is no mention of this sum.

Charlie looks back out at the tree. The birds have gone. He sees something come free from the branch and begin to descend, turning in the air. A sycamore helicopter. His mind scours itself for the appropriate explanation.

She's worried about the Revenue, I shouldn't wonder.

But I understood you were a schedule E employee? All your tax would have been paid for you.

I sometimes did extra shifts. Not at Gray's Inn Road. That was schedule D. Maureen did a bit of work for pin money. She never declared it. I expect that's the reason. I'm sure that's the reason.

So are you telling me that you and your wife are going to come to a private agreement about this sum?

Yeah, I'm sure that's it.

I see.

There is a heavy pause. Then the solicitor picks up a pencil and begins making calculations on a blotter in front of him. After about thirty seconds, he speaks.

At the end of the day, Mr Buck, if I may sum up, if we assume that your valuation of the house is correct, and we add on the other bits and pieces, and then deduct the proceeds of sale, and of course my fees and court charges and so forth, and we assume that you achieve 40 per cent of the capital value of your house . . .

What do you meant, 40 per cent?

Well, I'm afraid that since you are unable to pay your wife any significant maintenance, it may well be that she receives the lion's share of the capital in order to compensate for this. The courts are rather old-fashioned in this respect, I'm afraid. They consider that the woman has less potential for earning than her partner.

But my career is finished! There's not going to be any more work for compositors! Not with all these new computers everywhere. And I'm fifty-six years old. No one's going to want to employ me.

Nevertheless, the courts will still be liable to see your relative position as advantageous over that of your spouse and, in lieu of maintenance, are liable to make a favourable award bearing that consideration in mind.

Charlie shifts uncomfortably in his chair. The future, already thin, translucent, seems to stretch tighter.

What am I going to get left with, then?

Bottom line? I think you're probably going to make it out of here with around £40,000. If Mrs Buck plays with a straight bat.

Charlie repeats the sum very quietly. To his surprise, having turned it around in his mind, it still sounds like a considerable amount. He thinks of it stacked up in £1 notes, how much space it would fill.

Plus half what Maureen has got stashed, of course.

The solicitor smiles. To his surprise, Charlie notices that he seems to be smiling genuinely, with real amusement, for the first time.

Of course.

Charlie sits in the front room of Tommy's house in Chingford. He has just arrived. He looks around him disconsolately. In the hall, yellow emulsion. The living room is decorated with blue and white pinstriped wallpaper from Colefax and Fowler. His heels click as he walks across the bare floor.

When you getting some carpets in, then?

It's meant to be like this.

You're having me on?

Floorboards. All the rage. Ask Lolly. She gets all the magazines.

He gestures towards a matt-black magazine rack. Charlie notices without surprise that there are cuts all over his knuckles. The magazine rack is full of copies of *The World of Interiors*.

A baby bellows in the background

Lorraine! Do something, will you?

You do something! comes the retort.

It is from upstairs, where Lorraine is applying a sponge soaked in Autumn Verbena emulsion to the bedroom wall. She is finding it difficult to achieve the effect required. Her lips move as she struggles to pick up the tips laid out in the copy of *House Beautiful* that she has spread out in front of her. The waterfall of peach-coloured ruche that falls from beneath the pelmet has been carefully covered in transparent polythene to protect against paint splashes.

Do you want a cup of tea, Charlie? says Tommy, walking over to the kitchen.

We've just had a whirlpool bath fitted. Want a look?

Not at the moment, Tommy.

Go on. It cost me . . .

I'm really not in the mood.

Tommy, disappointed, returns with a cup of tea and sits with Charlie at a table by the window. Tommy has also placed on the table a bottle of Scotch and two glasses. Charlie pours himself a large glass and takes a hefty slug. The window is criss-crossed by leading that Tommy has bought at trade price and now features on every window in the house. Above them, replica wooden beams complete the country-house effect. The baby's cries louden. Tommy shrugs and pours himself a whisky also. Despite the fact that he has always thought of his brother as a *mug, a stiff*, it pains Tommy to see him in such a condition. For the first time in his adult life, he has that day witnessed his brother's tears. Charlie has been struggling to convey the enormity of his situation to Tommy, but so far little has emerged other than curses and blanket condemnations of the opposite sex, to which Tommy has nodded sympathetically. Now Charlie has entered one of his periodic glum silences. Outside there is a low grey sky pressing down on the estate of identical red houses, like a rag of ether on an invalid's face.

I never trusted him, not the first time I saw him, says Tommy.

Who? mutters Charlie.

That Peter Horn. He had that look.

What look?

Shifty. Scheming.

I don't remember, says Charlie.

I tell you what, Charlie, says Tommy, leaning forward conspiratorially. *I know some fellers.*

302

In what respect? says Charlie.

Some fellers. You know. They'll put him right. Nothing fatal. He'll learn a thing or two. He'll get what's coming towards him in his direction.

Charlie looks up, manages half a smile.

Can they do two for the price of one?

Well, I don't know, Charlie. I'll have to have a word. It's possible that it's cheaper for women. But I don't know about two for one. It's not as if . . .

Tommy, I'm not bloody serious, am I?

Tommy! Will you sort out Kylie!

Lorraine's voice is piercing, furious. Tommy ignores this demand from above and furrows his brow.

***Aren't** you serious?*

Of course not.

I'm surprised. After all, she robbed you. And I know what I'd do if someone robbed me like that.

She's my bloody wife.

Not any more she's not, Charlie.

He nods at the brown envelope that Charlie has brought with him, containing the decree absolute. It has all been over so quickly. More than a quarter of a century both contained and negated in a single tiny envelope.

Lorraine appears in the doorway. There are specks of paint on her face and a scarf is tied round her head. She sports a thin gold ankle chain, 24 carats, around just-shaved legs, goosebumped like plucked turkeys.

You fat useless lump! You never lift a finger.

Blah blah blah. Tommy mimics an enormous yawn, makes the shape of a mouth yapping by beating the four fingers of one hand against the thumb. *Never lift a finger, Charlie. Not me. All this house, the car, the stuff for the kid, it all falls through an enormous bloody great hole in the sky.*

You're bone idle!

I'm trying to talk to my big brother. He's going through a difficult time, isn't he?

At this moment, the baby stops crying. Lorraine's eyes move from side to side, soften slightly. She holds her position in the doorway for a few more seconds. Still the baby is silent. She takes a step towards where the brothers are sitting.

That's not going to help, is it? says Lorraine, nodding at the bottle of Scotch and pulling up a chair.

I suppose you're right, says Charlie, taking another mouthful nevertheless.

You look like death warmed up.

This is one of my better days, says Charlie.

What's this I hear about Maureen pocketing your life savings?

Lorraine puts an arm over her brother-in-law's shoulders. She smells a faint body odour, notices that Charlie is unshaved.

There was £25,000, or thereabouts. She's kept it all. It's in a box.

I can't credit Maureen doing that. There must be a reason. What did she say?

She said I lost my right to it when I . . . when I . . . She's going to save it for my grandson. Says I'll just drink it anyway.

Charlie voice falters.

When you what? says Lorraine.

I think I can hear Kylie again, says Tommy.

*When you **what**, Charlie?* says Lorraine.

Charlie paradiddles his fingers on the table. There is dirt under his fingernails. Without Maureen, his personal hygiene has been slipping.

Charlie gave her a little bit of a slap, says Tommy.

Lorraine withdraws the arm from Charlie's shoulders.

How much of a slap?

It wasn't just a slap, says Charlie miserably. His eyes meet Lorraine's, then, unable to bear it, he looks away. *I punched her.*

How much? Lorraine's voice is even, cut glass.

How do you mean?

To. What. Extent.

There was some facial bruising. A sprained wrist.

What else?

I busted one of her ribs.

Quite a slap, says Lorraine coldly.

He didn't mean to hurt her, says Tommy pleadingly. *He was at the end of his tether. Christ, she's been in like Flint with his fucking neighbour for the last two years, old Magnum Force there, old Peter-on-the-horn. It's enough to drive any man beyond the pale.*

That's no excuse. If I did everything I'd like to do to you, you'd be in half a dozen pieces in the waste disposal.

Tommy snorts, swigs at his drink.

Is she going to prosecute? says Lorraine.

No, says Charlie, eyes downward.

More fool her.

That's a bit harsh, Lol.

Now the baby really does starts crying again. Lorraine raises her eyes to the heavens, shoots a glance at Tommy and makes towards the sound. When she is gone, Tommy and Charlie sit in silence. Finally, Charlie looks up. There are tears in his eyes once again.

*What am I going to **do**, Tommy?*

Tommy shuffles his shoulders, adopting a position that suggests fresh starts, positive action.

Come on, Charlie. Don't be a moaning fucking whassername. Minnie. OK. Okey-dokey karaoke. Let's look at the pros and cons. There's no use crying over spilt milk. What's done is done. What's the bottom line here? First, you're going to need somewhere to live. How much are you going to get when the house is sold?

About fifty K. The lawyer says forty, but I think I'll do better.

Are you going to stay in MK?

I don't know. I suppose so. I can't come back to London now. The property prices are too high.

Well, if you stay there, you'll have enough for a deposit on a little flat and a good bit left over.

Who's going to lend me the money, Tommy? I got no job.

They don't care. What about redundancy?

Not much. Maybe ten grand at best.

So that'll be sixty grand. Get another property, borrow as much as you can. The price will carry on rising, and you'll be back on your feet in no time.

They can't keep rising for ever, Tommy.

Charlie, they ain't going to go down. Interest rates are down again. There's money all over the place. I'm in the trade, mate, I know the score. You can't lose.

At this, Charlie brightens somewhat.

Perhaps you're right.

Think about it. Bang twenty grand down on a property. They'll lend up to five times your declared income at the moment, plus repayment holidays, God knows what. They're gagging for business. Get some of that money that's sloshing about. The tumbledown effect or whatever they call it.

*I haven't **got** any income.*

Tommy touches his nose.

*I said **declared** income, didn't I? Declared. You don't have to be straight about it. They have these, what are they called, these types of mortgages where they don't check up on you. They just give you what you say you earn. 'Non-status'. I can tell them that you're on my firm. Adviser or something. I mean, don't go mad or that, but let's just say you told them you were earning twenty grand per a. Then they're going to give you 100 Gs. They're even doing 100 per cent mortgages, where you don't have to put down any deposit. I know a bloke in the Jewing trade, he'll sort you. You can get a* *lovely new place, low repayments, leave yourself plenty of capital to play with for doing whatever you want to do. Nice little shag-pad.*

Shag-pad?

Come on, Charlie. Look on the bright side, you miserable twat. You're free, mate.

Tommy lowers his voice.

It's a blessing in disguise. You ain't got to listen to some gash ear-aching you all day long. What a relief. You're still in pretty good shape for your age. There's plenty of muff out there for a man of property.

Charlie slumps again slightly.

A man of property with no job.

No one's *got a job any more. Work for yourself! It's the future. That's what I'm saying. No deposit, no check on your income. You'll have forty, fifty grand to set yourself up in whatever line you choose. There's loads of little earners. Everyone's making it, Charlie. This is your big chance! In five years, Maureen will be eating her heart out that she's dumped on you, because you're going to be driving around in a nice big Merc with a nice little bit of gash in the seat with her hand on your gearstick, if you know what I mean, while she's stuck with that gourd in the back of a Mini Metro going down to Kwik Save for some cut-price deep-frozen fucking turkey nuggets. You can go into* **business***, Charlie. It's not the end of something. It's a new beginning!*

Kylie pissed on my hand.

Lorraine has returned to the room, holding her right arm in the air, and heads for the sink. The screaming has grown louder. Tommy and Charlie fall silent as Lorraine washes herself and, with a dark glare at Tommy, returns upstairs.

Tommy speaks again in hushed tones.

See what I mean? Women are a bloody vexation. The times I've wanted to do to Lolly what you did to Maureen.

Charlie looks up at his brother's red, densely packed face.

Why didn't you, then?

Why?

Why?

Well.

Tommy screws up his face as if making a huge effort to uncover the answer.

It would have been wrong, I suppose.

Charlie nods. The thick knot of sickness that has hardly left his stomach since the day he split with Maureen seems to tighten once more.

*Anyway, never mind that, Charlie. Never mind me. This isn't **about** me. You've got what everyone wants. You got freedom. Now it's down to **you**.*

Some light at the back of Charlie's eyes flickers. He feels some faint pulse at the centre of himself, some emerging core of possibility.

Think about the future. It's Pennies from Heaven, Charlie. Every time it rains, etc.

*But what am I going to **do**? What kind of business could I set up?*

Whatever you like! There's money out there slopping around all over the place. Someone somewhere has spilled a big bucket of it. It's there for the people who have the guts and the get up and go to reach out and take it. The thing is to think of something you enjoy, try and find a market for that thing. It's A, B and C – it's arse, bollocks and cunt.

There's nothing I enjoy I can make a living out of. What am I going to do, open a card school? Start an off-licence?

A tobacconist's maybe, says Tommy, seeing Charlie reach for yet another cigarette.

Yeah, or my own railway station, laughs Charlie, his first laugh of that day.

Somewhere upstairs, Kylie has started crying again. A dog barks in the street.

Your own railway station, says Tommy. *Now there's a thought.*

Charlie stops laughing. His eyelids flicker.

Model railways, says Charlie, with a tone of dawning amazement. *Model railways.*

Hobbies and games . . . It's a massive market. People have got more money to spend than ever before. There's millions of the bastards out there who're into those toy trains.

***Model** trains.*

You could get a lease on a shop outright with your capital, have plenty left for stock. With those sorts of bananas in the bank, they'll lend you even more. It's a goer, Charlie, I'm sure it's a goer.

I don't know. I've never run a business in my life.

You'd never owned a house before in your life either, had you, and I remember how you moaned and groaned and dragged your feet before you bought that one. Now look at you. Five years down the line, you've got fifty, maybe sixty grand in the bin. If you'd played it safe, Maureen would have got the key to the council flat, cos they're all lesbians at the local council, and you'd have been living in a bleeding bedsit in Earls Court, surrounded by a bunch of koala-fuckers. You got to move up and move on, Charlie. This is a big opportunity.

Charlie nods, amazed at the simplicity of it all.

Maybe you're right, he says.

When you're right, you're right, says Tommy.

Tommy! Get your fat behind out of that chair! calls Lorraine.

Tommy doesn't move, but pours Charlie another glass of Scotch. He winks at Charlie.

Charlie goes to the lavatory and Lorraine comes back in, harassed, chewing her own teeth.

What did you tell him?

That he could start his own business.

What? That . . . loser?

There are worse things than being a loser.

Not any more there aren't. Not in this day and age. Not in 1987.

Anyway, he's not a loser. He's going to be OK. Just you wait and see.

Lorraine yawns theatrically, shakes her head and turns towards the kitchen. Charlie reappears with a vague smile upon his face.

Here he is, then. Donald Trump, says Lorraine with a snort.

Charlie simply looks puzzled.

Who's he?

15

15 October 1987. Margaret Thatcher has been elected for a third term this summer and she is triumphant, resplendent, invulnerable. She has cut taxes, and cut taxes again. Oil money flows into her coffers from the cold wastes of the North Sea. Interest rates are the lowest anyone can remember. The financial pages are sexier than the page-three girls, and the sell-offs of state property, the *family silver*, serve to top up coffers already overflowing. It can't last . . . but then again, maybe it can! Anything is possible! Even stupid people, mediocre people, *undeserving* people, are walking around with labels that announce their extraordinary, unprecedented success.

And suddenly . . . labels are everywhere, labels that were once reserved for the tiny layer of society at its pinnacle. There is Mulberry in Milton Keynes, there is Lacoste in Luton, there is Chanel in Chingford. Even Charlie has happily caught the bug, proudly wears the insignia for his new Ralph Lauren polo shirt, which sits this winter under a brand-new, pale yellow Pringle sweater.

Things have worked out exactly as Tommy has predicted they would. The house realized even more than they could have hoped, and there was a small pay-off from News International, and Charlie, at one golden moment, had £68,000 sitting in his deposit account, even though Maureen took close on 60 per cent, as the lawyer had predicted. Charlie has bought a new house, smaller but nice, a Barratt home, five years old, five miles away from the old one. He has a 100 per cent mortgage, but the house's value is rising so fast, the mortgage seems to be disappearing as he sits, eroded by the distant wash of larger forces. He is carried, like all the lucky ones, dipping and bobbing on a blue and green sea of banknotes.

It is the day of the opening of the Milton Keynes Model Railway Centre (prop. C. Buck). The lease cost him a £10,000 premium, then another £10,000 to fit the place out. He's spent £25,000 on stock and has borrowed £25,000 more from the bank. Tommy tells him he has to have a logo, and Charlie gets one designed for a grand – a railway engine with the name of the shop spelt out in steam. There's rent of £100 per week plus the rates, plus God alone knows what else. He's spent a few K advertising in the local paper, another on local radio. He's got accountants, book-keepers, a solicitor. There is a two-year-old silver-grey Mercedes saloon outside, which Tommy found for him, a bargain. Charlie would have been happy with some little Japanese job, but Tommy has explained that you've got to *walk the fucking walk*. No one's going to take you seriously if you don't take yourself seriously, says Tommy. So he got the Merc, and it feels good behind the wheel, it feels real, it lends him a dignity that he could never have imagined.

Sometimes Charlie thinks back to his days at the council flat in Fulham with Maureen, and thinks that it cannot be true that the same person occupied this skin, this same ghostly tenant who owns a shop, and a German car, and a lovely new house, and is single and very much available and open to offers, not that any have been forthcoming as yet.

And as he stands behind the plate-glass doors and gets ready to unlock them for his first day of trading, he realizes two things simultaneously. First, that he doesn't have a clue what he's doing. Not . . . the . . . first . . . damn . . . clue. But – Jesus God Almighty! – instead of frightening him, this thought uplifts him, amazes him with the power of his own resources in the face of such ignorance. And second, and connected to this, that this is one of the most exciting, most satisfying days of his life. He turns the key in the lock. Immediately, an ear-splitting alarm sounds. He scuttles to the control panel and punches in the code. The silence that follows resounds, feels sacred. Now Charlie sits behind his counter and surveys his empire. At the front of the shop, a giant garden railway arranged around replica fields and a single, four-foot-high snow-topped mountain. There are low waiting rooms, precisely copied signals, railway crossings where stationary model cars wait for moving trains to pass.

The railway is G Scale, and there is some sixty feet of track snaking around in an extended oval. A Lynton and Barnstaple tank locomotive sits at the miniature station, which is in this world called Chelfam Station, made of simulated stone with a tiled roof and bargeboards. A modular lattice foot bridge crosses from one platform to another. An Edwardian family awaits the train, a tiny but perfectly finished driver waits for the engine to be stoked. There are signal boxes, a station clock showing the real time: 10.03 a.m. A lone woman, who appears to be from an entirely different time zone, perhaps the 1940s or 1950s, waits for the train a few inches along from the Edwardian family. Charlie recognizes the inconsistency of these details, but views the creation of model universes with a catholic eye. He knows that artificial worlds do not need to correspond to actual ones.

He goes to a control box, which is concealed within a model signal box, and engages a switch within. There is a low thin whistle, and the train begins to move along the track, heading away from the station and towards the mountain. Its progress is predictable, inevitable, entirely satisfactory. Charlie watches it make the circuit with enormous pleasure. He does not care to make himself rich through this new business. He simply wants to be able to spend his time doing what he loves with a passion that sometimes feels evangelical.

For half an hour, he arranges scenery, polishes engines and models on the shelves, cleans dust and grit that remain from the refurbishment of what was once a hardware store off the floor. On a shelf behind the desk, alone, centred, he keeps the empty Leek and Manifold engine casing that was Robert's Christmas gift in 1980. He takes it down and dusts it off. *One day*, he thinks, but does not finish the thought. He carefully replaces the casing.

Still, no one arrives, but at exactly 10.35 a middle-aged man carrying a briefcase and looking faintly annoyed opens the door and walks in briskly.

Hello, says Charlie. *Do you know, you're my first customer? Welcome to the Milton Keynes Model . . .*

Where's the post office?

What?

Do you know where the post office is?

It's just over in the main shopping centre.

Where's that?

Charlie gestures faintly with his hand towards the north, where there is a large and obvious covered mall. Without another word, the man turns and leaves. Charlie regards the tank locomotive making its umpteenth ascent of the polystyrene mountain. It seems to struggle to reach the top. But it always makes it in the end. Thinks Charlie.

Maureen feels like shouting at Peter. She does not understand why he cannot grasp what it is she is trying to say.

We have to be absolutely realistic about cash flow, Peter. It is not important to our customers whether they have the full set of optional extras when they are learning to drive! It's just money down the drain. *Don't confuse your personal tastes for business. This business is about giving people what they want, efficiently, at the lowest possible price. It is not about having leather seat covers, or electric locking or all the other nonsense that the manufacturers load up the price with. Let's keep it simple, let's keep it basic. We start small, we start slow. We get ourselves known, we build up by word of mouth.*

But we have to advertise . . .

Of course we have to advertise. We're not in **contradiction** *to each other. But we have to target the right group. Who's learning to drive? Mostly people in their late teens and twenties. You advertise in the local paper, well, young people don't buy the local paper, it's for old fogies like me and you. You've got to go where the business is. Leaflet discos, the colleges. There's that huge university campus. Knock lessons out cheap for students. I've done the figures, Peter, you haven't. I know where we stand and I know where we have to get to.*

Peter feels winded. He is frequently amazed by Maureen, about how little she resembles the woman he first met, when he stumbled into her house with a bottle of wine. He had thought then that she was just a housewife, much like his own ex-wife, dull, kind, dutiful. But now he sees her pushing through the sheaf of papers, making precise marks in the margins, concentrated, even fierce. It still astonishes him, and he finds that he likes it, that he loves it, that he loves this woman who has so much direction and, well, get-up-and-go. She has transformed everything.

Have we sorted out that problem with the switchboard?

I think so.

You think so? Or you know so?

I'll check.

Maureen and Peter are sitting in the prefabricated building in the small car park from where they work. Peter is wearing no jacket, exposing purple City-trader braces unnecessarily supporting his snug trousers from Next. There are only two grey chairs and an ordinary desk in the room, and a small bench for anyone waiting in an even smaller anteroom. There are three second-hand Ford Escorts outside, bought by Maureen's divorce settlement, but they are proving expensive to service and maintain and the customers do not take to them. Maureen has made the decision to buy some new vehicles this autumn. Peter gets excited, wants a raftload of extras. He has all the big ideas, which Maureen has to water down with her instinctive practicality. As a partnership, thinks Maureen, it works well, it balances up. Peter gave up his job to take a chance on her. This evidence of faith she will not forget.

Has our ten o'clock come in yet?

He's waiting outside.

Where's Cathy?

Cathy is the newest of their five employees, a thirty-three-year-old whom Maureen has seen Peter eye with less than the indifference she expects of him. Flattered by Peter's attention, Cathy takes the security of her position for granted, and is thus sometimes tardy in both manners and time-keeping.

I don't know.

This is the third time in a fortnight she's been late. If she's not here in the next five minutes, she's out.

Maureen says this briskly and with absolute certainty. Peter looks suddenly uncomfortable.

What do you mean?

I mean what I mean.

The sack?

The sack. Yes, of course the sack.

But I've never . . . I wouldn't know how . . .

He shifts anxiously in his chair, stares past Maureen's head at the small window behind her.

What if she goes to the union?

Maureen almost laughs out loud.

Stop it, Peter. You're scaring me.

Peter blinks, still uncertain.

*Well, will **you** do it, then?*

I'll be happy to do it. Look, it's five past. You'd better take the customer. Apologize. Offer a discount.

I'm sure Cathy will be here in a minute.

This is business, Peter.

Maureen gets up, walks to the office door and pushes it open. An aerobic smile manifests itself.

Mr Connolly?

A young man with an attempted moustache, wearing Adidas trainers, a Nike T-shirt and ballooning track-suit bottoms, comes through from the waiting room.

Yes?

I'm most terribly sorry. Cathy Edwards seems to have been delayed. Would you mind taking our senior partner instead? Peter Horn? He's a far more experienced tutor. And of course for your inconvenience we would be happy to offer you a 20 per cent discount on the lesson.

The young man shrugs.

All right.

Peter picks up his coat and pecks Maureen on the cheek before leaving.

Go easy on Cathy.

Go and do your lesson.

Maureen watches as the Escort pulls out of the car park with the pupil at the wheel. A few seconds after it has disappeared, she spots Cathy Edwards's car, a five-year-old red Mini, appearing through the gap where Peter has just left. It screeches to a halt and the driver stays in her seat. She adjusts her hair, at length, gazing in the rear-view mirror.

A minute more for a little make-up. This fixes Maureen's decision.

When Cathy enters the office, Maureen does not look up.

Hello, Mrs B. Sorry I'm a bit late. But it looks like my client hasn't turned up anyway. So, no harm done, I suppose.

Could you give me a moment, Catherine.

Maureen makes a note in her diary to ring the local newspaper and place an ad for a new driving instructor. Then she looks up. And the smile on Cathy Edwards's face dissolves.

By late afternoon, Charlie has had precisely three customers. The first, a teenage boy, simply purchases a pot of blue model paint for £2.25. The second, a man in his sixties with an Amish-style beard and an aggressively friendly manner, talks to Charlie about the minutiae of German and European turn-of-the-century locomotives for thirty minutes, then departs without buying anything. The third is a sharply dressed working-class young woman, buying a gift for her husband. She reads from a scrap of paper her requirement for a working water tower kit YG628, manufactured in fibreglass resin with brass parts and wire mesh delivery bag. She departs with the water tower in a matter of three minutes, barely even glancing at the remainder of the layout.

It is not much profit for a day's work, reflects Charlie. But, he thinks, obviously there is going to be a period in which he has to get himself established. Success doesn't happen overnight. These things have to spread by word of mouth as much as anything. He feels sure people will come.

Just before five-thirty, which he has decided is the end of his working day, a thin rain begins to fall outside the shop. His spirits are a little low. Under the counter he keeps a hip flask of brandy, from which he has been taking nips all day. The removal of Maureen from his life is a constant ache. A faint feeling of sickness as ever presses at his stomach. Outside, through the skein of grey, he sees a police car with reflector windows pull up. A solitary officer emerges and heads for the shop. The alarm has accidentally gone off several more times. Perhaps someone has alerted the police station. Charlie replaces the hip flask swiftly in the drawer; he is not sure if there are certain rules *irregardless* of the fact that he is the proprietor. Maybe they've had a report. Then he dismisses the thought as silly, almost pulls out the flask again in defiance.

The policeman comes closer and now Charlie can make out his features. He removes his cap. Charlie sees that the policeman is his son.

Charlie's first thought is to hide, to retreat into the bowels of the shop and not emerge. A bolt of biblical pride surges within, too great, it feels, to swallow. But he sees that Robert has spotted him. There is no escape. Robert enters through the glass doors. It is only two years since Charlie has seen him, but he seems much older. His hair, which has been plastered down on to his head by his cap, is thinning badly.

Hello, Dad.

Robert folds his arms, surveys the shop with a thin, even gaze. Charlie fights with an impulse to throw him out, but the loneliness of the day has been too much. The confession to himself comes reluctantly, but comes none the less: he is pleased to see his son.

Got your security sorted out, have you?

How did you know I was here?

Robert looks surprised.

Mum told me.

Charlie, although he thinks of Maureen often, has not registered that she might also follow his progress in life, and so is vaguely pleased that his efforts have been acknowledged in another's consciousness. He regards Robert, remembers the night at Wapping. The boy is looking heavier, less of a boy. It strikes Charlie with surprising force that his son is now a fully grown man, not far off thirty years old.

Charlie ventures tentatively out from behind the counter.

I'm glad to see you, son.

Robert nods.

Yeah, Dad. I'm pleased to see you too.

The space between them trembles slightly, but cannot be stabilized enough for an embrace. Charlie touches him on the shoulder by his police number inscribed in silver.

Nice and shiny.

Take a look at this, then.

Robert removes his jacket. Underneath, three angled darts on the shoulder.

What's this?

*I'm a sergeant, Dad. I got promotion. I'm **good** at my job.*

Charlie fights with himself, wins the victory within that he seeks.

*Well . . . well **done**, Robert. I always . . .*

You always what?

Charlie hears the edge of irritation in his son's voice, feels an acid stab of regret.

I'm sorry, Rob. I suppose I never really . . . had enough faith in you.

Robert nods, makes no other acknowledgement of what it has cost Charlie to say so much.

I had some business to attend to up here. So I thought I'd come up and check out your new venture.

Oh.

How's it doing, then?

So-so. Early days yet. This is my first day.

I know. I've brought you something.

He hands him something in a small box. At once, Charlie flushes with pleasure. He knows what the gift will be. He glances at the casing of the Leek and Manifold locomotive that sits on the shelf behind his desk. Now at last it will have the engine that Robert promised him all those years ago. His son has done well, as he promised he one day would.

He tears off the cardboard. Inside is a plastic shopping bag. He takes out the contents. There is a paperweight with a model of a Miami Hotel inside and some kind of item of clothing. Charlie opens it out. The message reads 'My Son Went to Florida and All He Brought Me Was This Lousy T-Shirt'. Charlie manages a thin smile.

Clever.

It's a smile, ain't it? says Robert. He picks up a small model fire extinguisher and begins idly examining it. *Reckon you'll do all right, then, do you?*

Like I say, it'll take time. How are you, Robert? How's everything?

All right.

Robert looks up, past his father's head, at the gift he once bought his father so proudly displayed on the shelf. Charlie seems to see Robert's face soften and now, for the first time, Robert lets his eyes rest on Charlie's face for more than a split second.

Look, I'm sorry it has had to be this way between us, Dad.

Does it have to be this way?

Doesn't it?

Maybe.

Robert puts down the fire extinguisher.

I've got something else for you.

He turns back towards the blocked-out windows of the police car, makes a gesture. Charlie watches as the door opens. He does not recognize the woman who gets out at first. Her punky hair has disappeared, and the clothes that Charlie always described to Maureen as 'way out'. She is smartly dressed, with a short coiffed bob, a pair of pressed jeans and a navy cardigan. It is only when she beckons towards the open door and a young boy, maybe five years old, walks out after her.

Carol's a good mother, says Robert.

You and her are . . .

We're just friends, says Robert. *I see plenty of Chuck. He's a nice kid.*

The boy is a little chunky, with thick black hair, and he skips towards the train shop, Carol following after. He does not wait for Carol to arrive before pushing the door open and marching right up to Charlie.

Are you my grandad?

Charlie gazes down at him. Sees the cornflowers in his eyes. Thick black hair, his own hair magically transported down two generations. He holds out a hand. The boy grabs it, allows Charlie to shake it once, then lets go.

I suppose so, says Charlie.

The boy has already focused away from Charlie and is staring at the model railway.

Would you like to be a train driver? says Charlie.

Chuck answers without looking up at him.

No. I want to be a policeman.

That's good, says Charlie. *That's nice.*

Driving a train is boring.

Hello, Mr Buck, says Carol.

You should call me Charlie, says Charlie.

And he closes the space between them in three paces and enfolds her in a hug, wondering simultaneously why he cannot do this with his son. Carol submits, then gently pulls herself away. Chuck is pulling levers in the station box of the train layout.

He looks like you, says Carol. *Doesn't he, Rob?*

Worse luck, says Robert pleasantly.

Grandad's old, says Chuck.

That's right, says Charlie, almost to himself, surprised that he has been hurt by this. He turns to Carol.

You still playing that terrible music?

Yeah, says Carol.

You can borrow some of my Mantovani if you like, says Charlie, the lilt of a joke in his voice.

Who's he? pipes up Chuck. His voice has Carol's faint northern shadow.

No one, says Charlie. *Someone who used to matter.*

There is a stretched silence. The past weighs down. The air is still thick with unforgotten hurt. Robert checks his watch.

We have to be going.

Going? You've only been here five minutes.

To be honest, I've got more police work still to do and I want to drop Carol and Chuck off to see Mum. She's cooking dinner and that. I just wanted to see if you were all right.

Are you my grandma's husband? says Chuck.

Not any more, says Charlie. *We got unmarried.*

Why? says Chuck.

Things change, says Charlie.

It's the truth, says Robert. He shuffles his feet uneasily. *We're a bit late.*

That's fine. That's good. Give Maureen my best, eh?

Of course, Dad. Listen. The shop looks good.

Thanks.

He seems to be about to say something else, then turns away instead.

Sorry about everything that's happened. With you and Mum, I mean.

Well, it's just the way the . . .

Cookie crumbles.

Charlie smiles.

I'm like a stuck record.

No, you're not. You've had a go. Life's hard. People get things wrong.

Ain't that the truth, kiddo.

He puts his hand out to Robert, and Robert takes it firmly and shakes it. His grip is powerful, his hand far larger than his father's now. Eye contact is briefly made, then unmade.

See you, then, Dad.

See you, son. Be careful, eh?

***You** be careful.*

I'm proud of you, Rob.

I know. I know you are. He smiles. *Chuck, you want to give your grandad a kiss?*

No, says Chuck. *That's gay.*

Carol, Robert and Charlie all laugh, genuine laughter, this time full and unrestrained. Immediately Chuck begins to cry.

What's the matter, Chuckle? says Carol.

You all laughing at me.

Carol picks Chuck up and his snivels diminish.

Say goodbye to your grandad.

From the face pressed into Carol's shoulder a muffled voice emerges.

Bye, Grandad.

Bye-bye, Chuck. Come and see your old grandad sometimes. You can play with my toy trains.

Chuck emerges from the folds of his mother, nods at Charlie.

Bye, Carol. Bye, Rob.

Charlie watches them all as they climb into the police car and it revs up, then moves away, heads northwards, towards Maureen and Peter's. He wonders what is for dinner there. At home, Charlie has a Marks & Spencer Roast Pork Meal for one.

*

That evening Charlie celebrates his first day in business with two bottles of what he assumes is decent red wine since it costs £3.99 a bottle. He gulps down the roast pork, which he enjoys, although eating alone has seemed one of the worst things to him about being divorced. He and Maureen never used to talk much during dinner, but to have someone there made all the difference to the meal, made it not just about the trivial, animal compulsion to feed. By the time he gets to his pudding, a microwavable individual chocolate sponge, he is already at the end of the second bottle. He thinks of Robert, and Maureen and Peter, five miles away, as he spoons at the earth-coloured sponge. The television blares; the repeating patterns and dramas of *EastEnders* reassure him that there is a place to which he is still connected. It is he who is addicted to soaps now, he who requires a supplement to reality, like the vitamins Maureen used to take for her bones and skin.

While eating, he divides his attention between Albert Square and the local newspaper, which seems to be full of photos of unattractive children on bouncy castles, disabled people running marathons, and stories about crime, endless crime. Muggers, robbers, Rolex-snatchers, petty fraudsters. From Bletchley to Luton, the whole county is awash with people seizing other people's rightful property. No wonder Robert looks so drained, thinks Charlie, trying to hold the collapsing seams of everything, of society, together, even though there was no such thing, Mrs Thatcher said, and Charlie felt she'd got it right. Just people in their houses, like his house, trying to get along for themselves. That was about the size of it.

He flicks through the pages. The pleasure of his first day in business has entirely evaporated now. Worries press down on him about the repayability of the debts he has, the demands of the landlord, the price of stock. He looks about him at the walls, imagines the bricks and mortar underneath the plaster, and this comforts him. He knows the price is expanding as he watches, creating wealth out of nowhere. It is his safety net. House prices, as Tommy has predicted, are still rising and rising. They are an unstoppable force.

Relieving, by means of this thought, one set of anxieties, he exposes a deeper nerve pulsing within which, he suddenly realizes, has been with him from the day Maureen turned up alone driving a car for which Charlie thought she had no licence, the day Charlie assaulted her, the last day she wiped a crumb tenderly from the edges of his mouth. A feeling materialized then within him almost at that exact moment, like some strange cooling, some suffocation of the muscles of the heart. Through the years of his job, and with his family, in all his years in London, he had felt many varieties of ordinary unhappiness but never this odd constriction. Now he has named it and identified it, this twentieth-century curse, this refrigeration in his veins, this price that choice carries like a parasite on a living thing. This loneliness.

He cannot think what do with himself. Sometimes he has the feeling that he wants to vomit only he doesn't have a mouth. It is not just emptiness. It is also a soft choking, a terrible pressure for company, for human connection of almost any kind. It cries out silently and terribly down the new streets of the Barratt homes and carriage-lamped half-lit front doors. It is unbearable.

He sits at the table, not moving, not really watching the TV, not really reading the paper, not really finishing his pudding. He is in a daze of aloneness; it comes upon him like this sometimes. He drinks fiercely down to the dregs of his glass, but this he knows will not do the trick, short of rendering him unconscious.

His eye falls once more on the local newspaper. There is a column marked 'One to One' – 'People Like You for People

Like You'. He picks it up and begins to scan desultorily the advertisements listed underneath. The men seem to heavily outnumber the women. What women there are seem to favour long walks in the country, salsa dancing, wine bars and cinema. Many seem to be cuddly or full-bodied. Their primary requirements are for good physical height and a GSOH, but Charlie is unsure what this stands for. Many others claim to be happy and satisfied with their lives. He understands the code. He respects the execution of these carefully forged lies.

There is a form at the bottom of the page for new advertisements. *Why not?* thinks Charlie suddenly. *There's no shame in it. Not nowadays.* Perhaps he's a prize. Not *so* old, small businessman, own house, gleaming silver Merc. Yes. There would have to be a market out there for him.

He reaches for a piece of paper and a Biro, tries to concentrate. His first effort at composing an advertisement for himself he finds disappointing. 'Businessman, own Mercedes, late middle age, seeks lively lady to keep him company and share life's little up's and down's'. He is not sure where to put the apostrophes but feels sure that someone at the paper, a sub-editor, will sort it out. It is not the punctuation that worries him unduly, but the lack of the flavour of his life. It is too bland, too empty, too crude. But how can you trap an existence in so few words?

He tries again. 'Middle-aged gentleman, successful, nice home, recently divorced, seeks woman of similar age or younger for company and mutual . . .'

Mutual . . . mutual what? Nothing *goes* with mutual. However, he is pleased to have excised the 'late' from 'late middle age'. This modest bevelling of the truth's sharp edges is bound to widen the net. The softening of references to his prosperity also seems to succeed in rendering the ad less vulgar – to announce himself as a businessman seems to suggest that this, too, is a business, this seeking of love. Women, he intuits, will not respond to this. Also, Charlie thinks, it is a positive move to suggest that he is divorced. To never have married in middle age, never mind late middle age, would certainly suggest something fundamentally defective, inadequate. The Mercedes is gone. Again too nakedly transactional. Should he claim to have a GSOH when he does not know what one is? Obviously not, but he decides to claim to be tall, although he is only average, five ten. Mutual what . . . mutual what? The word is no good.

Ten minutes and three more drafts on, he settles on a final version. 'Tall middle-aged gentleman, successful, nice home, solvent, recently divorced. Seeks woman of similar or younger age for walks, company, maybe more?' He likes this, likes the open-endedness of the final question mark. He feels suddenly sure that it will draw replies. He cuts out the voucher, inserts it into an envelope and decides to go and post it there and then, in case his determination dissipates during the night.

There is a post box 100 yards away. A neighbour notices him and Charlie smiles at him with some embarrassment, as if he could guess what Charlie was posting, as if the humiliation shone clear through the envelope. For now in the cold night air, he cannot help but see it as a coming low, as a desperate cry. He is no longer Mr Charles William Buck, husband of Maureen Buck, father of Robert Buck, but Middle-aged gentleman. Recently divorced. He hesitates, drops the envelope into the gaping mouth of the box, and it falls with a faint papery flurry. Then he hurries home through the still-falling rain.

He is amazed at the strength of the wind. It howls and rages down the street, to such an extent that Charlie feels he can almost lean into it and not fall over. On the television that night, Michael Fish had said that the rumours of a hurricane were nothing to worry about. It was a hell of a breeze, though.

Three hours later, Charlie wakes up from a sleep in which he dreams of Margaret Thatcher shrunken to toy size and driving one of his model trains across a desert. She is lost, looking for her son, Mark. Charlie is helping her with the search. He wakes up just as she toots the horn, which makes a sound like Big Ben. The windows in his bedroom are rattling like a strong man is outside physically shaking them. There is an extraordinary rushing noise in his ears. There is the sense of a world in motion, of chaos descending. He panics momentarily, thinks of the atomic bomb. All that fear throughout the 1950s and 1960s has never quite left him, although the Russians have given up the game now, outbid by Ronnie Reagan. He admires Reagan, his common decency and the pleasant, folksy approachability of his smile.

The panic subsides as it gradually dawns on Charlie that the sound is merely the wind barrelling across the spaces between the red houses in the new town at a breathtaking velocity. He thinks he hears tree branches cracking, the sound of breaking glass.

Clad in his pyjamas, he makes his way to the window, which is shaking violently. He opens the curtains and there is enough light to make out the devastation beneath. Gardens are littered with rubbish, old branches, small logs. Several large trees have toppled at the backs of the houses opposite. A telegraph pole has been uprooted, the wires hanging crazily. Lights are on everywhere, although his watch shows two a.m. Several people are, like him, observing the spectacle through their windows.

The room is cold. He hugs himself. He wants to go back to sleep, but it seems to him somehow that the drama is too large to be ignored. He has always enjoyed storms, ever since he was a small boy, the sense of safety they produced within him, listening from the warm inside.

Charlie has been looking into the middle distance, searching for damage. He sees trees swaying at impossible angles. An entire branch detaches itself and takes flight, depositing itself on the roof of a small semi 500 feet distant. Diagonally across the way from Charlie, another light flicks on in a window. Children's faces appear.

Charlie has a bottle of Scotch in the room. He pours himself a slug, sinks it in one, then goes back to the window, glass in hand. Now at last, he brings his eyes down to the site of his own back garden. The noise intensifies, the wind threatening now to bust the windows of the house in. The sense of safety is supplanted by a vague awareness of real threat. Charlie peers through the darkness at his garden, which is at that moment illuminated by a flash from a neighbour's security lights as a frightened cat scuttles past infra-red sensors.

Charlie slams his glass down. Then he is running, running down the stairs, still clad in his striped flannel pyjamas, his soft cock protruding sadly through the open vent at the front. His breathing is heavy, strained, as he reaches the back door and fumbles with the key. He drops it, then retrieves it, this time engaging the mortise. He fears going out in this fierce wind. But he has no choice. Leaving the key in the lock, he turns the handle.

The wind is pushing directly against the back door and, to his amazement, Charlie finds it hard to open because of the air pressure. But it moves and then he is outside. He looks up at the house opposite. He notices the children he has seen before staring down at him from the window. He sees them laughing and wonders automatically what the joke might be. Then he realizes suddenly, and with revulsion, that they are laughing at *him*. He imagines himself seen through their eyes, his full head of dyed black hair standing up fantastically from his reddened, scared, distended face.

The swilling of wind and rain, the panic in his mind, conceal the fact from him that his cock still protrudes from the front of his pyjamas. There is nothing on his feet in the cold night air. He treads in the mud of the lawn like a padding animal, defenceless prey for larger beasts. The wind batters at him.

What he has seemed to see from the window of the house is confirmed. His own garden railway, his pride and joy, the models, the station houses and signal boxes, the fire extinguishers, the train, the track itself, have been uprooted and smashed to pieces. Some actually lie in neighbouring gardens, other parts, as he watches, are being carried across the lawn. He chases a nineteenth-century parson, but loses the model through a hole in his fence. The locomotive has been crushed by a small falling tree.

Now Charlie is on his knees in the mud, trying to gather up these scraps of his imagined world, but larger forces have scattered them irrevocably. All the pieces acquired meticulously and painstakingly down the years have been thrown, literally, to the wind.

Charlie desperately tries to gather together what is left. The sharp rain beats harder; he throws his head back at the heavens and cries out, an animal cry, wordless. The children watching are crouched over in laughter now. Their parents, joining them, close the curtains, scolding. They, too, find it funny but are disgusted by the old man's penis flapping around. They might report him to the police, but decide, on balance, that he is simply and harmlessly mad.

16

In the nights following the storm, Charlie begins to dream that the world is coming to an end. Or that some seed which has been planted somewhere in the darkness of the past is coming to terrible fruition. Signs and portents are everywhere. The Stock Exchange has crashed; money has been wiped off Charlie's small holdings in British Gas. There is a bomb in Enniskillen, a deadly fire at King's Cross.

And yet the centre holds. While 1987 leaves its trail of chaos, with astonished corpses in Hungerford, the drowned in Zebrugge and armies of abused children in Cleveland, in comes 1988 surfing on a waver bigger, crazier, richer than ever before. Now it has the desperation of the closing hours of a party, but the energy is none the less frenetic for that. Everyone – everyone! – has money, apart, of course, from the multiplying ragtags who find their way into shop doorways and camp out next to ATMs. More and more now, Charlie feels in his pocket for change as he passes. They no longer seem like scroungers and ponces. Charlie has come to understand how bad luck and bad choices can bring a man down, the brute power of circumstance.

Some of the money is even coming Charlie's way – as Tommy predicted, the shop is beginning to cover its costs. Rental values are going up, so he faces a hefty hike on the rent review, but even so; leisure and leisure activities are the future. Trade, if not brisk, is respectable.

And property! Nothing will stop property! In the spring budget, Nigel Lawson announces a cut in tax relief on joint mortgages – but has generously left four months before it comes into effect. So everyone is queuing up to buy, and the money flows in cascades, in waterfalls, rivers of income and expenditure running into oceans of credit and debt. Charlie knows that the value of his house has risen by 30 per cent in the last year, so he feels safe, protected by his hard, bricks-and-mortar cushion. So much money represented by such a small and ordinary little house in such an ordinary little town. Will it end? Will there be a fall? Tommy says no, not yet, and Tommy has been right all down the line thus far, so Charlie listens to him again, and borrows more money against the value of the house to fund greater stock investment and better computer accounting systems (*You got to have a computer, Charlie*, says Tommy. *Computers are fucking **tomorrow**.*)

Things could be worse, things could very definitely be worse, Charlie tells himself as he closes up shop for the day. They have taken over £1,000 on this very ordinary Wednesday afternoon. It doesn't add up to much profit when all the overheads are taken into account, but in the long run it's sound. It has promise.

Charlie has had replies to his ad in the personal columns. The first week it ran, he got only five responses. He then decided to take out a 'six weeks for the price of four' offer that the paper was running and over this period many more letters have come to his doorstep – nearly fifty in all. Each one he reads carefully, and responds to carefully, even if he is not interested. A good half of the women writing seem to him on the cusp of being dislocated by their solitude, and this edge of desperation, although it is one he himself feels daily, repels him. So tremendous is their plight, they barely bother to conceal it any more; the letters are not letters of courtship but of pleading for very life. This is expressed either explicitly, in the semi-literate text of the letters (*You sound like exactly the kind of dream bote I have been wating for*) or, more often, implicitly, in the tragic photographs, with rounded corners and flared red-flash camera pupils, as if some devil has already claimed them.

Those remaining are a mixed bag. Some letters are formal, polite, as if distantly interested in a mildly promising business proposition (*Dear Sir. I read your advertisement in the **Milton Keynes Inquirer** with some interest. However, I have a number of concerns . . .*). Others are too short, too terrified, a sentence and an address. Only half a dozen seem to contain, within the shape and content of the hand that frames them, some resemblance to a world which Charlie can recognize as normal or familiar.

He has so far met four of these six women. The first, from her letter, seemed an entirely promising prospect. She, too, was a displaced Londoner, from roughly the same district (Hammersmith rather than Fulham) and roughly the same age (fifty-two). She wrote well, grammatically and plainly, and was honest about her situation; about the extent of her loneliness, about how since her husband had died she had had trouble making new friends. But she had many interests, and still considered herself 'young at heart'.

Something in the tone of the letter made Charlie warm to her and, after a few nights of plucking up courage, he found the resolution to telephone her at the number she had inscribed in tidy copperplate at the top of the page. The voice that had answered his call was soft and attractive, and they had enjoyed a nice chat of some thirty or so minutes before agreeing to meet at a local steak house.

Charlie, on arriving, had spotted his date and found her immediately physically repulsive, with a parched, emaciated frame and thinned-out hair that somehow suggested cancer to him. To his shame, he had left without even introducing himself, turning on his heel in the lobby of the restaurant, and headed home to leave an apologetic message on her answering machine claiming that his estranged wife had suddenly returned to him and he was thus unavailable. He realized the improbability of the excuse, but he thought that she would be grateful for even so transparent a lie.

The second woman had been younger than him, in her mid-forties, and was surprisingly attractive. It had been obvious from the word go, from the way that she scrutinized his belly poking out over the top of his trousers, from the way she looked at him askance as he struggled to pick out the right cutlery from the array of possibilities at the fancy restaurant she had insisted on him taking her to, that she was simply out of his league. She had kept an air of studied indifference and tight politeness all the way through the short dinner. She had criticized the amount that he drank, which admittedly had been excessive even for Charlie, who was by now sinking the equivalent of three bottles of wine a day. In the end, the woman had left swiftly at the end of the main course without ordering pudding. Charlie had felt humiliated, but reasoned that it was poetic justice after his behaviour on the previous date.

Before contacting the third woman, Charlie had experienced a sudden renewed jag of grief for Maureen and had almost rung her up and begged her to return. How he ached for the familiarity, the dull worn groove of their shared life. This attempt to create newness at the end of so much time seemed increasingly repulsive to him and unutterably depressing. He had almost thrown the rest of the letters away but had finally rung up the third prospect.

The subsequent meeting had heartened him. The woman he met for a cup of coffee (she eschewed dinners, worrying that they implied too much too soon) at a shopping mall café was extremely kind and solicitous, and about, he estimated, as attractive a prospect as he himself, so the playing field was more or less level. A small woman, in good shape for her claimed fifty-one years, she possessed an unusual capacity for asking questions that were neither aggressive nor intrusive, simply well aimed. Charlie's impacted life began to loosen and drift out of him, in a swelling mist of stumbling words and sentences.

The woman, whose name was Ruth, had a daughter, Cassie, whom she clearly loved, an oral hygienist who worked at a dental practice in Luton. She showed him photographs, carried three of them around in her purse. A fresh-faced girl, twenty-one, almost blotted out by galaxies of freckles. They saw each other every week, were the best of friends. Charlie in turn told her about Robert. She had listened silently, but attentively, and soon he was talking about his falling out with Lloyd, about Maureen's infidelity, about the thin stretch of his life. At one moment when he found himself talking about the pain of his divorce, she had put her hand on top of his. He had found himself shocked by the electrical reaction this provoked in him, the establishment of contact, however slight, after so long. He had almost found himself crying; but had held himself back, thinking the situation ridiculous. Ruth and he had agreed to meet again, but then she had phoned him to say there was some kind of family crisis and that she would call him again when it had been sorted out.

Charlie had at first assumed this to be a brush-off, but she rang again, once more apologizing, explaining that her daughter was unwell and that she would be in touch the first chance she got.

In the meantime, Charlie felt, since no romantic bond had actually been established between them, and probably nothing more than friendship was likely to be on the cards anyway, that he would telephone one of the last three women on his short list. Her name was Susan Galloway and she had a slight Scottish burr when she picked up the phone to answer his call. It was immediately plain that they were going to hit it off, when Charlie found himself laughing uproariously at a rather risqué joke she told him after only about ten minutes of small talk.

It emerged that they were nearly neighbours, she living on the estate but one to the west of him, and that she knew of his shop and had probably seen him at the large supermarket that stood equidistant between them, and to which they both made regular forays for solitary chill-cook meals. They agreed to meet there and then at the café in the supermarket. Susan Galloway turned out to be a dapper pepper-and-salt-haired woman with an open, guileless smile and a slightly flirtatious giggle, only forty-five years old and, to Charlie's eyes, extremely attractive.

She had eaten teacakes with dainty hands and small fluttering gestures that strangely affected Charlie, who was still wearing his around-the-house jeans and the T-shirt that Robert had bought him. It had made Susan laugh. They'd spent an hour in the supermarket café, and at the end of it Charlie was convinced that this woman possessed all the attributes he had hoped for. She had a good sense of humour – a GSOH – she was attractive, she seemed to take herself lightly and, most importantly of all, she seemed, like Ruth, to find Charlie more than the absurd, silently fading creature that he sometimes glimpsed when he looked in the bathroom mirror. They had arranged to go out more formally for dinner some time the following week, and tonight is the night. Charlie feels some vague churning in his stomach as he locks up the plate-glass doors of the shop and heads towards the multistorey car park that contains his Mercedes. He feels good about the evening ahead. Nervous, but optimistic.

When he arrives home after the short drive, he immediately showers and lays out a new set of clothes. They are almost brand new, and mostly from Marks & Spencer, which once upon a time he would have considered slightly above his mark; British Home Stores or C&A had previously suited Charlie down to the ground, but now he was dissatisfied, not so much with their clothes but with what the label implied about who he was.

There is a pair of brown slacks with an iron-in crease, a generously cut shirt with a button-down collar in a shade of blue that Charlie thinks flatters his complexion. He wears a thickly knotted tie displaying an explosion of primary colours arranged in an abstract, apparently random pattern. This tie he thinks of as rather daring, rakish, even sexy. Under the whole outfit, a pair of plain cotton boxer shorts, which he finds uncomfortable but wears as insurance in case the evening becomes more passionate than he imagines is likely to be the case, given women's odd superstitions about first dates. He looks for a handkerchief. He cannot remember where he keeps them and therefore has to unload several drawers to uncover the small pile of folded white squares. It leaves a mess of photo albums, old books and magazines on the floor, under which, mysteriously, he has found the hankies, but he is in too much of a hurry to bother clearing up.

He has already decided that he wants to have sex with Susan Galloway, but is far from sure that the urge is reciprocal. You can never tell with women, he feels. They always have other agendas than those they confess to. However, nowadays – or so he has read, in the *Sun* and the *Daily Mail*, his current papers of choice – they can sometimes be upfront about sex in a way that women of his generation would never have been. Perhaps he will be the beneficiary of such a development tonight. Just in case, he has gone to a chemist's and bought a packet of three condoms, which he hides in the uppermost pocket of the navy wool 50 per cent cashmere jacket he tops his outfit with. It is tempting fate, he knows, but he'd rather be safe than sorry.

As the moment of their assignation approaches, Charlie feels his nervousness increase, and pours himself a third gin and tonic to relax. He goes to the bathroom and reaches automatically for the Hai Karate, which he has had for at least a decade. He pauses, then picks up the bottle and drops it in the bin. There is some Eau Sauvage that Maureen bought him but he never used because he wanted to finish the Hai Karate first. He realizes that this will take a lifetime. He tests the Eau Sauvage on his hand – fresh, lemony. A few dabs and slaps around the chin and neck. Perfect.

He regards his image in the mirror critically. The best view he can take of himself is that he won't look too bad after a couple of drinks in the half-light of the restaurant (dark, intimate booths) he has carefully chosen to begin his seduction of Susan.

He has called for a minicab. As he replaces the receiver, the phone rings almost at once. A sudden stab of anxiety. Perhaps Susan is going to cancel. He picks up a pencil out of habit in order to make a note on the pad that sits by the phone. Then he thinks it is the minicab firm calling back to announce a delay. When he answers, it is a woman's voice, but not Susan's. He works his memory. Ruth.

He is obscurely overcome with embarrassment, as if he is being unfaithful. She sounds frail, somewhat distant. Pointlessly, he writes the name 'Ruth' on the pad in thick grey pencil.

Hello, Charlie.

Hello, Ruth. How have you been?

A bit at sixes and sevens. But I'm a little better now. And you, Charlie. How have you been?

Oh, I shuffle along, I shuffle along.

Good. Look, I was thinking . . .

Charlie suddenly wants to derail her attempt to make a fresh assignation but cannot think how. He plays for time.

What's been wrong, Ruth?

Oh, it's just a bit of bother.

Come on, Ruth, don't be shy. No need for that type of attitude. I thought we'd become friends.

Well, I'm not sure that on the telephone . . .

Still Charlie cannot think of a way of leaving Ruth to her life without being unkind. He prods at the conversation for want of anything else to say.

*Are you in trouble? What's **happened**?*

Charlie fumbles for his cigarettes, drops them and retrieves them before Ruth answers.

It was Cassie. She's just had to have a few tests.

Tests? What for?

There is another long pause.

HIV.

HIV? What's that? says Charlie blithely.

He knows the acronym AIDS, but only vaguely apprehends the condition through which it incubates.

You know, HIV. She tested positive.

Oh.

It doesn't mean that she'll necessarily get the . . . you know. Full thing.

Full thing. What are you talking about?

His mind is scrambled. He is looking for his keys while propping the receiver up against his chest. He can hear the minicab approaching. Then the letters HIV find some resonance within him, some connection is made constructed of old newspaper cuttings and half-listened-to news reports. He suddenly stops fidgeting for the keys.

HIV? Isn't that . . . I mean, don't you get that before AIDS?

Not necessarily, Charlie.

There is a ring at the door. The minicab.

I've got to go, Ruth. I'm . . . I'm sorry about Cassie. I hope she's OK.

I think it was something to do with her dental work. She's a good girl. Not that type.

What?

Charlie, can I ring you again?

Ruth, I . . . I've got to be off now.

Will you ring me, Charlie? It would be nice to hear from you.

Sure. Yes. Look, I . . . The minicab . . .

His voice drops away.

OK, Charlie. Look after yourself.

Bye, Ruth. You too. And, uh . . . Cassie.

He hangs up. The doorbell is still ringing in his ears, although the cab driver took his finger off the button some time previously. Charlie – successfully – tries to block the thought of Ruth and Cassie out of his mind. Galaxies of freckles obscured by clouds of the urgent present.

He arrives at the restaurant some five minutes early, but to his surprise Susan is already waiting for him, sat at a table for two in a far corner of the half-full restaurant. She is wearing a long red dress that seems to him impossibly lush, exotic. Her hips are wider than he remembers, but he does not mind. Her hair has been carefully styled into a bob. She is heavily made up.

I know the lady is meant to arrive late but . . .

That's silly, isn't it?

I suppose so.

You look very pretty.

So do you. I mean . . .

She laughs.

Not pretty exactly.

I should hope not.

Charlie feels nervous, a slight film of perspiration dampening his shirt already. There is an indeterminate space between them of maybe two feet that Charlie is reluctant to occupy yet feels it obscurely necessary to do so. He is not good at flirting, never mastered the art even when a young man. He likes to get to the point, and yet he feels that women find this crude and clumsy. Already, before the evening has properly begun, he feels himself spooling forward to the scene that must round the night off. Should he try to kiss her? Should he even try to take her home?

A waiter approaches.

Would you like an aperitif, Susan?

Yes, please.

How about a cocktail? I hear they do an excellent martini.

Charlie has learned this as the decade has passed. He knows about single malt whiskies, and vodka martinis and grappas and aquavits and a whole cornucopia of once unimaginable tastes, brands, possibilities. Tommy has told him this too is necessary to conduct successful business, and it now comes to him naturally. The waiter arrives.

That would be lovely.

Vodka OK?

Vodka would do the trick.

Charlie turns to the waiter, feeling his confidence beginning to unfold. He pulls at his cuffs, speaks firmly and without deference.

A vodka martini, very dry, chilled, no ice, and nothing from Warrington either. Russian vodka. And for me a large whisky sour. And could you bring us some menus right away, and the wine list.

The waiter nods.

Certainly, sir.

Charlie has done some evening classes on wine since Maureen left and is keen to show off his knowledge. The wine list, when it arrives, no longer terrifies him. It is his ally.

Neither of them takes an hors-d'oeuvre, and Susan chooses roasted quail, while Charlie goes for a spatchcock chicken with rosemary.

Do you have any preference for a wine?

I don't know much about that kind of thing, Charlie. I suppose since you're having chicken we should choose a bottle of white. House white?

That's a bit of a misconception. You don't have to have white wine with fowl, especially not with game birds.

How do you know I'm game?

She doesn't giggle at this, but gives him a look beneath lowered eyelids. Charlie blushes slightly and returns to the wine list. He's not sure if quail is properly described as game but feels he's got away with it anyway.

A nice chilled Beaujolais would go. Or a Côte du Rhône. Red Burgundy, perhaps.

I'll leave it all to you, Charlie. You seem to know what you're doing.

And Charlie thinks, yes, yes, I do know what I'm doing. With each passing minute the confidence in him grows. *How do you know I'm game?* He finishes off his whisky sour. He has that nice warmth within him that he always gets after three or four shorts have been put away. He lights a cigarette, sits back with it balanced between two fingers. He is sophisticated, he is a rock, he is Rock Hudson. The divorce was a blessing in disguise. He is a successful businessman, late middle-aged it is true, but getting better, like good wine. A Côte du Rhône is ordered. When it arrives, Charlie smells the cork, swills the crimson liquid round his glass, takes a deep inhalation. There is little in the way of bouquet, but he nods all the same, then takes a full mouthful and swills it into all parts of his mouth and swallows. The wine tastes thin and unpromising but he smiles nevertheless. His new confidence has its limits.

That's lovely.

The waiter nods, pours the wine. When he returns with the food, this too is mediocre, but Charlie cannot be bothered to complain. He feels Susan's knees brushing against his under the table and, to his amazement, feels a faint erection develop, virtually the first non-self-induced erection since Maureen left. He hears himself laughing loudly, sees Susan blur into a gorgeous pattern of vivid pinks and reds and pepper and salt. The front of her dress strains against her good-sized breasts. Music plays; to his delight, it is 'Charmaine' by Mantovani. Now he knows beyond doubt that all will be well, a message has been sent to him from the gods. They also grant favours.

They both order pudding, some kind of tarted-up zabaglione, and Charlie picks up a fat bill, which he pays with a carefully displayed gold American Express card. By now Susan is leaning low over the table, her face only inches away from Charlie's. He can smell her perfume, something earthy; if it had a colour it would be blood and loam. Charlie has drunk around eight glasses of wine by now and he feels like nothing can stop him tonight, that he is on to a sure-fire winner. As they leave the restaurant, he ventures to put his arm around Susan, and almost naturally, so easily, she puts her arm round his waist as they set off towards a cab rank. She leans against him. He hears her breathing. Charlie is beyond amazed, then proud, then philosophical – why *wouldn't* she want to hold him?

Should I escort you home? says Charlie, as they reach the rank and a fat man with a ponytail begins to approach them. It is not really a surprise when Susan says, *Whose home?* and Charlie, easily, the easiest thing in the world, says, *Mine.*

The cab ride flashes past, as he begins to kiss her. He had forgotten kissing, hasn't kissed any woman but Maureen for close on thirty years; it's like a sweet kick in the heart. Now, close up, he sees that she is older than he took her for, and in her eyes he sees a familiar, faint desperation, but he does not care, he is at the centre of this moment, and it enfolds him and cossets him, package-holiday sun in winter.

At the door to his house, he pays the cab and fumbles the key in the lock. She removes his coat, he removes his jacket. They do not speak as they head up to the bedroom. Charlie retreats to the bathroom and scrubs his teeth and carefully folds up his clothes and puts on a pair of pyjamas. When he returns to the bedroom, he sees that Susan is already under the covers. Her shoulders are bare. She is looking at something. Charlie recognizes it as the photo album that he dropped on the floor earlier, while he was searching for handkerchiefs.

Sorry. I'm being nosy.

Charlie assumes it is photos of his wife and family and feels embarrassed. He peers over her shoulder. But instead of faces and smiles, there are dozens of shots of the development of the extension in the old house, catalogued with comments from the first brick laid. 'Here we go! The "great bodge" begins!'

He flushes.

Sorry. I'm a bit boring, I suppose.

No, you're not.

With a wonderful shock, he registers that she is naked. Suddenly he recognizes that his pyjamas are absurd and, in her full gaze, he removes them. He is already half erect. She is smiling, turning back the covers. He thinks he has never seen anything so beautiful in his life, although her skin is stretched in places, and although her belly sags, and although her breasts are smaller than he had expected, having been artificially accentuated, he presumes, by her brassiere.

They embrace and begin to kiss. He tastes his own toothpaste mix with her odd aniseed taste – mouthwash, he assumes. His erection grows. He moves his finger to between her legs. There is an astonishing moistness there, and a fleshiness that Maureen never had, a lushness, a generosity. Her clitoris, its soft topography prominent and clear under his finger, is swollen.

He wants to take her there and then, and manoeuvres himself on top of her, when she whispers urgently.

Do you have anything?

Anything?

Any kind of protection?

Protection from what?

Susan giggles, nips at his neck.

French letters. Do you have a sheath?

Charlie smiles with relief.

Of course. Of course I do.

He remembers that the condoms are in the pocket of his jacket downstairs, hanging up in the hall, and slips out of the covers and, naked, heads down the stairs.

It is cold in the hall, the central heating having clicked off some time ago, and he feels himself shrink slightly as he makes it to the jacket. He fumbles in the top pockets for the condoms, finds the pack of three, hopes it will be enough, then half laughs at himself for the vanity. More than enough.

The slippery silver foil falls through his fingers and lands on the telephone table beneath the coat rack. He reaches out to retrieve them, then, out of the corner of his eye, notices the name written on the notepad. Ruth.

He picks up the condoms. Ruth. Condoms. Ruth. Cassie.

Cassie is HIV-positive. Fresh, freckled Cassie. She said it was something at the dentist's. What did that mean? He doubts that she is telling the truth. You would say something. You would make an excuse.

Fear of AIDS now rises up in this cold hall like a spectre from the Spanish guitar barometer that adorns the hallway's approach to the stairs, one of the few artefacts he retains from the divorce. Susan Galloway. Who is she? How many men has she slept with? How do you get AIDS anyway? Charlie finds himself unsure. He is not 100 per cent that it cannot be got from kissing. He is not 100 per cent that it cannot be got simply by drinking from the same glass. Something in him recoils and shrivels. He stares again at the telephone pad. He looks up at the door to the bedroom, where Susan waits for him, the wetness between her legs, her infected wetness, her venomous gap.

Charlie! Come on! Come on, sweetheart.

His legs feel heavy. He makes his way slowly up the stairs, does not answer. On the way, he drops the condoms into a small wicker bin in the hall. He re-enters the bedroom.

Couldn't find any.

Oh. Oh.

Thought I had some. Sorry.

Never mind. Never mind. We can think of other ways to keep ourselves entertained. Can't we, Charlie?

She has pulled the covers right back now, to show the spreading vagueness of her body in the too-harsh light of the standard lamp in the corner of the room. She holds out her arms. Her lips a crimson line. Charlie feels an uprush of nausea within him.

Not feeling too well.

Can I . . .

It's OK. I just . . . just need to sleep.

Charlie lays his head in the crook of Susan Galloway's shoulder, closes his eyes. He feels her stiffness under the weight of his head, and hears, after a minute or two, the slight rhythm of her breath interrupted by the sharp intakes of air.

He knows this is sobbing withheld. And he searches for a way to soothe it, but finds none, allowing himself instead to drift into anaesthetic, remorseful sleep.

It's a stupid idea, Peter.

Maureen tucks into a large wedge of carrot cake. She has given up dieting, now eats what she wants, but finds that what she wants isn't very much at all. Since wholeheartedly giving up on this lifelong regime of denial, she has lost weight. Abandoning control has, amazingly, led to control.

I don't see what's stupid about it. And I don't see why you have to talk to me like that. I am your partner. In several ways.

The time is not right to start buying up more cars. We don't have the business to justify what we've got at the moment.

But the interest rates are low, there are some amazing deals at the moment. If we don't spend now, we're going to regret it in six months' time. It's boom time, Maureen. Everyone's getting rich. Why not us? In five years, who knows where we could be? That villa in Spain. A house with a swimming pool. Everything's going our way.

Maureen taps her finger on the stack of heavy books in front of her on the desk of the small Portakabin that serves as an office for M&P Driving Centre.

Nothing ever stays the same, Peter. Your investments can go down as well as up, as the small print says.

Listen, Maureen . . .

Maureen is aware of Peter puffing out his chest slightly, an affectation she finds sweet but occasionally irritating. This, she decides, is definitely one of the latter occasions. Peter continues.

. . . you live in the past. Everything's changed. All this boom and bust, it's a thing of the past. We've solved the problems. The unions have been whipped into line. We've got rid of all the dinosaurs. Britain's a great country again, Maureen! A great country! The

sky's the limit. With enterprise and a spirit of adventure, there are
fortunes to be made.

Maureen sighs.

Come on, Peter. I'm not going to have a discussion about 'this
country'. That's just silly stuff. That's just you taking newspapers
too seriously. I'm talking about the way things are. Things come
and go. Opportunities open, then they shut. You have to run to get
through the door, or you have to hold yourself back, to keep your
distance from the lemmings. Everything always changes, all the
time, but people always fool themselves that it will always stay
the same. If you want to be successful in business, you've got to
have a successful world view, every part of your life. It goes beyond
these *. . .*

She indicates the heavy black volumes.

At a certain point, business isn't about plans and figures and
investment and capital and cash flow. It's recognizing the way the
world is. It's sniffing things out. It's using your nose. And everything
I smell tells me at the moment that the economy, all of it, is . . . too
hot. *Too . . . I don't know . . . hysterical. There's something unreal*
about it all. I can't put my finger on it, but what I am sure of is
this. It's no time to be borrowing £50,000.

Well, I think you're wrong.

Well, I don't care.

I'm going to order the cars.

And I'm not going to sign the cheques.

You don't need to sign the cheques.

I do now. I instructed the bank as of this morning that no monies
could be released without joint signatures.

Peter sits down slowly in the plain grey office chair.

You don't trust me.

Maureen sits down beside him, puts a hand on his shoulder.

I trust you absolutely, Peter. I ***love*** *you. But this is my business*
too. And it has to be run like a business. We don't make the

investment unless we get my say-so too. And we don't have my say-so.

Peter sits still for several more seconds, feeling the weight of Maureen's hand on his shoulder. The warmth from it seems to be almost clearly discernible through the fabric of his suit. He looks up.

OK, Peter?

OK, Maureen. You're the boss.

And although this is meant as a joke, Maureen does not trouble herself to issue a contradiction. Her mind is on something else now. Important matters need to be settled, and a tide is running.

And there's another reason why I don't want to be taking on any more responsibility.

Why's that?

Maureen pauses. She only vaguely knows why she chooses to announce this now. Perhaps it is because Peter is beginning to acknowledge what she already knows. That she will, in the end, have her way.

I want to get pregnant.

Pregnant!

Yes, Polly Parrot. Pregnant.

Peter sits heavily down.

But you're forty-seven years old!

They've got drugs now. Being old isn't what it was.

I don't know, Maureen. I've already got three.

Then a couple more won't make any difference, will it?

A couple?

These drugs sometimes do that. Twins are common. I've looked into it.

Peter's eyes widen.

How closely?

I've been to see a doctor. He's referred me. I've taken up the referral. The specialists says there's a decent chance. Now all that's left is the fun bit.

She smiles at Peter archly. Peter wants to deny her, but he knows, he has learned, that she has become too strong to resist. He nods weakly, gives a matching smile in return.

17

Spring 1990. The beginning of a new decade, yet the spirit of the old is far from exhausted, is still not exhausted today. Charlie stares at the two letters spread out before him on the table. Tommy sits opposite him, in a Gabicci shirt and designer jeans. They have both sat in silence now for several minutes. Tommy realizes that he has run out of suggestions.

It's not possible. They've got it wrong, he says finally, picking up the letter nearest to him.

He has uttered this phrase several times already. And each time Charlie, sitting opposite him, has responded with an answering incantation.

I've had the valuation done four times. They all said more or less the same thing.

But it can't be worth so little. How can it go down from 120 K to less than seventy K in the space of two years? The valuations have got to be bent. There's some kind of percentage in it for them.

They're independent.

Who's independent? They're all in each other's pockets. They're out to snooker the little man.

They're succeeding.

Let's think this through. Run through the situation at the shop. That – what's his face . . . Buttercup.

Butterfield.

That Buttercup is coming to see us about.

Charlie sighs.

I've got creditors chasing me down hard. I'm way beyond the ninety days on most of them. The interest rates are hitting me too hard. *Business is way down. I've done all the arithmetic. Take a look at this.*

He reaches under the table into an old cardboard apple box which is full of sheets of A4 paper, scribbled on as if by a child with special needs. Figures spread across the white spaces like a virus, underlined, crossed out, added, subtracted, divided. Charlie fumbles among them, drops them, retrieves what he can, reshuffles them, trying to make sense. Tommy winces.

Has your accountant looked at all this?

*It costs me an arm and a leg to make a phone call to him. I can't afford to **do** it any more. I've got to sort all this out myself. I'm on top of it. I can get on top of it. Now where's that sheet for last month gone? Jesus God Almighty!*

He scrabbles hopelessly among the mounting nest of paper, eventually drawing out three dog-eared sheets with apparently random hieroglyphics inscribed on them. He studies these, face rapt with attention, as if their base metal can yield up gold through the alchemy of simple concentration.

See, the way I figure it, I can get out of trouble. I can capitalize the lease on the shop. I can return some of the stock perhaps. I can get a rate rebate. It's all a matter of cash flow really. That's what's killing me. If I could make it through to Christmas. That's when I do the best business. If I could get the other side of that, things might play out. Give back the Merc, get something smaller.

Much smaller.

Yeah. All right. Much smaller.

So what figure of money are we talking about?

Forty.

Forty quid? Forty buttons? Forty packhorses? How much, Charlie?

Forty grand. If I could get hold of £40,000, it would see me through to the other side of Christmas. I reckon I could save the business, the house, everything. It would be tough. But I could do it, I know I could do it.

Can't you borrow it again?

No one'll look at me, Tommy. They know my credit's up the Swanee. They've got it all on the computer nowadays. They won't touch me with a thirty-foot bargepole.

Charlie turns his eyes up towards his younger brother. The humiliation of this moment burns in his throat. He swallows. Tommy looks away as if he knows what is coming.

Tommy, if you could just . . .

The doorbell rings. They can see a dark outline through the glass. Neither of them moves. The doorbell rings again.

Best get it over with, Charlie, says Tommy quietly.

Charlie meekly gets up and opens the door.

The man on the other side of the doorway looks not at all like what he in fact is, consequence turned into flesh, fate's messenger. He is bright and cheerful, with sandy hair, a dense brown moustache and a blue-black suitcase with a gold combination lock. He gives Charlie an enormous grin and holds out a big ham-like hand. It seems he is delighted to see Charlie.

Mr Buck!

Yes.

Hello! I'm Leslie Butterfield from the National and North Bank. I believe you're expecting me.

Charlie nods him in morosely. Butterfield immediately walks across to where Tommy is sitting, glowering, in an armchair by the table. He reaches out a hand to Tommy which Tommy shakes unenthusiastically.

Hello! I'm . . .

I know.

Tommy doesn't offer his name but buries himself further into the cushions of the chair.

Mind if I take a seat?

Without waiting for a reply, Butterfield sits down at the

table and places his briefcase on the polished surface, then begins to fiddle with the combination. He looks up at Charlie.

Well, we've got one or two things to sort out, haven't we?

He opens the briefcase. Inside, everything seems to be arranged in perfect symmetry, with colour-coded files, papers highlighted with markers, knife-edge plastic wallets precisely labelled. Inside the briefcase is a world of order.

I suppose so, says Charlie, taking a chair opposite him.

Do you think I might have a glass of water? says Butterfield, as he removes a pack of A4 documents from some initialled recess.

Charlie gets up to go to the kitchen.

No hemlock in it, thanks!

He smiles at Tommy, who bites his lip.

My job doesn't always stand me very high in the league table of public affection, he confides, the smile growing broader than ever.

Charlie returns and places the water in front of him. Butterfield looks at it, looks at Charlie, then Tommy.

Any chance of a smidgen of ice, do you think?

No ice, says Charlie.

Oh.

Butterfield's face darkens momentarily. He nods, as if some understanding that has been eluding him till now has been arrived at. Then he seems to brighten.

Well, never mind!

He takes a pair of spectacles out of his top pocket, unfolds them and places them on his face in such a way that they sit on the end of his nose. This changes the aspect of him slightly; it gives him weight. For the first time, Charlie feels slightly afraid of him. Butterfield looks over the spectacles at Tommy.

Sorry. You are . . .

The victim's brother.

The victim's brother. Butterfield frowns. *I don't quite get what you mean.*

I'm Charlie's brother.

Oh, I see. He takes a swig of water. *It's rather warm. Are you sure you don't have any ice?*

I'm afraid not.

Never mind. He peers over his spectacles at Tommy. *You think your brother is a victim?*

Yeah, says Tommy, throwing a glance at Charlie.

A victim of whom? Of the National and North Bank?

This question is delivered in a slightly sharper tone than previously. Tommy is taken aback.

I was just having a bit of a joke really.

I can assure you, Mr Buck, this is no joke.

Butterfield leaves a long pause, then smiles at Charlie again.

Well, then, Charlie. Do you mind if I call you that?

No.

Charlie, you seem to have got yourself into a bit of a mess.

I suppose so.

Another long pause.

You have not met your payments on this house for the last . . .

He checks a single sheet of closely typed paper comprising more figures than letters.

. . . six months. My colleagues in the small-business unit inform me that you're in a similar situation with regards to the loan against the lease for your shop premises and your stock.

It's not quite as bad as all that. I've made one or two part-payments. I've explained it all to your other feller . . . Mr . . . I can't recall his name. The man with a type of greyish beard and . . .

Butterfield waves his hand in the air.

It doesn't really matter.

What?

Charlie looks startled.

What matters is that we can hardly allow this situation to continue without taking some kind of action.

Charlie nods. Tommy points a finger at Butterfield and starts to speak.

The thing is . . .

Butterfield clicks the top of his pen. It makes a surprisingly loud report.

Would you mind, Mr Buck – Mr Buck Junior, is it?

I'm his younger brother, that's right.

Would you mind if, for the sake of clarity, right now I deal solely with Charles?

You what?

With Charlie. Can I just talk to Charlie alone for a little while?

Well, I was just going to say . . .

Would that be OK with you?

This last phrase comes out clipped, suddenly impatient. Tommy, again taken aback, closes his mouth, shifts uncomfortably in his chair. He is not used to being in conflict situations he cannot end with a punch. Butterfield nods.

Good. Excellent.

Do you want me to leave? mutters Tommy.

Oh no. I'm sure that's not necessary.

He turns slowly back to Charlie.

When we arranged this meeting, Charlie, you suggested to me that you might have found a way out of our current problems. Is that still the situation?

If I could just get through Christmas, says Charlie desperately.

Christmas, says Butterfield, looking puzzled.

Yes. That's when the bulk of the trade is, see?

*Unless the tradition has been modified and no one has thought to tell **me** about it, Christmas is in December.*

Butterfield smiles hugely. It seems that he is about to burst out laughing at his own joke.

I've worked it all out, Mr Butterfield.

Charlie picks up the sad pile of scribbled-on paper from the table and waves it like a talisman.

I know that if I can find a way to . . . I've done all the figures again and again. Minimum projections, nothing fantastical. Irregardless of all the problems I've got, I can get through. All I need is one final loan.

He pauses. Knowing the audacity of the request he has just made paralyses his tongue. He coughs, clears his throat.

Butterfield seems amazed.

*A loan? A **further** loan? For how much?*

Forty grand. I mean, thousand . . . It's nothing. And then I can make it through.

A low-flying aircraft passes over the house, making it impossible to say anything for a few seconds. Then Butterfield speaks, in a completely neutral tone.

You want £40,000? To help you make it through the night?

He takes off his spectacles, cleans them, smiles broadly.

You want the National and North Bank to lend you a further £40,000?

That's right, says Charlie eagerly.

On top of the £100,000 they have lent you for your house and the £50,000 the commercial branch has lent you for your business.

That's right, says Charlie, less perkily.

Despite the fact that the most recent valuation on this property is . . . bear with me a minute . . .

Butterfield goes straight to a small pocket on the outer edge of the briefcase and extracts an immaculate set of three letters on headed notepaper. He examines each of them, then returns them to their pouch.

Despite the fact that the best . . . the best, Charlie, estimate of the current value of this house is £68,000.

Yeah, but that's silly. That's a moody valuation. The house just down the road, which hasn't even got as big a garden as this . . .

The best! That's the **best**, *Charlie. Less optimistic estimates put it at little more than sixty.*

But that's not my fault! says Charlie, suddenly outraged. *When you made the loan, you assumed the same as me. We all thought property would keep rising. Your bank even bought a string of estate agents, didn't it?*

Property consultants, corrects Butterfield.

You can call a duck a sausage roll, but it's still a duck. Whatever you want to call them, you took a hiding on them too. So to punish me now, I mean, to not give me a bit of support, is . . .

Butterfield hardly seems to be listening. He holds up a hand.

I'm afraid the fairness of things is neither here nor there. The fairness of the world is not the issue. The issue is the way things are, not the way that they might be.

Charlie says nothing.

The way I see it, continues Butterfield, *the National and Northern Bank is looking at a hiding on this one. A* **pasting**. *We're in a hole. You are in a situation of negative equity. So we're all in a hole. Wouldn't you agree?*

I suppose so, but . . .

Do you know what I think about holes?

Butterfield looks at Charlie brightly, as if he is expecting a serious answer.

No, mutters Charlie morosely, *I don't.*

I think that when we are in one, we should stop digging.

Oh, says Charlie, not really understanding.

I think, says Butterfield, *that the files need closing on this situation.*

The files?

Butterfield brings the flat of his hand down on the table in front of him, producing a resonant *thwack*.

We need to foreclose. On both the business and the house. Within thirty days.

Charlie blinks, once, twice, three times. He feels a tightness in his chest. He has tried not to drink today, but now he aches for the burn of whisky at the back of his throat.

Are you saying you won't lend me the money?

*That's **precisely** what I'm saying. Your track record simply doesn't justify it. It's sad for all of us. Particularly for us, as a matter of fact. You are just a man. A man, Charlie. But we are an institution, and an important one at that. Institutions like ours make this country what it is.*

Charlie nods, hoping that his approval of this lecture will buy him some goodwill.

Take consolation in this. You're not alone. I have to deal with cases worse than this every day. Men with wives and children. It's not easy, I can tell you.

Butterfield begins to close his briefcase. Charlie holds out a hand which, by a supreme effort of will, he keeps from trembling.

What if I could come up with half of it myself? Capital. To show you I still have resource . . . resourcefulness. Would you match it?

Butterfield pauses. The briefcase hovers half open, half closed.

*Is there **any** realistic possibility of that? Of you finding £20,000 further unsecured capital?*

There may be, says Charlie.

Hmmm.

Butterfield reopens the briefcase and this time goes to a flap that has been concealed. There seem to be thousands of them in there, thinks Charlie, far more documents than the case could ever really properly hold. Again, delicately poised between thumb and forefinger, Butterfield takes out five or six sheets of immaculately typed paper. He slips a calculator from another pocket and punches in a series of figures. There is a claustrophobic, anxious silence in the room. Eventually Butterfield speaks again.

If you could come up with a lump sum of £20,000 within the next thirty days, I think we could see our way to extending the loan by an identical amount until the end of the year. Until after Christmas. And we would extend the repayment holiday on these premises also. But it would have to be . . .

Butterfield now fixes Charlie with a stare that is glacial and seems to him deathly.

Not £19,999.99. Nor can it arrive in thirty-one days, or thirty days and fifty-nine seconds.

He smiles again, cheerily, as if things have now been resolved to everyone's satisfaction.

But if you can raise the £20,000 within thirty days, then I'm sure we can do business, for the time being at least, in the manner we have always done in the past. I know you're trying your best. I know times are difficult. You may find this hard to believe, but we at the bank always have our customers' interests at heart. And I honestly don't think, Mr Buck, that it is in anybody's interests to continue with this situation unless you can produce the required sum within the required time.

He clicks closed the briefcase and gets up, smooths down his suit. The darkness of the previous few minutes seems suddenly to leave him. He grins, takes a deep breath.

Thank you so much for the water.

He turns and offers a hand to Tommy.

Mr Buck Junior. Thank you for your contribution. I'm sure your brother is grateful for your support.

Unexpectedly now, he slaps Charlie quite hard on the back.

Buck up, eh, Buck? Worse things happen at sea, or so I'm told. Although myself, I get seasick, so I wouldn't really know.

He gives a small bark of a laugh, turns.

I'll see myself out.

Then he leaves, closing the door gently behind him.

Tommy and Charlie wait until they hear his car start and pull away from the road before they speak to one another.

Well, that wasn't so bad, says Tommy.

Wasn't it?

There's a chance anyway.

At this, Charlie glances up eagerly at his brother.

Is there, Tommy? I know you wouldn't leave me up there without a paddle. Is there any chance you could, you know, bail me out? Just for a few months?

Tommy pauses for a moment to take this in. It has genuinely not occurred to him that his brother would ask him for the money.

What?

Twenty K, Tommy. You could get hold of twenty K, couldn't you? I mean, you could borrow it. Your credit's good.

*You want **me** to front you twenty K?*

*We're **brothers**, Tommy. I don't have Maureen any more. I hardly ever see Robert, and anyway he hasn't got anything to lend. I lost most of my mates when the job went down. You're all I've got to turn to. It's just for a few months.*

Right.

What do you say, Tommy? Otherwise, I'm going down. I'm going down all the way, all the way down shit's creek. There's no safety nets any more. I'm in middle age. Late middle age. I'm not strong enough. Tommy. You got to help me.

Tommy has no idea what to say. Lorraine is pregnant again. She wants them both at private school. She wants a new kitchen. Smallbone. She wants to trade in the series three for the series five. The building trade has gone arse-upwards anyway. There's been no work for a month. He's reduced to bits and pieces, shifting bricks around yards. He makes up the difference working as a doorman five nights a week.

I can't do it, Charlie.

What?

I can't do it. Not without selling the house.

But I thought . . . if you could borrow it . . . My credit's shot, see.

Tommy shakes his head. Charlie's eyes begin to water.

Tommy, you talked me into all this. You said I should buy my own council flat. You said I should start my own business. You said that property prices would keep on going up. You made me . . . shoot for the pot.

Tommy takes a deep breath, expanding his enormous chest several more inches. He turns his gaze from his brother, inspects his great, salami-fat fingers.

*Come on, Charlie. It's not me, is it? It's just . . . you know . . . the way things turn out. The . . . the . . . fucking **times**. Suddenly along came all these . . . choices, didn't they? I mean, it would have been different twenty years ago. Mo would have stuck by you come what may, slaps or no slaps. You'd have been nice and cosy down in Fulham. There'd have been no business, no loans. But things don't stay the same. Everything's changed, mate. It's a different **world**, Charlie. You can't blame **me**. You know, it's like cards. Like stud poker. Shoot. Like you say, you shot for the pot. Used to be it was all just like Chase the Ace. That's what life was. No one won or lost that much. Pennies, buttons and matchsticks. Now it's all poker. Poker and shoot. High stakes. All or fucking bust. Kaboom.*

Charlie's hands are trembling. He goes to fetch himself a bottle of Scotch from the kitchen. When he returns, he pours himself a large glass.

And I went . . . kaboom.

Tommy spreads out his hands.

It's Chinatown. The way the old cookie . . .

All right then, Tommy. All right. Fair enough. I made a few bad

calls. But I can still make it back. I can still make the table money.
Listen, how much can you spare me? I know twenty's a bit rich. But
you could come up with ten, couldn't you? Surely you could make
ten. That's nothing to you. I could cash in my endowment on this
place, got to be worth a bob or two. I could make up the difference
somehow. What can you do, Tommy?

Tommy shifts uncomfortably in his chair.

*It's not really the matter of the **amount**.*

It isn't?

See, the building trade is pretty low at the moment.

You could top up your loan on the house.

Lorraine wouldn't stand for it. She wants the kids to go through
private school so they can become stuck-up cunts like her. She wants
*a new car. The whole **lifestyle package**. You know what women*
are like. If I could do anything . . . But I'm lumbered, mate.

*So you're saying . . . you're saying . . . **nothing** is what you're*
saying.

Tommy shrugs, kneads his forehead with his knuckle. Even
his forehead, thinks Charlie, is fat.

I dunno. I might be able to knock together a grand, I should
think. I wouldn't have to tell Lorraine about that.

Charlie nods his head bitterly, as if he suddenly accepts an
unpalatable truth.

A grand.

Maybe twelve hundred. Twelve hundred is tops, though.

Right.

Charlie puts his head into his hands. Through the meshed
fingers words come.

It's Lolly, then, is it?

Well, to be fair to her . . .

She's never liked me.

I'm sure that's not true.

Tart.

Steady on, Charlie . . . She is my . . .

I'll tell you something about Lolly, Tommy.

Calm down, Charlie. I mean it.

She's nothing. She's a tart.

What you talking about? You've gone off your . . .

Christmas Day, 1980. I saw them in his bedroom. They were together.

Tommy's eyes seem to bulge, his great bulk shifts slightly where it stands.

You're having a laugh. Together? Who was together? What do you mean?

Either that or Lorraine's got a damn peculiar way of cleaning her teeth.

What? Are you saying . . .

I'm saying that the turkey wasn't the only bird that was having a gobble. Lolly was south of the border, down Mexico way. With Robert. Think I'd make it up? It's true, Tommy . . . I saw it. What you think they were doing in there? Toasting marshmallows over the Christmas fire?

Tommy feels his face go red. All he can think is that his brother has searched inside himself and found the most destructive thing he knows how to say.

Then he realizes somehow that what Charlie says is true. He knows his brother well enough to be sure that he wouldn't invent this. But instead of making him hate Lorraine – that will come, that will come later – it makes him hate Charlie, hate him like poison, destroying what little thin sympathy has been unfurling inside.

*Fuck you, Charlie! You're not getting twelve hundred. You're not getting a penny. Lolly was right. Robert was right. Maureen was right. Everyone was fucking right, except you, you dopey cunt. You're a **loser**.*

Tommy turns to go. He considers chinning his brother, but

holds himself back as he sees Charlie's face suddenly drop. It is too pathetic.

I'm sorry. I didn't mean it. I made it up. You got to help me, Tommy. You got to help me out. I'm not going down. I don't want to go down.

But Tommy is gone, gone for ever into the deathly quiet new town twilight.

18

Three weeks have passed. There is one week to go before Charles William Buck's world stands to fall utterly and irremediably apart. He has so far managed to raise £8,763 towards the required £20,000. He has sold off his endowment policy for what is, to him, an astonishingly low figure, despite the fact he has held it for ten years. He has sold his shares in British Gas, in water, in electricity. Robert, to his surprise, has taken out a loan to raise £3,000 for him. He has sold everything in the house of value, leaving him living in a shell, without television, without video, without even cooker and fridge. The last item to go was his Mantovani collection. An enthusiast bought it all. A lifetime's work – £50. About 50p a record. No call for Mantovani any more. Tastes have changed.

Now Charlie sits on the floor in his empty house drinking his way through the one luxury he has not disposed of, his drinks cabinet. He has nearly completed a full pint of blended whisky. He can smell himself, the stink of failure. Taking the money from Robert, begging from his own son, was the worst part about it.

He has one last hope of raising the remainder of the money, but it is a desperate one, a terrible one. He turns it over and over in his head, arguments presented as increasingly blurred and fragmented sentences and questions and justifications.

I'll never get away with . . . But it's mine really . . . After all, she left . . . But where will she keep it? . . . What if I get caught? . . . She'll keep it where she always kept it . . . Alarms? . . . Maureen never believed in them . . . Bitch . . . how could she do it? . . . No,

no, not a bitch . . . my wife, my Mo. Kiddo. Sorry, kiddo. I need the
money, I need it so bad. You understand . . . I'm sorry, I . . . I didn't
mean to do that . . . Peter will . . . Peter, that fucking . . . I can't
*do it. I have to do it. Can do. You got to have **can do**. Winners and*
losers. On your bike, mate. On your bike and look for work. On
your bike and look for treasure. I know where you live. I know where
you live.

I know where you live.

Standing unsteadily, he realizes that this is not entirely true,
that he has never been inside his ex-wife's new house, since
Peter sold up his house and they moved over to one of the
grandest parts of town, some of it still old, part of the original
Milton Keynes village. But he had to drop some legal documents over there once, regarding some technicality about the
divorce, and remembers it vaguely, the nicely spaced houses,
the well-kept hedges, the 200-year-old pub a short walk from
the driveway. The coy name outside, in golden italics on a
varnished cross section of tree bark: 'Mowanpete'. He estimates it is about three miles away.

He grabs a light coat, a pair of suede gloves and, on impulse,
two plastic shopping bags from Sainsbury's, where he likes to
buy kippers for the morning, and places them in his pocket.
He staggers again. The drink is muddling him but makes him
feel optimistic, brave. He pats his half-full bottle of Scotch.

Outside, it is late afternoon. He assumes that Peter and
Maureen will be at work. They work hard. They must work
hard. Robert tells him that their business, despite the recession,
is doing well. People always need to learn how to drive. Robert
tells him that they work all the hours that God sends. Today
the house will be empty. He just knows it. He feels lucky.

He realizes quite quickly that he has come out of the house
under-equipped for the weather, but he does not really feel
the cold. He walks along deserted cycle paths, across road

bridges, past roundabouts where cars spin and reel endlessly. There are virtually no pedestrians. When he first arrived in Milton Keynes, he remembers the feeling of freedom this gave him, the lack of bustling crowds, of smells and noise. Now he finds the absence oppressive, sinister. He longs for the messy clamour of London.

He gets lost twice, but after about an hour he spots the pub he remembers from the time he dropped off the documents. It has a thatched roof and low small windows. Now he remembers the name: the Haystack. Somewhere behind here, a few hundred yards from where the car park ends, is Peter and Maureen's detached house.

The light rain and the penetrating cold has sobered Charlie up and, as he approaches Mowanpete, he finds his pace slowing. The absurdity, the desperation, of his scheme begin to dawn on him. He knows that he is liable to be first suspect in any investigation. And that the smallest inquiry into his financial affairs will reveal a large sum of money magically appearing from nowhere right on cue. He almost turns back then and there.

But he pauses. Surely the identification of the money by Maureen will attract the attention of the Inland Revenue. Charlie feels certain that the sum will have been topped up since their divorce, probably from undeclared income of some kind or another. And anyway, he could ring Maureen and tell her what has happened, promise that the money will be returned. She'd be angry, but he's the father of her son – surely she wouldn't turn him over to the police.

In the desperation of his mind, these reasons seem convincing enough. He pulls his collar up around his neck. A young man approaches on a BMX bike, riding on the pavement. Charlie turns his head away as the man cycles past, but he pays Charlie no attention at all.

Mowanpete is the fifth house on the right. Sure enough, there are no lights on this darkening afternoon and no car in the driveway. He feels sure that the place is deserted. There are six flowerpots along the front of the house, he notes, with a vague excitement. Maureen always used to leave a spare under the flowerpot in Fulham. As quickly as he knows how, he lifts them up, one after the other. There is no key.

He corrugates his brow in frustration. He checks the frame above the door, he checks under the dustbin, he checks through the letter box to see if it hangs on a string. Now he begins to worry that his presence will be noted. A house opposite sits in clear view of this house and there are lights on there.

A few more seconds, he decides, and he will give up. The idea now seems more and more absurd to him, and he feels himself seem to shrink inside his raincoat. What if Peter or Maureen were to turn up? His humiliation would be worse than imprisonment. Worse than anything.

He takes one last look at the house before retreating. He looks bitterly at the sign, 'Mowanpete', and invents another, more satisfying: 'Prickencunt'. Then, as he stares, he notices that the sign is affixed to the brick wall only by a screw at the top. Nothing fastens it at the bottom. On a hunch, he reaches out and pulls the bottom of the sign away from the wall slightly. The key falls on to the front path, jangles on the concrete. He glances around behind him, then picks the key up and palms it.

Still he is not ready. To be certain, he tentatively approaches the front door, presses on the bell, then retreats as quickly as he can to a hiding place behind the neighbour's privet. He waits, peering through a gap in the foliage. Thirty seconds, one minute. Nothing.

He feels in his pocket for the two bags, one for the money,

the other in case he should be disturbed and need to be disguised. He feels the plastic stretch between his fingers. Then he moves quickly down the front path again. He fits the key to the lock and turns. It opens easily.

He is as silent as he can be, although he knows there is nobody in. His shoes click on the tiles, so he removes them. He feels that silence is appropriate to the occasion, even though he knows the house is empty. He takes a Sainsbury's bag out of his pocket, pokes two holes for his eyes and one for his mouth, but does not place it over his head.

He cannot resist a snoop around the house before he moves upstairs to look for the money. He feels sure it will be under a floorboard under the bed; Maureen is a creature of habit.

He is impressed by the opulence of the place – the thickness of the carpets, the gleaming gold of the fittings in the bathroom. The bathroom cabinet is uncluttered, unlike the one they shared. There are expensive creams, hand lotions, perfumes. None of the Bonjela or verruca ointments that used to fall out every time he opened the cabinet they had together. There is a large box of condoms.

Charlie pads out of the bathroom and into the living room. There is an oil painting of Maureen above the fake open-fire hearth which makes her look ten years younger, a romantic heroine. There is a huge collection of heritage pottery pieces – dray horses, and cottages, and peasants chewing straws on benches. The whole place smells of good polish and air freshener. It is pleasant, but something is disturbing him deeply, although he cannot work out what it is.

Then it comes to him. He is in a *happy* house, a place steeped in goodwill, in fresh, unbroken promises, in genuine contentment. A place where love is. This understanding, this final reproof, pierces him, makes it almost unbearable to continue. But he does continue. He no longer has any choice.

There is a British flag framed in the toilet – Peter's sole contribution to the decor, imagines Charlie. There are framed photographs of Robert and Little Charlie. Any remnant of Charlie's marriage to Maureen seems to have been comprehensively erased. There is none of their old furniture, pictures, ornaments, nothing. He is a non-person. He has been erased.

He pads up the thick stairway carpet to the first floor. There are three closed doors in front of him, and one open: the second bathroom. He does not know which is the main bedroom, only that he will find the money there.

Suddenly, there is a noise. A kind of soft creaking, rhythmic, distant. He cannot decide if it is in the house or not. He freezes, waits. The noise stops. He reaches in his pocket, decides to put the plastic bag over his head. The faint smell of fish assails him. He feels sick but keeps the bag on, adjusts it so that he can see through the poked eye-holes. He waits again. Still nothing.

He decides to continue, that the noise must be from a heating duct or distant machinery. He opens the first door. It is kitted out as an office, with bookshelves, a desk and chair, and a computer that is active and running. This disturbs Charlie slightly, as does the image that drifts across the screen, toasters bearing wings, heavenly domestic appliances. He recognizes that this is the wrong room and moves away, pushes open the door to the second room.

This, too, is not the room he seeks. But to his amazement it is kitted out as a nursery. There is a crib in there, and a mobile, framed pictures of teddy bears and raggedy dolls, a rocking horse, all the paint in pale pinks and blues. Charlie cannot make sense of it; perhaps Peter has a young niece or nephew, although he never mentioned anything. There is no room in his imagination for the other possibility.

He finally opens the third door and squints through the holes in the bag in the half-light to make out the large king-sized bed in the middle. There is a moment's hesitation before his senses communicate to his brain what is going on.

Maureen is there, lying on her back, undressed, face turned towards Charlie, eyes closed. He sees the pregnant bulge of her stomach, the modest hill of her womb. He sees Peter on top of her, pushing at her with quick jack-rabbit motions. He actually hears the sound that the penetrations make, moist, like a swimming costume being wrung quickly after bathing.

Maureen is moaning in a rapid singsong rise and fall of breath, while Peter is grunting with the effort of his frenetic penetrations. Charlie sees the deep blush of Peter's face, the grim, delighted effort of withholding himself.

Charlie stumbles slightly on the carpet threshold as the last granule of his world falls into dust. At the slight noise, Maureen opens her eyes, which immediately stretch wide. She gives an infinitesimal gasp, as reflected light strikes her retina and describes this impossible apparition. Peter at first smiles in satisfaction, then, sensing that something is wrong, that this is not an exclamation of bliss after all, turns and sees a man standing in the doorway with no shoes, grey towelling socks and a white plastic shopping bag fixed over his head.

Neither Charlie, nor Peter, nor Maureen moves. The moment hangs in the air. Charlie thinks of these things: of running on an empty beach as a child, of how he still loves Maureen, of the sadness of his shoeless feet, of Robert as a baby trampolining on his lap. He sees a shotgun cradled on the wall, hopes suddenly and completely that Peter will use it, will blow his head clean from his shoulders. But Peter does not move. Charlie feels his hand come up, past his shoulders, above his head.

Slowly, quite indifferently, he pulls the plastic bag from his head. In a glance, Maureen sees all that is written on his face, and feels only grief. Peter tries to rise, but Maureen holds his arms fiercely, keeps him still.

Another moment passes before Charlie silently turns, takes slow steps down the thick carpeted stairs. He hears no noise behind him, so he keeps walking until he reaches the door. He sees his shoes but ignores them, continues to walk. It is raining now; the towelling socks absorb the moisture like sponges.

He vaguely hears Maureen's voice behind him as he moves hypnotically down the street.

Charlie. Come back.

But Charlie cannot come back, for he is no longer there. His shock and his shame have cracked open the unstable matter of what is left of his life, producing fission. Black energy pours out; he is lost, knows nothing. A blinding pain appears in his head. He puts his fist to his temple and rubs at it.

For hours he wanders the darkening streets, unable to think, unwilling to think. The bottle of Scotch in his pocket has been emptied. He feels for his wallet. There is money there. Enough. Enough.

He looks around him in the terrible gloom. As if beckoning, a few hundred yards off, there stands the railway station. He makes his way towards it, mumbles enough information to buy himself a one-way ticket to Euston. There is a train waiting. He gets in it and sinks into a seat next to a woman who is reading the *Daily Telegraph*. As the train begins to move, she glances at her companion, then moves quickly to find another seat. Already, he senses, he is moving beyond vision, beyond Mantovani, beyond the hurricane. The train moves unshakingly on determined tracks. He dreams he is inside one of his models. He feels he is an artefact, created by someone else, bereft of life. He falls asleep, and wakes somewhere else, someone else.

Charlie will not come back, for the person who can return is gone, has been shuffled, and scattered, and finally disassembled. Life has done this, at that far edge where it cannot be resisted.

Epilogue

1991. The funeral at the crematorium is poorly attended. In the front pew, Maureen sits dressed in expensive black. She holds two babies in her arms that whimper intermittently. Despite the sadness of the day, she smiles at them with cautious, shining eyes. Nothing can touch the deepest part of her happiness. Peter Horn sits on one side of her, Robert on the other. He is a detective now, prosperous, a man of status and substance. He has put on more weight, and the sullenness in his eyes, once an adopted expression of adolescence, has faded into an avuncular gleam.

He studies the coffin in front of him, as if inspection will solve some puzzle. His life in the police force has made him hard, yet he feels a strange lump in his throat. His father is in the cheap pine box in front of him, waiting for the priest to finish his vague ministrations, before the rollers will move underneath and deliver what is left of Charlie to the fierce, controlled heat of the flames. In the coffin, Robert has placed a model live steam engine, fitted into the frame of Charlie's Leek and Manifold (Peak District) locomotive. Robert is shocked by the unclenching that is now taking place within him. Tears begin to come. Charlie Junior, sitting beside him, puts his hand on his father's arm as if in consolation.

Seven pews back, Tommy Buck sits with his wife, Lorraine. He will not speak to Maureen, whom he believes broke his brother's heart, and he will not speak to Robert, since he knows what Charlie told him about Christmas Day and him and Lorraine was true. They will slip out quietly at the end, after Tommy has paid his respects. Charlie played his hand like a sap, thinks Tommy, but he was his own flesh and blood. He, too, feels an unfolding within his chest, a losing of part of himself. This goes beyond like or dislike.

Lorraine sniffs and looks around her. She is barely suppressing boredom, and this lack of respect irritates Tommy. She has a hairdresser's appointment later that afternoon and finds herself concerned about missing it.

Further back still, two faces next to each other, one black, one white. Mike Sunderland is a senior executive for Times Newspapers now. He is clean-shaven, dressed in an expensive suit and hand-made shoes. The silver Rolex glints in the half-light. He has no emotions left for Charlie – he came from a different time, from a different age. But the story interests him; he is thinking about putting one of his reporters on to the case. One man's life through the 1980s, highs and lows, so on, so forth. Too pat, maybe, but still . . . Poor old Charlie. Never did have much of a clue.

Lloyd George, no longer Snowball, now a night watchman who is distantly employed in some branch of a private security organization that Robert sells advice to, has heard about the funeral from Mike, who keeps in touch from time to time. For reasons of guilt, he supposes. The therapist did an incomplete job. He doesn't know why he is there really. Nothing else to do. He wishes he hadn't come, but it's interesting to see Mike again. He's done well. White people always do well.

Except for Charlie of course.

The vicar is making traditional noises about returning to the fold, about bringing in the sheaves, about green and pleasant lands far, far away. He knows nothing of the deceased or his life. No one knew about Charlie and his life, Charlie himself least of all. Fragments glimpsed in parts of moments were all there was.

An ersatz organ chord, pre-recorded, sounds and the pine coffin begins its slow journey towards the flames. It takes no more than a few seconds before the red curtains close behind the oddly small box. There are one or two choked sobs – one from Maureen, one from Robert. Then these are brought under control. There is silence.

At this point, at the special request of Maureen, the speakers located in the corner of the chapel come to life once more. Plunging, cascading strings issue forth. It is 'Charmaine' by Mantovani. And at this cue, the few people remaining in the chapel begin to file out, one by one, of the open door. Out there into the rest of the world, where choice, and accident, and things without warning will yet push each of their lives, desires and intentions unstoppably away from them and into a future barely imagined.